A
Refuge
Assured

Books by Jocelyn Green

The Mark of the King
A Refuge Assured

A Refuge Assured

JOCELYN GREEN

BETHANYHOUSE
a division of Baker Publishing Group
Minneapolis, Minnesota

Published by Bethany House Publishers
11400 Hampshire Avenue South
Bloomington, Minnesota 55438
www.bethanyhouse.com

Bethany House Publishers is a division of
Baker Publishing Group, Grand Rapids, Michigan

Printed in the United States of America

Library of Congress Cataloging-in-Publication Data
Names: Green, Jocelyn, author.
Title: A refuge assured / Jocelyn Green.
Description: Minneapolis, Minnesota : Bethany House, a division of Baker
    Publishing Group, [2018]
Identifiers: LCCN 2017036495| ISBN 9780764219078 (softcover) | ISBN
    9780764231438 (hardcover)
Subjects: | GSAFD: Christian fiction. | Love stories.
Classification: LCC PS3607.R4329255 R44 2018 | DDC 813/.6—dc23
LC record available at https://lccn.loc.gov/2017036495

Scripture quotations are from the King James Version of the Bible.

This is a work of historical reconstruction; the appearances of certain historical figures are therefore inevitable. All other characters, however, are products of the author's imagination, and any resemblance to actual persons, living or dead, is coincidental.

Cover design by Jennifer Parker
Cover photography by Mike Habermann Photography, LLC

Author is represented by Credo Communications, LLC.

18 19 20 21 22 23 24   7 6 5 4 3 2 1

To Susie
For Everything

Thou art my refuge and my portion
in the land of the living.

—Psalm 142:5

Prologue

Propping open the door to her shop, Vivienne Rivard listened to a distant rumble that vibrated the windows and shivered in her chest. A rumble that might have been mistaken for thunder.

"What do you think, citizeness?" Camille, the wine seller in the shop next door, mopped his brow and nodded toward the noise. The lines framing his chin resembled those of a marionette.

"The revolutionaries are gathering again. It's not so different from other times." Vivienne's nonchalance rang hollow. Shielding her eyes from the sun, she scanned the rest of the Palais-Royal complex of colonnaded storefronts. On the other side of the central garden, a book printer swept his entryway in the shade of the Roman arcade.

"Ah, but there is a difference. With the citizen soldiers arriving from the provinces, they've grown to twenty thousand."

"For the protection of Paris, they said." Not that she fully believed them. She could hear them singing a new song brought recently by the men of Marseille: *To arms, citizens! To arms!*

Slowly, Camille nodded. "To fight the enemies of liberty.

7

Wherever they may be. Have a care, citizeness. Stay inside today." Taking his own advice, he ducked back inside his shop.

Turning from the clamor, Vivienne moved about her boutique in a whisper of blue satin, readying for patrons unlikely to come. Sunlight glared upon papered walls and shelves holding ribbons, fans, and bonnets. Everything was trimmed in patriotic red, white, and blue, since all other color combinations were illegal. At the far end of the room, an armoire cabinet housed Alençon and Chantilly lace, expertly crafted by women formerly in Vivienne's employ. Relics of a different era, the unsold pieces were kept in the shadows, like an aged woman whose charms had faded.

Crossing to the display window, she looped a basket blooming with bouquets of tricolor cockades over the arm of a life-size fashion doll. A sigh swelled in her chest as she glanced around the shop that had once sold only the finest lace, some of it made by her own hands. Her work had been contracted by the fashionmaker to the queen, which meant Vivienne's lace adorned Marie Antoinette, the French court, and any woman who could afford to copy them. So high was the demand for lace in Paris that Vivienne had partnered with her aunt in managing a network of lacemakers to supply them. Alençon trim for one gown brought more than six hundred *livres*. Lace for a mantle brought three hundred or more.

But no one, save the queen, bought lace anymore, so the shop was forced to sell ribbons and fans to stay open.

The scent of rose water wafted through the room as *Tante* Rose emerged from the stairway leading to their second-floor apartment. "Did you manage to get any sleep, Vienne?" Even in this heat, Rose managed to look crisp and stately in her taffeta redingote gown.

Vivienne smiled and kissed the rouged cheek of the aunt who had raised her. "I slept enough." Far into the night, hordes had filled the air by singing "La Marseillaise" and shouting, "*No more king!*"

As if she, too, could hear the echoes of the haunting refrain, Tante Rose glanced toward the open door and whispered, "What do you suppose it all means? For the king and queen?" She nodded in the direction of the Tuileries Palace, a few blocks to the southwest, where the royal family had been kept ever since a mob of market women had driven them from Versailles three years ago. The war against Prussia and Austria had not been going in France's favor, and Louis XVI and Marie Antoinette were blamed. *Treason,* the people said. But why would the king and queen betray their own country?

"I wish I knew." Vivienne watched a marzipan vendor strolling between the clipped hedges of the garden, but her thoughts were with the queen, her most faithful patron and the scapegoat of France's every problem. *Whore,* Paris called her. *Madame Deficit. The Austrian.* "Surely the National Guard will do their best to protect the king and queen and their children. We can't have a constitutional monarchy without a monarch, can we?" Vivienne did not point out that not everyone wanted a constitutional monarchy anymore. Or a monarch at all.

Flies droned in the heavy air. The breeze was an unwelcome puff of humidity that stuck Vivienne's fichu to her skin.

"Citizeness?" A little girl stood in the doorway.

"Lucie!" Vivienne embraced the twelve-year-old child, bussing both her cheeks. "Come in, come in."

"Good morning, *ma chère!*" Tante Rose exclaimed. "How is your family?"

Lucie bit her lip as she entered the shop, glancing around until she found the armoire behind two green brocade chairs. She crossed the rug and pointed through the glass cabinet door. "My mother made that, didn't she? Nearly went blind with the working of it."

Vivienne clasped her hands in the uneasy pause that followed. She hated the toll lace exacted from the hardest-working women. "The details are very fine. Did you know the other length she made just like it was made into cuffs and a collar for the dauphin, Louis-Charles? Be sure to tell your mother her work was truly fit for a king."

A smile flitted over Lucie's face. "If you please, I'd hoped to tell her that all her work had been sold. And that—perhaps—you needed more? And just forgot to request it?" Her large eyes pleaded above cheekbones far too sharp. "We could really use the work, you see. I can help. I'm very good."

"I have no doubt of that," Tante Rose murmured. "Sometimes it's the little fingers that do the best work, yes? Did you know Mademoiselle Vivienne began making lace when she was four years your junior?"

"Please. *Maman* is having another baby—her fifth. We need employment."

Vivienne's chest squeezed. Lucie was not asking for charity, but for industry. Her mother, Danielle, was incredibly skilled and unused to idle hands. With a quick glance at Tante Rose, she nodded. "All right, then. An order for you and your mother. I need one and a half ells of Alençon trim for a mantle." She went to the cash box on the counter and opened it. There wasn't much left. Still, she counted out the livres the work would have earned in better times and pressed them into Lucie's palm.

"But you normally pay for the work upon completion," the child protested.

"And this time, in advance. I trust your mother to do a fine job, but there is no rush for it to be done. Make sure she knows, won't you? No hurry at all." *Lord, sustain them. Sustain us all,* she prayed.

"*Merci!* Merci!" Pocketing the money, Lucie flew out the door.

Vivienne met Tante Rose's gaze. "I know it won't sell. At least not for a long time."

"God will provide for us, Vienne. Just as He is providing for Lucie's family. Let us be instruments of grace in the lives of others for as long as we're able."

Before Vivienne could respond, a woman stepped inside the shop, and Vienne flinched with recognition.

"I'm sorry—" The woman took a long stride forward, hand outstretched. "I don't mean to upset you, I . . . Please, be at ease."

But Vivienne was never at ease when this woman was around.

"Sybille," Tante Rose breathed, greeting her sister. "Such a surprise." Though Rose was older by several years, their resemblance was obvious.

In the pause that followed, gunshots speared the air outside above the roar of a combusting crowd. Recovering her composure, Vivienne looked squarely into Sybille's familiar green eyes. "Are you here to shop?"

Sybille shook her head, white gauze trembling on the brim of her *bonnet à la citoyenne*. At forty-three years of age, she was seventeen years older than Vienne, but her expertly performed toilette gave her a timeless appeal.

"Then have you some other . . . trouble?" Concern softened Rose's tone.

Vivienne sharpened her gaze, alert for signs of affliction, the type common among women of Sybille's trade. *Courtesan,* she called herself, but her sins were the same, whether committed with one man or hundreds.

"There is trouble, I fear, but it isn't mine." Sybille fanned herself with bejeweled ostrich feathers. "I know how you pride yourselves on being independent. You're far more clever than I am, both of you. But if you ever need anything, anything at all, please think of me as a resource. I want to help." She swallowed. "Things being the way they are, it's a terrible reversal for you, and the rent on such a place as this . . . If, at any time—oh la! I have rooms," she finally blurted, along with the address on the rue Poissonnière, northeast of the Palais-Royal. "They're paid for."

Vivienne's cheeks blazed with heat. "And how often are these rooms—frequented?"

Rose snatched up a sandalwood fan and worked to cool her beet-red face.

Sybille's feathered fan slowed, then flurried again at her slender neck. A raven ribbon of hair curled and bounced near her jawline, the very shade of Vivienne's own. "Not at all. I am provided for, but I am alone. All alone, as it happens." Her voice trembled. "Forgive me if I've said too much. I meant no offense to either of you."

Guilt trickled through Vivienne, unreasonably. She had not asked to be born of Sybille's illegitimate coupling. Sybille had certainly never pretended to be Vivienne's mother in any sense of the word other than the biological. She had chosen her path, and it didn't include her own family. At least not until now.

"If you find yourselves exhausted, financially or otherwise, or there comes a day when your trade places you in danger—"

"What kind of danger? Why? We've done no wrong." Behind Rose's quiet alarm, the din of angry crowds crescendoed outside.

Sybille shrugged. "Lacemakers are as unfashionable as lace itself. It's like silk—a sign of aristocracy. And aristocrats are as unpopular as the monarchy right now."

Tante Rose slid a glance to Vivienne, brows arched high. She pulled Vienne aside and whispered, "Could Sybille's offer be God's provision?"

Vivienne's spirit groaned at the notion. "We'll be fine. It will all be fi—"

Her words were drowned in an explosion of noise. Cannon fire?

Vivienne rushed outside, where other shopkeepers streamed from arched doorways to investigate the sound. Heat shimmered in choking waves that smelled of yeast and coffee, of sweat and sulfur and sunbaked earth. Clouds of smoke boiled in the sky. Coldness spread from the center of her chest while perspiration slicked her skin.

His apron smeared with ink, the book printer pointed and shouted.

A loose knot of men stomped into the Palais-Royal from the southwest in bloodstained trousers and shirts, red caps pushed back on their brows. "No more king! No more veto!" they yelled. Two of them dragged bodies, swearing and complaining of the weight before they finally stopped. Kneeling, they stripped blue uniform jackets and red breeches from the dead Swiss Guards. Swiss Guards, the protectors of the king. A butcher's knife bounced light into Vienne's eyes as it plunged into a corpse.

She covered her mouth in a soundless scream. More people streamed into the courtyard, and the mob teemed and frothed around her, brandishing sticks and knives, axes and broken bottles. Scraps of uniform with flashing gold buttons. Gobbets of human flesh. Her heart hammered against her corset, urging her to flee, but the citizens of Paris were a living, writhing jail around her.

Several National Guardsmen rose above the crowd, eyes wide beneath shining brims, mouths open in shouts she could not hear. Would they restore order? Would they stop the carving up of the bodies in the street?

How tall the Guardsmen were. Giants. But the way their heads bobbed and swayed . . . A chill spiraled up her spine as she met their unblinking stares. The masses streamed past, and then the Guardsmen were directly in front of her.

No, only their heads. On pikes.

Strength abandoned her, and she dropped to her knees in the gravel. When she pushed herself up from the ground, her hands came away wet with blood. In horror, she looked around. Crimson streams trickled between the rocks at her feet. Flowed more quickly in the gutters where the dead were trampled.

A hand roughly seized her arm and propelled her toward the edge of the throng. "What do you mean by coming out here?" Camille hissed. "Paris has gone mad." He released her with a shove. "Go home. Be safe."

But she knew her home—like Paris, like France—would never be safe for her again.

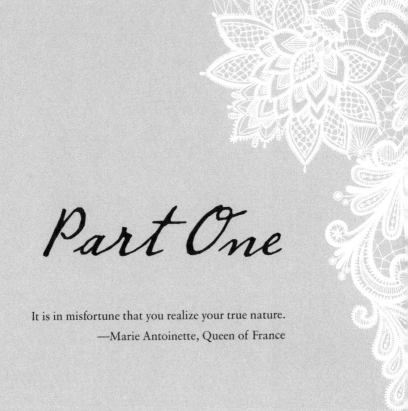

Part One

It is in misfortune that you realize your true nature.

—Marie Antoinette, Queen of France

Chapter One

She should be numb to this by now, the way skin exposed to cold eventually lost feeling. Instead, the repetition did not dull the pain but increased it, like the lashing of flesh already filleted.

"Where is Rose? She's not still vexed because I won't make lace with her and *Grand-mère*, is she?" Sybille's voice lifted weakly from beneath the yellow silk coverlet she had pulled over her disfigured nose. "Why won't she come to me? I miss her so."

Always the same question, until Vivienne feared she would go mad reliving the answer. She sat at the marble dressing table in Sybille's boudoir, mending a tear in a pillowcase. The needle slipped and pricked her finger, forming a crimson bead on her skin. What was one drop of blood, when the guillotines in the plazas spilled rivers of it?

"Where is Rose?" Sybille asked again.

With a sigh, Vivienne laid her sewing in the basket at her feet. "She is dead."

Sybille rolled to her side and struggled up on one elbow. "Oh no! My sister! But how did it happen?"

A hollowness expanded inside Vivienne. "In her sleep. She died in her sleep." She pushed the lie past her teeth, for it did no good to further burden a woman whose pox had addled her mind as well as her body. Sybille only remembered life before Louis XVI and Marie Antoinette had been guillotined while their children remained imprisoned, life before thousands were beheaded for not supporting the revolution. That Tante Rose had been arrested for lacemaking while Vivienne had waited for bread in the convent's charity line—Sybille would never understand this. That Rose had been guillotined and buried in an unmarked grave—this Vivienne could barely grasp herself. Lucie and her mother, Danielle, had lost their heads as well, for making the lace Vienne had ordered the day the monarchy was overthrown. In her tortured dreams of that day, when she pushed herself up from the gravel in the Palais-Royal courtyard, she knew the blood on her hands belonged to them.

Sybille's coverlet slipped from her face. Ulcered lips formed her next question, as usual: "No pain?"

"No pain." After all, the guillotine was the humane way to separate heads from bodies, the quickest path from life to death. Or so they said.

Closing her eyes, Sybille sank back into her pillow, sorrow etched into her features. Trembling fingers sought refuge in the few patches of hair that remained after the mercury treatment that did more harm than good. "Dear Rose. Did you ever meet her? We quarreled some, but I loved her so."

Vivienne crossed the worn rug to perch on the edge of her bed. "*Oui.* I met her." A smile stole across her face, though deep down, she felt again the prick of being forgotten. It had been a year, maybe longer, since Sybille last understood that Vivienne was the daughter she'd begrudgingly given birth to. Since then, she thought Vienne to be her lady's maid and nurse, whose name was neither relevant nor important.

Sybille wailed openly now, like a child. "My sister!" She sobbed with fresh grief, exposing the gaps in her mouth where several teeth had fallen out.

Vivienne pressed her lips together, bracing herself against the tide of sorrow. She had heard that it was possible to die of a broken heart. If that was true, how much longer could Sybille survive a heart that broke every day, with the same ripping force as if it were the first time? Vivienne's desire to steel herself was pierced by pity, yet again.

If she left Sybille, the former courtesan would not comprehend that her daughter had abandoned her, as Sybille had abandoned Vivienne to be raised by Rose. But Sybille would understand that she was alone, and despite everything, that was not something Vivienne could countenance.

Tears gathering beneath her chin, Vivienne gathered Sybille's failing forty-five-year-old body into her arms and rocked the bewildered child trapped within. What could cheer her? How could Vivienne ease her pain?

With a shudder, Sybille's sobbing faded almost all at once. "What . . ." She shook her head, clearly having forgotten why she was crying. It happened often. "I am sick to death of this place! Come, dress me in my green-striped polonaise, the one that matches my eyes. Where is my hairdresser? I want to be with my friends. Are they calling for me?"

Moving to the window, Vivienne drew back the drapes, and the room filled with the colorless sunlight particular to late March—or *Germinal*, as the new government now called it. She budged open the sash, and wind swept over her, damp and raw. It smelled of the Seine River several blocks away. Muted voices of fishermen mingled with those of the market women along the quays.

Sybille's rose above them. "Do you see my friends there?"

Leaning on the windowsill, Vivienne peered down at the slush-slick street, still dotted with islands of unmelted snow. From the north, a black horse pulled a tumbrel carrying six more victims for the "national razor," hair shorn to their necks. Around the wooden cart marched a crowd of *sans-culottes*, named for wearing revolutionary trousers rather than aristocratic breeches. Red caps waving in the air, their cheers ricocheted between the buildings, just as they had during Rose's transport. Several young ladies had joined the dark parade, laughing, their hair cropped as short as the soon-to-be-executed, and wearing bloodred ribbons tied at their necks in the style *à la victime*. Everyone but the condemned wore cockades—it was now illegal to be seen without one.

"Well?" Sybille pressed. "Are they calling to come up, or shall I meet them below?"

"They aren't there."

A pout. "They hate me, I know it. I've been forgotten."

Vienne spared one more glance at the street below and found her errand boy, Thomas, grinning up at her. She held up one finger, signaling she'd meet him at her door soon.

"I'll be back in a moment, Sybille. Thomas is here with some food." Vivienne tucked the coverlet back up under the sick woman's chin before gliding out of the boudoir and into the receiving salon.

Brushing past the sofa, Vivienne skirted an ivory game table and opened the door from the apartment to the hallway. Wind rushed through from the window left open in the boudoir, swinging the wrought-iron birdcage that hung in the corner, long since empty of the songbird it once held.

"*Bonjour*," Thomas mouthed, theatrically tiptoeing through the hallway, demonstrating that he remembered his vow of discretion.

Vivienne waved him inside and shut the door behind him.

"A nice harvest for you today." Beaming, he produced wrinkled apples from his bulging pockets along with a paper-wrapped wedge of cheese. The baguette in his arms he presented to her as if it were a ceremonial sword.

Stifling a laugh, Vivienne dropped into a deep curtsy and accepted the offering, then set the food on the turquoise-paneled commode. "Merci, citizen." She pressed a few *sous* into his palm, adding a tip to the agreed-upon wage for his errand.

"Don't you ever get out yourself?" Thomas asked. "Seems like, with the weather turning to spring, you ought to like a bit of fresh air."

"I like being here," she told him. With lacemakers still in danger all over the city, she could not risk being caught, for Sybille's sake.

Vivienne swept the salon with a glance. It was her sanctuary and her prison, both. It was her entire world, when outside these walls, all of Europe, it seemed, was at war with France.

Thomas nodded, and his red woolen cap slipped forward over one eye. He shoved it back in place over his unkempt brown hair. "I'd like it here, too. Lucky you found it first." Likely he assumed Vivienne had improved her station by moving in as soon as the aristocratic owners fled for their lives. But Sybille had never been an aristocrat—she had only served them, first as a fourteen-year-old girl in the opera chorus, and soon after as a courtesan. The fancy furnishings, financed by former lovers, did not change the fact that she'd always been an outsider.

Stepping on the heels of his shoes, Thomas peeled them off and left them near the door. One stocking hung halfway off his foot as he crossed to the globe by the sofa and spun it with one finger.

If only time could move as quickly, Vivienne mused. If only the revolutions of the earth would end the revolution's Reign of Terror. But terror, declared a man named Robespierre, was the order of the day, a virtue of the new French Republic. And so his Committee of Public Safety worked with neighborhood surveillance groups to execute France's own people. But she smiled for Thomas, rather than give voice to such thoughts. For who was to say he would not accept a sum of money for reporting her dislike for the government?

The corner of a muddied envelope peeked from Thomas's back trouser pocket. She hardly believed he was receiving mail.

"Thomas, do you have something else for me or Sybille? A letter, perhaps?"

He wheeled around. "Right. I forgot." Mouth screwing to one side, he fished out the envelope, shrugging as he handed it over. "I found it downstairs. Must have fallen from the postman's bag."

She slid her thumb beneath the flap of the envelope. "Unsealed?" She eyed him and his *bonnet rouge*—a political symbol worn by revolutionaries. Did Thomas lean more toward their camp than she realized? "Do you know your letters, *mon ami?*"

With a smile she could not read, he trotted back to his shoes and stepped into them. *"Au revoir,* citeness. I'm off to watch the beheadings.*"* With a salute, he turned and let himself out of the apartment, whistling the tune to "La Marseillaise" as he marched away.

Vivienne closed the door. Locked it. Lowered herself onto the damask sofa, the globe beside her slowing to a halt. The envelope was addressed to Sybille in round, curving letters. Feminine. She removed the letter within.

Come with me to America, she read. *Meet me in Le Havre. I have found a way for us to escape what our dear country has become. It is not too late, but waste no time in coming.*

After naming a *pension* where she would wait in the coastal city, the missive was signed with a single initial: *A.* Sybille's friend Adele, perhaps.

Vivienne brought the paper to her nose and closed her eyes, inhaling deeply. Faintly, she thought she smelled the sea, and longing swelled in her chest. She read the letter once more. *Escape.* The word leapt off the page, and her heart beat as if to be free of the bars that caged it.

The clock on the mantel ticked moments away as Vivienne stared at the globe beside her. There was France. There was Paris, a mere finger's width from the Normandy coast. And there was the Atlantic Ocean. Her finger traced its curve, stopping on the east coast of America. *It's not too late.* Wasn't it? Whoever wrote this letter could not have known how far Sybille's disease had progressed. Too far for hope, the doctor had said.

And whoever may have seen this knows we have reason to escape.

Thomas's parting grin came back to her. He was so eager to see heads roll. Had he read the letter? Would he betray them for coin or bread, a new set of clothes? For the thrill of sending another victim under the blade?

Forsaking the food still on the commode, Vivienne returned to Sybille's bedside, letter in hand. She was so thin, she barely altered the terrain of the coverlet that draped her form. Kneeling, Vivienne lifted the lid of the empty chamber pot beneath the bed and dropped the missive right onto the painted likeness of Benjamin Franklin. She replaced the lid and rose.

"Who are you?" Sybille's foul breath soured the air between them.

Vivienne bristled, though she knew the mercurial moods were part of the pox at this stage. There would be no discussing the invitation, and there would be no fleeing to Le Havre. She would pass her days and nights here, between these few walls that all but closed in on her. She would not discard her mother. She would pray, though France had banished God to worship Reason instead.

"I am Vivienne."

"Why are you here? Are you a thief, taking my valuables?" It was not the first time Sybille had mistrusted her.

"Nothing of the sort. I'm taking care of you. Do you want something? We have apples, cheese—"

"I don't want you! I want my sister, Rose!" Sybille wailed. "Where is she? I need my family, not a stranger! Oh!" She clutched at her chest, wincing, grunting. Sweat glittered on her sallow brow.

"Sybille!" Vivienne dropped to her knees beside the bed and gripped her shoulders.

"I am—dying," Sybille rasped. "Alone."

"No," Vivienne said fiercely. "You are not alone, Sybille. You must know this. I am here with you, I have never left you. You are *not alone.*"

Eyes glazing, Sybille's head jerked to one side. "But I don't— know you." She exhaled the words.

They were her last.

Grief touched Vivienne with the flutter of a moth's wing, and she swatted it away before its presence grew large and sharp enough to slow her down. After she had wrapped Sybille's body in muslin and summoned the wagoner who collected and buried the dead, a fury rushed in to fill the hollows of her heart and life, a white-hot combustion of hurt and anger and fear. Vivienne had stayed with Sybille, nursed her, wept with her, and in the end, none of that had mattered. Sybille was as alone as she felt herself to be. Vivienne was alone in truth.

At least until Thomas returned with any citizen who would arrest her on behalf of the Committee of Public Safety, for she was convinced now that he would. Dread turned innocent noises ominous. Pigeons flapping away from the windowsill echoed the frantic beating of her heart. The slam of a door became the fall of a guillotine's blade in her mind. Now that the only life at stake was her own, she would do what Sybille could not. She would leave the Paris she loved—and the Paris she hated—for a place and future she could not conceive.

Luggage in hand, she studied her reflection in the salon's floor-to-ceiling mirror. Sewn into the hem of her gown was the profit she'd saved from selling Sybille's antique furniture months ago. Her underskirt concealed the valuable lace she'd sewn into her petticoats, the pieces she had managed to save from the shop after Rose's death. Her cheekbones angled prominently beneath green eyes that stared back with startling intensity. It was the image of Sybille in younger, healthier years, the wanton mother who rejected Vivienne in the beginning and denied her in the end. Vienne could still hear her whisper, "*I don't know you.*" No matter how far she went, she could never leave that behind.

But leave she must, with no further delay.

Outside, her heels clicked over cobbled streets, and the scurry of rats amplified in her ears. On the next street over, a tumbrel clattered by with a roar. The fragrance of cigars and wine floated from cafés, mingling with the stench of refuse in the gutter. An old playbill skittered into her path for a performance of *The Marriage of Figaro*.

Clear the way, Vivienne prayed as she stamped the soiled paper with her heel. *Please help.* The portmanteau she carried was larger than a valise but small enough that by carrying it behind her wide skirts, it may not attract much attention. What madness was this, she wondered, that the size of one's luggage could be the difference between life and death? For the trunks of fleeing aristocrats had marked them for the guillotines, sure enough.

Alarm dogged her steps. Every puff of wind raised the hair on her neck as if it were the breath of someone following her. She kept her head down as she hurried past blocks of many-storied buildings and into the market as it was breaking up for the day.

"Please," she said to a woman loading her unsold cabbages. Vivienne had purchased produce from her before. "May I ride with you just past the gates? I'm to catch the water coach outside the city."

The woman eyed her. "Haven't seen you these past many months."

"I've been caring for my mother. She recently passed. Please, I'll be no trouble."

With a jerk of her chin, the market woman grunted. "Get in. Your bag at your feet, for I'll not be charged with concealment."

Vivienne nodded, her speech buried in hopes and dread. Climbing into the wagon, she sat up front, as if she had nothing to fear at all. Skinny mules pulled them through the city at a pace that stretched Vivienne's overwrought nerves tighter still. When they passed through plazas where the guillotines were raised, Vienne bridled her revulsion. Recoiling at the revolution's methods would be enough to guarantee her arrest.

Time slipped beneath her like sheets of ice on the Seine. While Paris passed by on either side of the wagon, she held tight to her bench and focused only on the mules before her, as if any diversion in her attention could cause the entire venture to break apart.

"Nearly there." The woman's words lashed through Vivienne. Her heart pounded with such force that she feared it would give her away.

Four market carts waited before them at Paris's west barricade. Citizen soldiers working for the Committee of Public Safety searched the carts before allowing them through the gates to their farms outside the city. It was great sport, she had heard, for the sergeants to find aristocrats in disguise and send them, at the last moment, to the Tribunal, which would ultimately call for their heads.

Vivienne tried to control her shaking. The guards numbered twice what she had expected. Some sat on casks, drinking to make the job more amusing. Laughter pelted her ears, from soldiers and wagoners alike. Up ahead, a scuffle. Jubilant shouts. A soldier kicked a barrel onto its side, then rolled it from a wagon to the ground. Out from his hiding place tumbled a man in women's clothing, cheeks caked with rouge.

"Two ruses at once, and neither good enough!" shouted a guard, pouncing on his prey. The man would lose his head tomorrow, while women knitted and gossiped as they watched.

God. It was all Vivienne could pray. Why had she packed a portmanteau? Was it too late to kick it from the wagon? Too late to rip the lace from between her petticoats and throw it all in the Seine? Fear stole her wits. *Too late, too late.* The words thundered in her ears with her pulse.

A sergeant approached the wagon.

"Relax," the market woman beside Vienne whispered.

Vienne nodded.

And suddenly, the soldier was right beside her. "Vivienne Rivard?"

Her name on his lips sliced right through her. "Félix," she gasped. She was exposed. He knew her. He knew she'd made lace, and most likely believed that a crime. "Please," she whispered. "Let me go."

Félix looked past her, nodding a greeting to the market woman, then turned once more to Vivienne. Scarcely could she believe that this man had ever promised his enduring love to her. But that was years ago. And they had not parted well.

His eyes glinted as he regarded her. Desperately, Vivienne scrolled through her memories of him, searching for tenderness and decency. When they were children, Félix had dried her tears when she'd torn her dress climbing—and falling from—a tree. Another day, poor though he was, he gave her his last coin so she could make a wish and throw it in a fountain. When they were older, they had crouched beneath the windows of the opera house, listening to Mozart's music in the shadows of a summer night. He had said he loved her, with words and kisses that had stolen her very breath.

It didn't last.

Félix had changed, even before the revolution began. The hunger and intensity with which he viewed Vivienne, she realized, was how he saw the world. With eagerness sharp as a blade, ever convinced that his way was right.

"Out."

She gripped the hand he offered and held on even when both feet were on the ground. "Please," she said again. "Have mercy." *God in heaven* . . .

The cabbage woman stood on the other side of the mules, watching Félix lift and shove at her wooden crates of vegetables in a routine search. Returning to the bench at the front, he glanced at the portmanteau no longer obscured by Vivienne's skirts. His gaze swung to hers.

"Where are you going, citizeness?" But his voice was quiet enough that he didn't attract attention. "Without your aunt?"

Vivienne's mouth went dry. "She was arrested already and killed," she managed.

Something twitched over Félix's face, something that might have been sympathy or regret, if such emotions still lived in him. She prayed they did. She prayed he remembered that he'd been fond of Tante Rose. That he had once adored Vivienne, or seemed to.

Aching for a father's affection, she had wrapped herself in Félix's instead, and he'd been more than willing to fill the gaps in her heart. "*It's all right, ma belle,*" he'd whispered in her ear. "*You don't need a father when you have me. I will love you and protect you forever.*" The irony stabbed. Now it was Félix who might send her to her death.

"I'm sorry." His words puffed white in the bitter cold, a ghost of his former sensitivity.

Vivienne's hood slipped back in a gust of wind. With trembling fingers, she pulled it back into place and fisted the fabric beneath her chin. "For what?"

He glanced at a soldier searching a wagon of unsold onions. As he stepped toward Vienne, the hard line of his jaw tensed. "For everything. The loss of your aunt. The pain I caused you."

She grasped for this flicker of humanity. "We can't go back and change anything. But I can move forward, if you'll let me. There is nothing left for me here. I beg of you, Félix. Just let me go."

Vivienne looked at him across the years and hurt that separated them. In the end, Félix had proved as faithless as Sybille's lovers. But before that, he'd shown compassion. *Please God, let there be some left in him. Just enough to spare my life.* Her heart drummed a tattoo on her chest.

At last, he helped her back into the wagon while the cabbage woman climbed in from the opposite side. Drawing himself to his full height, he stood aside. "Let them through," he called out, and Vivienne shuddered with relief.

"Merci," she mouthed to him, and to God, for she couldn't speak past the wedge in her throat. The mules pulled forward, and the wagon lurched.

"Au revoir, Vivienne." His rueful smile was a shadow of the man she'd once loved.

The farewell echoing in her mind, she passed through the barricade, leaving all she'd once held dear in her wake.

Chapter Two

Days and nights of sitting in the rocking water coach had felt like weeks as Vivienne floated on the Seine River from just outside Paris to Rouen, then changed vessels for the last leg of the journey to Le Havre. Now that she was here, she gripped her portmanteau with one hand and held her hood to her head with the other. Sea gulls squawked between sea and sky while wind lashed strands of her hair about her face. She had never been to the coast before, but she had marveled at paintings of the ocean. Thick brushstrokes layered on canvas had seemed a deep blue dream to her then, the stuff that art was made of. And now she stood on the very edge of it. Anticipation rippled through her.

Vivienne studied the *pension* before her, wondering if Sybille's friend really waited inside. White paint peeled between the glass panes, and window boxes tumbled over with last year's dead geraniums, the colorless stalks blending in with the limestone walls. Smoke curled from the chimneys, adding charcoal columns to the pewter sky. Except for an orange cat napping in the window, the entire scene was painted from a palette of restful gray.

Stomach flipping between hope and doubt, Vivienne knocked on the heavy wooden door. A short, round woman with pink cheeks answered, blond hair peeking out beneath her pyramidal muslin cap.

"Bonjour," Vivienne began. "I am in search of a friend who is a guest here."

The woman nodded at her luggage. "And will you be staying with us yourself? You may have your choice of rooms."

"Yes, of course. Merci."

The door swung wide, scraping the floor as it did so, and Vivienne swept inside.

"My name is Sophie." The proprietress shoved her hip against the door to shut it. Her blue gown was coarsely woven but clean and in good repair. "Welcome. We'll set you up with a room shortly." With a curtsy, she bustled to the counter, where another guest waited for service.

Vivienne lowered her hood. The parlor was small but comfortable, bathed in a warm amber glow. Above the roughhewn wooden counter hung a mirror flanked by brass sconces. A rust-colored rug worn thin and pale sprawled upon the floor, its fringe stretching toward the fire. Thin-legged furniture—a green damask-upholstered sofa, two armchairs, and a table between them—edged up to the hearth, and Vivienne could not resist doing the same.

After she set her portmanteau on the floor, she held her hands out toward the friendly flames. Her feet tingled as they warmed. River water had soaked her shoes and the hem of her skirts when she disembarked, and the cold had quickly spread right through her. Closing her eyes, she relished the heat wafting over her face and let it take her back to brighter days of sun-filled rooms and flaky croissants, of studying fashion magazines with Tante Rose, noting the trends for lace.

A book slammed shut. "Sybille?"

With a start, Vivienne turned. "No."

Firelight wavered over the man's face. The hair in his queue was a marbled blend of brown and gray, like driftwood. The way he stared at her, his eyebrows plunging, brow puckering—it was unmannerly. But then, if he knew Sybille, good manners were not likely to be his strong suit.

"But you—" A book in one hand, he reached for her with the other, then jerked his hand back into a fist when she stepped away from him. "I don't understand. I was expecting Sybille."

Vivienne did not respond right away. They faced each other before the fire, and she studied him so long that the right side of her body grew overwarm from the flames. "She isn't coming."

Lines fanned from his brown eyes. "But she received my note. She must have."

"It was a note from her friend." She paused, hesitant to reveal too much. "Adele, I think."

"Are you certain? Was it not just signed with the letter *A*?"

She stared at him. "I assumed . . . she spoke of Adele a few times. I didn't know of any other friends."

His thin lips quirked in a curious sort of smile. "You misunderstood. An honest mistake." He bowed gallantly. "Armand de Champlain, at your service. I am Sybille's friend, but more than that, if truth be told."

"Of course you are." Vivienne should have guessed her mother's friend would be a man. Mechanically, she lifted her hand, and he brought it to his lips, brushing a kiss on her fingers. "Vivienne Rivard."

"Vivienne." He released her hand, straightening slowly. "*Enchanté*. I am only too pleased to meet you. You are her very likeness." His voice grew husky, and he paused, composing himself. "But I don't understand why she did not come. I have been waiting many weeks now." He sat in an armchair and motioned for her to sit, as well.

Vivienne lowered herself onto the sofa, regarding him coolly.

Armand leaned forward. "She is vexed with me, I suppose. For making her wait years while I promised to leave my wife and marry her. But I did keep her in good custom as long as I could. . . ."

"So she was your mistress."

"For as long as I could afford her, yes." He didn't even have the decency to look ashamed. "I had hoped, however, she would stay true even after I lost my resources. For love, you see." His fingertip traced the engraved title on the book's spine.

Revulsion twisted her gut at hearing an adulterer speak of fidelity. She cast her thoughts back to the period when Sybille was supposed to be healed of her disease, reeling the scenes slowly through her mind. No man had stepped inside Sybille's rooms after Rose and Vivienne came to stay. But when they thought they could not survive another week for lack of funds, Sybille had disappeared for several hours and come back with bread. "*Make it last, if you please,*" she'd said.

"*What did you do?*" Rose had asked when Sybille dropped a dark loaf in her lap and another in Vivienne's.

"*What do you think, ma sœur? At least one of us can still ply a trade.*" She smoothed the rumpled pleats at her waist, and the bread turned to ash in Vivienne's mouth. Far worse than the idea that Sybille enjoyed her work was the suspicion that she didn't.

"Vivienne?" Armand's voice snapped her back to the present.

"She is dead, citizen. From the pox."

Unguarded shock and horror wrenched his features. Clearly, he was registering that Sybille had not stayed true to her affair with him. But he could not possibly understand what the pox had done to her mind and body.

Armand laid his novel on the table beside him. "I—I didn't know."

"No. Of course you didn't." Rose was dead by then. Sybille's friends had abandoned her as soon as her affliction marred her face. Aside from the doctor who had pronounced her case terminal, Vivienne had been the only person to see Sybille for those excruciating final months.

"You were with her, then?"

She sighed. "Until the end." A black-and-white cat bounded up onto the sofa. She presented her fingers to it, and the cat immediately pushed its head into her hand.

"And she did not speak of me, did not say my name?"

She met his imploring gaze. "Sybille did not say *my* name, citizen. And I believe it was she who named me, although I could be mistaken. Perhaps that honor, too, fell to my aunt." Bitterness laced her words, and she regretted them as quickly as she spoke.

He winced, then rubbed his hand over his face. "I didn't know."

The cat climbed onto Vienne's lap. Stroking its silky fur, she waited for Armand to speak. When he didn't, she prodded him. "Then what do you know?" The smell of oysters and cider drifted from the nearby dining room.

"I know I loved her, if imperfectly." He looked past Vivienne to the window facing the harbor. He seemed riveted and was so pale, as though he spied Sybille's ghost on the docks. "I know I made mistakes and would atone for them if I could." He turned to Vivienne again. "I lost my title and my land when France abolished the aristocracy, but I managed to protect some assets. All that I was planning to provide for Sybille, I willingly transfer to you." He shifted from the armchair to the sofa and fingered a lock of her hair.

She bristled at the gesture. "Unlike my mother, I am not for sale," she hissed, recoiling from him. The cat leapt from her lap.

He blinked. "She told you nothing about me? Not ever?"

A tart reply sprang to her tongue. How easy it would be to strip this man of his arrogance. It was ludicrous, the notion that she would have wanted to hear any sordid tale that featured an adulterous man and his mistress. Indignation flared within her, and she fanned it into full flame, for it was easier to burn with anger than to feel anything else right now.

"Forgive me," he said, "this all comes as quite a shock. But you must have come looking for me, or for Sybille's friend Adele, because an escape plan appealed to you. Because you want—dare I say, need—the help I offered in my note. You must allow me to give it, now that you've come so far."

Vivienne had not relied on a man for help since Félix, and it galled her to think of depending on the very one who had used and been used by Sybille. "Despite appearances to the contrary"—she

33

paused to force a smile—"I am not my mother. I will make my own way."

He draped his arm over the back of the sofa, his fingers dangling near her shoulders. As if she belonged to him, when she didn't belong to anyone. "If you want to sail, you will need my help to secure passage, I have no doubt," he whispered, the smell of Normandy cider on his breath. "I will give it to you. I promise."

Vivienne rose and dropped a cold smile on the floundering man before her. "I understand you've made promises before."

She picked up her portmanteau and left the warmth of the fire to approach the counter across the parlor.

"Ah yes. A room for you, citizeness." Sophie puffed a wisp of blond hair from her brow and named her fee. "How many nights will you be staying on?"

Vivienne set her luggage on the floor. "Until the next ship sails for America." She hoped it was soon and that the passage was affordable. Her gown was still weighted by the coins she'd sewn into the hem, but it was getting lighter. And the lace she'd secreted out of Paris would only be of use once she could sell it in America.

Armand appeared at Vivienne's elbow. "I said I would help you," he murmured. "I will pay for the room."

"I will pay for my own room."

Sophie's eyebrow rose. "There is a schooner that just delivered a load of lumber from Maine," she said. "It'll be taking French goods back with it, but all is not ready yet."

Vivienne glanced out the window at the end of the counter. The large orange cat still occupied the sill, soaking up the sun's last rays as it napped. "How much is the schooner fare? Have you any idea?"

Sophie offered an estimate based on the last time it came.

Dread drizzled through Vivienne. She could not afford more than a few days at the pension and the ship fare both.

"I can cover the cost." Armand's hand, heavy and damp, rested on her shoulder.

Vivienne angled away until his hand dropped. "Armand, this does not concern you."

Sophie cleared her throat. "A bit of privacy for my guest here, citizen. Stand back, if you please."

He lifted his chin. "You may change your mind at any time, Vivienne. You've only to say the word." Head high, back straight, he returned to the chair by the fire.

Sophie huffed as she watched him return to the sofa. "He's not the friend you expected to find here, is he?"

"No." Vivienne hesitated. "I'll be truthful with you, Sophie. After purchasing my passage on the schooner, my remaining funds will not last a full week at the pension. As you heard, Citizen de Champlain is willing to assume the expenses himself, but—"

Resting her ample bosom on the counter, Sophie leaned forward. "Persistent, that one. Wants you to be in his debt, does he?"

"So it seems." Vienne's stomach growled and twisted.

The proprietress pressed a key into Vienne's hand with a friendly squeeze. "Third floor, end of the corridor. Freshen up, then come to the dining room for your meal. We will take it one day at a time, ma chère."

"Merci, Sophie." Exhaling, Vivienne bobbed in a grateful curtsy.

Portmanteau in hand once more, she slipped the key into her cloak pocket and headed for the stairs. Fatigue came upon her all at once, now that she was so near a bed.

"Allow me. Please." Armand, again at her side, pointed to her luggage. "I will carry it to your room."

"Thank you for the offer, but I've managed this far." And she preferred that he not know which room was hers.

"It's the least I can do." He reached for the handle.

Vienne stepped beyond his grasp. "I bear my own burdens, Armand." She said it with pride.

But the slant of his brow bespoke pity.

1 FLOREAL, YEAR II

Salty mist chilled Vivienne as she gripped the schooner's rail. It had been nearly two weeks since she arrived at the pension at Le Havre, a lifetime since she'd seen Paris, and yet not enough time to prepare herself for leaving France. Chest aching, she cast her gaze starboard, across the Channel, and then looked back. The cliffs bracing the Normandy coast were chalk-white beneath low-bellied clouds and shivering with nesting kittiwakes. The birds were free to wing over land and sea, yet they came home to roost at the edge of the country she could no longer call home. Vivienne had come unmoored. Adrift, in more ways than one.

"You look lonely." Armand appeared beside her. His Roman nose had reddened in the damp, cool air, so that between his pale face and blue woolen collar turned up at his neck, he resembled a tricolor cockade.

She looked at him sideways. "A woman on her own is not lonely by definition." A concept that seemed to elude him. During her first full day at the pension, she had slept through two meals and found him waiting for her in the dining room for the third. He had peppered her with inquiries about her finances and about Sybille. He had been no less dogged the following day, his questions nipping her ears. He was lost, she had realized, without his wife, without Sybille, without the trappings of his nobility. But Vienne could not handle both his grief and her own.

"You are the most singular young lady I've ever met," he sputtered beside her now. "Most women take great pains to turn heads, and yet you seem completely content with isolation."

On the contrary, Vivienne enjoyed people, or she had before the revolution raised suspicion between neighbors and friends. It was Armand's company she could do without, for reasons he ought to understand.

He wiped at his nose with his wrist. "Ghastly way to begin a voyage," he muttered. "Sick from the start."

Vienne fished a clean handkerchief from her cloak pocket and gave it to him. "This wind does you no favors. You should rest." Elsewhere.

She rubbed her hands together, then blew on them. Her fingers were forever cold. Now they stung where the mist hit the cracks in her skin, for they were chapped from working, too. When the schooner had been delayed, Sophie had arranged for Vivienne to help in the kitchen to compensate for her room and board. It was out of mercy that they had let her cut vegetables and wash dishes, for the kitchen was fully staffed without her. Keeping busy had passed the time and paid for ten more nights of lodging, but it had also kept her away from Armand. She had eaten her meals in the kitchen, and at the end of the day she'd retired straight to her room.

Armand sneezed into the kerchief, then rubbed his nose, brightening it even more. "You can't avoid me forever."

She raised an eyebrow, unconvinced. "Philadelphia is the capital of America. The likelihood of us crossing paths in such a city is low, unless by appointment."

"Would that be so terrible? To see a familiar face in a strange land during our sojourn there?"

"Sojourn," she repeated. "When do you plan to go back to France?" New laws dictated that any émigrés who returned would be separated from their heads.

"When the time is right, of course. Won't you?"

"No. The revolution has killed my industry and my family. When I land in Pennsylvania, I will set about making America my home. Permanently." The deck rolled gently, and she planted her feet a little wider beneath her skirts.

"I am French through and through and have no inclination to playact the American. I'm sure our countrymen already in Philadelphia feel the same. There are thousands of us there, and I see no reason to venture beyond the French community or to bother learning the English language."

"You don't know it already?" Vienne had assumed that he did. Rose had been fluent enough to transact business in English and had taught Vienne. They often served British patrons eager to purchase French lace.

"French and Italian are enough for me. English never appealed. There is no music in that awkward tongue at all." Armand wrinkled his nose, then blew it again. "I intend to stick to my kind in Philadelphia. Birds of a feather, you know." He gestured to the colonies of kittiwakes nesting on the cliffs.

Sails snapped in the wind. Ratlines and rigging rattled. Vivienne leaned her hip against the rail and crossed her arms to warm her hands. "But the two of *us* will not be flocking together."

He set his jaw. "And why not? What will you do, *ma belle*?"

She chafed at the term. No doubt it was Sybille he saw when he looked at her. Blame volleyed in Vivienne's mind between Sybille, this man, and the untold numbers of others. If she never saw Armand again, she would not be sorry. Her gaze retreated from his and fixed instead upon a sailor cursing and swabbing the deck where a seasick passenger had missed his bucket.

"Then you must allow me to provide for your maintenance, as I would have for your mother," Armand pressed.

Vivienne hooked an errant curl behind her ear. "Until the last two years of her life, Sybille did not feel an obligation toward me. Neither should you."

"I must insist."

"I must refuse." She faced him, at the end of herself. "Regardless of how I must appear to you, I am not her proxy. Caring for me even materially will not atone for your past sins, or for hers."

Something flashed in his watery eyes. Was it surprise? Anger? Regret? "You are so hard." His voice was edged with steel.

She matched it with her own. "I have a head for business. I will make my own way."

"You senseless, stubborn girl!" he cried. "Can you not see? I do not intend to conform you to your mother's chosen lifestyle. My aim is to protect you from the need to follow suit!"

His outburst splashed coldly over her. "Tell me, Armand, if I depend on you for my security, is that not following in Sybille's footsteps, too?"

He vented his frustration under his breath. She could not read the lines in his face. "Vivienne, you doubt my motives, but there is a reason you should believe that I want only what's best for you."

"Is that so?"

Armand coughed, then swallowed. "This is a conversation I have rehearsed many times in Le Havre while waiting for a suitable opportunity to speak with you." He held his breath for a moment before exhaling. "Your middle name is Michelle. You reached your twenty-eighth birthday last month. Didn't you?"

She stepped back. "It doesn't matter."

He grabbed her arm. "I think it does."

"Let me go."

"I won't hurt you, just—I've known Sybille for many years. Thirty, to be exact."

"Many men could say the same." She wrenched her arm free and sailed beyond his reach.

He followed. "You must have wondered."

"Don't," she said in a voice no one could hear. The ocean slapped the sides of the ship in rhythmic waves. She told herself she saw no resemblance, nothing familiar in his features. But then, it was Sybille's likeness she bore so strongly, and she doubted there was any room left to even hint at the man responsible.

"Sybille was faithful to me back then," Armand insisted.

Vivienne rounded on him. "You don't know that."

"And you don't know that she wasn't."

"I have no father." She cut him off, almost daring him to refute this. "At least, none that ever wanted me. I accepted that long ago." Men who kept courtesans had their own wives and children. They did not need—did not want—any others.

He pulled his cloak tighter about him, and she noticed again the clean, trimmed fingernails on hands less callused than her own.

"Let it rest, Armand," she urged. "Your guilt does not concern me. Do not pretend to be something you aren't in order to ease your conscience, if you have any left."

"You know very well I could be your father. Why do you deny the possibility?"

"Because it doesn't matter." She spoke over whispers of doubt.

"It matters to me." But he left her, and Vivienne turned back toward the coast of France.

It was gone.

She stood staring into the distance until she forgot her face and hands were cold, and until thoughts of the man who claimed to be her father receded from the forefront of her mind.

It was over. She had escaped the revolution at last.

Little by little, the fear, the urgency, the constant vigilance that had been with her for so long, began to ease. In the void created by the loss of those constant companions, Vivienne felt as blank as the ocean expanding before her, nothing but blue sky and blue sea in each direction. She barely remembered who she had been before the revolution.

O Lord, thou hast searched me, and known me. Vivienne let the words of the psalm rinse through her. *Thou art acquainted with all my ways.* Her ways had been so troubled lately. She had forgotten how simple things could fill her with joy, because nothing had been simple for years. Eyelids drifting closed, she remembered roses in gardens and vases. Tea in painted cups. The crunch of a perfect baguette. White lace, and all things beautiful, whether it was a sonnet or a sonata or a sunrise.

Vivienne leaned on the rail and peered at the water. It was not a blank expanse at all. Bubbles ruffled the surface, fish gleamed silver beneath. Pelicans plunged for prey, and dolphins leapt in graceful arcs. A new thing to love, then. The ocean. New beginnings. And the God who was sovereign over all.

Part Two

French refugees . . . had formed in Philadelphia an ark of safety like that of Noah.

—Chevalier de Pontgibaud

In this unhappy time of revolution, a Frenchman is sometimes the worst company that a Frenchman can encounter.

—François-Alexandre-Frédéric,
duc de La Rochefoucauld-Liancourt

Chapter Three

Sunlight rippled over the Delaware River as Vivienne disembarked the schooner ahead of Armand, who engaged a stevedore to convey his trunks from the ship. For five weeks, sails flapped, waves slapped, and rigging and timber creaked with every breath of wind. Now that the constant rocking beneath her feet had ceased, it seemed the rest of her world had tilted.

Church spires, not guillotines, gleamed above redbrick buildings. Sea gulls looped overhead in a sky of brilliant blue. The shouts of dockworkers and the groaning of chains and anchors filled her ears as she put the wharf behind her.

Armand had made arrangements to stay with a friend who'd arrived in Philadelphia two years ago and now had his own home. Still, he'd insisted on sharing a carriage with her until she was safely in her own lodgings, as she had refused to join him in his.

A light carriage pulled near, and she hailed the driver. "I'm looking for a pension. Could you take us?"

With a broad, friendly smile, the ebony-skinned man said he could. "In the French Quarter, I'd guess."

"Yes, thank you."

With a nod, he straightened his cap over his coiled gray hair and loaded Armand's trunks into the rear. Holding her portmanteau,

Vivienne lifted the hem of her petticoats to clear the wheel, and Armand handed her up into the carriage. He climbed in beside her, not quite muffling a moan as he sat.

Sea travel had not agreed with him. Too sick for much conversation, he had asked her to read aloud to pass the time, and she had agreed. Unfortunately, *Romeo and Juliet* had only deepened his emotional misery, and *Robinson Crusoe*, adventure tale of a shipwrecked hero, had done nothing to ease his distress.

The horses pulled the carriage up the slope from the wharf to Front Street, their black tails swishing at flies. The land leveled, and the activity swirling about the carriage both bewildered and buoyed Vivienne. Iron-rimmed wheels and hooves rang over cobblestones. Sailors spilled boisterously out of grog shops, and street criers hawked their wares along the teeming riverfront. For three years, she had barely seen a carriage, for those who could afford them had fled Paris as soon as they grasped the danger. Now not only did she sit in one, but the earth fairly shook with the thundering of coaches, chariots, chaises, wagons, and drays. Bridles jangled and whips cracked above the horses pulling them.

"Ask him how big this town is," Armand prompted, and she complied.

"Well now, this here along the riverfront is the eastern edge, of course." The driver hitched a thumb over his shoulder. "Behind us a couple blocks is Vine Street, the northern boundary before the Northern Liberties suburbs. Seven blocks down the river from Vine—that's about a mile, I reckon—is Cedar Street, the southern end."

A mile from one end to the other. The entire length of Philadelphia was shorter than the distance between the Palais-Royal and the Bastille. "And to the west?" Vivienne asked. "How far does it reach?"

"Eighth Street."

A gust of wind sashayed against her blue silk gown, swaying the lace at her elbows. "So, eight blocks from here? The city is less than a square mile?"

The driver grinned. "And growing all the time. Forty thousand souls and counting."

Swallowing her surprise, she translated for Armand, who straightened his bicorne hat on his brow. "And they call this a capital." Lace ruffles bobbed beneath his chin as he muttered.

The carriage trundled over the street, rumbling the bench beneath Vivienne. At the large, brick London Coffee House, they rounded the corner onto a street that must have been a hundred feet wide. In the middle of this broad road, covered market sheds buzzed with noise and people. Her stomach clenched in envy at the sight of shoppers' baskets laden with golden rolls or rainbowed with fresh produce.

"Markets are open every Wednesday and Saturday," the driver threw over his shoulder.

Wednesday. Saturday. She rolled the English words over her tongue. No more ten-day weeks without room for the Lord's Day. No more months named for wind or flowers or snow or heat, no more counting the years from the birth of the revolution, rather than from the birth of Christ. The carriage driver could not have known the comfort his simple comment afforded.

The repetitive calls of rag pickers and chimney sweeps reminded her of Paris, where she could buy roasted chestnuts, wine, or *café au lait* on nearly any corner.

"Pepper pot! All hot!" an African woman shouted, banging a long-handled spoon on a large pot of soup. "Come buy my pepper pot!"

Smells of oysters and manure mixed freely with those of perfume and tobacco. Among the crowd, round black hats the size of dinner plates topped men in black cloaks and white neckcloths. Men walked, children played, and women swept along bricked surfaces between the buildings and the streets. Sidewalks, the driver explained. In France, pedestrians and horses and wagons all shared the roads.

Armand clucked his tongue, his spine straight as a lamppost in his mauve silk suit, hands clasped atop the walking cane between his knees. "You are a peacock in a dovecote, ma belle."

She frowned. "Armand, we are clear on our arrangement, yes? If what the captain said is true, there are five thousand French in this city. That's plenty of company for you without me." The voyage had blunted the sharp edge of her bitterness toward him, but his presence still scraped at her nerves.

"Come now. Aren't we at least friends after the last several weeks? And yet you stand ready to evict me from your life though you don't know another soul here."

They were not friends, but she left that remark uncorrected. In truth, he had surprised her during the crossing by guarding her from more than one sailor's advances. Though he was nearly green with nausea, he had summoned his strength and a voice like thunder to protect her. When storms had raged and waves had pounded the schooner, they had huddled belowdecks together. She could not remember who had reached for the other's hand first, but she did recall clasping his fingers in the dark as salt water streamed in around them.

But the voyage was over at last, and so was their forced companionship.

Persuading patience into her voice, she reminded him, "We have different goals here, you and I. You want to stay only as long as you must before you may return with your head intact. I have no desire to go back at all." If this was to be her new home, she would not waste time longing for a past that could never be restored.

Lines furrowed Armand's brow. He pursed his thin lips and looked out toward the street. For a moment, his posture flagged, as though pressed by the weight of all he had lost. His wife and their children had moved in with her sister's family somewhere in the south of France almost as soon as his title and estate were stripped from him. Armand had not been invited. "*And if your family had not abandoned you?*" Vivienne had pressed on the schooner. "*Would you have written to Sybille?*" For that, he'd had no answer.

Two blocks had passed, and they turned onto a narrower street lined with lampposts and passed through a blizzard of small white petals plucked by the wind from their tree branches. Gradually, the homes changed from brick to wood.

"What's that all about?" Armand pointed to some boarded-up homes whose gardens had been abandoned to weeds.

Vivienne repeated the question in English for the driver.

"The yellow fever," he replied. "It was worst in the blocks closest to the river. Fevers always come in the hottest months of the year, when the air is bad, but last year . . ." He shook his head. "Worst I ever saw."

"And these people never recovered," Vivienne added.

"These, and thousands more."

"What does he say?" Armand asked, and she translated. "Thousands? Are you sure he said that?"

"Pardon me, how many died, again?" She leaned forward. Perhaps she had misunderstood.

"Five thousand. In three months' time. Many said the French brought it with them, when they came from Cap-Français."

Vivienne gasped and quickly repeated this information to Armand. She knew the revolution had crossed the ocean to the West Indies and the French colony of Saint-Domingue. The colony was famous throughout Europe for the wealth gained by its cotton, coffee, sugar, and indigo. But the slaves, who outnumbered their French and Creole masters ten to one, rose up when the cry of liberty reached their ears from far-off France. Those who escaped the massacres there must have come to Philadelphia. If the city laid the blame for the epidemic at their feet, would they bother to make the distinction between French fleeing Saint-Domingue and French escaping France?

The carriage rolled to a stop in front of a building that slouched between a townhouse and a café with a red-striped awning. Above the front door, a wooden shingle reading "Pension Sainte-Marie" squeaked on its hinge in the breeze. A halo was carved above the words. Though Vivienne knew it had been named for the Virgin

Mary, it was still a jolting reminder of the late queen, whose name had never been paired with the holy.

"Here? Are you sure?"

She allowed Armand's question to drift, unanswered, while she climbed out of the carriage and took the measure of the small wooden pension, from its flaking yellow paint to the untidy lavender bushes stretching slender fingers toward the windows. The building's frame hunched slightly forward, like a woman whose shoulders were rounded with age. Tree boughs bent gracefully over the sidewalk toward the pension, and shadows fell like Chantilly lace at her feet.

Aside from the wasp nest in one blue shutter, Vivienne found the place charming in spite of—or perhaps because of—its gently weathered exterior.

The plodding of passing horses filtered through the birdsong, and she turned to find the carriage driver still awaiting her verdict before he would leave. Armand watched with a scowl, obviously unimpressed.

She climbed the four front steps and rapped the brass knocker on the door. At length, a maid of slight frame and florid cheeks answered. Wiping her hands on her greasy apron, she took one look at Vivienne and said, "French?" She looked to be no more than nineteen years of age.

"Yes," Vivienne replied. "Have you room?"

The maid blew a strand of brown hair from before her eyes and proceeded to speak in their native language. "We do. Two dollars a week for a room and one meal per day. You'll not find any cheaper, for the French Welcoming and Charity Society takes up some of the costs. The missus will tell you that—come in, I'll fetch her. That is, if you still want the room?"

"Yes, I do. A moment, please." Feeling lighter than she had in some time, she hastened down the steps and told the driver he could carry on. "Thank you."

The driver touched two fingers to the brim of his hat and smiled. "Fare thee well, as the Quakers say."

Armand clutched at her, countenance sagging. "When will I see you again?"

She unwrapped his fingers from her arm. "Forgive me, but that is not my chief concern. Please, do not seek me out. Au revoir." With one more wave to the carriage driver, she returned to the Pension Sainte-Marie, eager for a new beginning.

By the time she stepped inside the narrow foyer, another woman stood ready to greet her, a soup-spoon-sized hollow at the base of her corded neck. "I am Madame Ernestine Barouche, the proprietress."

Not citizenness. Madame.

"Vivienne Rivard." She bobbed in a curtsy.

"You are very welcome here. I understand you've met Paulette Dubois, my maid and helper in all things about the pension." Silver hair sparkled in expertly coifed curls upon Madame Barouche's head. Her dress, with its wide panniers at her hips and flattened bodice, suggested she had traveled to America nearly twenty years ago, when such were the fashions, and for whatever reason had never returned. "It has been months since we've had a new boarder. Do you come direct from France? Or have you been living in exile in England?"

"Madame, it is not three months since I left Paris."

A brown-spotted hand fluttered to her heart in a gesture that echoed Tante Rose. "Do come in." She beckoned Vivienne into the parlor and bade her sit in one worn velvet armchair while she lowered herself into the other. "You must tell me, then. We heard some months ago that the queen—" Madame clasped her hands firmly at her waist. "She is dead. Along with the king. Is this so?"

Dust flecked a sunbeam between them. "Yes, it is true," Vivienne confirmed.

Madame crossed herself. Lines deepened from the corners of her mouth to her chin. "We can never be certain of the news we hear. Some have held on to hope that the queen was still alive, though imprisoned, and that plans were under way to bring her here. To America, I mean."

Vivienne crossed her ankles, then uncrossed them, the chair squeaking with her movement. "I'm sorry. She is no more."

Stoically, Madame nodded, her hair framed by a white doily topping the cushion behind her head. "It is as I suspected, of course. And what of Louis-Charles? What news can you share of the boy king?" Her tone remained tight. "He lives, does he not?"

"Only barely." Vivienne pressed her lips together, unwilling to relay the story, common knowledge in Paris, that a cobbler had been tasked with beating the royalty out of him and making him into a revolutionary. A drunk revolutionary, at that, for otherwise surely the boy would never have signed that accusation against his mother, the one that tipped the outcome of her trial toward execution. Shameful depravities that should not even be whispered in secret were shouted by the town criers until all of Paris had heard. It was patently false that the queen had ever harmed Louis-Charles in those unspeakable ways. If the boy had signed a confession, surely it was under duress. "They keep him alone, imprisoned. Not even his sister shares his cell."

"But why? What harm could there be in letting him live with his relatives in Austria?"

Vivienne rested a hand on the chair's arm, fingertips dipping into the carved wooden scrollwork. "He's a threat to the government because of those who wish to restore him to the throne." She could not bring herself to repeat that he'd been abused so much that rumor had it he no longer spoke. "*Insensible,*" the story went. "*An idiot.*"

Madame Barouche looked past her, toward the window. The minute hand twitched inside the clock on the mantelpiece before she smiled again, her eyes crowded by wrinkles. "You must forgive me for pouncing on you like that, and you no doubt are eager for your room. It's hard, you see, wondering about the truth. But then, it's even harder once we know it."

It was an unfashionably early hour for sleep, but soon after Madame Barouche led Vivienne to her room, she hung her three gowns on pegs in the wall, then fell exhausted onto a bed that did not sway. The small garret chamber held dried roses and the lingering scent of coffee from the café next door rather than that of salt and tar. Toile curtains matched the counterpane. The wallpaper's pale green print of milkmaids and sheep on a creamy background was reminiscent of Marie Antoinette's made-to-order village at Le Petite Trianon, where sheep were groomed and beribboned, and eggs were wiped clean in the chicken coop before royal fingers touched them.

Questions about Vivienne's uncertain future surrendered to the overwhelming need to sleep. Before she could finish the prayer she began, she tumbled into an unrestful slumber, where memories distorted and twisted together. Rose whispering, "*Save yourself. Do not object,*" before climbing the platform to the guillotine. Sybille drifting home with a loaf of bread in one hand, hair disheveled. Armand begging for forgiveness. Louis-Charles screaming for escape, scratching his uncut fingernails against stone walls.

When she awoke, she was filmed with sweat. Light from the streetlamp seeped through her open window, and the breeze swept a chill down her spine. Swinging her legs over the side of the bed, she went to the washstand and laved water over her face and hands, but she could not rinse the images from her mind. She crept back to bed and waited for her pulse to calm, gaze fixed on a cobweb strung in the corner near the ceiling. Outside, the night watchman called out the two-o'clock hour and added that all was well.

All is well, she repeated to herself with a series of deep breaths. *It was merely a dream.* But it was more than that. An ache filled the empty spaces her losses had carved away. It was not only Rose she missed, or Paris. But to her dismay, her thoughts looped back to Sybille. The footing they had found themselves on was complicated and cautious. "*I don't expect you to forgive me for being who—and what—I am,*" she had told Vienne one day, before the pox stole her senses. "*I ask no loyalty or love. Just courtesy.*" But Vienne was loyal. Eventually, she even grew to love Sybille, more from choice than natural affection. Once, Sybille had told Vivienne she loved her. She was mad by then, but Vienne had longed, beyond all reason, to believe it anyway. Now Sybille was gone. And Armand made it impossible to forget her.

Vienne had been wrong about grief, to think of it as mere sadness, to believe it could be dammed while inconvenient, or set free to run its course and then dry up. It was a crush in the chest, a sharp pull in the gut, pain that circled back without warning. No respecter of time or will.

Life and lacework with Tante Rose had seemed so stable and enduring, when in fact it was only an opera set struck down by revolution, and Vienne was the only one left standing on an empty stage. Where exactly did she find herself now? What role would she play here, and with whom? How quickly the relief of escape had faded. Now all she felt, besides loss, was lost. *Lord, guide me.*

A child cried out.

Vivienne sat up, heart drumming, and turned her ear toward the sound. Listening closely, she heard it again. On the other side of the wall, a child was crying. A woman consoling.

She might have guessed as much in a pension full of refugees. There were nightmares enough for them all.

Morning poured into Vivienne's chamber through the tree outside her window, and the sounds of a city waking met her ears. Pushing her black curls from her face, she peered at the street below. Buggies and wagons rolled toward the center of the city, and the smell of the river carried on the cool spring breeze. Iron scraped brick as the café staff next door set bistro tables and chairs beneath its awning. Her stomach cramped at the thought of food.

Quickly, she dressed and performed her toilette before going downstairs to the dining room. Three others were already at the table.

"G'morning," said Paulette, her cap slightly askew on her hair. "I figured you'd come when you smelled the coffee, and here you are. I'm Paulette, if I didn't say so, should you need to call for me. Which you probably won't, as I've a keen sense of what needs

doing and when and where, and I make it my business to do it."
Breathlessly, she pointed to an empty chair, set a basket of baguettes on the table, and stood against the wall, poised to be of
service.

Vivienne smiled at this magpie of a maid. "Thank you. I'm
Vivienne Rivard." She eased into a seat.

"Welcome." The only man present was the first to speak. "I am
Father—excuse me. I am Alain Gilbert. Once a priest, but no longer. Not for lack of faith." He was dressed in plain clothing rather
than clergy's garb, a sad smile in his eyes, and Vivienne guessed
the rest of the story. He'd likely been defrocked for not taking the
revolutionary oath that placed Reason above God.

Vivienne nodded, warmed by his quiet convictions already. If
he were corrupt, as many priests were, he'd have had no qualms
agreeing to terms that would have allowed him to stay in France.

"This little lamb is Madame Suzanne Arquette of Saint-
Domingue." Father Gilbert placed his hand on the back of the
woman's chair. She was not little, however, and neither was she
young. Her eyebrows were painted high on her brow, and her expression was blank and simple, as Sybille's had been once she'd
lost her faculties.

Madame Arquette stared at Vivienne. "Have you seen my husband and children? I hate to eat without them, but the hour is
getting on."

Father Gilbert answered before Vivienne could reply. "There
is no cause for alarm, I'm sure. They would want you to break
bread without them. Here, allow me." He filled her coffee bowl.

The steam curled toward the woman's face. "But where are
my servants? They should pour, not you." She looked about the
room, lips buttoned tight, before cupping the bowl in her hands.

"You may call me Martine," the woman beside Vivienne said
quietly. "I believe we are neighbors."

So this was the woman whose voice Vivienne had heard in the
night, although perhaps she was mistaken about the child. A beauty
patch adorned Martine's drawn but pretty face. Her unpowdered

hair was white, far ahead of her years. There was gentility in Martine's voice and grace in the tilt of her elegant neck, but dark bands beneath her eyes spoke of sleeplessness, or sorrow, or both. Her hands shook as she tore off a piece of bread and dipped it into her coffee bowl.

"Martine." Vivienne handled her name gently, for she appeared as fragile as spun glass. "Your lace is familiar."

Martine glanced up, face tight, the cords of her neck tensing. Arms crossing at her middle, she covered the lace cuffs at her elbows. Was she so haunted by ghosts that she thought the observation a threat?

"I meant only to say that I knew the woman who made that lace," Vivienne clarified. "She was in my employ in Paris. My *manufacture* supplied lace to those who made Marie Antoinette's fashions and sparked trends for the women of France."

Martine relaxed. "You're a lace mistress?"

"At least until I can sell the inventory I smuggled out." Vivienne poured cream, then coffee, into her bowl, then took a drink.

Madame Barouche made her entrance as they spoke. Eyebrows raised, she stood at the head of the table, hands clasped loosely in front of her skirt. "How lovely! How very clever! Was your family in the lace business long?"

"Five generations in France, starting with my great-great-grandmother Gabrielle. My grandmother's sister, Isabelle, moved to England to make and sell lace near Bath. I believe she passed the tradition down to her daughter, too, but we lost touch over the years."

Suzanne sniffed imperiously, clearly a class above those who worked with their hands.

Madame ignored her. "And does your family await your return to France, or . . ."

Vivienne set her coffee bowl down and dropped her cold hands to her lap. "No."

Nodding heads ringed the table. Everyone had lost someone. Spouses. Children. Friends. Parents. Siblings. Names were spoken in somber tones, for the names were all that remained of them.

The young maid sighed as she cleared away some dishes, her timing somewhat irreverent. Suzanne pushed back from the table, and Father Gilbert excused himself to chaperone her.

"Well!" Martine clapped her hands in the first display of animation she'd shown. "We all adored your lace at court. I would love to purchase some from you. A few of my gowns need to be retrimmed, and the lace here in Philadelphia . . . well, it isn't French. It isn't yours."

Vivienne smiled, even as she dreaded where this might lead. Like the queen, members of the court were accustomed to acquiring on credit, quite comfortable with debt. But she could not give her lace away. "I'm honored, Martine. But I hope you'll understand, I can no longer transact on credit."

"I can pay right away, you needn't worry." She leaned in close. "I had the Privilege of the Candles at Versailles, and I put my advantage to good use. I don't plan to purchase an extravagant amount of lace, just enough for one gown's repair, maybe two."

Madame Barouche sat in the chair Father Gilbert had vacated and rested her hands in her lap. "Privilege of the Candles? I'm not familiar."

Color rose in Martine's cheeks, but she explained. "It was the custom at Versailles for new candles to replace any that had been lit for any length of time in the queen's presence. This was not Marie Antoinette's demand, understand. It was only the custom. But it did mean that if she was in a room for even as little as five minutes, all the perfumed tapers in that room were lit for only five minutes, snuffed as soon as she exited, and then new candles immediately replaced the used."

"And the used candles? What was their fate?" The frown on Madame Barouche's face reflected Vivienne's sentiment, as well. Such waste! On the edge of the room, Paulette scowled and rolled her eyes.

"Four ladies-in-waiting were given the privilege of collecting them," Martine explained. "'The Privilege of the Candles,' you see. We sold our shares and found ourselves fifty thousand livres richer for it each year."

Behind a mask of polite interest, Vivienne reeled at the sum. Little wonder starving peasants harbored so much hatred toward the court.

"Other women spent their money on gowns and gambling, and I admit to some of that as well," Martine continued, "but I saved the lion's share. And it brought me here. So you see, Vivienne, I am able to buy your lace."

"I see," Vivienne breathed. Any sale would help, and the sooner she unloaded her lace, the more secure her position in America would be. "In that case, I will bring some samples to your room so you may see how they suit your gowns."

"Oh no, don't!" Martine brought her fingers to her lips. "That is to say, the light is so much better in the parlor." She gestured to the chamber next to the dining room. "I shall meet you there, instead. In an hour?"

Vivienne contained her surprise at Martine's outburst. "Yes, of course." She added a smile. "In an hour."

Martine exhaled in apparent relief. "Merci, Vivienne." She stood, and when Madame Barouche swept from the room, Martine snatched the roll from her plate and tucked it into her pocket.

Vivienne pretended not to notice.

Chapter Four

Rain fell hard and cold outside. Tucked into the Four Winds Tavern between Philadelphia's French Quarter and Market Street, Liam Delaney waited at a round, ale-stained table in the corner. It was only big enough for two people, three if they squeezed in tight. It suited him. Crowds didn't.

Swallowing the last of his cider, he stretched his travel-sore legs beneath the table and spread yesterday's newspaper out before him. The headlines from France's revolution were almost too violent to credit. Columns of essays followed, written by Americans feverish for America to support France's war on Europe. Meanwhile, French refugees flocked here, to Philadelphia. Liam shook his head as he folded the paper and tossed it onto an empty table nearby. Opinions raged in this city. That much was nothing new.

Damp spring air crackled in the heat from the nearby fireplace. Outside the window, rainwater gushed from the downspout. It sounded faintly like a river, which made him think of home. It was peaceful there and full of promise, unlike this place, which only reminded him of what he'd lost. The eggshell-colored walls embraced by sage green moulding seemed blank and forlorn without his mother's needlework samplers and his father's bookshelves.

Impatience tightened his chest as he watched his sister Tara refill uplifted tankards. She was tall for a woman, and for that, and for giving no quarter to disorder in her tavern, some had called her mannish. Statuesque and capable, she called herself, and he agreed. Glancing his way, she smiled and lifted a finger. A moment longer. Fine.

A few minutes later, she set her empty pitcher on his table and plopped into the chair opposite him. Weariness etched her face. "Don't give me that look. You know as well as anyone that liquor is what they come in for. If I can't sell drink, I can't afford to stay in business at all."

"You look tired," was all he could think to say.

She threw her hands in the air. "Such a gentleman you are!"

Liam shrugged. "Pardon me. You don't look a day over—how old *are* you now, anyway?" He knew full well she was thirty-three, five years his junior by the calendar. But with the sorrow she'd borne losing her young husband in the war, he reckoned she'd aged a sight more than her birthdays told.

She thwacked him on the arm. "William Michael Delaney!" She straightened her cap before crossing her arms. Her hair matched his chestnut brown in this dim light, but in the sun it shone like burnished copper.

He grinned, tempted to tease her about the freckles that still sprayed her nose and cheeks after all these years. But today, he was playing no games. He leaned forward. "Come away with me. I've got a nice little house on good land now. It's quiet—"

"Too quiet for the likes of me, I'm sure. What would I do there, aside from cook for you? I make a decent living here, I do."

It was not the sort of living Liam would call decent. But then, Tara had always taken after their mother, who had loved living here right up until her final breath last summer, when yellow fever took her life. Liam, however, favored his father. A schoolmaster, like Liam had been until last year, Da had longed for land of his own, land denied him when the English rulers redistributed Irish properties, taking land from rightful owners and giving it to English supplanters instead. Land and freedom were the two dreams his father had for his family when he immigrated to America, and the two causes he died fighting for in the French and Indian War.

The group of men dining at the long table nearby rudely bounced their forks and fists on its surface until one of the staff returned bearing bowls of steaming mashed potatoes and a platter of roasted chicken. The savory aromas clashed with the smells of pipe smoke, rum punch, and ale, forming a veritable hammer to Liam's head. Rising, he turned and shoved open the window to get some fresh air, even if it was wet. He shook his head and eased back into his chair. "You don't belong here."

"*You're* the one who can't abide being here. This is exactly where I belong, and you know it." Tara's tone softened. "You didn't fancy living here even when we were children. You were none too pleased to share your home with boarders, but the Four Winds has been good to us. When you ran off to the war, Mother and I made this tavern into what it is now. This place has been a part of me since before I can remember, and I won't be throwing it all away."

Liam spread his hands. "I had to offer." It was all he had, that new plot of land, but it was the finest he'd ever seen. With his crops already sown, it was sure to yield a harvest, even in its first year. It would have been selfish to keep from his family the dream their father cherished.

"You're a good brother. Stop trying to be anything more than that. You have your dream, Liam, and I have mine."

He met her gaze, then immediately looked behind her, where a one-eyed Scots-Irishman stood dripping, his blond hair curling from his head like foam. Rain darkened the shoulders of his oiled deerskin cloak. The leather patch over his missing eye lent a hardened quality to his wiry frame.

Tara swiveled. "Why, look what the wind blew in!" Her laughter was deep and rich, the kind that others might call unladylike but which suited Tara Kate McFarland just fine.

Liam stood and pumped the man's hand. "If it isn't our favorite whiskey rebel!"

Finn O'Brien was more like a brother than a cousin. When his parents died in a carriage accident, he had moved in with the

Delaneys at the age of four. Tara was seven at the time, and Liam was the man of the house at twelve. He could still see his mother gathering all three children to herself. "*I've lost a husband and a brother and a sister-in-law,*" she would often say, "*but the good Lord saw fit to bless me with another son.*" For years, Finn called Liam "Uncle." It must have tried his mother's faith something fierce when Finn lied about his age and joined Liam's regiment.

"Liam!" With a voice bigger than his body, Finn boomed above the noise of the tavern. "Speaking of dreams, I brought mine, too. Sit." He tossed his hat onto an iron hook protruding from the wall. Water dripped from its rim to the floor.

Tara hurried away and returned with a glass tumbler. She slammed it on the table before Liam. "Be polite," she whispered, clearly recalling he didn't drink hard liquor. When Finn pulled a bottle from inside his cloak, she said, "Tell me you've brought barrels more of the stuff. We've been clean out for months."

"I already unloaded them from my wagon, and they're safely in your kitchen as we speak. Now, Liam, it's high time you tried the famous Monongahela rye. Home brewed by yours truly." Finn poured the dark brown whiskey into the glass.

Liam brought the tumbler to his nose, and his nostrils burned at its mere proximity. It wasn't only the sickly heat of whiskey he smelled, though, but something earthy and sweet. Honey, perhaps, or maple. It smelled almost smooth, if such a quality could be smelled. He took a small sip. Then, shaking his head, he whistled low. "Whiskey is not my drink, old friend. But if it were, I'd choose yours."

Finn dropped into the chair beside Tara. "Just as well. You could never afford my prices." His laugh was a merry roar and impossibly contagious. The teasing about Liam's slender resources was well justified. Until he'd acquired his land last year, his frugal lifestyle as a schoolmaster in small towns outside Philadelphia had included boarding with students' families for six months at a time. It was no way for a man to live, especially one on the wrong side of thirty.

Liam pushed the tumbler across the table toward Finn. "Speaking of prices, how are you getting along with the whiskey tax? Doesn't that cut into your profits?"

Finn cursed under his breath and finished off the remaining whiskey. As he leaned his elbows on the table, his face shifted from mirth to fury. "Tyranny if ever we saw it, eh, Liam? The British taxed us, and we resisted. We fought a war and won. We were patriots. And now our government has the nerve to tax our whiskey, and as soon as it's made, even the barrels we never sell. They must know we use whiskey to pay our field hands and barter for trade. So, the tax would not just cut into my profits, it would eat them up altogether. If we let it."

"Meaning?"

"Meaning we've agreed to disagree." His one brown eye sparkled mischievously.

Liam squinted at his cousin. "You and the tax collectors?"

"Almost all of us with stills and the tax collectors. They stopped coming around long ago. Didn't take but a couple of them getting tarred and feathered for them to learn their lesson."

Liam clasped his hands behind his head. "You can't think they're done trying to collect, though."

"If anyone else proves fool enough to come for the tax, I'll be hanged before I give him the first coin. A fellow by the name of Fisher paid the taxes. Wanted to do the right thing, he said, but it took nearly every last coin. He was going to get out of Washington County and start over in Kentucky. Ain't no way he can leave now."

Liam's forehead knotted. "An ill-advised tax, to be sure." He knew what it was to feel stuck and out of options. So did Finn, and more than most. Militia veterans had not been paid for their service during the war except in worthless paper bonds, which Finn had traded for land in western Pennsylvania. The men there were even rougher than the terrain, and Finn lost his eye in a brawl, ending his days as a carpenter. The whiskey trade was all he had left.

"A right shame," Tara said, shaking her head.

"'Tis tyranny, plain and simple," Finn added. "I resisted it from the hands of the British, and I'll resist it now." His declaration crescendoed over the din of the tavern. Heads turned to listen. "I gave the best years of my life for the cause of liberty—so did you—and I'll not see my freedoms trampled on by British-aping easterners with no concern for us on the frontier. Mark my words, the West will split from the East if this keeps up."

"Hear, hear!" a diner shouted, fist raised. "Resist! *Vive la* whiskey rebels!" He pounded the table, making dishes clatter.

"*Vive la liberté!*" cried another. "Down with King Washington and his puppeteer, Hamilton! Down with tyrants! *Vive la France!*"

Liam had heard enough. Exhaustion weighting his eyelids and limbs, he pushed himself up from the table. "I sympathize, Finn. I do. Just remember that this is the capital before you raise any liberty poles around here." He bade them good night.

"So early?" Tara kissed his cheek. "Well, I don't doubt but that you're worn to the bone with travel."

"How much travel are we talking, from here to your place?" Finn asked.

Liam kneaded the muscles in his neck. "My farm is on the edge of a settlement more than a hundred and sixty miles north of here."

Finn whistled. "You've got to be near the border of New York up there."

"Not too far from it."

Finn's brow rippled. "That's no easy journey. What is it that brings you here?"

Liam placed his hand on Tara's shoulder. "Aside from the chance to see my darling sister? The mail. I'm an express postman between the settlement and Philadelphia. I'm on rotation with a few other riders, so I only make the trip once every four or five weeks. It puts a little extra cash in my pocket and lets me keep an eye on Tara." He winked at her.

Standing, Tara gave him a halfhearted punch in the arm. "I have work to do. Finn, I'll send up a plate of food for you, all right?" She hurried away.

Finn thanked her, then turned again to Liam. "You're talking about a round trip of more than three hundred miles over rough terrain. Don't tell me you use your farm horse."

Liam shook his head and rubbed his hand over his jaw. "The manager of the settlement owns a Narragansett Pacer, and we use her. He covers the cost of keeping my horse, Red, in the livery while I'm gone, on top of paying the fee for making the trip." Since Liam didn't own any livestock outside of Red, he could leave the farm for short periods. "There's no better horse than a Narragansett for the journey, but it still takes a good four days in the best of weather." Liam covered a yawn. He and his mount both needed to rest and refuel. "I'll be here two more days."

"Glad to hear it. Good night to you, then. See you on the morrow." Finn saluted Liam, who returned it.

Greeting Jethro, the barkeep, as he passed, Liam wended through tables to the stair that took him to the third floor. Tara had assigned him his old bedroom, though it hardly bore any resemblance to childhood memory. The mattress creaked as he sat and pulled off his boots.

After lighting the oil lamp on the bureau, he shuffled to the washstand in the corner of the room. He poured water into the basin, then splashed it over his face and toweled dry in front of the looking glass on the wall. Two floors below, American voices sang the French revolutionary song, "Ça Ira." The jaunty tune was fast-paced and bright, and the patrons were no doubt swinging their tankards and pints to the French lyrics. The men below might not understand what they were saying, but since Liam had learned the language while training to be a schoolmaster, he had no trouble translating. *It'll be fine . . . the aristocrats, we'll hang them!*

Liam stared at his blue-eyed reflection, catching a glimpse of the father who was fading from memory. "Hang the French," he muttered as he turned away, for it was the French who had killed his father when Liam was seven years old. True, King Louis XVI and Lafayette had helped America win its independence from Britain, but the French people had since beheaded their king and imprisoned

Lafayette. Liam had no stomach for the head-chopping tactics of the revolutionaries, and the aristocratic refugees he'd met were an idle and arrogant lot. Taken all together, Liam was hard-pressed to invest himself in the fate of the French Revolution—especially when the fate of his own country's still hung in the balance.

Chapter Five

For the third consecutive night, Vivienne was awakened by blood-curdling cries from the other side of the wall. There were two people in Martine's room, though no one ever mentioned the child. The crying tonight was awful, and Martine was weeping, too.

Pulse trotting, Vivienne left her chamber and brought her fist to Martine's door—then remembered to open her hand and scratch against the wood instead, for this had been the custom at Versailles. "Martine?" she called to the queen's former lady-in-waiting. "It's Vivienne. Please, won't you let me in? I'm worried about you."

Martine opened the door only as wide as her slender shoulders. How frail she looked without the trappings of the court. She sniffed at the hem of her sleeve. "Oh, Vienne!" she cried in an urgent whisper. "I have a secret."

"If you'll pardon my saying so, you're not keeping it very well—at least not from me. You might as well share the burden you bear."

"I have to trust someone, even if he doesn't."

Vivienne frowned. "What do you mean?"

She looked over her shoulder toward the sound of a whimpering child. "I can't do this alone anymore. I need a friend."

"So do I," Vienne choked out, surprised to find her throat suddenly tight.

The door swung wide enough to admit her, and she stepped through. The chamber smelled sweetly of Martine's orange-scented perfume, but it looked much like Vivienne's. A washstand, a chest of drawers, pegs on the wall draped with gowns—one of which was half retrimmed with the lace Martine had purchased from her.

But there, huddled on the bed in a pale pool of candlelight, was the shuddering form of a child, perhaps eight or nine years old. His knees were tucked under his chin, and he rocked back and forth, the mattress squeaking with every movement. Untidy waves of blond hair lay on his head.

Vivienne took a few steps closer but dropped to her knees when she was still a yard away. "Hello there, monsieur. I am Vivienne, your new neighbor. I should also like to be your friend, if you'll let me. I haven't many others here, you see."

The boy lifted his head to peer at her over his knees. Tears welled in his wide blue eyes. "I don't know you."

"Perhaps we can get to know each other," she offered.

He curled onto his side and faced the wall.

"Is he unwell?" Vivienne asked Martine, rising.

"Pains in his legs and back keep him in bed most of the time. And he is terrified. I cannot console him, though I've tried. Nights are the worst, as you've observed. He dreams he is still in Paris, and relives scenes too dreadful . . . too dreadful." Martine pressed her fist against her mouth. When her shoulders shook with silent sobs, Vivienne pulled her into her arms. If this woman had been lady-in-waiting to the queen, there was no end to the terrors she had seen.

"I don't know what to do for him," Martine rasped as she released Vivienne's embrace. "The governess at the palace was much better with children than I've ever been. I want to help him now, but how can I, when I cannot face down the past myself?"

Vivienne didn't know much about children. But she knew about fear. And she knew what it was to feel trapped.

"What is his name?"

"Call him Henri."

Slowly, Vivienne approached the boy and sat on the edge of the bed. "It's all right, Henri. You're all right. No one will harm you now." She laid her hand on his back, and he flinched. "I won't hurt you. We are all friends here." Martine stood over the bed, her nightdress gleaming in a moonbeam. "You are safe." Vivienne hoped Martine believed it, too.

When the boy's breathing steadied, Vivienne spoke in low tones. "In the daylight, could we not tempt him to come outside with us? Perhaps he would like to watch the boats in the harbor, or the horses at auction on market days. Would he be amused by catching a fish?"

"But his pains. I can't make him walk when it hurts him so." Martine's smile felt apologetic. "To bed with you, now, Vienne. I'm sorry we stole your slumber—and yet so grateful that you cared enough to come."

In the morning, Henri was still on Vivienne's mind as she hurried through an early breakfast. While he and Martine both seemed chained to the past, Vienne must look to the future. She needed to sell the rest of her lace. Perhaps she could even establish a partnership with a dressmaker or milliner. Fueled by hope, she bundled three lengths of lace into her satchel and headed out.

Along South Second Street, she heard more French spoken than English. With the exception of City Tavern near the corner of Second and Walnut, many of the storefronts advertised French specialties: baguettes, pastries, ice cream, cheeses, wines. As she headed north toward Market Street, display windows showed various imported goods. At last, she came to a dressmaker.

A bell tinkled as she opened the door to the shop, and memory rushed at her—of her own lace shop and apartment in the Palais-Royal. She should remember who she was, she decided. Lacemaker for the queen of France, not to mention other European royalty. Taking a deep breath, she strode to the counter and gazed appreciatively at the radiant bolts of silk lining the walls.

"May I help you?"

Vivienne turned to smile at the shopkeeper. "I hope so. I hope we can help each other. My name is Vivienne Rivard. I've just come from Paris, and—"

The woman was clearly unimpressed. Thousands had come from Paris during the last year.

"I made lace for the queen," she started again, hastening to add, "and for anyone else who wanted it. I employed the finest laceworkers in and around Paris. Here, I have brought samples." She withdrew each one in turn, unrolling the delicate netting onto a black velvet-covered board the shopkeeper set on the counter.

"Oh, la!" the woman said quietly as she studied the patterns and workmanship of the pieces. "This is very fine."

Vivienne felt almost weak with relief. She had much more lace to sell, and who better to buy it than a dressmaker who could put it to good use?

"Think of how this would complement the dresses you create for your patrons." Vivienne described a few fashions that would display the Alençon or Chantilly to best advantage.

"How much?" the shopkeeper asked bluntly. "The cost for this lace. What are you asking?"

Vivienne named her prices for each piece and offered a discount if they were taken together.

The shopkeeper wrinkled her nose and counteroffered with an insultingly low figure.

Alarm shot through Vivienne. "Are you in earnest? Do you understand the months it took my laceworker to create this work of art?" She looked more closely at the six yards of trim for a gown's hem and remembered with a start that it was made by Lucie and Danielle. And those billowy cuffs with a scalloped edge were made by Tante Rose. They had lost their heads for this work, all three of them.

"You cannot expect to charge your fancy prices here, where refugees land with their fortunes already ruined. They may want to look like royalty, but they cannot afford to pay for it."

Vivienne swallowed her dismay. "Will you not take one piece and see if a single patron would value it?"

"On consignment, perhaps."

She shook her head. "Women died for this work, madame. I'll not part with it for less than it's worth."

The shopkeeper sniffed. "Then I daresay you'll not part with it at all."

Heat washed over Vivienne. She had to sell this lace. She had no other way to support herself. Crawling back to Armand was simply out of the question.

That the idea even crossed her mind jarred her.

With her fingertips, she carefully rolled the lace and returned it to her satchel. "I regret I'll not have the pleasure of doing business with you. Perhaps later, for the right customer, you'll change your mind," she offered.

"I won't."

Vivienne forced a smile to her lips. "Good day."

She marched out of the shop with her head held high and resisted the urge to slam the door shut behind her. Disappointment felt remarkably like anger.

Her rapid steps propelled her from the shop and out of the French Quarter, into American Philadelphia, before she knew what she was about. North of Market Street, she stopped in every dressmaker and milliner shop she found, testing her English with the same speech she had given in the French Quarter.

"*Too expensive,*" said one. "*I can get something cheaper that looks almost the same.*"

"*Consignment only,*" said another.

"*We specialize in British fashions, not French.*"

Vivienne pressed on, until shops catering to women gave way to furniture makers, blacksmiths, grocers, coopers, and carpenters. When she hit Vine Street, the northern edge of Philadelphia, she looped west, then headed south toward the pension on Third, but with no better luck.

Her mission had failed. And she didn't know where to turn next.

What on earth was she going to do? How long would she live in borrowed rooms? Would she pawn away this lace for mere survival? Surely not. Surely someone would appreciate its value, for the lace industry was dying along with those who made it. What once proliferated in France would soon be impossible to find at all. She shook her head with a sigh.

As she waited at a corner for carriages to trundle by, a flash of red across the street caught her eye. Shock prickled her skin, and her breath stalled.

The *bonnet rouge*.

It can't be. Not here.

Exhausted and shaken, Vivienne returned to the Pension Sainte-Marie.

"Welcome back, dear." Madame Barouche halted Vivienne's steps before she could climb the stairs. "You missed tea, but if you'd like, we can certainly put that to rights."

Paulette rounded the corner with a stack of folded bed linens, her thin face red and glistening beneath her starched white cap. "Tea service is over, thank you very much, and I'll not be dirtying the dining room again today."

"In the kitchen with me, then," Madame tried. "If you don't mind the informality."

Vivienne clutched her satchel tighter to hide the tremor in her hands. "Not at all."

"Fine, although a visit to your washbasin wouldn't harm you much, either." Paulette scurried off.

The color rose in Madame Barouche's cheeks. "There's no putting a lid on that girl, and I've given up trying. She means well, even if her tongue is hinged in the middle."

Vivienne managed a smile. "I agree with her on this matter. Allow me to freshen up, and I'll meet you for that cup of tea in a moment."

In her room, Vivienne washed her face and hands and re-pinned her curls before exiting through the rear door of the building. English ivy covered the ground in a carpet of glossy green points except for a well-worn path from the pension to the kitchen door. With a quick knock, she entered.

Bunches of herbs hung from exposed ceiling beams, releasing their scents into the room. On the wall to her right, copper pots, ladles, and long-handled spoons dangled from a wooden bar above the brick fireplace. A kettle already hung on a crane over the flames. On the opposite wall, a pine dresser held blue-and-white plates and matching serveware.

While Paulette tied and hung a fresh bundle of lavender with the rest of the herbs, Madame Barouche sat at a worktable and pointed to a Windsor chair opposite her. "Please."

The pine table was satin smooth beneath Vivienne's fingertips.

"You're troubled," Madame observed.

"I saw some things today I believed—with relief—that I should never see again. The *bonnet rouge* and the tricolor cockade." The words snagged in her throat, for the mere mention of them contained enough memory to choke her. "Why would Americans wear these symbols?"

"Ah. That." Madame folded her paper-skinned hands together. "Pro–French Revolution sentiment is strong in this city. They believe France is following in America's footsteps, and they are cheering them on by their dress. Did you know that the same man who wrote the pamphlet called *Common Sense*, which sparked the American Revolution, also penned *Rights of Man* for the French? Thomas Paine. A professional revolutionary, it would seem."

"But do they understand here that we barely have any rights at all in France anymore? Anyone can be arrested for the smallest offense, and it's no longer limited to aristocrats. Half the victims are of the Third Estate, at least."

Steam wafted from the kettle's mouth. Paulette swung the crane on which it hung away from the fire and poured the boiling water into a small teapot to steep the tea leaves.

Madame reached across the table and held Vienne's hand. Her touch was cool and dry. "Do not fret, ma chère. Some Americans may foam at the mouth because Washington declared this country neutral in France's war, but this city has also proven to be quite hospitable to the French who are here." She released her hand and leaned back in her chair.

Hospitable was not how Vienne would describe the shopkeepers she'd met. Briefly, she told of her failed errands that day. "The sale from Martine was a good start, but it cannot sustain me long," she added quietly.

Paulette poured two cups of tea and set them on the table. She then took up the sugar nippers, pinched two pieces from the sugarloaf, and dropped one into each cup. "Well, you'll not be getting any business from Suzanne, in case you were wondering." Wiping her hands on her apron, she hustled to the end of the table, floured the surface, and yanked a cloth from the top of a large earthenware bowl. A golden yeasty aroma wafted from the risen dough. "She has nothing—less than nothing, if you consider she's lost her mind. And I've had about enough of her complaining, though in that she's no different from the rest of the aristocrats who wash up here." Sleeves rolled to her elbows, she lifted the dough onto the table.

"Shhh, Paulette," Madame scolded, then sighed from a deep well of untold stories.

"It's all right," Vienne said, absently watching Paulette shape the dough. "That is, I understand. I once cared for someone who had lost her senses." But she was not about to confess the rest.

A breeze lilted through the open window. Vivienne straightened her posture in the Windsor chair, resolving to do what she always had. She would make a way forward, no turning back. Peering over her shoulder at the ghosts of her past would serve no purpose here and now.

Paulette leaned into the heels of her hands as she rolled the dough away from her, then refolded it and began again before dividing it into pieces. "Idle hands always put me in a foul temper. No doubt you'll feel better when you've got a little something to dirty your fingers." Dipping hers in a small bowl of flour, she powdered the table in front of Vienne's chair and shoved a large lump of dough at her. "Pinch this much off the loaf and work it between your hands like this"—she demonstrated—"to form a nice round ball. About this size, see. I know you're used to making lace, but you never know. You might take to making something practical, too."

In all her life, Vivienne had never made bread. At first, there was no need to, with the bakeries so nearby. And then, there simply hadn't been the means.

Madame clucked her tongue. "You need not do this, my dear. You've paid me in coin. I'll not demand your services."

Paulette shrugged. "She looks dour, if you'll pardon my bluntness. And work is a right good remedy for a host of ailments." She tore off a chunk of dough and deftly rounded it into a perfect sphere. "There's oils, and there's Epsom. There's cold compresses, broths and gruels, and then there's good old-fashioned work. I never go without it if I can help it."

A smile crept across Vienne's face as she dusted her fingers and palms with flour and then set to forming balls from the dough. "I don't mind, truly." She had learned basic kitchen work at the pension in Le Havre, and breadmaking seemed far more interesting.

For a few moments, the women sat together in companionable quiet, the only sounds that of birdsong and hoofbeats and wagon wheels from outside. The dough rounding between Vienne's palms was smooth and soft, and the sight of the rolls filling the pan Paulette set on the table offered a certain satisfaction. Life remained complex and unreliable, but this was simple and predictable. A comfort.

Madame Barouche rapped her knuckles on the table. "It has just come to me."

Vivienne tore off another piece of dough. "Yes?"

"The way to sell your lace, and in a hurry. All you need is an introduction to Philadelphia society. Individual fashionable women will benefit you the most. You may have heard the name Alexander Hamilton?"

"I may have." She swept a bit more flour onto her hands.

"He's the Secretary of the Treasury for the United States," Madame explained. "Despite being made an honorary citizen of the new French Republic, he remains staunchly opposed to the bloody turn the revolution took and is particularly concerned with the welfare of French émigrés. You must meet his wife, Eliza." She wrapped her hands around her teacup, though surely by now it had gone cold. "She has the heart of an angel and such influence over her friends. When Eliza learned that a portrait artist and veteran of the American Revolution was in debtor's prison, she marched in and commissioned him to paint her right there in the jail. Paid him handsomely for work well done, and got her friends to do the same until he had earned enough money to pay his debts and be free once more."

Paulette's mouth pinched.

Vienne's fingers stilled on the dough she was shaping. "Society women went to a prison? To sit for hours for a portrait?"

"Exactly," Madame Barouche said.

"Who would do this?"

"Women intent on making a difference, one person at a time," Madame replied. "We only need to introduce you."

Fingers sticky with ragged bits of dough, Paulette propped her fists on her slender hips. "I have it. The very thing. We'll send Father Gilbert with you, of course, as a chaperone. Are you up for attending a ball, Cinderella?"

Spreading her hands, Vienne glanced at her soiled and rumpled gown, the best she owned at present. "And who is to be my fairy godmother?"

Paulette began rolling another ball of dough. "Oh, come now. Between Martine's gowns and your lace, I'm sure you can make your own wish come true."

Chapter Six

If it didn't affect his cousin Finn, Liam would have left the matter alone. But since it did, he trudged toward the corner of Third and Chestnut Street.

A mere handful of blocks separated the Four Winds Tavern from the Treasury Department, but the two establishments were worlds apart. Liam felt a change in the atmosphere as soon as he neared the financial center of Philadelphia. Men stuffed into suits formed knots on the sidewalks, the urgency in their voices hinting at dire consequences if their advice went unheeded. Such was the manner of a finance man, and there was none so convinced of his own rightness as Treasury Secretary Alexander Hamilton.

Veering into the street to avoid a trio of men steeped in their own conversation, Liam narrowly missed a patch of horse manure wheeled flat by carts and buggies. He stepped back onto the sidewalk and found himself before a brick, two-story private home. Roughly converted for use as the Treasury Department, it proved an underwhelming façade for one of the largest—and most powerful—of the federal government's departments.

Liam stood for a moment, a rock around which a stream of people flowed. There had been a time when he and Alex were easy together. Friends, even, or so Liam had thought. He'd been among several officers invited to dine with Alex and Washington. They had eaten lentil stew and braised rabbit, with Martha's famous whiskey cake for dessert. But that had been during the war, when the ideals of independence and democracy had been toasted, and the tyranny of Great Britain denounced in unison. "*Give us liberty,*" they all had said, and had fought to set a nation free.

Liam entered through the front door and into a flurry of activity that smelled of tobacco and ink, courtesy of the clerks scribbling at humble desks against the walls. Upon giving his name to the stoop-shouldered usher who greeted him, Liam was conducted to Hamilton's ground floor office.

It was a plain space for a man of his position. Planks and trestles along the walls held financial volumes, ledgers, and papers. On one such makeshift sideboard stood an imitation Chinese vase and a plate holding glasses next to a decanter of water. The desk at which Hamilton sat was a simple pine table covered with a green cloth, and remarkably clear. But then, Hamilton could not abide a cluttered desk any more than he could a cluttered mind.

"Well! William Delaney." The secretary rose, revealing his short stature. Small black eyes shining in a face that had gone jowly in office, he circled his desk and shook Liam's hand. Surprising, since their last meeting had not ended well.

"I would say that I hope I'm not intruding, but you never stop working, so . . ."

"Indeed." Alex returned to his chair. "You cannot imagine how the work piles up. I trust you will sit."

Liam pulled a heavy oak chair closer to Alex's desk before taking a seat. He wasn't accustomed to sitting in the presence of Alexander Hamilton. As long as he'd known him, Alex's nervous energy had rarely surrendered to a chair but sent him pacing instead. Today, however, the small man with big ideas looked wilted beyond his thirty-nine years.

Liam leaned forward, elbows on his knees, his cap in his hands. "Are you unwell?" he asked. "Ghosts of the fever haunting you today?" Last summer, Alexander and his wife had succumbed to the yellow fever epidemic. Though they both recovered, it had stripped Alex of his typical physical and mental stamina for some months.

"Fever? No. I'm plagued by something far more virulent and pernicious than that, my friend." A muscle twitched in his cheek. "Republicans. But you haven't come to hear about my political rivals. Make your request, and we shall see how I may assist you."

Alex had risen to an astonishing level of power since they'd first met. Not only that, but he had a wife and children who adored him. Liam had never pined for a cabinet position, but he had hoped—had expected—to have a family of his own by now, which was more important to him by far. Or at least it had been, when he'd imagined that goal within reach.

"It's the whiskey tax, Alex. Are you aware of the hardships it imposes?"

The secretary frowned. "Is this about those rebels in the frontier?"

"It wasn't so long ago that *we* were the rebels, and Washington besides. Fighting against taxation without representation. You must know that's how the whiskey rebels view this tax. They feel singled out. Their interests aren't represented."

Alex opened his mouth to speak, but Liam barreled on.

"The roads between their land and any markets are pathetic. The most economical way they can get their grain here is to distill it into barrels of whiskey and cart them behind a mule over dangerous mountain paths. The Mississippi River would be an ideal way to transport their goods, but you—that is, the government—have failed to even open negotiations with Spain for permission to navigate its waters."

"If you haven't noticed, we're barely keeping out of a war which we are disastrously ill-prepared to fight—"

Liam held up his hand. "I'm well aware of that, and I appreciate the delicacy the situation requires. But for argument's sake, allow me to present a perspective contrary to popular opinion. Western Pennsylvania is as much a part of this country—this state—as Philadelphia is. Those men are patriots and veterans, the same as you and me. And you know better than anyone that they were never paid for helping secure America's independence. Is it any

77

wonder so many traded those bonds in when speculators promised fertile land? Except the land they got in exchange isn't fertile for anything but barley."

"The states were flat broke after the war. *No* militia were paid. You could have been, though, as an officer, if you hadn't refused."

Liam's militiamen had risked and sacrificed as much as he had. Of course he'd wanted to get paid for his service, but to accept money when men like Finn got nothing—it didn't suit. And Alex knew that. He knew Liam had scrimped and saved as a schoolmaster until he had enough money put together to finally buy his land. "It's called principle," he said simply.

"You say it as though I'd not heard of the word."

"From where the whiskey rebels stand, the liberties they fought for have vanished. Whiskey is used for trade, for bartering. It's their currency, Alex. When you demand taxes on whiskey as soon as it's produced, you're taking coin they do not have."

Hamilton rose and went to the sideboard along the wall. From the glass decanter, he poured two tumblers of water. "I'm doing everything I can to finance this country. We need taxes to do it. And that rebellion in the West, as you put it so mildly—it smacks of revolution inspired by the French." Returning to his desk, he handed a glass to Liam before taking a drink. "We cannot afford to allow perfidy to go unpunished. Law and order hang in the balance, Liam. Laws are to be obeyed, even when one does not agree with them. Otherwise we're left with anarchy. I can almost hear the guillotines slam. Can't you?"

Liam's glass perspired in his palm. "This isn't about the French. This is about America."

"Indeed, it is. On this we agree."

"And you."

Alex cocked his head. "How so?"

"Some say you are a monarchist."

"Ah, yes." He nodded. "Many do."

"They say you would turn America into another England if you could, and put yourself on the throne with crown and scepter."

Alex finished drinking his water. "I've heard it all. I've read it all. Obviously, you have, too. The debate between friends of liberty and friends of order is a significant one."

The usher returned and announced the next petitioner.

Alex looked at his pocket watch. "But unfortunately, not one I have time to explore in detail just now. I do welcome a good spar, however, and seeing as you have some fight left in you, may I suggest you come to the Binghams' salon this evening?"

Liam set his glass on Alex's desk. "William and Anne Bingham?" William was a successful merchant of Federalist persuasion and had been a warm supporter of the Constitution. He and his wife were the most fashionable couple in Philadelphia society, renowned for lavish parties at their mansion. The Washingtons and Hamiltons both held public levees and receptions, but Bingham salons were strictly by invitation only. "I've never had the pleasure . . ."

"I'll see that you're added to the guest list. I rarely have time for these gatherings, but tonight's will prove to be most stimulating. French refugees will be there, fresh off the boat in the last week or so. We'll hear the latest news straight from eyewitness sources. Those from the Jeffersonian camp will be there, too. Verbal dueling will abound." Smiling, he rose, and Liam did the same. "Do say I can count on your presence at the Binghams'. Eliza will be pleased to see you again."

After promising to come, Liam shook Alex's hand, then brushed past the next petitioner on his way out.

In the middle of Martine's chamber, Vivienne turned in a slow circle, the folds in her silk skirt whispering with movement. "How did we do?"

Martine smiled broadly from her perch on the edge of the bed, hands clasped beneath her chin. Henri lay curled beside her atop the counterpane. Blue veins mapped his translucent skin. He blinked, watching with mild interest.

"*Magnifique!*" Martine pronounced. "The gown is perfect on you, and your lace will be the finest they've ever seen."

Vienne touched the lace fichu she'd added to the square, low-cut neckline, grateful for the modesty it brought. She felt strange—dishonest, almost—wearing Martine's saffron court gown, even though it was a relatively simple one. The revolution may have leveled the social classes, but as a lacemaker, Vienne was raised with one foot in the world of the working people and the other tiptoeing through the doors of the aristocracy, catering to their whims. As such, she'd never fully belonged to either realm. Well practiced at straddling two worlds, she now belonged neither to France nor to America. Untethered, like a loose thread, while every other strand was woven into place.

Martine's manner turned wistful. With nail-bitten fingers, the young woman patted her own coiffure, shocked white from un-named trauma.

"Come with me," Vienne urged, for Martine was already dressed, as always, in court finery. "It would do you good to get out. Wouldn't you enjoy dancing?"

"Oh no, I can't leave."

"You're not in prison here, you know. Surely Paulette or Madame can sit with Henri while you're out. It would do him some good, too, to have a little variation to his routine. Would you mind, Henri?" Still painfully quiet, he rarely initiated conversation but did respond when spoken to.

The boy frowned. "You both want to go? But why?"

Martine pressed her lips together and shook her head. "I don't. I'm afraid I've lost all taste for gaiety. And I haven't the strength to pretend otherwise."

This, Vivienne understood completely. "Of course. Another time, perhaps."

Footsteps sounded in the hallway, and Paulette rapped on the doorframe before poking her head into the room. "Mademoiselle," she huffed, "your escort has arrived."

Hastily, Vivienne bussed Martine's cheeks, whispered good-bye to Henri, and followed Paulette down the stairs. Just inside the front door, Father Gilbert conversed in French with a tall young man in an American suit, complete with knee breeches and buckled shoes. Hat in his hand, his black hair shone like lacquer, and his brown eyes held golden flecks.

"I am Sebastien Lemoine, and I'll be escorting you to the Binghams'," he said in French, then bowed to her. His narrow features were animated with energy, and Vienne judged him to be a few years younger than herself.

"*Enchantée.*" She curtsied.

"The pleasure is mine. Shall we?" He offered his arm, and she took it.

"Find Eliza," Madame mouthed, then crossed herself. Father Gilbert followed as they exited the pension and climbed into the waiting chaise.

The journey to the Bingham mansion was not long but afforded time enough for Monsieur Lemoine to share that he had arrived from France three years ago and was now in the employ of a Senator Robert Morris, who had personally financed much of the American Revolution and had lent his townhome at Sixth and Market for the use of President Washington and his family. Also a particular friend to French refugees, Senator Morris had helped finance a settlement for them in the woods in the north of the state. French Azilum, they called it, or Asylum in English. Place of refuge.

Vienne smiled politely but concluded she had no interest in such a place, for she could not imagine her livelihood would thrive there. Far better were her chances here in the city. And that, she reminded herself as the horses drew into a circular drive, was why she had come to the three-story mansion before her. To find buyers for her lace.

In a few blinks of the fireflies around her, she entered the double doors with Monsieur Lemoine, aware of Father Gilbert behind her. The bright hum of conversation met her ears, punctuated by the occasional clinking of goblets. Large parlors flanked the wide marble staircase of the vestibule.

At the base of the stairs, Monsieur Lemoine facilitated the introductions with William and Anne Bingham, while Vienne noted with some surprise the French influence in their home: bright red arabesque wallpaper, silk curtains, and painted ceilings above dentil moulding. From classical alcoves, the busts of Rousseau and Voltaire looked on.

Having greeted the hosting couple, Monsieur Lemoine led Vivienne and Father Gilbert into the enormous dining room. A gleaming table bore every dessert she could have wished to see in France: flaky *vols-au-vent*, trifles adorned with candied orange peel and pansies, exquisitely molded ice creams on beds of sculptured ice, candied almonds, fresh fruit. Fat tallow candles stuffed every candelabra and chandelier. Full-length mirrors doubled the space, the light, the imported furniture, and the people.

Heads turned, and gazes fastened upon Vienne as she made her entrance. Did they admire her gown? Or hate it?

"Is it polite to stare at strangers in this country?" she whispered to Monsieur Lemoine.

His lean face warmed with a smile. "You're too modest, mademoiselle. But tell me, how did you come upon such finery? I was told you are a lacemaker. Of the working class."

"I borrowed the gown from a friend."

"And is this friend a member of the Versailles court?" Raising an eyebrow, he laughed.

She gave him a pointed look. "Lady-in-waiting, as it happens."

"Why did you not bring her, too? She would have been welcome." He signaled a waiter and plucked a goblet of wine from the tray. "Thirsty?"

She declined. "Her son is unwell, and she won't leave his side."

Monsieur Lemoine sipped his wine. "A pity."

Father Gilbert laid a hand on Vienne's arm. "My dear, if you'll excuse me, I believe I see an old friend. May I leave you with this young man here?"

"By all means."

Vienne watched as the older man made his way across the room and exchanged a few words with another gentleman. With a cry of recognition, the second man threw open his arms and embraced Father Gilbert. Both gentlemen stood straighter upon releasing the other. She hoped it was happiness, not envy, that tightened her throat.

Monsieur Lemoine touched Vivienne's elbow. "I believe you know Armand de Champlain?"

"Do you?" She turned to him and felt the pinch of whalebone stays laced tight against her middle.

"I make it my business to know all the refugees who arrive in Philadelphia. I met him a few days ago at Senator Morris's office. He's headed this way."

Vivienne started at this last sentence and turned. Armand's aristocratic red-heeled shoes clicked over the floor as he approached. After the men greeted each other, Monsieur Lemoine stepped a polite distance away to afford them a modicum of privacy.

Lines bracketed Armand's mouth as he smiled, and his appraising gaze swept from her hair to her hem. "The very likeness," was all he said, and she knew he saw Sybille in her place.

She had not meant to look the part of a courtesan. The small degree of warmth she had felt on seeing Armand quickly cooled. Her fingertips grazed her fichu to be sure it was still in place. "You are fully recovered from the voyage, I see."

"In body, yes. But my heart . . . I miss her, Vienne, more than words can tell. She would have dazzled everyone here with her beauty and grace. As you do. She would have made everything right just by being at my side." Violin music floated between them. "Say you'll dance with a lonely old man?"

The suggestion crawled over her skin. Vivienne had softened toward Armand during the crossing, and some days she'd even pitied him. But she could not put herself in the arms of the man who betrayed his wife to sin with Sybille.

"I have other matters to attend to." She looked at Monsieur Lemoine, and he joined them.

"But how are you faring at the pension? Do you have all you

need? May I help in any way?" The same questions Armand had asked at Le Havre and during their journey across the sea.

"I am managing, Armand." But she could not be distracted from her purpose here tonight. "If you'll excuse me. Monsieur Lemoine, I need to find Eliza Hamilton. Do you know her? Could you introduce us?"

He surveyed the room. "Of course. Follow me."

Armand remained behind while Monsieur Lemoine led her to a woman who was breaking off her conversation with someone else. Hunger walked beside Vivienne, prodding with sharp jabs to her middle, for she had strictly rationed her food until her means could be secured. The monsieur introduced Vivienne to Eliza, then left the two ladies alone to speak.

Quickly, Vivienne dropped a curtsy, then extended her hand in the American way, flushed at her awkward mixing of customs.

"You're among friends here, my dear." Eliza Hamilton's warm smile was disarming. Her chocolate-colored gown echoed her soft brown hair. "Tell me, how did you come to be in America? That is, if you have the heart to describe it."

Touched by the compassion in those few words, Vienne quietly explained, "I left to save my life."

"What charge did they have against you?" Eliza's voice was gentle.

With a rueful smile bending her lips, Vivienne pointed to the billows at her elbows. "I made lace."

Faint lines grooved Eliza's brow, as if unsure Vienne's English could be trusted. "You made this lace? You made lace," she repeated. "And this put your life in danger?"

"Yes. The laceworkers in Chantilly were all executed, every one of them. My aunt made lace, too, and she was killed for it, along with several women in our manufacture. Some of them were only girls." She had not planned to reveal so much. "I escaped alone." Her empty stomach cramped.

Eliza took Vienne's hand and squeezed it. "My dear child. If only I could comfort you with mere words. May the Good Shepherd keep you in His tender care." Tears shone in her dark eyes, dissolving a knot in Vienne's chest. "What will you do, now that you are here? Do you have means?"

She had been warned of the American habit of asking after private finances. But this conversation was exactly why she had come. "I have lace." She explained how she had smuggled it into Philadelphia, what it was worth, and her inability to sell it through the shops at which she'd inquired.

Eliza scanned the crowd, and then she brightened, signaling someone. Vienne turned to find Anne Bingham gliding toward them, her plum-colored satin skirt skimming the hardwood floor. In the next moment, Eliza retold Vienne's tale to the hostess.

Anne touched the lace at Vienne's sleeve. Candlelight made a corona of her upswept hair. "You made this?"

"This and more, which I spirited out of France."

Anne stood back to take in the gown from head to toe. Lace trimmed the neckline, sleeves, and the edges of her skirt. "Gorgeous," she whispered. "Simply stunning." Crossing one arm over her middle, she cupped her elbow and tapped her chin. "Come back Thursday at two o'clock sharp. Bring everything you have. If I don't miss my guess, you'll sell it all to my ladies' club by the end of the afternoon. And don't you dare drop your price one cent less than what the lace is worth. I daresay it's among the last French lace we'll see for quite some time."

Eliza squeezed Vivienne's hand. At the gentle pressure, bittersweet relief pressed into her. She bowed her head, grateful to hide the tears glossing her eyes. "Thank you."

Chapter Seven

When square-toed black boots edged in beside Eliza's hem, Vivienne looked up to find two gentlemen facing her. The elder of the two, if one could judge by the hair receding from his high brow, took Vienne's hand gently, without shaking it, and swept her a gallant bow.

"Alexander Hamilton, at your service." He released her, then presented his friend. "William Delaney. A veteran of the American Revolution. A true patriot and lover of liberty."

Mr. Delaney bowed stiffly, regarding Vivienne with intensely blue eyes. She curtsied as she gave her name. His jaw tense, he held his broad shoulders back in the impression of one still in military service.

"Liam, so lovely to see you again." Eliza clasped his hand. "How is your sister?"

A smile transformed his sun-bronzed face from severe to almost charming. "'Tis a pleasure to see you again, too, Mrs. Hamilton. Tara is as stubborn as ever, which can only mean she's in good health." His jacket pulled at the shoulder seams, and the sleeves hung an inch short at the wrists. Either he'd borrowed the suit from a smaller man, or he'd outgrown it since he'd last had reason to wear it. Vienne wondered why he had come and if his discomfort, like hers, was the price for his present purpose.

As Mrs. Bingham whisked away to engage another guest, a

wiry man noticed the Hamiltons and strolled over from the buffet, candied almonds cradled in his palm. He popped a few of them into his mouth, chewing noisily. This was Charles Whittaker, a prominent Philadelphia attorney, Eliza explained.

"Liam came to my office today, apprising me of the sentiments among the rebels in the western part of the state," Hamilton supplied. "Advised me to repeal the whiskey tax."

Mr. Whittaker nodded, and the yellow glare of candlelight slipped up and down his spectacles. "The excise tax was folly from the start. An oppression of frontiersmen already besieged with trouble."

In moments, the men's voices rose in pitch and volume, turning heads, drawing an audience. But from across the room, a fiddler's jaunty tune jerked Vivienne's attention. At once, she lost her appetite. Heart banging she looked around, astonished to find some of the guests actually raising their goblets and singing along with the "Ça Ira."

"My dear," Eliza murmured, "are you unwell?"

"That song. Do they know what they are singing?"

Mr. Hamilton held up his hand, breaking off his conversation. "Do tell us, mademoiselle, what this song means to you."

Armand appeared on the fringe of the gathering, face drawn in grave lines. He, at least, knew what she felt. Alone, though surrounded. Shadowed, despite the constellations of light thrown by crystal chandeliers. "Tell them. Tell them what I do not have the language to say," he urged. His shoulders pulled a little higher as the chorus gaily condemned men like him.

Drawing a fortifying breath, she spoke. "This was the anthem of the people. The cheerful rallying cry among citizens who styled themselves 'patriots' of France. The song says 'to the lampposts,' but they were really taken to the guillotine. With great relish, I might add."

Mr. Whittaker waved her comments away with one bony hand. "Because the excesses of the French monarchy drove them to it. Versailles represented a deplorable waste in a country already mired in debt." He sipped from his goblet.

Frowning, Mr. Hamilton crossed his arms. "Much of that debt came from supporting America in the war, not from court luxuries, though I cannot deny their mode of living a superfluous one. Still, if it weren't for Louis XVI and the Marquis de Lafayette, we might still be British subjects right now."

Mr. Delaney chuckled without mirth. "The French hatred of the British worked in our favor, I'll give you that."

With a few short sentences, Vivienne quietly translated the English to French for Armand's sake.

"All the more reason for America to fight alongside France now." Mr. Whittaker grew red in the face. When Vienne turned to Armand again, Mr. Delaney stayed her. "Allow me," he said and encouraged her to participate in the conversation while he translated.

"My good man, you suffer from selective memory loss," Mr. Hamilton seethed. "The French heroes who helped us win our war are now victimized by the revolution. For advocating a constitutional monarchy, Lafayette is imprisoned. Those revolutionaries exalt liberty to the exclusion of order, religion, even common morality. No, Mr. Whittaker, the United States cannot stand up for that, no matter how often or how fervently you and your Democratic-Republican Society say otherwise."

"Society?" Vienne interrupted. "What society?"

Mr. Whittaker pushed his spectacles up the bridge of his nose. "Fashioned after the *clubs des Jacobins* in France. Gatherings of like-minded people passionate for the cause of French liberty, equality, and fraternity."

Vienne's mouth went dry. A glimpse of Armand's blanching face proved that he understood Mr. Delaney's translation perfectly.

Jacobins were the radical revolutionaries bent on rolling the heads of anyone not enthusiastic enough about their new government and the leveling of wealth. They were enemies of the French court, aristocracy, and anyone associated with them. It was a Jacobin who'd arrested Tante Rose, Jacobins who condemned her to death. And if what Mr. Whittaker said was true, Jacobin societies had spread across the ocean. The news sent a chill through Vivienne.

Tucking a few almonds into his cheek, Mr. Whittaker continued. "There are thirty-five sister societies like ours at present in America, but the one here in Philadelphia was the first. We are professionals, craftsmen, tradesmen, and French citizens in support of the French Revolution."

"And what exactly do you do?" Mr. Delaney asked. "In support of the revolution?"

"We vow solidarity. Correspond with Jacobin clubs in France, and influence as many as we can here. Shall we Americans, who have kindled the spark of liberty, watch the bright flame burning in France go out?"

Vienne shook her head. "It's not a bright flame of liberty. It's a raging wildfire of bloodthirsty discontents. The guillotines know no rest in Paris."

Whittaker shrugged. "The end justifies the means. I still say the royal couple, mostly the queen, is to be blamed for the dissatisfaction that bred the revolution. Marie Antoinette spent—what was it?—five hundred thousand livres in one year on her wardrobe. And what of her artificial village, Trianon? Not to mention all that flour to powder towering wigs when people starved for lack of bread. And what did the oblivious queen say? 'Let them eat cake!'"

"She never said that. She *never* said that." Heat flashed through Vivienne. How many other vicious rumors had winged their way across the ocean? "Her spending was excessive for a time." Without realizing it, she'd slipped back into her native tongue. The low timbre of Mr. Delaney's voice echoed her words in English now for the benefit of those gathered. "But she scaled back dramatically and was famous for her generosity to the poor she encountered. Did you know she even adopted children into her care? And let us not forget that Louis XVI and his queen came into power when France was already in dire financial straits, even before they sent funds for your American war. Surely you don't believe one woman could have plunged a nation so thoroughly into debt single-handedly?"

Whittaker sneered. "Another royalist in Philadelphia. Just what we need. No wonder you and the Hamiltons get along."

"Faith, Vivienne, take care. He is a jackanapes as bad as the rest." Caution edged Armand's tone.

She pressed on. "I was in favor of the revolution when the aim was a constitutional monarchy. But I cannot abide the monsters who have taken over. I doubt you would think so highly of it yourself if the next neck on the block could be yours. No one is safe now. No one."

The hum of the crowd around her amplified in the pause that followed. Eliza clutched her handkerchief in one hand and her husband's arm with the other. Armand nodded solemnly. Mr. Delaney, she could not read at all. Hands clasped loosely before him, his jaw locked tight. Candlelight glinted on his chestnut hair and cast shadows beneath his cheekbones.

Whittaker swallowed. "Thomas Jefferson says that if half the earth must perish for the French Revolution to succeed, then he would rather see it done than for the revolution to fail. And I, for one, agree."

"Half the earth!" Vivienne gasped. "Women and children? God-fearing souls?"

"If victory required it. The liberty of the whole earth depends on this contest."

Hamilton glowered. "You're mad. You would gain the whole world, and lose your own souls."

"There would be no honor in such a victory," Mr. Delaney added.

"*Vive la France! Vive la liberté!*" With one long stride to the dessert table, Mr. Whittaker picked up a knife and chopped the head from a bright red lobster molded out of ice cream. Scooping the severed head onto a plate, he began to eat it, looking straight at Vienne.

All others in the room fell out of focus as she stared at his horrible smile, stained red.

Loathing for Charles Whittaker snaked under Liam's skin, along with an urge to knock the plate of garish ice cream from his hand. While Alex verbally lashed Whittaker, Liam crossed to the Frenchwoman. Her face was pinched and pale. Though he held no love for aristocrats, he was no brute. "Enough of that," he said to her. He took her hand and placed his other hand at the hollow of her waist. "Shall we dance?"

She startled before settling into his hold, as if she only just then registered that the music had changed to a waltz and that couples twirled about them.

Turning her head, she avoided his gaze as he swept her away, the steps returning to him with surprising ease. A few ribbons of black hair coiled at her neck, and lashes just as dark fringed her green eyes. The hollow of her throat pulsed between collarbones far too prominent. He'd forgotten what it felt like to have a woman in his arms. Liam sensed that, unlike Maggie, who had seemed to mold herself to his touch, the only thing keeping his dance partner with him now was the music. The mademoiselle was rigid. Brittle, even.

She finally faced him, composure restored, her steps never faltering as he guided her through the room. "Mr. Hamilton said you spoke to him on behalf of whiskey rebels. So are you, how do I say it, in favor of only obeying the laws you like?" Her cheeks flushed pink with what he guessed was anger. Perhaps even hatred, no doubt fanned by Whittaker's macabre theatrics.

Her clothes and her sentiments proved she was an aristocrat, the type who curried no favor with the likes of him. Yet how different she was from the woman who had stolen—and squandered—his heart. If Maggie had been half as direct just once during their courtship, Liam would have understood that she had neither patience nor patriotism enough to wait for him while he fought for America's liberty.

"This is what you call liberty?" Mademoiselle Rivard asked, and Liam returned from his thoughts with effort.

"I'm in favor of a representational government that acts justly for all its citizens," he responded.

"And if the government does not act the way you want it to, is this grounds to call it tyranny and overthrow it? You fought in the American Revolution, yes? So will you keep revolting and rebelling every time you don't get your way? And I suppose you will call this patriotism." She spat the word, even as she danced with grace and precision. "Freedom. Freedom for whom? Freedom from what?"

Liam almost forgot to lead. His hands grew warm as he held her. "The whiskey tax is an American issue, inspired by taxes Hamilton introduced, whatever he may say. You're taking this all a bit personally, aren't you?"

She tensed. "Did you not hear the 'Ça Ira' played and sung but moments ago?"

Cringing inwardly, he made no response. It was folly, this borrowing of one nation's revolution and proclaiming it as one's own battle cry. Didn't America have its own share of tangles to sort?

"Mr. Whittaker and his Thomas Jefferson seem to be taking the French Revolution personally, too, wouldn't you say?" she continued. "I cannot comprehend why they applaud the lawlessness that reigns in France. I can only imagine they believe it will prove some point about what kind of government is best for you."

"Mademoiselle, you have just summarized the split between the Federalists and the Democratic-Republicans. The two parties divide along their response to the French Revolution. The former is for a strong central government, the latter for the people's individual freedoms."

She stared at him, brow furrowed, but said nothing.

In the corner of Liam's eye, he caught Eliza Hamilton's stern glance as Alex waltzed with her nearby. Clearly, she disapproved of his irritating effect on his dance partner.

Liam relaxed his grip on Mademoiselle Rivard's hand. He hadn't intended to hold her so firmly. "I did not mean to upset you. In fact, I meant only to put a little distance between you and the source of your distress."

She eyed the small space between them. "Did you?"

"Do not blame me for your agitation. You're safe now, whatever rhetoric tickles your ears."

She tilted her head. "Safe," she repeated in a tone that had lost its sting, "but not altogether welcome."

The music stopped. He let go of her hand and waist and bowed to her, at a loss for words, and she curtsied. As she rose, he followed her gaze and found it riveted on the tricolor cockade pinned to another man's lapel. He was talking to two other self-styled Jacobins, loudly enough to be heard all too clearly.

"No doubt you've heard that the boy under guard in Paris is not the son of Marie Antoinette at all," said one. "Some poor street urchin pretends to be Louis-Charles. Paying with his life so the real Capet boy can live in hiding somewhere safe."

Another man rocked back on his heels. "All the better for the revolution if they bring the boy out publicly—imposter or not—and send him to the guillotine for all to see. Have it over and done with. Then perhaps the royalists will stop resisting. The time for kings is past the world over."

"But what if Louis-Charles is elsewhere? Waiting to emerge and claim the throne again?"

The third man, quiet until now, spoke up. "We'll find him before that happens. And what a prize that will be. The head of Louis-Charles will seal our success."

The coarse talk repulsed Liam. No wonder the mademoiselle paled once again.

"Monsieur Lemoine," she called to a young man, who quickly approached. "I've had enough amusement for one evening. Allow me a moment to collect Father Gilbert."

"Not so soon, surely," the Frenchman whined. His black hair was in perfect order, as was his well-tailored suit. Liam disliked him immediately. "There are others who wish for an audience with you. They are most insistent."

"And I am more so. Take me home at once, monsieur."

The young man barely disguised a scowl. "It isn't fashionable to retire so early." He tossed a glance Liam's way. "If this American oaf has soured your evening, allow me the honor of sweetening it."

Oh, good. An insult. Liam smiled. "Actually," he said in French, "I'm exhausted, too. We American oafs tire easily, you know." The look on Lemoine's face was worth all the unpleasantness that preceded it. Swallowing a laugh, Liam went on. "Fancy clothes, fine drink, dancing—stimulating company . . ." He blew out an exaggerated sigh. "I'm spent. Why don't I save you the trouble and escort the lady and her friend home myself?"

The hint of a smile curved the mademoiselle's lips, but she shook her head. "Au revoir, gentlemen. I do believe we'll walk." With that, she turned and swished away, leaving Liam and the Frenchman in her wake. Finding the man who must be Father Gilbert on the edge of the room, she exchanged a few words with him before looping her hand in his elbow. Together, they wended from view.

Chapter Eight

Clouds muttered above Liam's room at the Four Winds Tavern, refusing just yet to drop their heavy cargo. The humid breeze through the window carried the smells of canvas, tar, and timber from the shipyards. Live oak from Georgia, mulberry from the Chesapeake, and red cedar of the Carolinas met here in Philadelphia to be turned into the masts, spars, and planks of the best sailing vessels in the world. The sawdust that never seemed to clear the air prickled Liam's throat. He poured himself a glass of water and downed it.

His evening at the Binghams' echoed in his mind, especially the sound of Americans cheerfully singing for the death of French aristocrats. Was it a giant leap to suppose they would sing for the death of their American counterparts? Federalists, with Alex Hamilton at the head, were already being skewered in the press. Liam had meant to persuade Alex regarding the whiskey tax after Mademoiselle Rivard took her leave but had instead walked away with more questions than ever. Finn's reasons for opposing the excise tax were sound of their own accord. But the idea that a larger force was at work in the west, aiming for the downfall of the American government, stayed him.

Last summer, the French minister Genêt had been recruiting American soldiers and sailors for France's war. Pro-French spirit had been at a fever pitch in Philadelphia and all along the eastern seaboard. When Washington proclaimed neutrality, thousands of Philadelphians mobbed his house in protest, day after day. If the yellow fever hadn't interrupted, scattering the discontents like roaches, there was no telling how far the rioters would have gone. Could people of the same mind—French, American, or both—now be attacking Washington's leadership by aggravating the poor folks in Washington County, Pennsylvania? *Diabolical. But not impossible.*

Throat still itching, Liam went to the bureau and grasped the pitcher, only to find it empty. Without bothering to comb his hair, he headed downstairs to refill it.

The dining hall was empty when he entered, and only Finn and Tara still lingered at the bar. If she stood a little straighter, she'd have two inches on their cousin, easily. From the other side of his Dutch door, Jethro responded quietly to something they said, the towel slung over his shoulder stained brown with Monongahela rye.

At the sound of Liam's footsteps, Finn looked up and beamed. "Well, if it isn't the fashionable gentleman from the Binghams' party," he teased. "'Twas enough to make you thirsty, was it?"

Liam held up his pitcher as he approached. "For water."

Jethro filled it from an urn along the back wall before returning it to him, his large brown hands dwarfing the vessel.

Tara kissed Liam's cheek. "Didn't see you come back. How was your evening? How did it go?"

He pushed her coppery hair back from her face, and she swatted him away. Stifling a sigh, he loosened the knot in his neckcloth. "If you're asking if I convinced Hamilton to repeal the tax, I didn't. Not yet." Pouring himself a glass of water, he slaked his thirst. "You know how stubborn he is."

"As stubborn as you?" Finn prodded. "If anyone can find a way to make him see, it's you." He raised his glass. "To Liam, the cousin closer than a brother. You've never let me down."

Yet, Liam mused darkly as his cousin drained his cup. But Finn had always looked up to him. When they were children, the orphaned boy had attached himself to Liam like a puppy to its master. He taught Finn to read, write, and figure, while his mother turned their home into a tavern to pay the bills. Defending Finn against a neighborhood bully had earned Liam his first black eye. And when Finn joined Liam's regiment at the age of fifteen, he kept him out of the action as much as he could. Somehow, after all these years, Finn still held Liam in higher estimation than he probably deserved.

Tara covered a yawn. "I'm done. Let Jethro close up for the night, will you?" After one more kiss for Liam and a slap on Finn's back, she left the room.

Jethro poured himself a shot of Finn's whiskey. Rare was the occasion when he shared a drink of any kind with anyone, especially when the hour was so late.

Liam eased onto a stool and cupped his tumbler of water in his hands, relishing the cool against his palms. "What's on your mind?"

The barkeep shoved his fingers through his coiled charcoal hair before responding. "I've been walking this earth for better than four decades. And what have I got to show for it? A rented room on Fifth Street no bigger than the one you're sleeping in now. I'm too old for this."

Liam recognized defeat when he heard it. His chest knotted in sympathy for a man, older than he, who had no land of his own.

"Go on," Finn prompted, his expression keen and hawklike.

"Day after day, night following night, I pour drink into white men's cups. They come and go, only staying a short while on their way somewhere else to do important things. And I stay right here. I wipe this liquor-slick shelf with my filthy towel, never going anywhere." He whipped the towel off his shoulder and leaned on the bar with straight arms, head bowed. "It don't suit a man my age. It just don't suit."

It was the longest speech Liam had ever heard him give at once. "I don't blame you."

Jethro threw back his whiskey, then brought the glass down

with a bang. "I don't mean to complain. Your sister's been good to me, and you know I've been loyal to Miss Tara."

"But there's nothing like land for a man," Finn said. "You need land."

Jethro frowned. "How's that?"

"At some point, a man's gotta be loyal to himself, doesn't he?" Liam pushed back his stool and stood. "If it's an opportunity you seek, I know where you can find one."

Finn nodded, clearly aware of where he was leading.

Jethro eyed them both warily.

"Did you not hear me telling Tara I could use a hand on my land?" Liam continued. "I had the domestic sort in mind, cooking and laundering, but I truly would appreciate another set of strong hands to share the heavier labor. Do more than pour drinks and wipe counters and haul drunk men to the door."

Jethro looked at his broad, dark hands, knuckles prominent as he gripped the edge of the counter. "You want me to work for you now, instead of your sister?"

Liam shook his head. "No, no. I want you to work *with* me. I've got land still needing to be cleared of its trees before I can begin to cultivate it. My cash is tied up in the crops right now, but if you'll come and help me work the land for a year, at the end of that time, you'll have earned yourself a portion of it to own outright, in your name."

Jethro's eyes burned with purpose and promise. "My own land."

"That's it," Finn agreed. "There's nothing like it."

Liam's plan unfurled. "Listen. I'm to purchase another Narragansett Pacer at the horse auction while I'm here to add to the stable for us mail carriers. I was planning to lead the second horse behind me on the way home, but it might as well have a rider." He grinned. "Eventually, we get ourselves a few sheep and dairy cows. We breed the sheep, and you can have your pick of the offspring. It will be a strong start for you, and you'll have the very best neighbor there could be."

Jethro drew himself up tall. "Deal straight with me now. It's good land? Fertile, close to water?"

"Ah, my friend." Liam squeezed the barkeep's shoulder. "Once you're there, you'll never want to leave."

Jethro's smile gleamed. For the first time that night, he seemed to exhale. "When do we go?"

Rain tapped against Vivienne's window, faintly scented with a hint of wine and veal fricassee from the café next door. Faint strains of "La Marseillaise" bounced off the cobblestones behind the pension, coming from the nearby Chestnut Street Theater, which closed every performance with revolutionary songs. Beyond the warm glow of Vienne's pension garret, it might as well have been France.

Disoriented, she traded the Versailles court gown for her night-dress and dislodged the pins from her hair. But tricolor cockades and a knife blade beaded with blood assaulted her vision, sweeping her back into the Terror in her mind. *Not blood. Ice cream,* she reminded herself. But the uncanny resemblance unlocked something inside her. Not fear itself, but the memory of it—and that alone was so strong as to leave her breathless. This was not what she'd expected from America. Martine had been right to stay home.

A light scratching sounded at the door, and Vivienne called to her friend to enter.

Martine appeared in the darkened doorway, the light of her taper ethereal against her white nightgown, white skin, white hair. An apparition, until she spoke. "Henri's asleep. How was it? What happened?"

Caging up her fluttering nerves, Vienne sat on the edge of her bed and pointed to the chair. "Come in."

Quietly, Martine closed the door and glided to sit in the chair. With rapt attention, she listened as Vienne spoke of the Binghams' mansion with its Corinthian pilasters and French style, of Eliza Hamilton, and most importantly, Anne's invitation to return on Thursday to sell her lace.

"Why, that's wonderful!" Martine clasped her hands. "You must be so relieved. I'm so glad for you." She narrowed her gaze. "And yet you don't seem altogether pleased. What aren't you telling me?"

"Only what you already know." Vivienne crossed to the bureau to retrieve her brush and pulled it through her hair.

"Ah. Let me guess. You met people who support the bloodshed we escaped, for the cause of liberty. Yes?"

Vienne returned to the bed. "Complete with cockades and hateful songs. One of the men whacked the head from a lobster-shaped ice cream to prove his point."

A giggle burst from Martine's lips. "No." She covered her mouth. "Truly? He beheaded—an ice cream?"

"And it made me furious!" The corner of Vivienne's lips twitched up as she set down the brush. The act that had so disturbed her now seemed ridiculous beyond words.

Martine's shoulders bounced with quiet laughter until tears streamed down her cheeks. "He killed an ice cream! Such villainy! Oh, la! Did it bleed very much?"

"Just picture it, if you please, melting from its severed neck! Ghastly!" But Vienne was laughing, too, until her sides and cheeks ached.

With a shuddering breath, Martine wiped the tears from her face. "We had the most delicious ice cream you can fathom at Versailles. You'll think me petty indeed when I confess I miss it. Of all the things to miss. Well, so ice cream is among them. The real question is . . . how did it taste? Tell me you at least sampled some."

"The lobster? I couldn't possibly. I doubt you would have, either, had you been there." Combing her fingers through her hair, Vivienne separated it into sections and began plaiting it for the night.

"No, no, something else. Surely they had more than one flavor."

Indeed they had. "French vanilla with caramelized banana and Jamaican rum—Thomas Jefferson's favorite, I'm told. Pineapple. Strawberry. Pistachio."

"Ah. The queen's favorite." And suddenly the levity leaked from the room. "Well. Which did you try?"

Vienne tied a ribbon around the end of her braid and tossed it over her shoulder. "None. I don't care for it."

"You what! Then you must never have had the good kind."

But she had. The very best, in fact.

Ever since she'd learned Tante Rose was her aunt and not her mother, she'd begged her for the chance to meet Sybille. When Vivienne was eight years old, they agreed that a brief visit would be acceptable. So Sybille treated them to ice cream at Le Caveau in the Palais-Royal.

Vienne was awestruck as soon as she met her mother. Every detail remained embroidered onto her memory. The ankle-baring *robe à la polonaise* in pink-and-white-striped silk, her white-powdered *pouf* towering above her head. Sybille was in the prime of her years at twenty-five, and she struck Vienne as the most beautiful woman in the world. She was determined to be so well behaved that Sybille would find her irresistibly charming. That she would love her. Want her. This was before she knew her mother was a courtesan, of course.

In her nervousness, Vienne had allowed her ice cream to melt, and it dripped all over her new gown, including the lace trim at the neckline, which Tante Rose had made for the occasion. She was devastated.

Vienne's childish voice still echoed between her ears. "*Oh, I'm sorry! I didn't mean to! I'll do better, I promise. Please, can't I live with you anyway? With Tante Rose, too? Don't you want me?*"

Sybille's laughter was the bright tinkling of bells. "*Want you?*" She paid the bill and sailed away, leaving Vienne, the jetsam in her wake, rubbing hopelessly at the dark chocolate on her lace. It was a very long time before she did not feel stained herself.

It was the end of her love for ice cream, the start of her devotion to lace. And the more pristine the white, the better. Failing to capture Sybille's affections, she committed herself to pleasing Rose—and her patrons—with her handiwork.

"Vienne?"

Rain coursed down the lead window panes in silver streams.

Outside, lanterns smeared the dark. "Forgive me. I was a world away."

"What will you do, once your lace is sold?" Martine asked. "I have no doubt that Mrs. Bingham's friends will purchase whatever you show them. So what then? How will you fill your time?"

It was a question that had needled Vienne, as well. But she did not want to just *fill time.* "I want to work."

Martine leaned forward, inclining her ear. "To work, you say?"

A small laugh bubbled in Vivienne's chest at the look of confusion on her friend's face. Martine clearly had no such desire, but Vivienne itched to be industrious. There was comfort in an orderly routine, joy in seeing a task done well. When she was a girl, she had once complained of the concentration required to learn her trade. In that gentle way of hers, Tante Rose served her a cup of sipping chocolate along with the reminder that creating was a form of worship. "*God is the Creator, is He not?*" she had said with a smile. "*So when we create, even if it is a mere length of lace and not the stars in the heavens, we honor Him. We bear His likeness when we work.*" That truth had lingered in Vienne ever since. When the government turned cathedrals into houses of reason, and when the church bells ceased to ring, Vienne had still quietly honored the Lord with the work of her hands.

"You will make lace again, then," Martine offered.

Vienne curled the end of her braid around her finger, twirling it in circles. Outside, the rain softened to a low hum at the threshold of her hearing. "I doubt it. Making lace is so tedious, and the market for it here so small. Besides, for the past several years, my income was not from the actual craft, but in managing a network of hundreds of laceworkers in my manufacture. I assigned and delivered orders to dressmakers and fashion moguls like Rose Bertin."

Martine smiled. "How I miss Madame Bertin and her fashions. She styled all of us at court." With fresh animation, she talked of card parties and tables piled high with the most decadent desserts, of trips to the opera and theater.

Only half listening, Vienne looked toward the window, her own reflection blinking back at her. The past suited Martine, but Vienne could not content herself on reminiscences, or even with her previous trade. It was time to lay aside the shape of her old life.

Chapter Nine

Aside from leaving Tara and Finn, parting with Philadelphia was as easy for Liam as retiring from the Binghams' party. He didn't belong beneath painted ceilings and crystal chandeliers, just as Jethro didn't belong caged behind his bar. Nature's beauty outshone any man-made ornamentation, and the drink Liam craved most flowed from the spring on his land.

The month of June passed as quickly as it had bloomed, thanks to Jethro's company as they worked, watering the earth with their sweat. By the time it was Liam's turn to deliver the mail from the settlement to Philadelphia again, summer's heat and humidity were at full boil.

It was worse in the city, where paved streets and brick buildings made him feel positively oven-baked. Were it not for the chance to see his sister, the trip would be more trouble than the extra income was worth.

"Ach!" Tara wrinkled her freckled nose as soon as she saw him dismounting his favorite mail-run horse, Cherie, behind the tavern. But after he handed the reins to the stableboy, she hugged him all the same. Apparently, she'd forgiven him for "stealing" Jethro away from her employ.

"That's the smell of my devotion to you, it is!" Grinning, he flapped his hat at the shirt sticking to his chest. "Nothing else could compensate for this."

"You flatter me, sir." She hooted in laughter, then dug a key from her pocket. "Wash up and change into something less . . . devoted-smelling. Then meet me downstairs."

After a little bow, he was only too glad to obey.

A quarter of an hour later, he descended the steps clean, dry, freshly shaved, and in desperate need of coffee. It was only mid-morning, but since he'd risen well before dawn to finish the journey, his body needed a little convincing.

Though the dining room was all but empty, the lingering aroma of eggs and potatoes cramped his hollow stomach. Sunshine turned the creamy walls a friendly, golden hue and bounced off the hard-wood floor in stabs of light. As he strode to the bar to place his breakfast order, he wondered whose face would greet him, now that Jethro was gone.

"Uncle!" Finn O'Brien slapped the bar, his greeting ricocheting off the tavern walls. This room had been their informal parlor once, where Liam coached Finn with his early reader, following in his schoolmaster father's footsteps when he was fifteen and Finn seven.

Laughing in surprise, Liam grasped Finn's hand and shook it. "I thought you were going back to Washington County right after Jethro and I took off."

"I thought better of it. Tara needed a barkeep in a hurry, thanks to you." The shallow box Finn stood on behind the bar allowed the men to see eye-to-eye.

"So you signed up for the job?"

"I couldn't very well leave her alone until she could hire a re-placement. What would she do if a man became unruly and she couldn't wrestle him out the door herself? She'd lose her license to run the tavern, and perhaps more than that." He shook his head. "Perish the thought. It takes such little effort on my part to keep an eye on the rowdies." He glared at Liam with his one eye to demonstrate.

"I see very well. You've been a better brother to Tara than I have in this. Well done."

Finn's cheeks turned ruddy with satisfaction.

"But what of your own crops?" Liam asked. "Do you have a hand to help tend them while you're away?"

"The barley grows whether I'm there to stare at it or not. And no one would bother stealing it before it's good and ripe anyway. It'll be ready for harvest at the end of this month, though, so I'm on my way back soon. Tomorrow, actually. The new barkeep starts this afternoon. You can meet him. Providential that you came today."

"Providence, is it?"

"We'll call it God, if you like."

Liam nodded, pleased to hear Finn make even the slightest reference to the Almighty. During the war, young Finn had been so taken with the brotherhood of his fellow soldiers that he was less than discerning in the company he kept at camp. For a time, he fell under the influence of those keen to pull the impressionable off the straight and narrow. It had taken all of Liam's powers of persuasion and even more prayer to draw him back. Even now, he wondered how God and Finn were getting along out in Washington County. Some of those rough-and-tumble soldiers were now his neighbors and fellow whiskey rebels. The sort that defied all authority, God and governments both. Providential, indeed, that Finn was back here, away from all that, for this long.

Tara swayed into the room, strands of russet hair sticking to her glowing cheeks. Her work-worn hands carried a steaming tray of breakfast, including a tall mug of coffee, bless her. "Sit." She stopped at a nearby booth. "Finn, join us."

Gratefully, Liam obeyed, thanking God for the food and his family before diving in. "Well? Have you been pushing your famous Monongahela rye on Tara's patrons?" he asked between bites.

"If they order whiskey, I can only give them the best. If that happens to be mine, then . . ." Finn spread his hands, smiling broadly.

"He's been good for business, he has." Tara picked a fried potato off Liam's plate and popped it into her mouth. "Despite what he'd have you think, he never oversells the drinks. Keeps the gentlemen in line." She palmed the roll from Liam's plate and knocked it on the table. "Hard as a rock, as usual. You'll break a tooth on it."

"The rest of the food makes up for it, though." Liam savored a swig of coffee, the pewter mug nearly burning his hand. Flies buzzed in through open windows, circling and swooping about his eggs. He waved them away. "Any update on the whiskey tax?"

Finn shifted in his seat. "The papers say the federal courts here issued writs for the arrests of those who won't pay."

Liam eyed him. "You seem relatively unconcerned."

"It's more hot air. We sent tax collectors back empty-handed often enough, didn't we? Whoever is fool enough to bandy about a writ will meet with the same amount of success. None." A shadow passed over his face as crowds formed on the sidewalk outside.

"Perhaps." Liam brought his coffee to his lips, aware he was about to sound like the schoolmaster once again. But so be it. "Let's talk it through. You've protested the tax, sent letters to your government—and tarred and feathered tax collectors, along with those who've given them quarter. The tax still hasn't been repealed. It was made into law by the government elected to represent the nation's interests as a whole. For better or for worse, they've decided this tax is a reasonable way to bring in income. At what point do you submit to the law?"

The corners of Finn's mouth pulled down. "We're the patriots, remember? King Washington and Hamilton are the tyrants. They want a monarchy for us, wait and see."

Rising, Tara retied her apron strings behind her waist. "Not this again. Have fun, boys. I have work to do." She slid away, taking Liam's dirty dishes with her.

"For the sake of argument, Finn, humor me. Is it right to only submit to laws you like?"

"It's never right to submit to injustice. You used to know that. Has Hamilton been bending your ear?"

Ignoring the jab at Alex, Liam leaned back. "What I know is that America is still in its infancy. It would not take much to destroy her, and I don't want to see that happen."

"I'm not talking about destroying the nation. I'm talking about my rights."

"My point exactly. Perhaps you ought to spend less time talking about your rights and more time considering what's best for our country as a whole. You'll have plenty of time for that on your ride back west. Put some thought into the balance between government law and individual freedom—before you're back with the rest of the whiskey rebels."

Finn's eye darkened. "Before they can do the thinking for me, is that it?"

Actually, it was. "I don't want you to get caught up in escalating violence."

Grunting, Finn pushed himself out of the booth. "Still trying to keep me in the rear of the action after all these years, are you?" He chuckled. Outside, voices gathered and crescendoed on the street. At Liam's questioning look, Finn said, "It's Independence Day, remember? They're waiting for the parade."

Liam had completely forgotten the date after four days on the road. Standing, he held his mug aloft. "To independence, a war nobly fought and won."

"Indeed. To *independence*." Finn swiped up his tankard with a smirk and drank.

Sun streamed through the branches above, warming Vivienne's straw hat and the brick sidewalk beneath her feet. Beside her, Sebastien Lemoine matched his long stride to her pace. But she paid little mind to his attentions, nor to Martine and Henri, who walked behind them, so immersed was she in her thoughts.

Though her feet moved her forward, she felt for all the world like she was stuck. Weeks had passed since she'd sold her lace to Anne Bingham's friends, and she still had not found employment. The shops in the French quarter had already hired more than they really needed. Other émigrés taught fencing or dancing lessons to Philadelphia's elite. One former nobleman had opened his own ice cream shop on Front Street, and another now sold books. But Vivienne had yet to find a new occupation.

Refusing to be idle, if not employed, she gave herself to learning from Paulette in the kitchen until she'd acquired enough skill to actually be of help.

When she was not kneading bread or rolling pastry crusts, she made it her personal mission to coax Martine and Henri from their isolation. The first time Vienne convinced Henri to leave the pension, it was only to catch fireflies in the rear yard. Enthralled, he at first cupped only those insects that flew near him, but eventually followed their glowing paths. He added a few steps to his delicate chase every time, until he forgot or simply ignored his pains. The dark grew less frightening as he learned to look for the light.

In the heat of the day, Martine often found reason to stay inside with her cards while Vivienne took Henri for brief walks. When he circled the entire block, they celebrated with crepes at the café. So far, his record was three laps, which would make today's outing a victory.

"Can we slow down? He's not very strong." Martine made no effort to lower her voice.

"Bah. He's stronger than you think. And so are you." Vienne stepped aside and motioned to them to walk in step with her, offering a hand to Henri. He took it with fingers cool and thin, and kicked a crumpled newssheet in his path.

Roses swooned on a windowsill behind an iron gate, bringing a smile to Vienne's lips and sweetening the breeze that ruffled the hem of her cotton round gown. Her blue-and-white-striped dress was not nearly so fine as Martine's painted silk, but far cooler.

"Are we almost there?" Shading his eyes with one hand, Henri peered toward Market Street.

"Don't pull ahead, Henri," Martine warned, though he was doing no such thing. She twisted the handle of her parasol in her white-gloved hand. "Ghastly hot. I don't know if this is a good idea after all. All these people, too . . ." Her voice trailed away. Flapping a hand to fan herself, she resembled an exotic bird among the Quakers that peppered the streets.

"She hates crowds," Henri supplied matter-of-factly.

"And you aren't much for walking," Martine inserted, "so we make a fine pair, no?"

Vienne squeezed Henri's hand to reassure him. Odd that Martine had pointed out his weakness when she could have cheered his progress. "One more block, and it will be worth it. The parade honors an important event for both this city and America. Did you know, Henri, it was right here in Philadelphia that the American Declaration of Independence was signed?"

"And that's what started the revolution?" Uncertainty threaded his tone.

"Not exactly," Monsieur Lemoine answered. "The revolution inspired the declaration."

The heat cut short a detailed history lesson. By the time they reached Market Street, Henri was flushed, and poor Martine's complexion was mottled with peony-pink blotches. Hoping for a few degrees of relief, Vienne stepped beneath a tavern's awning, and the rest of them followed.

Matched horses clip-clopped over the cobblestones, a stately beginning to the celebration.

"I can't see!" Henri cried, releasing Vienne's hand. When she turned, he was already gone.

"Henri!" she shouted, and Martine's face flooded with horror before they spied him scrambling up the few steps of the tavern to get a better look. Martine flew after him, and Vienne held back with Monsieur Lemoine while Martine scolded her son.

He leaned close to her ear to be heard. "I hope you don't mind. I told a friend he could meet us here."

The air was full of English, French, German, and the rich accents of slaves born in the West Indies. The gathered masses pressed them together. She laughed. "I hardly think I'll notice another person."

"You'll notice this one, I wager." He looked toward Martine, who was waving them up the stairs. "Shall we?"

Lifting the hem of her skirt above her ankles, Vivienne climbed the stone steps with Monsieur Lemoine right behind her.

Following the sleek horses came veterans of the Continental

Army in blue and buff uniforms, their faces red and glossy beneath their cocked black felt hats. Stars and Stripes billowed in the heat-laden breeze, while fife and drum played "Yankee Doodle."

Cheers erupted on both sides of the street, and Martine clutched Vivienne's arm. The crowd. The shouts. They must have sounded like an angry mob to her ears. Vienne patted her hand, for no words could be heard over the roar. Discreetly, however, she pointed to Henri, whose eyes were alight as he watched, though he leaned on the iron railing for support. Lips pressed in a thin, tight line, Martine nodded. She would stay, enduring heat and clamor, for her boy.

At the touch of Monsieur Lemoine's hand on her elbow, Vienne turned her gaze back to the throng. A man was weaving his way toward them, a French émigré, judging by his embroidered silk suit. When he looked up, her breath hitched.

"Armand?" she said to Monsieur Lemoine. "Your friend is Armand de Champlain?"

His smile was sheepish. "He told me not to tell you."

Eyebrows spiking in his aristocratic brow, Armand waved, then continued jostling his way toward her, his blue suit shimmering like the sun-sparked ocean. She sighed. When she was a child, she would watch the men in the street, wondering which of them might be her father. From the safety of her imagination, she shopped for a papa—or at least an uncle, by way of marriage to Tante Rose—the way ladies shopped for jewelry. She was looking for a man who was brilliant and dazzling, but even more important, a man of integrity. A man who was honorable, through and through.

She would not have chosen Armand. And yet here he was, clicking up the tavern steps in silver-buckled shoes, ornately carved cane in his pale hand. He gave a firm handshake to Monsieur Lemoine, a gallant bow to Martine and a kiss to her fingertips. Another handshake for Henri. The smile he offered Vivienne was tentative, a reflection of her own restraint, perhaps, as she gathered her manners about her.

He bowed to her but did not reach for her hand, as he had for

Martine's. "I would speak to you, Vivienne. Somewhere I can be heard."

How easy it would be to look away from the entreaty in his eyes. If she allowed the crowd to overwhelm his presence, if she could submerge herself instead into her new life, her new country, she might be able to ignore the pain that accompanied his person. For to face Armand was to face rejection. Her own, and Sybille's—and the family he betrayed. To Vienne, he was a reminder that she had been unloved and unwanted.

"Vivienne?" he tried again.

Before she could respond, a commotion on Market Street caught her eye. A tangle of men jumped into the parade behind the veterans' band, red sashes at the waists of their red-and-white-striped trousers. Their red, white, and blue flag was not American, and they were celebrating not just July 4 but July 14, as well: the *fête nationale* celebrating French revolutionaries' taking of the Bastille. The sans-culottes waved red caps on poles and marched and shouted and sang.

The crowd went wild. But were they for the French Revolution or against it? Or were the shouts merely in support of the French, whose fleet hemming in the British at Yorktown had helped the Americans win their own revolution?

Martine seized Vivienne's arm again. "We're going," she mouthed.

Monsieur Lemoine half shouted, "I'll escort you back to the pension."

Vienne began following Martine down the steps, but Armand's hand caught her wrist. "Stay, I beg of you."

Martine, Henri, and Sebastien were already disappearing into the crowd, but Armand held her firm, and standing on the steps of the tavern, they caught the eye of one of the sans-culottes.

"Aristocrats to the lampposts!" he shouted. "Long live the French Republic! Join the war for liberty! Death to tyrants!"

The words were ice picks in Vivienne's ears. Chills raced over her skin despite the sodden heat.

Laughing, the rogues flung insults, then rocks and handfuls of horse manure at them. Vienne stepped back as Armand banged his cane on the railing and raised his fist, his shouts weak and lonely against a sea of so many others. One sans-culotte downed the last of his drink, then smashed the bottle on the street. With a sloppy grin, he plucked up the shards of glass and hurled them at Armand.

Vivienne's arms bent over her head as bottle fragments flew toward them. Then came the bright sound of breaking glass and a rush of air that smelled of coffee and eggs and bacon grease.

Shouts crashed against the jeers. The door behind her flung open, and a strong arm cinched her waist, pulling her inside. Armand stumbled in, as well, and the door slammed shut again.

Pulse throbbing, Vienne felt sun-blinded until her vision recovered enough to recognize the man who'd pulled her to safety. The hand still on her shoulder belonged to none other than the American veteran she'd met at the Binghams' party, William Delaney. The man who favored liberty and freedom above all.

"Mademoiselle Rivard? Are you hurt?" The concern in his tone surprised her.

She shook her head, awash with relief that at least Martine and Henri had been spared that scene. Mr. Delaney released her and angled toward Armand, who was sputtering beside her.

A tall woman with copper hair looked out the window, fists on her aproned hips. "What in the name of all the saints in Christendom is going on out there? Another one of them so much as lifts a finger in my direction, Finn, you have my permission to blow it right off!"

"'Twould be my pleasure!" came a voice from outside. Through the broken window, Vienne caught a glimpse of a man holding a gun to his shoulder.

"I'm sorry about your window," she managed to say.

Mr. Delaney shepherded Vienne and Armand away from the door. "As if it were you who broke it. Never mind Tara and Finn. They enjoy getting mad, and they aren't upset with you. Besides, the pane can be replaced."

A curse fell from Armand's lips. Wincing, he cradled his right arm. The silk sleeve was sliced open, the hanging shred of fabric blooming a darkening shade of red.

Vienne stepped forward to inspect it. The gash on his forearm was not long, but deep.

Tara rounded on them, her milky complexion paling further still. "Ach. Is it bad? We have bandages." With broad, strong cheekbones, her face was honest, if not refined.

"I'm afraid we'll need more than that." Vienne watched Armand's face. "Stitching."

Tara covered her mouth.

"You'll have to excuse my sister." Mr. Delaney swiped a clean napkin from a nearby table and pressed it to Armand's arm. "Never could stand the sight of blood. Nor the suggestion of it."

Vienne thanked him and took over holding the cloth to Armand's wound. "If we could exit from the alley door—"

"Will you not stay and call a doctor?" Tara asked from a safe distance.

The front door swung open to admit a lean, blond man with a musket in his hands. Finn, Mr. Delaney had called him. With one appraising eye, he seemed to assess the situation.

"No need, my pension isn't far." Vienne kept her hand clamped over Armand's arm, though the cotton grew warm beneath her palm.

"The rascals have moved on, but they could still be lurking about, eager to pounce on wounded prey." Finn leaned his musket against the wall. "I'm sure Tara has what you need right here."

"Then I'll stitch you up posthaste," Vienne told Armand.

His brow creased. "You would do that? *Ma foi!* I don't require this of you."

"I was a lacemaker for the queen," she reminded him. "I believe I can handle a needle and thread."

"And I confess I never could. Not even for a sampler, to my dear mother's everlasting dismay. I'll send up what you need!" Tara called over her shoulder as she hustled from the room.

Mr. Delaney ushered Vienne and Armand out of the dining hall and down a long central hallway toward the rear of the tavern. He glanced at her. "I thought you were an aristocrat fleeing for your life."

"Half correct," she said. "I did flee for my life. But I've worked since I was a child." If he'd intended to disguise his astonishment, he failed. "Should I be flattered or insulted that this surprises you?"

Rather than answer, he called back to Finn to bring some whiskey to the yard in the rear, then opened the door and led them out. Rubbing a hand over his jaw, he glanced around. "You would rather sit for the procedure, yes? I'll be but a moment."

While he ducked back into the tavern, she tucked the lace at her elbows up into her sleeves, then helped Armand remove his coat. The gold embroidery on his vest shone in the corner of her eye as she rolled his linen sleeve above his elbow, refolded the napkin, and placed it over the wound once more.

Armand winced. "Hang the sans-culottes," he muttered. A grasshopper flitted among the blades of grass near his shoes. "I have missed you."

"You miss Sybille. You don't know me." Her voice was calm.

"I miss you both. And I would like nothing more than to know you better. But you—"

Mr. Delaney and Finn returned, bringing an end to the exchange. They set ladder-back chairs on the ground. With them came a woman with skin the color of walnuts, her black hair bound up in a red kerchief. After spreading an apron over Vienne's lap, she extended a threaded needle. "Boiled it myself. I'm Rachel, by the way. I do the cookin' for Miss Tara here at Four Winds. I do a great many other things, too."

Briefly, Vienne made introductions while Mr. Delaney peeled the napkin from Armand's skin. Bottle in hand, Finn came forward, his body sinewy and taut, a strung bow arcing over the émigré clutching his cane.

"Drink." After Armand obeyed, Finn poised the bottle above the wound. "Mind you keep your tongue free of your teeth, now. You'll feel a pinch."

Armand held his arm away from his body, over the grass-tufted earth. "Do it." Whiskey splashed into his wound and onto the ground. The cords of his neck tightened with the force of the groan he trapped.

"Mercy." Rachel backed away.

Swallowing, Vienne untied the ribbon beneath her chin, lifted her straw hat from her hair, and hooked it on the back of her chair. She leaned forward and with one hand squeezed the edges of sliced flesh together. The arm in her grip had embraced Sybille, then clasped his own wife to himself. Inwardly, Vienne recoiled at the feel of his skin against hers.

Shoving the thoughts aside, she began to stitch.

The silver needle winked in the sun as it pierced Armand's skin. Vivienne pulled the thread through and adjusted her grip on his arm, slick with blood and whiskey, the smells unsettling her stomach. Mercifully, a broad, tanned hand gripped Armand's arm to help reunite what the glass had separated. Mr. Delaney, on his knees beside her chair. Finn leaned against the well, carrying on in Armand's ear, no doubt trying to distract him. Rachel stood in the background, flapping her apron to create a breeze, prayers lifting from her lips in quiet bursts.

Sweat trickled from Vienne's hairline as she worked with fingers quick and sure. "I'm sorry," she whispered, grimacing.

"Don't be." Armand panted between stitches. "Go on."

With his free hand, Mr. Delaney dug a handkerchief from his pocket and pressed it to Vienne's brow before the sweat dripped into her eyes.

Nodding her thanks, she continued until the work was done. "Finished." She released a pent-up breath and knotted the thread as Armand, too, exhaled. "Well done," she told him, for he'd managed the pain as well as one could.

Rachel stepped forward again to snip the slender strand, then produced a small pot that smelled strongly of some herbal ointment Vienne didn't recognize. "It'll aid the healing. Keep it from sticking to the linen." Tenderly, she dabbed salve on the puckered skin and stitches before Vienne wound a fresh bandage around Armand's arm.

He grunted when she tied it, then sucked in a breath through clenched teeth. "Merci," he whispered.

Mr. Delaney brushed the dirt from the knees of his trousers as he stood.

Rising, Vienne gathered the apron from her lap and handed it back to Rachel. "Thank you. Thanks to all of you."

"Stay a moment. Tara told me to fetch her once the sewing up was done," Mr. Delaney said. "Then, when you're ready, I'd like to escort you back."

She agreed, and he turned and walked back into the tavern, followed by Rachel and Finn.

Armand leaned back in his chair, as wilted as the lace at his neck, his face twisted in obvious pain. Wind ruffled through the branches overhead. With nothing more to say, Vienne went to the well and washed her hands before donning her straw hat and sitting again.

He sighed. "This was not the encounter I hoped to share with you today. I'm embarrassed to be in this state. That you would soil your fingers with this task is almost unbearable."

"My fingers have been 'soiled' before." But Armand wouldn't want to know the extent of Sybille's humbled condition. And it would certainly bring Vienne no comfort to explain it.

"Sybille hurt you. So have I. And yet you have tended to us both. I am sorry, Vivienne, for your burdens, especially those I myself have heaped upon you. Many are my mistakes." He looked away, squinting, perhaps, into a past that haunted them both.

A cloud drifted in the sky, a scarf of gauze diffusing the sun's golden rays. His fist tight on his cane, Armand looked at the white linen swathing his forearm. "Could any miracle of stitching thread my life and yours into the same fabric? Need we be estranged forever?"

Vivienne swallowed against the ache in her throat. Oh, how she had longed for a father as a child, and even as an adolescent.

117

But the time for reconciliation was long past. "I am fully eight and twenty."

"Ah, ma chère. One is never too old for a father's love. Nor is one too old for a daughter's."

Tears of frustration gathered on her lashes. She untucked the lace from her sleeves and smoothed her gown from her waist with shaking hands. Her spirit rolled like a schooner on angry seas until Tante Rose's oft-repeated words came back to anchor her. "*You are not forsaken. You are mine, and you are God's. Rest secure in that Father's love.*"

"Please," Armand whispered. "Don't pretend I don't exist."

At this, Vienne lifted her chin and speared him with her gaze. "Forgive me, monsieur, but it was you who pretended I'd never been born. Is it not so?"

He flinched as though she'd struck him. "And what would you have had me do? Bring you home to my wife and children?"

"So you knew of me. And ignored me, just as Sybille did."

His jowls quivered as he shook his head. "I sent money for your upbringing every month, faithfully, until you came of age."

"Faithful, were you?" There was ice in her tone.

Armand huffed. "It was more than any other man in my position would do for his—"

She drew up straight in her chair, nostrils flaring, silently daring him to lay that ugly label upon her.

"It was more than I was expected to do," he finished.

Vivienne squeezed her hands together on her lap. It was for family, not money, that she had wished upon every falling star. But Armand and Sybille were not the parents she'd longed for. She drew a fortifying breath. "Your wife's children." Her mouth turned to cotton. "My half-siblings. What are their names?"

Shadows deepened beneath his eyes. "This is so unpleasant. Must we?"

"If I acknowledge you, I acknowledge them. They are my blood, by half. I will never meet them, but I wish . . . I wish to know about them, at least." As she had wished to be known, as well.

The heat grew oppressive, even in the dappled shade of an elm. The heady scent of lilies puddled in the air, mixing with odors of spoiled food and dishwater wafting from the alley trench. With slow strokes, she fanned mosquitoes away and willed her heart to calm. "Gustave is one and twenty. Angelique is seventeen. Hyacinthe returned to heaven before she could say her name without a lisp." Armand adjusted his hat on his head. "She was spared so much heartache. She was the lucky one."

Tears rose and fell as quickly as she wiped them away. After all these years considering herself an only child, if not an orphan, hearing her siblings' names unleashed something inside her. Something tender and raw and unrelenting. "Do they know about me?"

Armand's lips pressed tight, as if to lock away the answer written plainly on his face. With manicured fingers, he worried the buttons of his vest. A terrible sadness issued from the ballooning silence, pressing the air from Vienne's lungs.

She stood and turned from him, one fist gripping the back of her chair. Head bowed, shoulders shaking, she wept silently for Gustave, Angelique, and little Hyacinthe, the family she never had. This reunion with Armand, this bungling attempt to sew the rift between them with mere words and what-ifs and wishes—this did not feel like the hurt of healing. It was the pain of being ripped apart anew.

"Put it behind you, Vivienne." Armand's cane slowly tapped the ground as he approached her. "There are some things I cannot fix. But there are some that I can. It has been some time since I sent funds for your keeping. You must have needs. Allow me to supply them."

She squeezed her eyes shut, collecting herself. More than anything, she wanted to tell him she was fine, that she was already secure. But she was neither, and they both knew it. Even so, she was loath to accept his money.

At the scrape of wood on stone, she angled to see Mr. Delaney filling the doorway to the tavern's cellar kitchen. Taking his hat in his hands, he stepped closer, then halted in a shaft of sunshine that set his chestnut hair ablaze. Questions lined his brow. After a fleeting glance at Armand, his gaze held Vivienne's. "May I be of some service to you?"

Tara emerged behind him.

Sluicing the tears from her cheeks, Vivienne took in Tara's flushed face, her hands rough from working and doing, while her own had gone shamefully soft. An idea bloomed, and Vienne stepped toward her. "Please. I have no letter of introduction, but if I may be so bold, Tara . . . may *I* be of some service to *you*? In the kitchen, perhaps?"

A cry broke from Armand. "So you do need resources. I will help you, you needn't work!"

"I don't want your money, Armand. What I want is employ."

The color rose in his cheeks. "As a scullery maid?"

"If that is the work that needs to be done, then yes. I would do it." She hid her smooth hands in the folds of her skirt. "But I can also bake, if that would serve. Baguettes, croissants, pies, and tarts." It was time to put to use everything she'd learned helping Paulette in the pension kitchen. "If Monsieur Collet can open an ice cream shop, why should a former lacemaker not bake bread?"

Mr. Delaney's eyebrows arched for a moment, but an easy smile chased the surprise from his face. "If you can bake half as well as you stitch—" He looked to his sister.

Tara nodded, one fist on her hip. "It so happens that Rachel could use some help with bread. Come tomorrow morning, and we'll see how you do."

Agreeing to the trial, Vivienne clasped Tara's callused hand, hope fluttering through her.

Armand shook his head and muttered, "I don't understand you at all. You are so unlike your mother."

Genuine laughter escaped her at the consternation on his face. Gratitude and relief swelling inside her, she swept him a low and elegant curtsy. "Thank you, Armand, for noticing."

Chapter Ten

The mademoiselle was becoming more interesting to Liam by the moment. Standing a respectful distance away, he waited while she said good-bye to Armand and added instructions for the care of his wound. As soon as the monsieur took his leave, Liam offered her his arm.

"If you're ready to go home, I'll take you," he said in French, thinking to put her more at ease on a day that was already taxing.

"English, please." The frankness of her gaze was arresting. "Though your French is passable. Have you lived abroad?"

"My parents came from Ireland, but I was born here," he told her. "My father, a scholar and teacher, spoke as much French as English to me as I grew up, and I continued to learn through my formal education after he died. But no, I've not used it in France. America is my only home."

"And now it is mine," she replied. "I wish to speak the common language."

A smile tugged at the corner of his mouth. "As you wish."

"Good. And I'll thank you to correct me when I make mistakes. Yes? It will be a favor to me." She placed her hand on his arm.

"You want me to tell you when you're wrong."

Something glimmered in the eyes that looked up at him. "Only because I so want to get it right."

"In all my years as a schoolmaster, I can count on one hand

the number of students who specifically requested correction." That she was an émigré, and eager to assimilate, made it all the more surprising. "'Twill be a pleasure to coach you, if you ever give evidence of needing it." He guided her to the alley and then along the sidewalk in the direction she pointed.

"You're a schoolmaster!" She looked so pleased, he was sorry to disappoint her.

Liam steered her around a puddle before responding. "I was. Now I'm a farmer. And a mail carrier between my village and Philadelphia, but that's mostly so I can visit Tara and our cousin Finn, when he happens to be in the city at the same time. You met Finn briefly." A grin slanting on his face, he held one eye shut as he looked at her, a reminder of the backwoodsman's most distinguishing characteristic.

Her laugh was light and musical. "Yes, I remember." A butterfly swooped before them, alighting on the tip of an iron fence before winging away again, a blur of orange and black. "You changed your trade. Surely you don't find it odd that I'm willing to bake instead of make lace now, do you?"

"Not at all. You're adapting to a new life. Besides, both occupations are about creating something with your own two hands. Lace is beautiful and no doubt requires more skill." He glanced at the trimming on her neckline and sleeves, realizing she likely created it herself. "But bread is life, isn't it? Gives a person the strength to do what must be done. 'Tis a noble thing, that. To create that which sustains."

The mademoiselle nodded. "And this is why you farm. Is that right? To bring a harvest from the land by your two hands?"

"Two hands, one back, and a whole lot of sweat. But there's nothing sweeter than living by my own labor. Before I had my own land, as a schoolmaster, I lodged with the families of my students a few months at a time. Always moving around, beholden to strangers for the roof over my head and the food on my board . . . Well, it seemed a poor way for a man to live. I needed to sink my roots deep into a place of my own. Sounds strange to you, maybe, but my land and I take care of each other." It was a matter of independence and pride.

They paused at a street corner, waiting for a horse and chaise to trundle by. On the other side of the road, a couple of Quakers in black suits and round hats weaved through a group of aristocrats, like crows among peacocks. Next to Liam, a woman exited a perfumery, the pungent waft that followed her cloying in the summer air. The fresh air and peace of home seemed far away.

Mademoiselle Rivard peered at him around the brim of her hat. The ribbon beneath her chin flirted with the breeze. "It sounds like you and your land have a special relationship."

Her smile drew a laugh to his lips as he ushered her across the street. "That we do. And speaking of relationships, is Armand de Champlain your kin?" Today was not the first time he'd noticed a tension between them. At the Binghams' house in May, there was a strain he'd not managed to decipher. "You have the same chin."

"Do we?" Her hand floated up toward her chin but dropped again before she reached it. "We don't get along very well. In fact, we barely know each other."

When she didn't elaborate, he said, "I don't mean to pry. But you seemed so upset earlier, and you don't seem the type to cry over spilled blood." He cringed, aghast at his choice of words, for he could only imagine what she'd seen in Paris. "I meant Armand's wound, of course. You handled it with calm efficiency. Was it the sans-culottes in the street who distressed you?"

"Of course they distressed me." Her voice was quiet, but steady.

"They are fools. Parading about for a cause they don't understand, drunk on violence and heedless of who they harm. You must know I don't approve of that, for all my love of liberty." Why Mademoiselle Rivard's perception of his stand suddenly mattered to him, he could not say. But he could not abide being lumped in with those rogues in her mind.

"I know that." She shifted her gaze from one lamppost to another as they passed them on the sidewalk, as if they were anchors for her thoughts. From behind, a barking dog shot around her, tearing after a squirrel. "My pension is just there." She pointed to the next block. "The Sainte-Marie."

Liam spotted it. A few more steps brought them to the door of the property she called home. A shrunken thing it was, held up by the two buildings squeezing it from either side. His chest constricted just looking at it. "Are you happy here?" he asked. "It's not what you were used to in Paris."

Her lips curved in a winsome grin. "I did not expect to find the equal of the Palais-Royal in so young a town. But I am—what is the word? Adaptable?"

"Yes." Slipping back into French customs, he took her hand and bowed over it as he bid her adieu. "Tell me," he said as he released fingers that were porcelain smooth, and as delicate. "Would you—who have lived and worked in the most fashionable district in all of Europe—would you really agree to be a scullery maid?"

She crossed her arms, tucking her hands beneath the lace at her elbows. "If it was the only alternative to accepting funds from Armand, yes. I would do that work and be grateful."

Liam could tell from the lift of her chin that she meant it. There was a defiance in her eyes he recognized. It was liberty she wanted, from Armand. She was fighting for her own independence with more than a little pride. And that, he understood.

Before the sun awakened the next day, Vivienne arrived at the Four Winds Tavern, ready to prove she could bake well enough to be hired on to the staff. Amber light from the fire and candles cast a glow about the cellar kitchen. The low, timbered ceiling and bricked walls gave the space a close atmosphere, which would no doubt be sweltering later. For now, however, it felt to Vienne like being enfolded in a warm embrace.

"Mercy, if that don't smell like heaven itself." Rachel pointed to the bowl Vienne had brought with her. "What is it?"

Breathing in the yeasty aroma, Vivienne set the bowl on the stout worktable and peeled off the cloth covering to reveal a white, bubbly mass. "It's called a sponge. I made this at my pension yesterday afternoon, because it needs to rest at least twelve hours before it can be used to make dough for the baguettes." Madame Barouche had been a dear to let her borrow ingredients from the pension pantry.

"Well, anything you need this morning, you go ahead and use it." Rachel poured a steaming cup of coffee and handed it to Vienne before showing her where the sugar, salt, and flour were. "Just say if you need something you can't find, all right? I'm working on some berry preserves this morning before the breakfast orders begin, but I can sure enough point you in the right direction with one hand while I stir my pot with the other." Her laughter matched that of the crackling fire in the hearth.

Thanking her, Vivienne busied herself with her work. Not that it felt like labor. A bit of sugar, a pinch of salt, a few cups of flour, and the sponge transformed into a dough that turned stringy and difficult to turn in the bowl. Perfect. She dusted the table with flour, then turned out the dough on the surface, kneading to the rhythm of Rachel's humming. The soft dough yielded beneath her hands as she shaped it into a ball and set it back in the bowl. Vienne's hope rose along with it.

With the better part of an hour to wait, her memory scrolled through recipes she'd learned from Paulette. With Rachel's blessing, she made a lattice-crust cherry pie. After the last strip of dough was pinched into place, she punched down the baguette dough and let it rise again. At last it was time to roll it out and divide it into three equal rectangles. These she formed into oblong loaves, using the heel of her hand to seal the folded edge along its entire length. Covering these, she set them aside to rest again, which gave her time to put together a blueberry and strawberry tart.

Morning sun crept into the kitchen through the windows near the ceiling, washing the room with a pink blush. A girl arrived to begin boiling eggs and peeling potatoes, with Rachel presiding from her pots of raspberry preserves. Once Vivienne's creations were in the brick oven, the kitchen was near to bursting with mouth-watering aromas of fresh baguettes and simmering berries. Time seemed to slow until the baking was complete.

As if Tara somehow knew when Vienne's masterpieces had cooled enough to sample, she descended the stairs with her lanky cousin and blue-eyed brother in tow.

"Saints alive!" She feigned a swoon upon spying the bread and pastries. "I brought Finn and Liam to help taste what you've made, but my appetite just grew three times larger. Off with you now, boys, I've got this covered." She flashed a cheeky grin at the men, then ordered them to sit on the stools at the worktable and wait to be served.

Vivienne pressed the back of her hand to her sweat-dampened brow, then offered the first baguette to Tara. "Break it open, but mind the steam."

The golden crust crunched as Tara tore it, revealing the perfect airy bread inside. Rachel nudged a crock of butter toward them, and Tara passed the baguette around. When it was Vienne's turn to place a piece in her mouth, the bread melted on her tongue.

"Oh, is that good." Mr. Delaney closed his eyes while he chewed.

Finn rubbed a hand over his mess of short curls. "Man does not live on bread alone. Don't hold back now."

With cautious confidence, Vivienne served slices of the pie and tart before sampling them herself. The tart was perfect, but the cherry pie wasn't quite as sweet as it might have been. "I can add more sugar to the pie next time."

"No need." Mr. Delaney swallowed another forkful. "This is just the way I like it. Sweet enough, but with a little kick to it." He finished the rest of his piece and glanced at his sister. "Like Tara here."

Tara elbowed him in the ribs, holding her hand over her mouth as she laughed. With one large-knuckled hand, Finn banged the table in agreement, rattling the dishes on the board. The kitchen was barely large enough to hold their merriment.

"Mmm-mm!" Rachel licked her lips. "Well, are you going to

let the lady do this again and pay her for it? I sure would count it a blessing to have the help around here."

Vivienne held her breath and looked at Tara, who told her the terms of pay.

"What do you say? Will you join us, Mademoiselle Rivard?"

"Please, you must call me Vivienne, or Vienne." She drew in a breath. Released it. "And yes. I agree."

Tara beamed as she pumped Vienne's hand. "Then welcome to the Four Winds family. 'Twas Providence that brought you to our door yesterday, though it was Liam who pulled you through it."

More laughter, and this time Vienne joined in. "Indeed." She wiped her hands on her apron. "Well, thank God and Mr. Delaney for that."

"It's Liam." His broad hand enveloped hers as he shook it. "And you're very welcome." The warmth in his voice hinted that he knew how much all this meant to her.

Finn announced that he needed to journey west straightaway, and he snatched up the second baguette. "For the road?" he asked Tara, who nodded.

Liam lifted the third long loaf and raised it toward Vienne in a kind of toast. "To your noble work and your new life in America. May you and the Four Winds take good care of each other."

His smile filled Vienne with hope.

The days and weeks that followed fell into a pleasing rhythm for Vivienne. Rising before dawn became routine, and she looked forward to the quiet walks over dew-studded bricks while the lamplighter snuffed out his wicks. Rachel, always first in the kitchen, greeted her with a pot of coffee, and their morning together began.

Fire popping in the hearth, bowls scraping across the table, a knife thumping on a board. This was the music that heralded the dawn. Vienne added more specialties to the Four Winds menu: scones, cobblers, trifles. But her favorite remained the daily baguettes, a bittersweet tribute to France. Outside the tavern, tricolor cockades were still seen on Philadelphia's streets, and revolutionary news from across the ocean grew ever bloodier. But it was easier here, while she focused on work, to forget that. Energy thrummed through her as she baked, while Rachel cooked and others peeled or scrubbed, and Tara blew in and out like a strong gust of wind.

Despite the swirling activity, Vienne's spirit calmed as her hands worked the dough. The way it became firm and elastic with pounding, and the way it rested and doubled in size afterward, became to her a kind of truth. A picture of resilience she hoped to mirror. Martine remained limp and deflated by her trials, but Tara, who Vienne learned had lost both parents and a husband, had risen above, with an even larger capacity for joy and compassion.

When Vienne punched through the air pockets in a lump of dough, she prayed, *Fill my empty places with Your love and faithfulness.* As she rolled and sealed her baguettes: *Make smooth my rough edges, Lord.* And so with flour dusting her hair and sweat beading her face and neck, Vienne shaped her bread, and believed that God was shaping her, too.

Chapter Eleven

Parasol in hand and a willow basket swinging from her elbow, Vivienne waded through humidity that dampened her white muslin gown to her skin. The texture of the August air was nothing to the heat of the tavern kitchen, but the incessant whine of mosquitoes did grow tiresome.

Beside her, Martine panted for breath beneath her own fringed parasol. Henri's flushed face glowed with perspiration, and his golden hair curled at his neck.

"Perhaps this isn't good for him." Martine stepped over an apple core crawling with ants. Light danced over her tangerine silk gown, radiant as the sun, while her skin and hair remained pale as the moon. Though Vienne had been too busy at the tavern to notice, Paulette reported that the former lady-in-waiting had grown even more reclusive since the sans-culottes had jumped into the Fourth of July parade last month. Jacobins were now printing essays in the newspapers and growing more boisterous in the streets.

"On the contrary, it's the very thing for a boy," Vienne said, glancing to the Four Winds Tavern as they passed it, as grateful for her job there as she was for this afternoon off. She had not seen Armand since the day she had stitched him up, nor had she missed him. Neither had she seen Liam since the morning he sampled her baking, though the memory of his kindness on Independence Day stayed with her. If Vienne had been young and naïve, she might have been taken in by it. She might have found pleasure in his attentions, their conversation, or even in the endearing relationship he had with his sister. But she was no trusting maiden. Armand and Félix had taught her how faithless men were, and Tante Rose had taught her how satisfied a woman could be without relying on one.

"My legs ache," Henri puffed as they neared the covered stalls on Market Street. "How long will this take?"

"Just a few things, Henri, and then we'll go look at the ships." Vienne closed her parasol and looped its cord over her wrist.

"Promise?" His eyes widened, too large for his thin face.

"As long as your legs don't pain you overmuch." Martine pinched a mosquito off his neck and flicked it away. "And as long as we're not eaten alive by then."

Vienne felt Martine and Henri trailing her as she moved from stall to stall. The press of perspiring shoppers added a muskiness to air already thick with odors of raw fish, beef, and the smells of warming produce. Chickens clucked and scratched inside a pen littered with feathers and corn.

After paying a dairy farmer from Jersey for a wheel of cheese, Vivienne added a pint of cherries to her basket. As she dropped some of the ripe fruit into Henri's waiting palm, a conversation behind her veered into news of France's Reign of Terror.

"More than ten thousand people have been executed by now," one said.

"No, more than fifteen thousand, I read," countered the other.

"Ah yes, it was ten thousand assumed to have died in prison, without trial."

Her gut twisting, Vienne remembered with a jolt the horrors that had been so easy to forget during the past month of her employment.

"But Louis-Charles is still alive," one woman offered. "Louis the XVII."

And the other: "If it's actually him at all. They say the real Louis-Charles is hidden away until it is safe for him to be crowned king. The poor boy in prison is a decoy. His physique is different, as is his mental capacity."

"Then where is the young king?"

"Who can say? Austria? Belgium? If I was charged with his well-being, I'd send him as far away from that turmoil as possible. An ocean away, in fact."

Vienne looked at Martine, whose expressionless face assured her she'd not understood, or perhaps even heard, the English words. Henri pulled a cherry pit from his lips, and red juice dribbled from the corner of his mouth down his chin.

Pulse racing against reason, Vienne led Martine and Henri out of the shadows of the covered market and into the blinding sun, where she opened her parasol once more. Carriages clattered past coachmakers, goldsmiths, and ironmongers. Quakers sweltered in black suits, children skipped rope beside their mothers, and birds sang from poplar trees. This was America, she told herself yet again. Here in Philadelphia, she was safe. She could stay beaten down beyond all logic, or she could rise above her fears.

She chose the latter and offered a smile to Henri. "Are you ready to see the ships?"

He grinned and, with the back of his hand, smeared the cherry juice on his chin.

They walked down the slope from Front Street and turned south. A dog ran by with a live crab in its mouth, its wet fur reeking. Henri's steps were quicker now, if not entirely strong, as they came to a familiar wharf studded with packs of planks and shingles ready to be shipped.

At the end of the dock, the little boy sat on an overturned crate beside Abel, a fisherman they'd met before. Wrinkles carved his leathered face. Just as he had on their previous visit, he cracked open oysters and loosened the meat from the shell, allowing Henri to slide it into his mouth. The two exchanged few words, neither speaking the other's language, and contented themselves with oysters. The sight of them together—Henri in his green silk breeches and gleaming white stockings, and Abel in his fisherman's slops—lifted

131

the corners of Vivienne's lips. The smile Abel offered in return was more subdued than last time, but who could blame him in this heat?

The river doubled the sun's intensity. Grateful for her parasol's shade, Vivienne set her basket at her feet and watched the activity around the piers. Stevedores clambered over the wharves, some shouldering slabs of salt fish, others carting barrels of molasses from the West Indies, which would no doubt be made into rum in the nearby taverns.

Abel scooped another oyster from his bucket. He moved stiffly, slowly, as if it taxed him. "See here, son, and maybe next time you can do this yourself—" He winced. Leaning forward, he dropped the oyster with a clatter back into the pail. A guttural groan escaped his gritted teeth.

"Abel!" Vienne placed her hand on his back. "What ails you?"

"The oysters," Martine gasped, and knocked Henri's from his hand.

"Something you ate?" Vienne asked.

"I don't know," Abel moaned. "But there's a tempest in my belly sure enough!" He dumped the remaining oysters onto the dock. They skittered across the wood planks while he vomited into the bucket.

Martine grasped Henri and the basket of food, pulling both away.

Vivienne stayed and offered the fisherman her handkerchief. "Keep it," she said. "I have more."

Abel kept his head bowed as he accepted. "Thank you kindly. 'Tweren't fittin' for you to see that." He wiped his mouth. Before he could fold it and tuck it away, Vienne saw that the stains on it were black. "I was feelin' poorly for a while there but thought I'd licked it."

"Let me help you to a doctor."

Abel spewed a stream of curses. "I ain't goin' to any doctor so's he can bleed me to death. Get away from here, miss, and don't come back to the docks until after the first frost. It's unhealthful by the water."

Vienne's mind spun.

"And don't you dare tell anyone you saw this, or there'll be a panic, and you Frenchies will be blamed for every death. Now git!" He ended his speech with a growl and a stomp of his boot.

Barely daring to breathe, Vivienne pivoted and hurried to join Martine and Henri, who waited for her at the end of the wharf.

"What is it? What is it?" Panic raised Martine's pitch.

It is nothing, Vivienne longed to say. *You are too fearful, as ever. All is well.* But all was not well. Neither did she want to admit it. "Come." She steadied her voice. "Madame will be waiting for her cheese."

Martine skewered her with a narrowed gaze, but Vienne glanced at Henri with hiked eyebrows, willing her friend to understand they should not speak of it before the boy.

"Fine," breathed Martine. Her face blanched as white as her hair.

"Can we come back tomorrow?" Henri asked. "If Abel is sick, can't we bring him some broth? Oysters are no good for the gripe, you know. Too squishy."

"If Abel is sick, he'll stay abed and would not want you around to catch it." Vivienne placed her hand on Henri's shoulder, firmly turning him toward the pension.

Mosquitoes hummed in her ears as they passed taverns along Front Street. A door slammed open and closed again as a sailor stumbled out of a grog shop a few yards in front of Vienne. Clutching his middle, he struggled to the alley and retched into the dirt.

Martine grabbed Vienne's arm. "What is wrong? What's happening?"

"He's drunk," Vienne tried. But the vomit, she'd seen, was black.

Summer burned away like chaff. By the time news arrived that the radical French revolutionary Robespierre had been guillotined, ending the Reign of Terror, a different terror had taken root in Philadelphia. Yellow fever was upon everyone's lips, if not on each person's brow. Thousands fled the city before the sickness had a chance to reach epidemic proportions. Among them were Eliza Hamilton and her children, and Father Gilbert and Suzanne Arquette, who went to Asylum, the French settlement up north. At least they were safe, Vivienne told herself.

But Henri was not. Surely it could not have been Abel's fault, since Henri contracted the fever weeks later. Yet Martine was certain the fisherman was to blame and that Vienne was at fault for taking the boy from the Pension Sainte-Marie in the first place.

"We never should have gone to the docks." Martine wrung her hands. "He can't die. Not after everything we've survived already."

Exhausted after her day of baking at the tavern, Vienne knelt by Henri's bed in the stiflingly hot garret room and felt the scorching temperature of his skin. "Martine," she murmured, "we can't keep him here, you know. He needs a doctor's care."

Paulette entered the room, her face glistening, and laid a cool damp cloth upon his brow. "She's right," the maid said. "This is a pension, not a hospital."

"If it's necessa—" Martine wavered and began to crumple. Vivienne caught her before she hit the floor and eased her onto the bed.

Paulette flapped her apron to stir a breeze. "Those ridiculous clothes she insists on wearing, even in this heat. Silk! And all those layers! I do the laundry myself, and I can tell you for sure these gowns are a nightmare to clean beneath the arms. She'd do well to remember she's no longer at court. Little wonder she fainted."

Vivienne laid her wrist to Martine's forehead. "*Mon Dieu*," she prayed in a whisper. "Her clothes are not to blame."

Chapter Twelve

Perhaps it was not her fault that Martine and Henri contracted yellow fever.

Then again, perhaps it was. So when the doctor who came to examine them sent them by wagon to the only hospital that would accept such cases, Vienne went with them and entered a world of new horrors.

"It is the only way, the proven way." His apron flecked with bile and blood, Dr. Benjamin Rush lanced Martine's arm as she lay in the bed, and her lifeblood drained into a bowl. Dr. Rush then dosed Martine with calomel.

"Mercury?" Vienne asked. The treatment had been used for Sybille, too, but had only caused extreme salivation and the loss of some of her teeth. "Must you?"

"Young lady." Dr. Rush peered over his small, iron-rimmed spectacles. "You were not here last summer, so you do not understand how wretched a way to die the yellow fever truly is. Allow me to enlighten you. What appears to be a simple cold or flu is followed by sharp pains throughout the body, which intensify until the patient believes an arm or leg is snapping. The pulse whimpers, soft and irregular as the beating of moth wings. Skin becomes sticky hot, followed by sudden uncontrolled defecation. If the patient does not improve at this point, he will die. But not before his vomit turns black from blood in the stomach, while skin, fingernails, and even eyes turn yellow with jaundice."

Feigning calm, Vivienne struggled against a rebelling stomach.

"So you see," the doctor went on, "we must purge the body of the fever through every means we have. Through the blood, through vomiting, and through the bowels. Twice a day, thrice for good measure. It's a regimen I had my assistant use on myself last summer, and it's the only reason I'm still standing here."

Noxious odor stuffed the ward, though the windows remained open to the humid outside air. All around them, patients moaned in fever or while clutching their stomachs before retching into a pan. Henri lay in the bed next to Martine's, awaiting his treatment.

"I know you are here for your friends," Dr. Rush continued, "and I'll allow you to stay and help. After last summer's raging epidemic, those willing to nurse are few. If you want to help these two, need and common decency demand that you help as many as you can while you're here." His bald pate glistened with the sweat of his labors.

"Yes, of course," Vienne agreed, though she would need to talk to Tara.

"One other observation I'll share with you, since the patient's mother is in no state for discussion. Were you aware Henri has rickets?"

She glanced at the young boy, his limbs as thin as rails except for the knobs of his knees barely raising the sheet that protected him from flies. "Rickets," she repeated. "He's complained of pain in his legs and back."

"I shouldn't doubt it. His bones are weak, and I suspect he's sedentary due to the pain, but that most likely makes it worse. Movement is good for children of any age."

"Is there any other treatment?"

The doctor's reply was clipped. "None we have yet discovered, other than to keep him moving. There is much yet to learn about the condition. Now, if you don't mind, we both have more pressing matters to attend to."

When Vivienne explained the situation to Tara, the tavern keeper readily agreed to a leave of absence from baking, adding that her own mother had died of the disease last summer. "Take care of yourself," Tara whispered and crushed Vivienne in an embrace. "And come back to us."

So with Tara's blessing, Vivienne became a nurse, along with several black women volunteers considered immune to the disease. The small compensation she was paid for her labors offset the fees for two patients' care, but the rest she paid with her own funds, for Martine's had all but run dry.

Mechanically, Vivienne emptied chamber pots and bedpans and bowls of blood. She kept a handkerchief dampened with peppermint oil pinned to the strap of her apron to help combat her revulsion. Her world shrank to the confines of her ward, and the natural division between day and night ceased to carry meaning, for illness never slept. In the span of one week, which felt like six, Martine and Henri made progress, only to worsen without warning.

Outside the hospital, fires blazed on the street corners to help keep the fever from spreading, the smoke wafting in through the open windows. If anyone dared walk within sight of the hospital, it was on the sidewalk opposite, and with handkerchiefs covering their noses. Some wore bags of camphor around their necks, while others, Dr. Rush told Vienne, chewed garlic or carried dried frogs in their pockets as talismans to guard them from the disease.

Fresh wind blew through the hospital, however, when a new doctor, Edward Stevens, took over. Dr. Rush left for a different hospital, and his radical treatments went with him, to everyone's relief. Instead of mercury, Dr. Stevens had Vienne administer Peruvian bark and aged Madeira. Following his orders, she gave Martine and Henri cold baths, then glasses of brandy topped with burned cinnamon. Rather than emptying the patients' bodies, Dr. Stevens's aim was to build them up. Laudanum was the bedtime drink, and for patients with upset stomachs, it was one of lavender spirits, chamomile flowers, and oil of peppermint.

Still, their patients expired. Exhaustion weighted her as Vienne changed the linens on a bed recently vacated. She had not grown accustomed to this. It was not the stripping of soiled sheets that troubled her, but the quickness with which one patient must be forgotten so the next could take his or her place. There was no time to feel regret or loss for a life snuffed out. Her back aching, she stuffed the linens into a basket to be laundered, then straightened before going to check on her friends.

A smile cracked Henri's lips when he saw her. "Mademoiselle." He reached out his hand, and she took it, cringing at the bruising on his arm where Dr. Rush had drawn his blood. But the boy's skin no longer burned.

Hope flared. She knelt beside him, and he twirled one of her curls around his finger.

"Your hair," he rasped. "It's very messy."

She chuckled. "It is."

"Where is Maman? Is she well?"

Vienne swallowed. "She is here in the hospital, too. Resting. They moved her to a different area, but she asks after you often." She did not tell him that Martine's case was severe, that neither doctor had been able to pull her back to health, or that her fevered mind flipped between present and past.

"Well, you must tell her I'm feeling better. I should like to go home. Is the pension still our home?" The words were in English. Perfect English.

She blinked in surprise. "As soon as you are well enough, yes, indeed. But Henri, I didn't know you could speak English. When did you learn it?"

"At court, of course. The royal tutors."

"Then why have I not heard you speak it before?"

He shrugged. "Maman doesn't like it. She told me to speak only French and not to tell about my tutors. Oh no." He frowned. "I forgot. You must forgive me, there have been so many things to remember. And so many things to forget."

The forgetting, she understood very well. But the remembering . . . "What else have you tried to remember?"

He settled back into his pillow and scanned the ceiling for a moment before his eyes drifted closed, his delicate blond lashes sweeping his cheeks. Barely a trace of purple showed under his skin, which meant the hemorrhaging had stopped.

"I'm sorry, Henri. I've tired you. I'll go tell your maman you're feeling better. For now, you rest." She pressed a kiss to his forehead, rejoicing that his skin was no warmer than hers on this late August afternoon.

Rising, Vienne turned to go and nearly ran into Sebastien Lemoine. With his black hair tied neatly in a queue and his suit immaculate, he was a vision of health and vigor and wholly out of place in the fever ward. She was suddenly keenly aware of her own soiled apron and rumpled cotton dress.

She straightened her white ruffled cap over her hair. "What are you doing here?"

His hands cupped her shoulders. "I was looking for you. Madame Barouche told me I could find you here—indeed, she insisted I fetch you. You must come home and take care of yourself, or you'll occupy one of these beds soon. Those black circles beneath your eyes prove you've been denying yourself the sleep you need. What good can come of this?"

At the mention of sleep, her body betrayed her, swaying ever so slightly.

Sebastien looped an arm about her waist. "I'm taking you home. It isn't safe for you on the streets alone."

"More sans-culottes?" Her voice hoarse with fatigue, she swallowed and wiped her palms against her apron.

"Sans-culottes? Oh, there are plenty of those, as ever. But some of the Americans' hospitality is waning toward émigrés. It's the fever. Reasonable or not, they grow resentful all over again, believing that the French brought it on the ships."

"How resentful?" She licked her dry lips.

"So far it hasn't gone beyond rude insults. However, we both know where that can lead." He raised an eyebrow, clearly recalling the Fourth of July parade. "I insist on escorting you home."

Vivienne fought back a yawn. "A moment, please." She stepped out of his hold. "I must check on Martine first. It will do her good to hear that Henri is faring so much better."

"Mademoiselle?"

Vienne turned back to the boy, surprised to hear his voice again. His eyes were still closed.

"My name is Louis."

She stared at him, waiting for an explanation. "What did you say?" she whispered. But he had slipped back into sleep.

Sebastien inclined his head and cut his voice low. "Did he say his name is Louis-Charles?"

Louis-Charles, the boy king? Was it possible? "That's not what he said."

Sebastien stayed right behind her as she threaded between the beds toward Martine. "Louis. He said his name was Louis," he insisted. "I thought his name was Henri Chastain. Why would he say otherwise?"

Through the fog of sleep deprivation, her mind fished for a way to make sense of it. Rumors were strong that Louis-Charles was not in prison but in hiding. Philadelphia would seem a perfect haven. But Henri's mother was Martine, not Marie Antoinette. A lady-in-waiting to the queen.

But was it possible that Martine was not his mother at all and had only been charged with his care? Was there more to her hermit-like tendencies than she'd been free to explain?

Vivienne stilled and looked back to where the boy lay, a pale white face in a sea of yellow patients. One thing was sure—he was not delirious with fever.

"What can it mean?" Sebastien pressed.

Vivienne rubbed the heels of her hands over her eyes. "I don't know." After all, it could all be coincidental. What were the chances that she'd been living with the exiled king of France all these months? A shock spiraled through her at the notion. "I need to check on Martine."

He followed. When Vienne arrived at her friend's bedside, Sebastien was an arm's length away. Dr. Stevens was already there, stooping to feel the pulse in Martine's wrist. Straightening, he turned to Vienne. "She is sinking."

Vienne's heart slammed in her chest. That couldn't be right. Henri was recovering, and so must she. "What do you mean? She isn't . . ."

"There is nothing more I can do for her. She's as comfortable as she can be. You're her friend, yes? Say your good-byes sooner rather than later." He bowed and walked to the next bed.

Vienne lowered herself onto the stool beside Martine. A warm hand on her shoulder told her of Sebastien's presence, but she did not look away from her friend. She took Martine's hand. "I'm here, *mon amie*."

Her eyelids fluttered. "Henri?"

"He is better, or nearly there. I have no doubt he'll make a full recovery. He asked about you." She meant to sound bright, cheerful. It only came across as strained.

"He is a good boy, Vienne. You must take him as your own son now. Protect him." Martine's eyes shot open, the whites of them full yellow and fierce.

Sebastien swore under his breath. Vienne did not blame him for being startled.

"Keep him safe," Martine labored to say. "Or they will kill him."

A chill shuddered through Vivienne. "What?"

Martine tightened her grip on Vienne's hand, her untrimmed nails digging into her palm. "Keep him safe. Keep him hidden. It is the only way."

"Martine—" Vienne faltered. She should not expect an answer she could count on, not now, when the poor woman was at death's door. Still, she had to ask. "Henri said his name is really Louis. What did he mean?"

"Shh!" Martine's face twisted in agony. "No one was supposed to know. No one can know. They will kill him if they so much as suspect him to be the king."

Tears ran down Vienne's face. Her friend was sliding away from her in body, mind, and spirit. "Who? Where is the danger?"

"The Jacobins, here. The danger is right here."

Sebastien muttered an oath.

"Promise me!" Martine rasped, yellow eyes wild.

Vienne did, and the dying woman exhaled.

"Stay." Martine's breath came in shallow sips, and her grip on Vienne's hand relaxed. Jaw slackening, her mouth hung slightly open as her lids fluttered closed.

Sebastien knelt on one knee beside Vienne. "She is as gone now as she'll ever be. I'm taking you home."

Vivienne shook her head. "My place is with her, until the end. Leave us, please."

He did.

Whispered prayers formed on Vienne's lips as tears ran down her cheeks. "Mon Dieu, mon Dieu, receive her. Be her refuge, at last. Be ours." It was all she could manage.

She and Martine had not divulged the details of their pasts, for sharing the present had been enough. Their friendship had been woven from slender threads, with blank spaces where secrets were kept. It was precious, nonetheless. A piece of lace, gently worked. The empty places were as meaningful as the strands that embraced them.

In the morning, Martine was gone, and it was Vienne who felt unraveled.

Willingly, Vienne paid for a coffin and a plot of ground, and for a priest to speak words over Martine's ravaged body, though no one else was present save herself, Henri, and Madame Barouche. Everything Vienne had not been able to do for Sybille and Tante Rose, she did for the queen's lady-in-waiting. Once the priest and Madame took their leave, she knelt at the grave and wept silent tears, not only for the friend underground, but for all of her losses combined. And for Henri, who was an orphan now, as she had been.

She glanced at him as he sat slumped on the earth beside her, rocking himself, clutching Bucephalus, the small stuffed horse he'd brought on the crossing from France. It was always in his hand now, even in sleep. She wondered if he noticed or cared that the velvet on the ears had grown threadbare.

Her heart squeezed to look at the boy, who appeared two summers younger than his actual nine years. She had reduced her hours at the tavern to mornings only, with Madame and Paulette insisting Henri was no trouble while Vienne was absent, but she hated not being there when he woke each day. He barely spoke lately and cried in his sleep. Last night when Vienne had tried to comfort him, he only sobbed more despairingly upon finding her, and not his maman, in the dark.

His pain touched a bruise inside her, a soreness she had learned to protect. Though she had not physically buried her mother until this year, Vienne was younger than Henri when she learned Tante Rose was actually her aunt. That her real mother had never lived with her and never would. The day Vienne had struck the word *maman* from her vocabulary had felt like a death to her. *Lord!* She prayed desperately. *Fill me with his mother's love and with Your strength. Make me brave enough for both of us until he can have courage on his own.*

Late summer heat made pungent the tang of freshly turned earth and the perfume of the roses laid atop the mound. Vienne inhaled the fragrance forever tied to Tante Rose in her mind. The breeze wafted the smell over her, a vivid reminder that even in the presence of loss, there could be sweetness and beauty and life. Her aunt had been all those things to Vienne. She prayed she could be as much to this forlorn boy beside her.

"How are you, Henri?"

He waited so long to reply that she wondered if he'd heard her. Then, a shrug. "My stomach hurts." Still holding his horse, he pulled a blade of grass from the ground and chewed on it absently.

"Do you need a doctor?" she inquired.

"No, merci. I've had quite enough of those lately, if you please."

Worry wormed through Vienne as she looked at him. She knew nothing about raising children, especially boys. "Have you ever heard that keeping secrets can make one sick? If they are big enough, and you hold them long enough. If you ever had secrets hurting you, I would want you to let them out. All right? You can talk to me." Vivienne was all he had left. If he would confide in anyone, it should be her.

Martine's last words were stones in the pit of her stomach. Who was this boy left in her charge? What unseen dangers did he summon?

"Did you know," she tried gently, "you told me your real name is Louis?"

Wind ruffled his blond hair. His troubled eyes revealed that Martine had bequeathed to him her fears. "Did I?" He rubbed his toy against his cheek. "Strange. You know my name is Henri. Don't you?" The wrinkle in his voice brought a sting to her throat.

"Yes. I know your name. I know you," Vienne whispered as one singing hymns against the darkness. For in his question she heard echoes of what haunted her most. "*I don't know you.*" Sybille's words scraped her ears. Vivienne kissed Henri's silken hair, breathed in his smell of soap and grass. "Of course I know you, Henri."

But she wondered now if she didn't. If he had barricaded himself behind his fear, intent on hiding who he really was. An ache filled her, for she knew too well the loneliness that lived behind such walls.

A flock of birds undulated against the violet sky, and snatches of a psalm scrolled through Vivienne's mind. *O Lord, thou hast searched me, and known me . . . thou understandest my thought afar off.* She drew comfort from that, and from the idea that the same God who knew Vienne knew Henri, as well, whatever his name may be. In time, she prayed, Henri would trust her with the secrets he now locked away.

Chapter Thirteen

Shoulders and arms burning from the day's work, Liam balanced on a ladder leaning against a new house in the settlement. Jethro handed him a flat gray stone, and Liam climbed a few more rungs until he could heave it into place at the top of the chimney. "That was the last!" he called below.

Jethro stirred the mortar in his bucket one final time before climbing the ladder on the opposite side of the chimney with it in tow. Liam fished his trowel from his pocket, scooped it into Jethro's pail, and applied the mortar between the stones. Metal tools scraped as they worked with practiced efficiency.

Liam climbed onto the roof and perched carefully on the ridgepole to fill the chinks from that side. When every remaining crevice had been filled with mortar, he dropped his trowel to the ground and indulged in the view. A broad smile spread over his face. There, near land he and Jethro had labored to clear this summer, were both Liam's home and Jethro's. Forested, rolling hills dwarfed the two-story houses from behind. The tips of the leaves were barely starting to turn, so that the hills were flecked with orange and gold and crimson. He may grow weary of the one-hundred-sixty-mile

145

journey between here and Philadelphia, but he would never tire of living here.

"Jethro, come on up here. You have to see this."

With a grunt, Jethro climbed up to sit beside him. He let out a low, appreciative whistle. "Now that's the land I'm most interested in."

"I feel the same. But we'll not turn down good work, either, will we?"

"True enough." Jethro mopped his glistening dark brow with the cuff of his linen sleeve.

"And if the work is plenty, all the better." The settlement sprouting up so near his land offered plenty of employment for when his own chores were complete, which they were, for now.

The fact that Liam spoke French worked to his advantage here. Most of the people who had flocked to this bend in the Susquehanna were nobles and priests, with a few merchants and artisans. Not one of them knew how to build a house, or fell a tree, or plow a field. Which made them only too eager to hire their American neighbors. Dressed in their laces and silks and buckled red-heeled shoes, they could turn up their noses at Liam as much as they wished, as long as they continued to pay him.

Jethro climbed back down the ladder to solid ground. Before Liam followed suit, he looked in the opposite direction of his land and over the French settlement hugging the river. None of this had been here two years ago, and now two dozen houses lined the broad dirt roads, each home about thirty by eighteen feet, like the one he and Jethro had just finished building. They were four-roomed, two-story structures built of hewn and squared logs from the nearby forests. Separate from the main house were a kitchen house and a dining house, with a cool cellar beneath them. All the houses had papered walls, glass windows, and wooden floors, and the women took pains to beautify their spaces with flowers, Lombardy poplars, and fruit trees. For all the evidence of civilization, Liam far preferred the beauty of the land. His gaze swept back to the hills as he climbed down the ladder.

"Oh la! There you are!"

A voice, sharp as a pickax, turned Liam's head to find a woman with frizzled blond hair and wide gray eyes addressing Jethro as if she knew him. Her green dress shone in the sun, its enormously wide hem dusting the earth. Liam had glimpsed her once or twice before but hadn't officially been introduced. Beside her, Father Gilbert, whom Liam had grown to respect in the time since he'd moved to the settlement, laid a hand on her shoulder.

"Father Gilbert." Liam wiped his hands on a towel and tossed it into a bucket. He knew he smelled ripe enough to offend.

"Greetings, friends. This is Madame Suzanne Arquette. This is her house you've built. Magnifique! May we look inside?"

Liam gestured toward the cabin. "Door's open."

But Madame Arquette was not so easily distracted. She shook her finger at Jethro. "I've been looking all over for you! What does this mean, you sneaking around without so much as a hint as to your whereabouts! Why, it's enough to make me think you're of a mind to run away. I'll rid you of that notion one way or another—"

Liam held up his hand to stop her, grateful that Jethro couldn't understand her language. "What's this all about, madame?"

"Oh dear," said Father Gilbert. He pulled at the flesh beneath his chin. "I do apologize."

Liam glanced at the woman's pinched face before responding. "I don't know who she thinks he is, but Jethro Fortune here is a free man, working for pay, same as any of the rest of us American laborers."

Madame Arquette clenched her fists. "He is *not* free. He is my slave. Did you think you could steal him from me? He's branded with my mark. I'll show you."

"What's going on?" Jethro asked as Father Gilbert held her back.

Liam shook his head. "She's lost her senses, from what I can tell."

"What does that have to do with me?"

"You must remind her of someone she once knew." Or owned. But Liam saw no need to say it. "Head on home, our work is done for the day. I'll clean up here."

"Let's see your new house." Father Gilbert steered Madame Arquette through the door.

Liam followed them. While she was inspecting the wallpaper pattern, he pulled Father Gilbert aside. "Is this going to be a problem?" he whispered, looking pointedly at the woman.

Father Gilbert kept his voice low. "She escaped Saint-Domingue after the slave revolt, and her mind hasn't worked right since. I don't know how to help clear it. Her family was killed by her own slaves, you see. She hasn't yet accepted that. Keeps looking for them to arrive any day. And she doesn't understand why she no longer has her retinue of servants."

"We have laws in this state against slavery," Liam said. "Jethro earned his freedom fighting in our war."

"Oui, monsieur. I understand. I have no stomach for human bondage, myself. Yet I'm at a loss as to how to reason with a mind that has grown unstable." He sighed. "Your friend may want to keep his distance from her."

Liam watched Madame Arquette make a face as she surveyed the room. "Noted."

Her heels tapped across the wood floor. "It isn't nearly large enough."

"It is the same size as every house except the Grand Maison, and that was built for the queen." Father Gilbert's voice held an astonishing amount of patience.

She threw up her hands. "How on earth am I to host my parties? Where will we dance? No, no. This will never do. It is so—rustic."

"May I remind you that you are in the woods, madame." Liam smiled.

"Even if I lived on a desert island, I would require mirrors, chandeliers, and paintings," she snapped. "If I wanted an ugly house, I would have ordered one."

Well aware he would win no fight with her, Liam bowed and bade her good night.

Father Gilbert stopped him at the door. "I do apologize," he said again. "Her temper flares during times of change, and she still has not recovered from the arduous journey from Philadelphia. I don't suppose she can help it. I keep praying for guidance."

"I don't blame you," Liam assured him. But heaven help her if she ever came after Jethro.

"Aha! I nearly forgot. The other mail carrier brought this back with him a few days ago. It means little to me, but perhaps my American friend may want it." Smiling, Father Gilbert drew a thrice-folded newspaper from his coat. "It looks to be weeks old, I'm afraid, but I thought you'd enjoy reading the news from Philadelphia."

Liam gladly accepted the offering. "I would indeed. Thank you." After bidding the mild-mannered Father good-bye, he stuffed the paper into his trousers pocket, loaded his tools into his wheelbarrow, and made his way over the broad road toward his house.

The wind at his back was scented with apples and woodsmoke, and the walk passed in simple splendor. White and purple clover lined the road, and the sun winked at him from the windows of the houses he passed along the way—many of which he'd built himself. Cicadas droned and crickets clipped at the evening's quiet. Somewhere, a bullfrog twanged. How his father would have loved to call this land home.

At the edge of the settlement farthest from the river, Liam's property came into view. He wondered if the pride Tara felt for the Four Winds Tavern could possibly compare to what he felt for this. Built with the same dimensions as those in Asylum, his house had four square rooms, two to each floor. Outbuildings included a spring house over a nearby creek, a barn with more space than his crops and horse currently required, a dining house, and a cookhouse he barely frequented, taking most of his meals at the settlement's inn.

In the barn, the sweet smell of hay was made more pungent by last night's rain. A mouse skittered into the shadows while he cleaned his tools and set them back in their places. Red, the farm horse named for his bright chestnut color, twitched his tail against flies, watching Liam from his stall. Red would never win a race against Beau and Cherie, Monsieur Talon's surefooted Narragansett Pacers, but he worked hard plowing fields and pulling loads of hay or rocks or wood. Drawing an apple from his pocket, Liam offered it in his open hand, and Red took it, his dry and hairy lips tickling Liam's palm.

Leaving Red to his feed, Liam took a brisk jump into the creek to wash away the residue of the day's toil before entering the dining house. He spread the newspaper from Father Gilbert over his thick oak table. Tearing off a piece of bread, he turned his attention to the news as he ate.

What he found nearly caused him to choke on his food. Could this be right?

He lit the taper in its glass hurricane. A golden glow reflected off the whitewashed walls and gleamed on the pewter plate and cup sitting on a shelf. In the wavering circle of candlelight, two-inch columns of black text told a story in vivid color.

On August 7, President Washington issued a proclamation demanding that the insurgents end their resistance to the whiskey tax or face military action. On the same day, he called for a muster of 12,950 militiamen from New Jersey, Pennsylvania, Maryland and Virginia.

Insurgents. Resistance. Military action. Was this a revolution all over again, not twenty years after the first began? Liam's skin crawled to think of it. No matter who was right, could this country survive another war? He could almost hear England laughing from the far side of the ocean.

Between his trips to the capital on the mail rotation, Liam relished living apart from politics and debates. Isolation did have its charms. But how set apart could he allow himself to be? In Philadelphia, there were certain aspects of the Quakers that he admired, but their stubborn neutrality during the American Revolution was not one of them. If there was a conflict, Liam Delaney always picked a side and prayed to God in heaven it was the right one.

Slamming the door behind him, he left the dining house and stormed into the main house. He climbed the stairs to his room, pulled off his linen shirt, and eased into bed. Outside, fireflies throbbed against a dark purple sky beginning to be studded with stars. Night draped the hills in a velvet mantle of deep green and gray. Sleep, however, did not join him.

He knew he could not stay neutral in this fight.

Chapter Fourteen

This isn't working. Vivienne had only to look at Henri's sharpening cheekbones and lusterless eyes to see that her best efforts for him were not enough. A late-afternoon breeze lifted the hair from his brow as they walked beneath burnished trees. The air held a note of spiced cider and roasting chestnuts, but autumn's pleasures were lost on him. He curled inward like a drying leaf, clutching his stuffed horse Bucephalus to his chest.

His fingers were spindles in her hand as they crossed the street. He still wasn't eating, and getting him out of the house was a continual struggle, as much from his disinterest as from the rickets in his legs. But what bothered Vienne most was the time he spent alone while she earned the funds to support them both. Though she did not fault herself for working, she could not help but be concerned that, according to Paulette, Henri stayed alone in their room for hours, missing breakfast, the only meal the pension provided.

By the time Vienne returned home each day, exhaustion combined with worry made her fractious—and unreceptive when Monsieur Lemoine came calling. "*Has he said anything else about being Louis-Charles?*" Always the same question. And always the same

152

answer: "*No.*" There was a wall of mistrust between Vienne and Henri, and she'd not been able to breach it.

Tante Rose had been so much better at this. But then, she didn't have to leave Vienne alone while she worked.

"Here we are." Vivienne led Henri to the rear of the Four Winds Tavern, where the scullery maid scrubbed dishes near the pump in the yard. Food waste and grease floated in the trench near the alley.

Henri wrinkled his nose but said nothing as Vienne greeted the young woman, then pulled open the door to the cellar. "Come," she told him. "You'll get to see where I spend every morning."

"Why did you bring me here?" He followed her down the stone stairs to a kitchen steaming and snapping with supper preparations.

"I need to make the sponge for tomorrow's baguettes," she replied. "It needs to rest overnight so I can work with it in the morning. It won't take long."

"I don't see why I couldn't stay home like I usually do."

"Because I miss you." Vienne smiled at him as they reached the cellar, but he did not look convinced. The ache she felt was familiar by now.

"Well now! Who is this handsome young man escorting you today?" Rachel called out from her place at the fire. She pushed a spatula through a pot of caramelizing onions. A soot-smeared girl next to her turned a spit of chickens and squab. Juices dripped into a roasting pan in the fire below.

Henri gave a charming smile while Vienne introduced him, but he did not bow. The kitchen hands eyed his courtly silk suit while their hands stayed busy whisking sauces and shaping salmon corn cakes.

"We're just here to make the sponge, Rachel," Vivienne said. "We'll stay out of the way and be gone before you know it."

Rachel dabbed the hem of her apron to her glistening brow. "You never in the way, sugar, and I'm pleased to meet your boy. Reckon Miss Tara will want the privilege, too, mind you, so if she don't come down in time, go on up and find her."

Thanking her, Vivienne gathered what she needed and scooted

Henri toward a small table in an empty corner of the bustling kitchen.

"She called me your boy." Henri peered up at her with an expression she couldn't read.

"Did that bother you?" Vienne spooned yeast into a bowl of warm water.

He rubbed the ear of Bucephalus. "We don't seem to belong together, do we?"

"Let's talk about that. But in English, please. You can even correct me if I get the language wrong. How about that?" She smiled at him. "Your English is excellent, from what I heard earlier."

"You see," Henri said a little louder, still in French, "we don't even speak the same language."

Vivienne saw that very well. Fist on her hip, she looked him full in the face. "And we must. English, please."

He screwed his little mouth tight, glaring at her. "Why do you get to decide? Don't you care that I prefer French?" But the words he spoke now could be understood by the entire room. "I lost my country, my father, my mother, and now you take my language, too."

The kitchen's heat closed in around her. "I am sad for you. I miss your mother, as well. But this is our country now."

"No." He stomped his foot. "My country is France. I will go back there some day. I must."

Suspicion needled her. "Why must you?" *To rule as king?*

Henri pulled a wooden stool from the wall and climbed up onto it. His dangling feet knocked into the rungs. "Paulette says we must not give up on France. She wants to go back one day, too. Did you know that? I miss Versailles. I want to go back as soon as we can."

Vivienne clenched her teeth before responding. "We stay." If he was the future of the monarchy, France was the most dangerous place of all for him. Breathing deeply, she pressed floury fingers to her pounding temples. She had no evidence at all he was Louis-Charles. But what if he was? What if she had the next king of France right here in a tavern cellar?

She bent to look him in the eyes. She would not have chosen the kitchen for this conversation, but here it was. She lowered her voice. "Henri, I know you're upset, perhaps even in ways you don't understand. I am sad and upset, too. But we must try to get along. Your maman gave you to my keeping."

"She would have wanted you to be *nice* to me," he spat. His legs swung again, and he kicked her shin through her skirt. "Everyone at court was nice to me. They gave me whatever I wanted and let me do whatever I pleased."

"Is that so?"

"It is *so*. Didn't your maman give you what you wanted?"

"No." She rested her hands on the table, where uncomplicated work awaited her attention. "She did not. And neither did my aunt, who raised me." Hissing filled Vienne's ears, but it was only bacon cooking in a skillet and husks being stripped from cobs of corn.

"So you were an orphan." There was an edge to Henri's tone she didn't like.

"I had my aunt." Vivienne added flour to the yeast and water and began to stir.

"If you really cared about me, you would spend more time with me and do what I wanted."

Whether his blood was royal or not, this rudeness would not stand. She turned to him, her spoon resting in the bowl. "You are a big boy, and so I will treat you like one, yes? My job is to raise you to be a mannerly young man, not cater to your whims. Part of growing up requires you to accept facts, even the unpleasant ones, and adapt to them. And the fact is that I must work, as I have always worked. I work to pay for food and clothes and the roof over our heads."

Henri flinched at the thudding of a knife on a chopping board nearby. "Maman didn't work. I never knew anyone who had to, or wanted to."

"Now you do." She forced a smile. "I'm different from the people you knew in court. In Paris, you lived a different life. And as you pointed out, this"—she spread her hands—"is not Versailles. I will never replace either of your parents in your affections, but my dear young man, neither will I treat you like royalty."

From some corner of the cellar, an eavesdropping kitchen hand grunted in agreement. "Ain't no princes in America."

"What if I was?" It was a whisper so quiet, Vienne wasn't convinced it was Henri who had said it and not her imagination. And yet a charge went through her as she met the boy's glittering blue gaze.

They were surrounded by people busy at work, a couple of them children. Work had been good medicine for Vivienne. It would be good for Henri, as well.

After covering the bowl containing her sponge, she placed it out of the way and whisked back to Rachel. "We have some time," she told her. "May we help peel carrots for you? Not for pay. In fact, it will help me more than it helps you."

Rachel glanced at Henri, who slumped on his stool, Bucephalus held to one cheek. "Busy hands make a happy heart. Good thinking, Mama." Her smile dazzled white, all the more endearing for the small space between her two front teeth. "Go on and see if he don't enjoy making those orange strips fly."

Resolve steeling her spine, Vivienne thanked her, then carried what she needed to Henri.

"What are you doing?" he asked. "I thought you said we could leave after you made your dough thing."

"Watch this." She demonstrated how to set the peeler at the top of the carrot and slide it down in a long smooth motion, sending an orange ribbon curling into a pail. "Do you think you can do that? Look how shiny the carrot is beneath the peel. Once you get really good at it, look how fast you can go." Turning the carrot, she shredded its outer layer with practiced speed.

He stared, a wrinkle between his brows, as she held out a new carrot and the peeler for him to try. "This is peasant's work." In perfect English. For the entire kitchen staff to hear.

Vivienne was mortified. "It is honest work. It is good work, and it is *your* work now, because I say so."

Henri crossed his thin arms over his sparkling white blouse and silk jacket. "I won't do it!" He clambered down from the stool, Bucephalus dropping to the ground.

She picked up the soft velvet animal in one hand, still clutching the hard carrot and metal peeler in the other.

"Give that back before you soil it!" Henri cried. "It's mine!"

She straightened. "You need to find your manners again, young man." Her thumb grazed the bottom of the horse's hoof and recognized at once the feel of embroidery. She turned the horse over to inspect it and read in beautiful golden script, *Louis-Charles*.

The toy in her hand belonged to the child king of France.

Her gaze snapped back up to the boy before her, heart thudding against her ribs. *"My name is Louis,"* he'd once confessed. Every story she'd ever heard about Marie Antoinette's missing son slammed to the front of her mind.

"This was—" she whispered, but she dared not say the name of Louis-Charles aloud with so many listening ears. "Where did you get it?"

"It was a gift." He glowered.

Questions stalled in her mind. This was neither the time nor place to discuss them.

"I'm getting out of this filthy stinking place! I can't believe you'd rather be here than with me!" Snatching Bucephalus from her loosened grip, Henri stumbled away on rickety legs.

"Whoa, lad." Liam Delaney caught Henri by the arms. "What's all this?"

Vienne had not seen him come in, but the sound of Liam's voice nearly undid her. She dashed a tear from her cheek, set the carrot and peeler on the table, and tried to smile. "Liam, welcome back." She should have remembered he was due this week for his mail run. She stifled a groan that it should be this particular moment.

Liam kept Henri in his grip as he knelt on one knee to speak to him. "My name is Mr. Delaney, and this 'filthy stinking place' is my sister's property. That's my friend you've just insulted with that smart tongue of yours." He gestured toward Vienne. "Explain to me how such a lad as yourself could make a grown woman cry?"

When Henri was silent, Liam asked again in a tone that bespoke his days as a schoolmaster.

"Liam." Vivienne placed her hand on his shoulder to stay him. "It's all right." Her questions about Henri's identity nearly drowned out her dismay over the boy's rude manner.

"Oh, to be sure. It looks just splendid from where I'm kneeling. Now answer me, lad, for I'm tired and more than a little hungry after four days' riding to get here."

Henri's voice quavered. "She—she wanted me to peel a carrot. To work."

"And so? What's the trouble?"

"I don't want to." Tears glazed his wan cheeks.

Liam stood again and lifted Henri back onto the stool. Feet planted wide, he crossed his arms. "You don't *want* to? Listen to me, lad. I—"

Oh, the kitchen staff were getting an earful tonight. Vienne touched Liam's arm, and he bent low enough for her to whisper in his ear. "Henri is my charge. His mother died of the fever last month and placed him in my care. We're still learning to get along."

Liam stilled. She felt the tension leave his body and dropped her hand as he straightened. "Henri. Let's go outside and have a talk." Nodding to Vienne, he ushered Henri up the stairs.

Still buzzing from Henri's outburst, Vivienne stayed and peeled the rest of the carrots while her pulse slowed and her cheeks cooled. When the chatter in the kitchen resumed, she cleaned up her table and, with Rachel's blessing, packed a basket of food to take to Liam, whose hunger must surely be clamoring.

Tara whirled into the kitchen in a blur of aproned blue calico. "Going for a picnic, are you?" She eyed the basket at Vivienne's elbow.

"Liam's back."

"Is he now!" A smile lit Tara's face. "And he'll be wanting his supper, is that it? Don't let me stop you. He'll come see me when he's good and ready." She winked.

"It's not like that," Vienne burst out, and then out tumbled a brief version of what had transpired. "Liam's talking to Henri outside. Do you think—is it because the two of you lost your own mother to the fever?"

Growing serious, Tara touched a silver locket at her neck. "Partly. We lost her just last year, which isn't near what it is for a child to lose a mother. Liam's sympathy runs far deeper than that. Did you know our cousin Finn moved in with us after his own parents died? Four years old he was, and full of sass. If it weren't for Liam, I don't know what my widowed mother would have done. Poor Finn, grieving fierce—he didn't know which way was up."

Rachel's voice cut through the kitchen as she called for fresh herbs. Tara wiped her hands on her apron, rubbed the side of her freckled nose, and went on. "The first time Finn disrespected our mother, Liam took it upon himself to steer the boy right, and fast. After that, Finn knew better than to try anything—with our mother or with me." She smiled with the same tenderness in her eyes that Vienne had seen in Liam's but moments ago.

"He sounds like quite a brother. And cousin." Vivienne shifted the basket to her other arm with a pang of longing for the bond these three shared. And yet gratitude quickly followed that she should call these Americans her friends.

"A natural father is what he is. Has been since he was twelve. My guess is Liam has taken your Henri into his heart in the time it took you to pack that basket. Pity he has no children of his own. Yet."

Ignoring the tease in Tara's tone, Vivienne went to the pie safe and pulled out the last piece of the cherry pie she'd baked that morning. "For Liam. You don't mind, do you?"

Tara raised her eyebrows. "His favorite. Good choice."

Vienne tilted her head. "He's hungry."

"That he is."

Outside, spokes of sunlight fanned down through the trees in the tavern's side yard. Scarlet and saffron maple leaves glowed like pieces of stained glass. Liam sat with his back to a trunk, one leg stretched out, hands clasped atop a bent knee. Sitting cross-legged near him, Henri pulled a stick through the dirt and nodded at whatever Liam was saying.

Vivienne held back, not wanting to interrupt. But when Liam looked up and saw her, he spoke a word to Henri and pushed up to his feet, making his way to where she stood.

She held out the basket as soon as he was near enough to take it. "You must be famished."

A smile creased his face when he peeked inside. "Worth the wait." He met her gaze, holding it as gently as he had just been holding Henri's. "I'm sorry if I came on too strong. When I was scolding Henri in the kitchen," he added. "I couldn't abide how he was treating you. But now at least I know where it's coming from."

"He's right about one thing." She kept her voice low. "I don't know what I'm doing. When I'm kind, I worry I coddle him. When I try a firm hand, he rebels. Whether I'm with him or away from him, he's never pleased."

Liam set down the basket. "Your job is not to please him. Your job is to show him the right path, and from what I can tell, you're doing your best."

"And you know this because I tried to get him to peel a carrot? I wouldn't call that a success."

"You were right in that. And it looks like you've been thinking this through." Lips slanting in a lopsided grin, he looked at her hair while pressing his fingers to his own temple.

Oh, mercy. She brushed at the hair that had drawn his notice, and her fingers came away dusted with flour. "You don't understand," she said as she continued to rake through her hair. "My mother was no example at all—you have no idea—and Armand simply was not around." She bit her lip. She had not intended to let his name slip, but Liam did not look surprised. "Thank God for my Tante Rose, but I don't know how to parent. I've never seen it done, so how can I be the right person for this role?"

Liam took her hand to still it and clasped it between his own. "God placed Henri with you for a reason, Vienne. He'll equip you with the wisdom and grace for the task. And I heard—from a certain monsieur who seems to know—that you are nothing like your mother." He released her.

Dried leaves cartwheeled across the yard in the strengthening wind. Her skirt billowed before her, and a lock of hair blew across her eyes. She tucked it behind her ear, searching for an adequate response. The small thank-you she finally managed did not begin to express what she felt.

"Henri needs you," Liam told her. "Even if he doesn't say it, he does."

She peeked around him to glance at Henri. How small, how frail he looked. But was he Martine's son, or Marie Antoinette's? Had the queen spirited her son into the care of her lady-in-waiting? "I still don't know who he is," she whispered.

Liam frowned. "I doubt he knows himself. He's unmoored, isn't he, without his parents, in a new country—"

"That's not what I mean," she interrupted. The uncertainty surrounding Henri was a weight she could no longer bear alone. "He told me once that his name is actually Louis. Right after the fever, but he was lucid. He's been hiding something from me ever since." Though she hadn't planned to, Vivienne told him the slender threads of what she knew and the gaps of what she didn't. Taken together, it was an unfinished pattern, where order had yet to emerge from all the loose and dangling ends.

A muscle flexed in Liam's jaw. "You don't think . . ."

"I don't know what to think. Or do. Or say to him." Faith, but she sounded as desperate as she felt.

"Give him time. Royal or not, he'll let you in once he's secure in your love for him. Give yourself time, too." Liam stooped to retrieve the basket of food. "In any case, I doubt he'll give you any more cheek."

"At least not while you're around. How long can you stay?" Vienne smiled.

Liam didn't. "Not long enough."

She agreed.

Chapter Fifteen

The next morning, with Vivienne's fresh baguette in his belly and her situation fresh on his mind, Liam headed to the Treasury Department and shifted his thoughts toward the encounter ahead. This time, he did not wait to be shown to Alex's office. Blowing by the clerks just inside the front door, he marched straight into the spartan room where Alex sat bowed over some writing on his green felt-topped desk.

"Do you really want another war?"

Alex looked up, not quite as ruffled by the outburst as Liam might have hoped. He didn't even stand. "Dispensing with pleasantries, I see."

"Suppose we save the time."

Alex leaned back. "Have out with it, for I can see you're set to explode if you don't."

Liam pulled a chair closer to the desk. "Washington called out the militia against the frontiersmen in the western part of the state." Against Finn.

"You mean the rebels. Call them what they are, and do not tire me with stories of days gone by when you and I fought against England. These men are no patriots. They must be made an example of, or else who would obey any laws at all?"

Liam narrowed his eyes. "Calling out the militia is an extreme measure—"

"An extreme measure? My friend, is it possible you are not aware of their violence?"

Liam held his tongue, bracing himself as Alex pushed back from his desk and began pacing the small room.

"On July 15, whiskey rebels fired at two tax collectors, U.S. Marshal David Lennox and John Neville, when they attempted to serve a writ to a distiller for failing to register his still."

Liam was not surprised that the frontiersmen refused. For many, the absence and expense of travel across the state would be grievously costly. Still, they should have known better than to shoot at the collectors.

"On July 17," Alex continued, "a crowd of hundreds of men went to Neville's home, which was guarded by a group of soldiers. Shots were fired by both sides, one man killed. The troops guarding the house surrendered, and the rebels burned much of the property to the ground." He faced Liam. "How's that for extreme?"

Finn O'Brien surged in Liam's mind. He'd left the Four Winds Tavern on July fifth, so he may not even have been present by the seventeenth, so long was the journey. And with only one eye, even if he'd been there, it was unlikely he'd taken a shot at the tax collectors. But was it possible he took part in burning down Neville's house? Having survived one revolution, was he now taking part in another?

"I'm not through," Alex continued. "In early August, thousands of western Pennsylvanians marched on Pittsburgh but were dissuaded from destruction when plied with food and liquor." He gave a dark laugh. "Imagine! Several thousand of the lower class, beguiled by bread and beer. It only shows that they've been roused by some instigators. It smacks of the Jacobins and the French Revolution all over again."

Liam frowned, failing to make the same leap. "Indulge me, Alex, because the connection is blurry from where I stand."

A scowl pleated Hamilton's face, betraying his impatience for those who couldn't keep up. "It's the work of those Jacobin clubs—they call themselves Democratic-Republican Societies, recall—that have sprouted up all over this country. It's a Jacobin movement, I'm convinced." More pacing. "There is precedent. Last year these societies worked with French ambassador Genêt to recruit Americans to fight with France—after Washington had already declared us neutral. They planned for the backwoodsmen of Kentucky to seize Spanish-held Florida and New Orleans, and if I don't miss my mark, these American Jacobin clubs are behind the whiskey revolt in western Pennsylvania right now. Anything to overthrow the administration of our government, even by the most irregular means. If they can remove us Federalists and get Jeffersonians in power, their agenda is for America to fight alongside France in their war against the rest of Europe. It's madness."

Liam rubbed his chin before responding. Fomenting insurrection was a serious charge. "Genêt was dismissed," he pointed out.

"Yet indications are strong that his replacement, Fauchet, now lends his support to the whiskey rebels."

"Rumors, Alex? Tread carefully now."

"No, Liam." The Treasury Secretary shook his head and sat at his desk once more. "More than rumors. Western Pennsylvania has become a center of terrorism under the leadership of Albert Gallatin, the French-speaking, Swiss-born Jeffersonian politician. And look at this." He pulled out a *Pittsburgh Gazette* and spun it around to face Liam.

Liam parsed the text. A man named David Bradford, one of the Whiskey Rebellion's leaders, likened himself to Robespierre. Eyebrows raised, Liam's mouth went dry when he read the ill-conceived comparison. It was Robespierre who had initiated and enforced France's Reign of Terror before finally being beheaded himself. Under Robespierre's leadership, tens of thousands had died. Shaking his head, Liam scanned the next column and found that Bradford's followers talked about setting up a guillotine in the upper reaches of the Ohio Valley as a political solution.

"If you're about to advise me to let the states handle their own messes," Alex continued, "you can stop right there. The Supreme

Court certified that the judicial system in western Pennsylvania could not restore order."

"Which prompted Washington to call out the militia," Liam supplied. "At your behest, I suspect."

Alex slammed his fist on his desk. "Absolutely, at my behest! I'll be hanged by the nearest lamppost before I stand by and allow this country—*my* country—to be ripped apart by lawlessness and anarchy! I will not have it, not as long as I have any say whatsoever." His face purpled, and he dabbed a kerchief to his glistening brow.

A pocket watch on the felt clicked away several seconds before Alex spoke again. "I know you have friends out there. But if you could set aside personal loyalties for any length of time, perhaps you could understand what's at stake here. Everything I built."

"You mean America. *You* built it? Really?" Leaning forward, Liam whispered, "Does President Washington know?"

"Blast it, Liam. We all know what Washington means to this country, but if I didn't labor to put some kind of financial footing beneath the whole of it, we'd fall apart like thistledown. We must put down this rebellion, or our democracy has failed."

Liam raised an eyebrow. "What kind of 'we' are you referring to?" And then he knew. "You're going, aren't you? Didn't see enough combat during our own revolution, eh?" As Washington's aide-de-camp, Alex hadn't attained the pinnacle of military glory he'd hoped for.

Alex straightened his waistcoat, then polished a button with his thumb. "The Secretary of War has a leave of absence right now."

"Now?"

"Yes, so I'm going with Washington. Look, we've given the rebels plenty of time. The tax was passed three years ago, for pity's sake. Last month we sent a commission to western Pennsylvania to negotiate. They offered the rabble amnesty in return for ending their resistance to the tax."

"And the rabble didn't take it," Liam guessed.

Alex thumped two fingers on the page in front of him, dated September 24. "This is their report. Conclusion: the rebels are unwilling to submit to the government. I wish it weren't so. But it is, and it cannot stand. We leave in two days. You'll join me. You did travel to Philadelphia by horse, didn't you? You'll need him."

Liam shot to his feet. "Are you in earnest?" He couldn't imagine marching against his own cousin.

Rising, Alex skirted the desk and stood nearly nose-to-nose with him. "I checked the militia rosters. You're still on record with a Philadelphia regiment. If you don't comply, you'll be deserting. And I know where to find you."

"This could take weeks. Months. I can't be away from my farm that long."

"You'll be gone from it longer if you're in jail." Alex let the words settle between them. "Surely you have someone, a neighbor perhaps, who can look after your land in your absence. Send word tomorrow."

"Send word with whom? I'm the mail carrier, Alex, remember? And the horse I rode here doesn't belong to me. There's no way I'll take her on a military campaign. She'll be expected back in Asylum within the week."

"You're not the only postman for the settlement. Stable the horse at your sister's tavern until the next carrier arrives. He will know enough to look there, will he not? He can find out what happened to you from Tara and lead your horse back to Asylum when he returns. My clerk will procure a different horse for you to ride. No more excuses. You're coming."

Liam barely bottled his frustration. How could he leave Jethro to manage the farm alone? "You cannot ask this of me."

"I'm not asking. You'll be my personal guard, one of six men I trust to protect my life, for they're burning me in effigy already. Being hung from a lamppost is not a hypothetical possibility." Alex tapped the newspaper article calling for the guillotine to be put to use.

Liam knew his old friend better than to doubt that this was true. Alexander Hamilton was arrogant and self-important, but he was no liar. If he said his life was in danger, it was.

"Perhaps now you see what's at stake here." Alex smoothed down the tie of his neckcloth. "Hang the Jacobins. They may have toppled their monarchy, but the American government will not yield."

"Henri, I'm pleased to see your appetite has returned." Vivienne smiled across the small round table as the boy spooned another bite of ice cream into his mouth. Bucephalus was splayed on the table beside him. "But I had rather hoped," she added, "that it would be for something a bit more nutritious."

"You sound more like a mother every time I see you." Sebastien Lemoine dropped his spoon into his empty bowl and leaned back in his chair. Behind him, a large window placed the bustle of Front Street on display. "Sure you don't want anything? It's not too late to change your mind. They have strawberry, orange, pineapple, banana, blueberry, pistachio, chocolate . . ."

"It's like a rainbow under glass." Henri pointed with his spoon to the colorful presentation of ice creams lining one wall of Mr. Collet's shop. "And the rest is a cloud." He smiled as his gaze bounced from the white marble floor to the white plaster ceiling with bas-relief crown moulding. Even the tables and chairs were of white-painted iron.

"No, thank you," Vienne repeated. If it hadn't been for Monsieur Lemoine's insistence on treating them, and for Henri's sudden animation at the mention of it, she would not have come. And she would have missed this rare glimpse of Henri enjoying himself.

While the boy tilted his bowl and slid more ice cream onto his spoon, she tried to untangle the emotions he evoked within her. Always, an urge to protect him. Joy when he smiled or laughed—which was not as often as she wished. Guilt for not being a wiser guardian, and fear that her mistakes would cost him. And she knew with a clarity so sharp it felt like pain that she would do anything to keep him well and healthy. Was this what a mother's love was made of? How she hated that she didn't know. Though this ice cream parlor was worlds away from the Palais-Royal, the smells wafting over her triggered a terror of making Henri feel as unwanted as Sybille had made Vienne feel the day she stained her lace with chocolate.

"Why don't you want any?" Henri asked her, licking his lips. At least he now spoke English, and his attitude seemed a bit improved. Whatever Liam had said to him a few days ago seemed to have taken hold. "It's very good, you know. If you try it, you'll see. Just a little taste. Here." His tongue poked out of the corner of his mouth in concentration as he held out a spoonful for her to sample.

A quiet laugh escaped Vivienne. "I should be doing this with you but with venison stew, no?" But he remained so earnest, she could not refuse him. A hand over her lace fichu to protect it, she leaned over the table and took the bite.

"Well?" Henri asked. "How is it?"

She closed her eyes and let the sweet cream melt on her tongue. The flecks of grated vanilla infused it with unparalleled flavor. She opened one eye to squint at Henri as she swallowed. "Lovely," she said, and she meant it.

The smile on Henri's face rivaled her own.

"Then it's settled," Monsieur Lemoine declared. "A bowl of the same for you."

She lifted a hand to stay him. "Perhaps next time, monsieur, if there is occasion."

His eyebrows rose. "Of course. There will be. And please, you must call me Sebastien." He turned to Henri. "And what should we call you, young man?"

Vivienne held her breath at such a bold grasp for Henri's identity. Sebastien proved relentless, even here, in a shop where other customers were close enough to hear.

The child hesitated but a moment. "Call me next time you go for ice cream!" Dimples starred his cheeks, transforming him into a charming, blue-eyed imp.

With a squeeze in her chest, she laughed in surprise at his clever rejoinder. Sebastien had the good sense to join in and let the matter go.

But then her laughter died on her lips. The voices of Sebastien and Henri grew dim, and the people strolling outside the window faded into blurs of moving color. The lace collar at Henri's neck was familiar, she realized, not because she'd seen him wear it before, but because she'd been the one to make it. On the left side of the collar, entwined in flowering branches, were the initials LC for Louis-Charles. On the other side, the number XVII was tucked into the design. It had been a special commission made for the boy when his older brother Louis Joseph died, making Louis-Charles next in line for the throne, the new Louis XVII. His royal portrait had been painted while wearing that collar. And here was Henri, eating ice cream in it as though it belonged to him.

Did it?

Her glance darted to Bucephalus before she felt Sebastien looking at her. Had he asked her a question? He rose and helped her pull out her chair. Ah, so it was time to go.

"Vivienne, how you pale. Have you seen a ghost?" Sebastien asked.

A ghost indeed. The apparition of a monarchy which lived or died in the body of one person: Louis-Charles. She fought to keep from looking again at Henri. "I'm just tired."

"You work too hard. Would you not prefer a life in which you have no need?" A bell tinkled above the door as Sebastien opened it, and Henri slipped out ahead of Vivienne. "A life which includes a partner with whom to raise the child?" He caught her hand.

Wariness crept through her as she studied the youthful shine of his face, the pomaded black hair in its queue. The hand squeezing hers was distastefully smooth compared to the gentle calluses she remembered on Liam's. She tugged Sebastien outside where Henri waited, but he would not let go of her.

The door slammed shut behind him. "Every boy needs a father, and this one deserves one even more. If he's to be a leader of men—"

"And if he is not?" Vienne pulled her hand free. "If he is an ordinary boy, what would he deserve then?"

"So he is not . . . ?"

Exasperated, she broke from Sebastien to close the distance separating her from Henri, who lingered at the corner ahead. Scuffing the toe of his shoe at a broken brick, he swung Bucephalus behind him. Henri's golden head lifted when a man in sailor's clothing addressed him. The boy responded to the stranger with a bright smile and French words.

A French sailor? Her pulse quickened. This close to the river, the smell of oysters and rum breezed in from Water Street, and she could hear sea gulls crying, could imagine them plunging into the water to snatch their prey. Her hastening steps were muted by a mat of fallen leaves. "Henri," she called, a tocsin sounding between her ears. How had he gotten so far from her already?

He turned and waved. "I get to see his boat! But I have to do it right now, he says, because—"

A yank, and the child disappeared.

"No!" But it was only a whisper and not the scream she heard in her mind. Panic exploded in her chest. "Stop!" Fisting her skirt, she ran toward the alley, but Sebastien darted past her, hurling himself into the shadows after Henri and the man who had taken him.

Breathless, she reached the alley's edge and saw the boy being dragged by his elbow through drifts of spotting yellow leaves, his thin legs buckling from a pace he could not match. "Mademoiselle?" His small voice pierced her to the core.

"Halt! Unhand him!" Sebastien's shouts ricocheted between walls that seemed to be closing in. Barely slowing his stride, he snatched an empty wooden crate from the ground and launched it. It crashed into the man's head, stunning him enough that he let go of his prize. Henri staggered to a halt, and the sailor hesitated, eyeing him, but then sprinted toward the end of the alley. Sebastien gave chase.

"Henri!" Vienne shouted, running toward him.

His white silk stockings gleamed among the shadows as he

scampered toward her as fast as his legs would allow. Kneeling in the dirt, she captured him to her, and he collapsed on her lap, panting.

"He seemed nice," Henri whispered against her neck. Her shoulder grew damp with his tears. "He spoke French, you see, and I thought it would be nice to see his ship."

"Oh, Henri!" Vienne pressed a kiss to his hair. "You must never go off with a stranger."

"But you were very close by."

She shook her head. "Never again. Do you understand me?"

He nodded, and she held him close, her heartbeat thundering. She had come so close to losing him.

"I lost him." Sebastien loomed over her suddenly, for she had not heard or seen him approach. "He's probably hiding under a dock or in a grog shop somewhere. I'm sorry. But the important thing is that Henri is safe." He helped Vivienne to her feet. "Do you see what I mean, now? That was no random attempt. Faith! If I hadn't been here . . ."

"Yes, thank you. I am grateful." She struggled for composure.

"Can you keep him safe, Vivienne?" Doubt infused his tone. "This is important. *He* is important. And we are not the only ones who know it."

Vienne recalled the heated exchange between herself and Henri in the tavern cellar. Any number of the kitchen staff could have repeated the story afterward. This was how rumors took flight, scattering like seed in the wind.

"Oh no. Bucephalus!" Henri wailed. "He took my horse!"

Dread rattled through her. Whoever had tried to abduct him now possessed evidence that possibly, quite possibly, the young king of France was in Philadelphia.

Inside their pension garret at last, Vienne locked the door, then turned and leaned against it. Henri curled on his side on his bed, face blotchy from crying over the loss of his favorite toy.

Crossing the room, she knelt beside the bed and placed a hand on his back, feeling the gentle rise and fall of his shuddering breath. "I'm sorry you lost Bucephalus, *mon cher*."

"I didn't lose him. He was taken from me, which is ten times worse."

"Yes, that is worse," she agreed. "But do you know what would have been the very worst of all? The worst thing that could happen to me?"

He blinked at her, and one more tear rolled down his nose. "What?" he whispered.

"If *you* had been taken from *me*." Slowly, she rubbed his back.

"Oh. Would you have cried, too? Even more than you already did?"

"Like a river." She smiled, eyes burning.

"For me?"

"Of course." Her hand moved up to his collar, and she fingered the lace. "Henri, do you know why that man tried to take you? Any idea why he chose you among all the other children today?"

"No."

She dropped her hand to her lap. "You have heard the stories all over the city that young Louis-Charles is not imprisoned, but hiding somewhere else, no? And stories that say he is here in America. Perhaps even in this city."

His face revealed nothing.

"Do you know, some people might even believe he is you?" She waited a moment, watching him, ready to catch any flicker of expression that might offer some clue. "You are wearing his collar today. I made it myself. And I cannot forget that you once told me that your name is really Louis. Please, you can trust me. But it's important that we are honest with each other, so I can take care of you in the way you need. I'm going to ask you a question, and I want you, please, to answer me."

He nodded, pushing the hair back from his brow.

She rolled her lips between her teeth and folded her hands. "Are you Louis-Charles, the son of Marie Antoinette? Are you Louis XVII, the king of France?"

"Would you love me more if I were?" His composure crumbled, and he pulled his knees under his chin. "Would you love me more if I were king? Or less, because I could not belong to you, after all?"

"I love you either way," Vivienne gasped, devastated that he should even wonder if his value came from his parents. Was this what he had learned from her and Sebastien? That Henri could win or lose their affections based on his answer to their questions? Fearing that she'd just pushed him further away, she sat beside him and drew him into her arms. "I love you," she said again, "no matter what."

But I still don't know who you are. Prayers for help spiraled through her as she held him, but she could think of no other words to say.

A knock sounded. "Vivienne?" Paulette's voice floated through the door. "You have a caller."

Vienne crossed to the door and opened it. "Thank you, Paulette, but would you please tell Monsieur Lemoine that we are tired after our outing and wish to rest instead?"

Paulette's eyebrow quirked up with the corner of her mouth. "I would do that if it were Monsieur Lemoine calling. A Mr. Delaney for you. Says he's sorry he can't wait till tomorrow at the tavern, but he's got something to say to you now. You and Henri both."

Vienne glanced over her shoulder at Henri, who climbed out of bed, pulling at his shirt to straighten it. "All right," she told the maid. "We'll meet him in the parlor in a moment, thank you."

After washing the tears from their faces, Vivienne and Henri went downstairs.

Liam stood when he saw them, hat in his hands. "What happened?" He waved his hat at her skirt.

She had completely forgotten that she'd soiled her gown when she knelt in the alley with Henri. She pressed a hand to her aching head.

"Sit." Liam waited until she and Henri sat on the sofa, then hung his black tricorn hat on the stand and lowered himself into an armchair. He leaned forward before clasping his hands between his knees. "Tell me."

With her arm around Henri's shoulders, Vivienne briefed Liam in whispered tones and watched a fire kindle in his eyes.

"Well, that was exciting, wasn't it?" His words to Henri were buoyant, but his tone—and the color flaming in his cheeks—betrayed his concern. "You're all right?"

Henri's chin bobbed. "But he took my horse."

Liam clicked his tongue. "A dastardly thing to do. Every man needs his horse, eh, lad?" He leaned back, his broad shoulders looking out of place against Madame's doily-topped velvet armchair. His gaze shifted back to Vienne. "And you? How are you?"

The clock ticked loudly on the mantel. A blade of sun struck between the curtains and across the parlor, landing on a beveled glass decanter on the table between them. Prisms of rainbowed light trembled high on the toile-papered walls.

"Vienne?" Liam asked again.

"Pardon me," she breathed. "I am not myself quite yet. But there was something you came to tell us?"

"To be sure. I'll be leaving tomorrow morning, early."

She had expected this. It was the personal good-bye that surprised her. "You must be looking forward to getting home."

"I am, indeed. But that won't be where I'm headed." He squeezed his hands into fists. "I'm going west. With the army that will put down the insurrectionaries."

"The whiskey rebels?" she clarified at the unfamiliar word, and he nodded. "But I thought—"

"Are they like revolutionaries?" Henri interrupted, crushing a fold of Vienne's skirt in his small hand. "Watch out for them, Mr. Delaney. Please."

"I will take care," Liam assured him.

He had not said he would be fine. Vivienne told Henri to say his good-byes and wait for her upstairs in their room. When she could no longer hear his faint tread on the steps, she turned her focus to the man before her. "I thought you were on their side. Isn't Finn a whiskey rebel?"

"It doesn't matter what I think. I've been called up for militia service, and I cannot refuse." He explained what his role would be, and how his land would be managed in the months of his absence.

"There will be fighting, then." Vienne's fingers worried the furbelows on her sleeve.

"I pray not. But likely so." He stood, his message thus delivered. "Keep Tara in line for me while I'm away."

Dazed by his brevity, she rose, as well, standing in his shadow as she smoothed the wrinkles from her filthy gown. "We will pray for your safety and well-being."

"And I will pray for yours." He retrieved his hat and tapped it against his leg. "I want you to remember something while I'm gone. That boy upstairs is a child of the King—the only King that matters—no matter who his parents were. And so are you."

His tender words drew a knot to Vivienne's chest, and a burn to her eyes. Nodding, she attempted a smile.

He settled his hat into place, lips pressed tight as if there were more he might say, but wouldn't. Then he left, releasing a flock of hopes and fears inside her.

Part Three

If the laws are to be trampled upon with impunity, and a minority is to dictate to the majority, there is an end put at one stroke to republican government.

—President George Washington

My imagination presented the evils [of the French Revolution] so strongly to my view, and brought them so close to probable experience at home, that, during the whole period of the [whiskey] insurrection, I could scarcely bear to cast my eye upon a paragraph of French news.

—Hugh Henry Brackenridge, Pittsburgh attorney

Chapter Sixteen

Henri put a pillow over his head when Paulette knocked on the door and quietly called his name. Surely she knew by now that he wouldn't be coming down for breakfast. Ever. The longer he stayed in bed in the morning, the shorter the wait, it seemed, until Vivienne came home.

The knocking stopped, and Henri pushed the pillow aside to look out the window. Bare branches tapped the glass, as persistent as the maid, while wind haunted the pension with the sighs and whispers of a hundred ghosts.

Shuddering, Henri reached beneath the sheets to draw Bucephalus close, then remembered afresh that this small comfort was gone, like so many other things. He was ten now and shouldn't need a child's toy, but the truth was, he missed it desperately. Naming the horse Bucephalus after Alexander the Great's famous horse had been his father's idea. But the gift also reminded him of his mother—it had carried her scent, or the memory of it. Years ago she'd sprayed her perfume on its velvet for him until the fabric was nearly drenched. It made him choke at first, but after its potency mellowed, the smell sank him into calm, like a stone in deep water.

Without it, he felt himself folding inward. Sometimes he hated that about himself. He knew Vivienne would be pleased if he let her in. Still, he'd been trained to build a cage about himself and found that he could not find the key to unlock it. Not yet, anyway. But oh, how lonely was this secret place of his own making.

A pain unfolded in his belly, but it wasn't hunger. Cringing, he turned onto his side, curling into a ball. Teeth clenched, he had to fight not to hold his breath. Inhale, exhale, inhale, exhale. Sweat dampened his forehead with the effort of merely breathing until the pain passed. It made him feel so weak.

Moments passed, or maybe minutes, and then he swung his legs over the bed and hopped to the floor. In the corner of the garret room, Henri knelt in his nightdress and swept his hand over the floorboards until his finger caught in a small hollow knot in the wood. With one more glance toward the door, he yanked up the board and set it aside. His tongue poked out of the corner of his mouth as he fished out a small velvet bag. Plucking it open, he poured the contents into his palm and smiled.

He didn't feel weak anymore.

Taking it out like this, handling it, even just to look at it— Maman had said it would be dangerous. But she'd been so often afraid, and the signet ring of Louis XVI was the last treasure he possessed. The gold was so heavy in his hand, and yet he felt a lifting in his spirit, a sense of something important. He wondered when it would be safe to go back to France and be who he was supposed to be, and who would take him.

Outside the pension, the sky was bleak and gray, with wind that grabbed the trees and shook them. But contained in Henri's palm, the ring glowed golden, the color of sunshine. It was a symbol of power, and the promise of power to come. But most important, it held the fingerprints of his mother, who had touched it last. He tried to remember what Maman was like before the revolution had changed her. She'd been happy to see him and quick to laugh. Her smile had been the sun that lit his days. Closing his eyes, he slipped the ring over his thumb and tried to believe that cool touch was his mother, holding his hand.

But of course it wasn't.

He returned the ring to its hiding place, and the snap of the floorboard back in its place felt to him like the snipping of a bond that was not meant to break.

Henri still missed Bucephalus. Rising, he went to wash his face at the basin and peered at his reflection in the mirror. His throat hurt, he noticed. He must be getting sick.

ALLEGHENY MOUNTAINS, PENNSYLVANIA
OCTOBER 21, 1794

Rain poured in sheets from the sky, plastering Liam's shirt to his body. Drenched and shivering, he rode Shadow, the gray horse secured for his use, in a long line of soldiers through ankle-deep mud. Towering rocks and ancient pines would have dimmed the narrow mountain pass in daylight even without the rain. It was well that Washington had returned to Philadelphia already. This terrain would not have been kind to the sixty-two-year-old president, whose back was already stiff from decades of riding.

This left Alexander Hamilton in charge of the troops.

Shadow stumbled on a rock in the path, and Liam dipped with the borrowed horse, bracing himself for a bumpy ride down the east side of the mountain. "Easy, boy." He poured all the calm he could muster into his voice, and Shadow regained his footing. The poor beast was ill-used, with as little to eat as the men. Some horses had fallen in the mud and simply never gotten up again.

Alex rode directly in front of Liam on the path. As he stared at Alex's back, he could scarcely conjure a charitable thought.

Hamilton's army was a joke. No, worse. It was a disgrace, and everyone knew it. Nicknamed the Watermelon Army, much to their chagrin, it was made up of men from Virginia, New Jersey, Maryland, and Pennsylvania. Gentlemen officers itching for a battle and the subsequent glory, and militiamen, most of whom were inexperienced and undisciplined. In Carlisle, soldiers had accidentally killed two civilians—an innocent boy and a tavern drunk. Rations were days behind them, if they were coming at all, and Liam, like the rest of the army, was desperate for food and decent clothing.

Thunder rumbled overhead, and lightning split the sky. Night was falling. In the mountains, that meant utter darkness would be upon them all too soon.

"We gonna stop for the night?" a soldier called from behind. "Or do you intend for us to plunge to our eternal sleep instead?"

A series of echoes followed, but Liam ignored them. He was tasked with protecting Hamilton from those who would harm him, and it was not his job to answer. Besides, he was in no mood to waste breath pointing out the obvious—there was simply no place to stop, unless they wanted to sleep in the mud where they were.

Finally, the grade leveled somewhat beneath Shadow's hooves.

"There!" Alex called out, pointing up ahead, where the path turned. Beyond it, hovels crouched between oak and sugar maple, chestnut and birch trees. Army horses were tied to the trunks, and wheeled carts sat beside them, ready to be loaded. Alex turned to Liam. "I see the quartermaster corps has paved the way for us."

No doubt they had. Washington had given strict parameters that there should be no illegal plundering of civilian property, so Alex had made it legal. *"If we don't impress it, either the army will starve or take to thieving. What choice do I have?"* he had said. And so instead of the soldiers going hungry for the journey, these mountain people would starve for the winter, for the army went through their provisions like a plague of locusts.

A great whoop went up from the men behind them when they realized their treacherous march was at its end, at least for the night. Liam clucked his tongue to his horse and steered him off the path toward the glow of firelight coming from the wretched huts.

That night, while most of the militiamen slept outside beneath canvas army tents as ill suited to their job as the soldiers beneath them, Alex camped inside a hovel and insisted Liam and two other guards named Simpson and Cooper come, too, baleful though their hosts may be.

In a dirt-floor shelter no bigger than twelve feet square, a family of seven scowled at their four "guests," and Liam could not blame them. From the parents on down through each of their five sons, the youngest aged about two, their faces were marked by dirt and soot, poverty and resentment.

"I s'pose you'll be taking our dinner." The mother's voice was far younger than Liam expected, for her face was sun-blasted and tough.

"Only what you can spare," Liam said, his stomach clenching in protest.

Alex, unperturbed, said, "Yes. Per the order of the United States government."

Pointedly, the mother took bowls from her children's hands and shoved them at Liam, Alex, Cooper, and Simpson. Black dirt lined her fingernails. Shame filled Liam, because God help him, he took that child's food. It was the worst-tasting gruel he'd ever had to muscle down. After a few bites to placate his belly, he handed the bowl back to the little boy, who eyed him from beneath his thatch of tangled, greasy hair.

When it was time to sleep, the sharp-faced father threw a filthy blanket at his intruders, who bedded down on the hard-packed earth. The family of seven filled a pallet on the opposite wall, with one thin blanket to cover them. The ramshackle dwelling shuddered in the storm. The roof, such as it was, leaked in several places, and a rivulet of rain rushed over the ground beneath Liam, so that the mud chilled his back.

"Alex," he whispered once he heard snores from the other side of the room. He felt something crawling over his neck and pinched it hard between his fingernails. Lice. He threw his share of the blanket aside, preferring the cold to vermin.

"Mm."

"These people have nothing. Less than nothing, now that we're here to clean them out."

"Orders." Alex rolled onto his side, then returned to his back.

"This is the type of poverty you'll find on the other side of the mountains. They barter—they don't have cash. This is why the tax was bound to fail from the beginning!"

Alex exhaled sharply through his nose. "Our course is set. Even Washington said so in Carlisle. An army in motion will not be stopped. Do not vex me. Good night."

His breathing steadied and slowed, but for Liam, sleep could not be had. He lay awake and listened to the rain pelting the ratty canvas tents outside—or worse, the men lying in the open rain. Those who didn't already have dysentery or fever could surely expect to contract it now.

"Blast it!" Cooper had scrambled out of the hovel, apparently tripping over some men as he went to empty his own distressed bowels. Someone shouted at him for not getting far enough away from the tents.

Rain sprayed through the door he left ajar.

Simpson groaned. "There had better be a fight, for all this," he growled. "I didn't come here to get the runs and starve to death in the mountains! I will have me some action, even if I have to create it myself."

That was exactly what Liam was afraid of. With nothing but cold and dread to cover him, he let his eyes close and tried not to think of tomorrow.

Compared to Valley Forge, this discomfort was nothing. He'd been twenty-two then, with hope of a reunion with Maggie to pull him through that bone-numbing winter in Washington's camp. The irony was that while Liam had been dreaming of Maggie, she had been swooning for the British officer billeted in her townhome during the British occupation of Philadelphia. The woman who held his heart had given hers to an enemy twice over, for England had subjugated Ireland, where Maggie's people had come from, too, even before tyrannizing the American colonies. Either Liam hadn't known her at all, or she hadn't even known herself.

He could consider the matter coolly and without passion now, with no regrets for what might have been. Maggie was not the one he wanted to see in his dreams.

The urge to take Vivienne in his arms when he saw her last had been sudden and strong, but she'd been upset from nearly losing Henri, and it hadn't seemed right to take advantage of that vulnerability, even in the interest of comforting her.

Tara had been right when she'd teased him on his last visit. *"You'd sooner risk your life in battle before risking your heart again,"* she'd said. *"You'll woo a horse but not a woman!"* There was more truth in her words than he liked.

Rolling to his side in the hovel, Liam put his arm beneath his head for a pillow. As his ribs and hip pressed into the ground, Vivienne filled his mind, a vision of green eyes and soft curves and strong hands eager to work. And now she bore the added responsibility of raising Henri. She could do it. He had faith in her, and in the God who had sustained his own mother as she raised Tara, Liam, and Finn. Still, it was a sobering role, even without the added stress of attempted abductions.

Rain pounded overhead, gurgling in small streams from the roof. A frown aching on his brow, he prayed for Vivienne and Henri, as he had every night since he'd left. He should have held her to comfort her before leaving her alone. He had done as much for Tara. He could have embraced her in a brotherly manner. She was part of the Four Winds Tavern family now, after all.

Liam stared into the dark with a frustrated sigh. For there was no mistaking Vienne for a sister.

PHILADELPHIA
NOVEMBER 1, 1794

"Ready?" Vienne asked Henri, slipping her arms through her woolen cape. The fur muff she wore had been Martine's.

In truth, she did not feel quite ready herself to take Henri outside again after his near-abduction, but it was time to break through her fear. No matter who he was, she could not imprison him in the pension and declare it was for his own well-being. She drew what comfort she could from the fact that his new broadcloth coat and American-style hat would help him blend in with the city better. As he outgrew his courtly suits, she would replace them with more sensible, sturdy clothing, as well.

Henri fastened his top button and pulled on his hat. "Ready." Together, they left the Sainte-Marie.

Trees stretched bare arms against a sky of pale blue silk. Wisps of cloud, like ostrich feathers, floated by. "When is Mr. Delaney coming back?" the boy asked. "It's been a long time. Long enough, wouldn't you say, for his trip?"

Vienne put her hand on Henri's shoulder as they passed a lamp-lighter on his ladder, trimming a wick. "He said it might be months before his return." And it had only been thirty-one days, though it felt far longer than that.

She missed Liam. More than she wanted to.

"Oh." Henri hopped over a broken pipe stem on the sidewalk. "Where are we going?"

"We'll stop at the tavern on our way home so I can make the sponge for the baguettes, of course. But we have time to go some-where else first. Your choice."

He grinned, nose already pink from the cold. Smoke curled from chimneys behind him. "I want to see the ships, please."

"Again?"

Henri shrugged. "It's been a long time." There was a bounce in his step. "You can't say there's a danger of fever now."

She conceded the point. Toes tingling with cold, Vienne agreed to his destination, and in mere minutes, they turned onto Front Street. Just below it, the Delaware River lapped at wharves and ships. Even in November, smells of tar and wood from the nearby shipyard mingled with the spice of rum floating out of the taverns and grog shops lining the street.

"Mademoiselle, look!" Henri pointed to the sky. "Look how they fly! In a V! V for Vivienne!"

Smiling, Vienne watched the graceful formation of Canada geese as they soared above the water.

"I should like to see them make other letters in the sky." Henri shaded his eyes with one hand.

"An H for Henri, perhaps?" She laughed. "Now that would be something special indeed." The birds' honking echoed faintly even after they had flown from view.

"Vienne!"

She wheeled toward the voice. "Armand."

He hastened toward her, small white clouds puffing from his nose. His hair had grayed some since July, or perhaps she just hadn't remembered this shade of weathered driftwood. No longer thinned by hunger, his face sagged in fleshier folds. "Vienne," he said again, and the familiarity chafed her. "Have a drink with me."

She glanced at Henri beside her. "Where? Don't forget, women and children are not welcome in taverns." Unless they were working for them, she mused.

"Ah." Deflated, Armand blinked down at the boy. "Hello! Henri, is it?"

Wagons and carts rumbled past. "Yes, monsieur. Pleased to see you again." Henri swept him a courtly bow.

Vivienne cupped the boy's shoulder, marveling that they recalled each other when their previous encounter on July 4 had been so brief and full of distraction.

Armand returned his attention to her. "Monsieur Lemoine told me the boy's mother died of fever. A pity, that. You're to be commended for taking him in." He turned his collar up against the wind. "You look well. I can't tell you how glad I am of that. When the fever came, I worried more than you would believe. But Sebastien kept me informed of your welfare."

Henri tweaked her skirt, likely impatient to get to the docks. She tucked her hands back in her muff and told him to wait. To Armand, she asked, "Sebastien Lemoine has been playing the informant?" Two chimney sweeps ambled toward them on the sidewalk, smelling of soot and ash. "You paid him to *spy* on me?"

"To keep an eye on you. Don't be cross. He didn't mind the

assignment—quite the opposite, as it happens—and you cannot blame me. I try not to be hurt that you never ask after me."

Vivienne swallowed the tart reply that sprang to her tongue. "I don't know what sort of relationship you expect to have with me."

Armand rubbed his nose. "Whatever you're comfortable with. Which I know isn't much. Regardless, hear me out. Sebastien tells me that most of the funds earned by your lace sales were required for hospital and burial fees, and that your work at the tavern doesn't pay as much as you need."

Sebastien certainly didn't hold back in his reports. Irritation warmed her. "I had to cut back my hours, I—"

Armand held up his hand. "No need to defend yourself. Of course you cannot work all day, leaving Henri alone. And now you have two mouths to feed, two bodies to clothe. It's an impossible position for you. I told Sebastien to extend my offer of help to you, but he refused, saying it would only drive you away. But if you are as desperate as he suspects you are, you owe it to yourself and to the boy to hear me out." Behind him, a tavern door scraped open, and out spilled a tangle of jocular fishermen. Ever the aristocrat, Armand wrinkled his nose and stepped closer to Vienne, giving the men a wider berth on the sidewalk. "I would not be so bold, ma belle, if what I had to say could wait. I am moving to Asylum and invite you to join me, you and Henri both."

She held him in her narrowed gaze. "What do you mean?"

Chapter Seventeen

Henri moved behind Vivienne to allow three fishermen to pass. He was so tired of waiting for her and the monsieur to stop talking. The cold pinched his nose and prickled his hands and feet, and they hadn't even reached the docks yet. Bored, he kicked at a broken piece of pottery, sending it into the street.

A flash of orange caught his eye. A kitten the color of peach preserves rubbed up against his ankle, mewling pitifully. Enthralled, he knelt to pet it. "Bonjour, little one!" The fur beneath his hand was soft as eiderdown. Fishing one of his mother's ribbons from his pocket, he dangled it, bouncing it up and down, and the kitten batted at the green satin strip.

Henri laughed. "Look! He likes this!"

But Mademoiselle and Monsieur were deep in their conversation. The damp wind seemed to wrap around him and seep right down into his bones. He cast a glance toward the docks, but the way his legs ached, he was no longer eager to go.

Squatting behind Vivienne's skirts, Henri tempted the kitten again. The small feline crouched, rear end high, tail pointed like a spear. It rocked on its tiny back feet from side to side before pouncing on the ribbon. Henri laughed again.

He repeated the trick several times, until at last the kitten caught the green satin with its tiny claws and teeth. It tugged, and Henri's fingers were so cold that the ribbon slipped from his grasp. Down the sidewalk the kitten scampered, and suddenly the game wasn't nearly as fun.

"Wait, kitten!" Henri lunged after him. "That's mine! Here, kitty, kitty!" Down the street he followed his tiny feline friend, but when he reached an alley, he gave up the pursuit. He'd had enough of alleys the last time he was out. Besides, he had two more ribbons in his pocket still. Next time he would not be so careless with them. They still smelled of his mother's perfume.

"Henri?" Sebastien Lemoine stood in the open door of a tavern. The many-paned window near it glowed with warmth and light. "I thought I saw you through the window! But where is Vivienne?"

Henri pointed down the street. "Just there. She is talking with Monsieur de Champlain."

"And you ran off? Again?" He cast a glance toward Mademoiselle before pulling Henri inside. "You should not be alone on the street."

"It was only a minute," Henri protested. "Maybe less than that. A kitten stole my mother's ribbon right out of my hand." He slipped his hand in his pocket and rubbed the remaining ribbons between thumb and forefinger, over and over, but it wasn't the same as having Bucephalus. His fingers and face began to burn with the welcome change in temperature. Untidy men sat at thick oak tables, and ladies refilled their tankards. The uneven floor was dirt, not wooden, and had turned to mud where boots dripped melting snow. These Americans spoke and laughed too loudly. "I should go back before Mademoiselle wonders where I am."

"No." Sebastien's hand clamped over his shoulder. "Stay with me and get warm while she finishes her conversation. There's no use in you waiting for her in the cold when you could wait for her here."

Henri swiped his hat from his head and squeezed it in his hands. "But will she not worry?"

"Well, looky here!" A tavern maid with bright yellow hair and pink lips approached. "Just look what the wind blew in! The finest-looking chap here, that's what!" She grinned.

Henri felt his cheeks grow hot. Her shirt was too small for her chest.

"Ah!" Sebastien smiled at her. "Would you seat my young friend at my table? And bring him something to drink. Something to warm him, if you please. Henri, I'll dash out and tell Vivienne you're with me."

The woman showed Henri to a high-backed wooden booth and assured him she'd be back soon. He climbed onto the bench, grateful for the chance to sit. Under the table, he pinched the ends of two ribbons between his thumb and forefinger, then wove them between his other three fingers, over, under, over, like the lattice on Mademoiselle's cherry pies.

Moments later, Sebastien returned and joined him at the table. "This is better than waiting in the cold, isn't it?"

It was. Maybe after this, he would have energy to go to the docks after all. He swung his dangling, aching legs from his perch on the too-tall bench. "Pardon me," he said when his shoe knocked into Sebastien's shin. "My legs hurt."

Sebastien winced but quickly smiled. "Does swinging your legs make them feel better?"

Henri shrugged. "The doctor said I have rickets and that nothing will help, but I think moving them does. I didn't mean to hurt you. I'll take greater care from now on."

But Sebastien looked more interested than offended. "Rickets? I just thought you didn't much care for exercise." He smiled again. "I'd like to get to know you better, Henri. Shall we start from the beginning? Tell me why you came to America."

"The revolution, of course," Henri replied. "My father lost his head. I was supposed to be safe here." He thought Sebastien already knew all this.

The waitress returned with a pewter mug. "On the house."

Dropping the purple and white ribbons on the table, he took a drink and shuddered at the spices in what he guessed was apple cider.

She laughed and patted his back. "Such a pretty fellow. Ye'll warm up in no time, only be sure and drink it all down." Then she swirled her finger through the ribbons. "What have you got here?"

"They were my mother's. Her favorite colors." The drink burned as it went down his throat, but the warmth in his belly was worth it. It spread through his limbs to his toes and fingers.

"Lawsy, but you're a charmer. Dimples, too? I'm smitten!" She pinched his cheek and swayed away.

"Those were the queen's favorite colors, too," said Sebastien. "Marie Antoinette's."

"Yes, of course." Everyone knew that. "But did you know she once had a dream that her fashion maker, Madame Bertin, presented her with a box of ribbons, and when she picked purple, white, and green out of the box, they turned black in her hands? Black for death. And this was before the king was beheaded." He could see Sebastien was impressed with this story. Henri felt important, talking this way.

"And how do you know what the queen dreamed of?" Sebastien whispered.

"I heard her tell Madame Bertin. They didn't know I was close enough to listen."

"I see." Sebastien took a drink from his own tankard, then set it down and licked his lips. "A few months ago, you told us your name is Louis. Why?"

"Because it is." He took another drink. "Louis." It felt so good to say his real name. Sebastien Lemoine could be trusted, after all. He was friends with Vivienne.

"Remind me, Louis, where did you live in France?"

"Versailles, and then the Tuileries Palace in Paris. Until it was no longer safe."

Sebastien raised his eyebrows, an unsteady smile on his lips. "Tell me about Versailles. Tell me about the Tuileries."

Henri warmed to the attention. "I spent most of my time in the queen's rooms," he admitted. "And with the animals."

"What animals?"

"There were cats everywhere, and dogs. Madame Elisabeth,

Louis XVI's sister, loved greyhounds, and the Mesdames Tantes favored spaniels. Such a racket they made when they set to chasing and hissing and barking!"

Firelight played across Sebastien's face. "What else?"

Henri told him that the Duchesse de Polignac, the Royal Governess, had fled at the beginning of the revolution for her own safety and was replaced with the Marquise de Tourzel, whom the children all called Madame Severe. He spoke of the daily carriage rides through the queen's English-styled gardens, the secret tunnel between the queen's bedchamber and the king's, and about the horrible attack by the mob of market women in October 1789, and Sebastien seemed quite interested in that. "And then we had to leave Versailles and live at the Tuileries Palace, until they attacked us there, too." A day Henri would never forget, though he'd tried. He finished his drink and thought, though his thoughts moved slower now. He looked for the waitress.

Sebastien found her and waved. "Another drink for my young friend here!" he shouted across the room.

She threw her head back in unrestrained laughter and went to the bar. When she returned, she refilled Henri's mug. "I'll bet you're feeling lovely warm, now, eh?"

He was. And it was lovely. Sighing, he fumbled at the buttons of his cloak.

Chuckling, she unfastened them for him, peeled off the cloak, and set it on the bench beside him. "Ooh, how fancy!" She lifted the edge of his lace collar. It was the one he'd worn to get ice cream. Mademoiselle had told him not to wear it again, and he hadn't meant to disobey her, but his other collars were soiled at the moment, and he couldn't be fully dressed without one.

The waitress flitted away again, and he wrapped his hands around the mug to warm his fingers. He took a drink, and contentment filled every inch of him. He rattled the cup back onto the table.

Sebastien stared at Henri's neck, reached out his hand, and grasped the chain that hung there, pulling it free from his blouse. "What's this?" His finger hooked inside the gold ring on the chain.

"That's mine!" Henri cried out, suddenly alert. He'd started wearing it to feel close to his parents, and important. "Don't let anyone see!"

"The signet ring," Sebastien whispered, eyes hard and sharp. "Where did you get this?"

"It was my mother's."

"A little large for a woman's hand, don't you think?"

"Please. It's special to me. Don't take it away."

Sebastien cupped the gold circle in his hand. "Louis XVI's signet ring." He swore under his breath, then dropped it on the table. "Isn't it? Tell the truth now."

"It is mine now." Henri hurriedly tucked it back under his clothes, feeling the metal against his skin. It was so hard to think anymore. His eyelids were so heavy. "I'm so tired," he admitted.

"A little nap will do you no harm. I'll wake you when it's time to rejoin Vivienne. Go on. Lie down on the bench and rest. I'll stay right here to make sure no one bothers you."

Agreeing, Henri balled up his ribbons and stuffed them in the pocket of his cloak. Then he made a pillow of his cloak and stretched out on the seat. He missed Bucephalus.

"Ah, yes. That was the stuffed horse that man took from you, wasn't it?" Sebastien asked.

Henri blinked. He hadn't realized he'd spoken aloud. "He was my favorite toy. My name is stitched on the bottom of its hoof."

"Which name? Did it say Henri?"

"No," Henri corrected him. "It said Louis. The name on the hoof is Louis-Charles." It was the last thing he said before he slept.

Chapter Eighteen

Vivienne's chest throbbed with the pounding of her heart. She could scarcely catch her breath. Snowflakes powdered her wet lashes and cheeks and stuck to the shoulders of her cloak. *Lord!* she prayed, desperately. *Keep him safe, wherever he is! Help me find him. Don't let him be afraid.* But she was terrified.

She had no sense of how long she'd been searching with Armand. They had combed the wharves and the shipyard, the taverns and shops along Front Street, and even the covered stalls on Market. How could she have been so careless? What if they never found him? How could she live with herself, not knowing where he was or how he fared, or even if he was alive or dead?

Shame and guilt dogged her as she hurried over Philadelphia's streets, her cloak dragging through mud and slush.

"Go home, Vienne," Armand urged.

"How can I return without him?" She'd go mad with the waiting.

"Henri might be there even now. Or if he isn't yet, he may be soon. You will want to be there for him when he arrives. I'll keep looking and asking around." He laid a hand on her shoulder. "All is not lost, ma chère. My daughter, Angelique, once ran away from my wife and me during a Carnaval parade. Can you imagine the confusion? We did not see her for two days. My wife was beside herself with grief, and I suffered an agony of suspense. But we were reunited, and she was fine."

Vivienne looked at him through the lace of falling snow. If she were not consumed with worry for Henri, she might have pointed out that a tale about his real family—the wife he was unfaithful to with Sybille, the daughter he raised while Vienne remained fatherless—failed to comfort.

"Go home," he said again.

She turned and ran, hood falling backward off her head, for her galloping pulse would not abide a slower pace.

When she slid around the corner to Third Street, her gut wrenched. Sebastien Lemoine was climbing the cracked stone steps to the Pension Sainte-Marie's front door. He held Henri's limp body. Her legs turned to leaden weights, but she forced them to carry her.

"Henri!" she called out as Sebastien knocked on the door. "Take him inside." She opened the door and burst into the pension before them.

Sebastien laid Henri on the couch in the parlor, and Vienne knelt by his side. "Is he—he isn't—" Breath puffed from his parted lips, and the odor slapped her face. "Drunk!"

She rose and faced Sebastien. "What is the meaning of this?" she whispered.

"I could say the same thing to you, Vivienne. Twice now I've recovered him while he was to be in your care."

Shame writhed through her anew. "Where was he?"

"I found him outside a tavern on Front Street, and I called him in from the cold. When he told me you and Armand were speaking outside, I went to find you, to tell you Henri was with me. But by then, you both were gone. He—" He stopped at the sound of footsteps in the hall.

Paulette entered the room and gasped at the sight of Henri. "What on earth?"

"He drank what didn't agree with him," Vienne explained simply.

"He looks right green! Not to worry, I'll make a peppermint tea." The maid scurried toward the kitchen.

Sebastien lowered his voice. "He was so cold, Vienne. I gave him something to warm him."

"You made him sick with it!"

He shrugged. "Not my intention. But the drink did loosen his tongue. I know who he is."

"He is—he is Henri Chastain." But even she was not fully convinced.

Sebastien shook his head. "He admitted again, his name is Louis. He told me his name was stitched on the bottom of his lost horse. His name, Louis-Charles."

Unsteady, Vienne grasped the back of the armchair and lowered herself into it. "He told me that horse was a gift. How do you know he is not simply who Martine said he is, the son of one of the queen's ladies-in-waiting?"

"The collar you told him not to wear." He pointed to the initials she had knotted into the lace herself.

Shocked to see it on him again, she licked her dry lips. She knew how it looked. And yet, "Could there not be some other explanation? The dauphin cast it off, perhaps."

"He complained of rickets," Sebastien pressed on. "Louis-Charles suffers from rickets."

Vivienne bit the inside of her cheek. "You are certain?"

"Most certain. I am a member of the Royalist Society of Philadelphia, and we make it our business to know all the details of King Louis XVII." With one finger, Sebastien hooked a gold chain from about Henri's neck and drew it out. In his palm lay a gold signet ring. "How do you explain his possession of King Louis XVI's ring? He removed it from his finger just before he was guillotined and sent it to his wife when she was still in prison with her children. As she is dead, God rest her, where else should this be, but with their son, Louis XVII, rightful king of France?"

Speech abandoned Vivienne.

"He cannot wear this ring on his person any longer, Vienne.

Keep it hidden away until the time is right for him to assume the throne. If it had been the Jacobins who found him wandering the street and not me—things would have ended very differently."

Vienne could barely hear over the pulse roaring between her ears. The king of France in her charge? The magnitude of it nearly crushed her.

She brought her hands to her cheeks. They were trembling. She hadn't thought to question Martine. Why would she? That Martine was a lady-in-waiting to the queen was beyond question. But Vienne could as easily believe that her friend was simply his guardian, protecting his identity to keep him safe. In some ways, Martine had seemed as overwhelmed as Vivienne felt to raise a child.

Sebastien knelt on one knee before her, brown eyes burning like coals. "The question is, can you keep him alive until he can rule? Today's fiasco is evidence to the contrary. Not to mention the incident which put Bucephalus in Jacobin hands—proof that Louis-Charles is in Philadelphia. If the Royalist Society knew what I know, they would say the boy needs to come under their protection. Do you hear what I'm saying? They would want to take him from you. They would say that you cannot care for him alone, and they would have reason."

"I will keep him," she whispered, though she didn't deserve the assignment. "You cannot take him away."

Paulette reappeared with a mug of steaming tea, the peppermint cloying with the lingering odor of hard cider. "He should rest in his own room."

Sebastien scooped up the boy, and Vivienne led him upstairs and unlocked the door to her room. After he laid Henri on the bed, Sebastien paused in the doorway. "Tell no one about this, unless you want to lose him."

Paulette pushed past him, forcing her way into the room as he left. She set the mug on the table beside Henri, then crossed her arms and eyed Vienne. "What was all that about?"

She swallowed. "Thank you, Paulette, for the tea." She pressed her lips tight.

Paulette did the same and, lifting her chin, left the room.

Vivienne had not grown up like other girls, dreaming of suitors and marriage and children. During the brief period when she did imagine motherhood, she expected she would be so much more for her child than Sybille had been for Vivienne. More caring, more attentive. And yet, Henri had come near danger twice now.

"*You cannot care for him alone.*" Sebastien's words filled her ears.

Vienne smoothed the hair back from Henri's brow, wrestling with her thoughts. At least Sybille had lost Vivienne only once, and for Vienne's good, when she placed her in her sister Rose's care. It was better that way, far better, Vienne knew. Just as it may be better to give up Henri to someone better qualified.

In a single beat of her ragged heart, Vienne saw herself at eight years of age, that moment at Le Caveau when, with chocolate ice cream staining her lace, she watched Sybille turn her back and walk away. For the first time in her life, Vienne wondered if Sybille had fled not because she didn't want Vivienne, but because she did.

The floor tilted and pitched beneath Henri as he hunched over the bucket in his lap. Mademoiselle knelt beside him in her night-dress, her hand on his back. Her long black braid tickled his cheek. She was saying something to him, but all he could think about was the angry sensation in his gut. It was dark when he began retching, and it was dark outside still. He feared this night of misery would not end.

Never in his life had he felt this awful. Even when there was nothing left in his stomach, his body cramped and heaved as if unconvinced. The walls seemed so close tonight, closer even than they had been during the past few weeks. Alone in the pension's garret room, he had thought much about those famous English princes Edward and Richard, who were just twelve and nine years old when their uncle locked them in the Tower of London. For their safety, it was said. But even there, they were not safe.

The fire in the hearth laughed at him, yellow and orange tongues wagging. *And what of the nine-year-old imprisoned at this very moment?* Henri asked himself. *Have you no thoughts to spare for him? You, who were once so close a friend?*

Henri groaned with guilt, for he had earned this agony. Perhaps his body was trying to expel the secret he'd held for too long.

A cool rag swept the sweat from his brow. The cramping in his middle eased enough for him to straighten his back. He set the bucket on the floor and shoved it away.

"Feeling better? Has it passed?" Mademoiselle's voice was layered with hope and worry. She draped her arm around his shoulders, and he leaned into her. They huddled together on the bare floor for so long, Henri wondered if she'd fallen asleep. But then a silent sigh gently moved him before she whispered, "Forgive me for not being the mother you had, or the mother you need."

"The mother I need?" Henri leaned back to look at her. "What do you mean?"

"Sebastien told me about your conversation with him. And showed me your ring."

Henri clutched suddenly at his neck and found it bare. "Where is it?"

"In my drawer for now, but it needs a much better home than that, no? Just as you need a better home, too. A better protector than I have proven to be."

Tears pooled in his eyes. "You don't want me anymore?"

"Want you?" she repeated, then covered her mouth and turned toward the fire. When she looked at him again, her face was wet with tears. "I want you," she said with a fierceness in her tone. "I love you. But I fear I am not the best for you."

"You are!" Panic raised his voice. "I'm sorry, Mademoiselle, perhaps I should have told you sooner, but—"

"But what?"

"At first, I didn't know you thought I might be Louis-Charles. And then I didn't mind you wondering. I have never felt important before." Oh, how bitter that truth was on his tongue. "I wanted you to have a reason to love me, and if you thought I was the missing king, wouldn't that make you love me? Everyone loved Louis-Charles, just everyone. But then I worried, later, that if you found out I'd let you believe such a thing, and you learned I was just an ordinary boy, you'd be disappointed, and I couldn't bear the thought. I didn't know what to say to make it right." He swallowed the sharp knob in his throat. "I still don't. All I know is that keeping everything bottled up inside is making me sick, just like you said."

Mademoiselle turned to face him. The right side of her face and gown shone in the firelight, and the other side remained shadowed. "Start from the beginning, mon cher, and don't worry that I could love you any less—or any more—than I already do. But I do think it's time to meet the real Henri, don't you? Starting with your name."

He nodded. "I was named Louis after the king. Maman said it was a way to honor the king, and it seemed a good strong name for a baby boy. My name is Louis Henri Chastain. I am not Louis-Charles, I vow it. Though if I could be the young king and someday save France, I would." He looked at his thin legs. He wasn't strong, but neither was Louis-Charles, who had rickets, too.

Vivienne slowly exhaled. "Go on."

He could see she measured his every word. "People stopped liking King Louis XVI, so it didn't seem like such a good name to be called anymore. Maman said it would be safer if we used my middle name. But I don't understand why she insisted on it even after we came to America."

Mademoiselle rubbed her hands together, then blew on them. "You and your maman saw a lot of scary things in the queen's service, didn't you? During the revolution. A lot of things you're trying to forget. Perhaps your first name reminded your maman too much of the king for whom you were named, and the queen. Perhaps it was easier to forget if she didn't say it many times a day."

"Perhaps." He pulled his knees up to his chest. "Maman's hair was blond once, I think. Like mine. I remember thinking it looked like gold. Sometimes I even remember her by the smell of your gowns—the ones she gave you. Sometimes when you wear them, they still smell like her. But I don't remember her smile." His lips trembled, and he pressed them into a flat line until they stopped. "She stopped smiling the day her hair turned white. White, like the queen's. So we could never forget Marie Antoinette, you see. I have lived that day over in my nightmares so many times. Do you remember the tenth of August, 1792?"

She nodded. "Very well."

"Then you remember that mobs of soldiers and citizens came to the Tuileries for the royal family, and that they killed lots of people who were in their way. Louis-Charles and his family escaped in time, but we weren't allowed to go with them. We—the ladies-in-waiting and children—we hid in a corner of a drawing room. The sans-culottes who found us spared us. Maman kept telling me that Papa was fighting to protect us, for he was in the National Guard that was meant to keep the palace safe. She said we would be all right in the end. But did you know, Mademoiselle, that the National Guard turned on itself? Did you know they cut off men's heads and put them on pikes, and carried them through the streets?"

Tears rolled down her face, and she wiped them away with the sleeve at her wrist. "You saw the heads?"

"One of them was Papa's."

"Oh, Henri!" A sob choked the whispered words. She enfolded him in an embrace that was both soft and strong at once, and he thought he smelled his mother on the fabric of her nightdress. But Maman had never held him so, had never rocked him against her, or kissed his hair, or comforted him in illness as Vivienne did now. Maman had parceled out those jobs to nurse and governess, and seemed out of her depth to be alone with him in America, though he pretended not to notice.

"And I miss Louis-Charles!" Henri shook against Vivienne, and she laid her cool hand on his cheek. "He was my best friend. I never saw him again after that. Did you know, they didn't let him take any clothes or anything with him when he left the Tuileries? Maman saved one of his collars before the public came in and went through everything. They ripped up whatever they didn't take to wear themselves." He twirled his finger in the end of Mademoiselle's braid, which was just as soft as his mother's satin ribbons. "Bucephalus really was a gift from Louis-Charles. He gave it to me one day when my legs were aching because he knew how that felt. He was kind like that. The best friend I ever had."

He closed his eyes, spent from the effort of so much talking. A log crumbled behind the grate, and a whoosh of warm air billowed over him. The fire was dying down, he could tell. Mademoiselle swiveled on the floorboards so that she faced it, which meant he, whom she did not release, absorbed all the heat from its flames. Her embrace was an oasis of warmth that covered and infused him completely.

"And the signet ring, mon cher?" she whispered. "How came you to have it?"

He drew a deep breath. "Just before the king was guillotined, he gave the ring to be delivered to the queen. And before the queen was killed, she smuggled it out of her prison and into my maman's keeping, knowing that those who wished to steal it would be searching for it among more senior, higher-ranking ladies-in-waiting, or among relatives. Maman was neither. She was ordinary. Like me."

The air crackled. He listened to Vivienne's heartbeat for several moments, lulled by its steady, comforting rhythm. And then, she said at last, "I believe you."

Henri forced himself to speak once more but kept his eyes shut tight. "I'm sorry for every hurtful thing I ever said to you. I'm sorry I'm not who you thought I was."

Her arms came tighter about him. "I want *you*, Louis Henri. With all my heart."

Tension uncoiled inside him. Fear and dread, guilt and shame felt like arrows launched far away. Henri opened his eyes, to be sure he wasn't dreaming.

Harp strings of light fell through the cracks between the curtains.

Vivienne kissed the top of his head, though she knew now that he was no king. "We made it through the night," she whispered. "How are you feeling now?"

Henri leaned back to smile up at her, the end of her braid still wrapped around his finger. "Better. I think now, at last, I can rest."

Chapter Nineteen

Liam awoke in the dead of night to the thunder of hoofbeats. Encamped west of the Allegheny Mountains, near the Monongahela River, he could see by the light of the moon that he was the only one left in the tent. Though fully dressed, chilblains burned in his fingers and toes as he slung his musket over his shoulder and burst outside. Cavalry galloped in three directions, pocking the freshly fallen snow.

He bolted to Simpson, who was saddling his horse, and grabbed his mount's bridle. "What are you doing?"

"Didn't you hear? Hamilton finally set us loose!"

Liam cursed under his breath. Now that the Watermelon Army was west of the mountains and in the heart of the Whiskey Rebellion, he'd known the time to act was soon. But he had no idea orders would come in the dark. "Are you arresting the people on the lists? Now?" he asked Simpson. One list held the names of people who were within amnesty. The second carried names of those suspected of treason. The third listed material witnesses, also to be brought in. "Do you all have copies of them?"

"No need." Simpson put his foot into the stirrup and mounted.

Liam held as fast to the bridle as he could. His hand had lost feeling near the freezing cold metal. "What's that supposed to mean?"

"It means that the generals gave us discretion to arrest anyone we suspect might be guilty. Of anything. Regardless of whether their name is on a list."

Confusion throbbed between Liam's temples. "You mean to tell me you can grab anyone you please?"

"Lighten up, Delaney. We're using our *discretion*. If we think someone might have tarred and feathered a tax collector, or refused to pay the tax, or harassed someone who did pay the tax, then we are to arrest him."

"And what if you think someone might have raised a liberty pole, or published something in the paper that was disrespectful to the government, or attended a meeting with the rebels?"

"Fair game, all of it," replied Simpson. "Plus those who might have been witness to any of these events. They're all to be captured, and this order comes from the top."

"Hamilton."

"Friend of yours, isn't he?" Simpson beamed.

Liam glowered.

"And I, for one, have been waiting for this for weeks. Hyah!"

The horse ripped from Liam's numbed hands.

Liam charged toward Shadow and saddled him as fast as he could with fingers almost too cold to cooperate. He may have come out here as one of Alex's personal guards, but right now it wasn't the secretary's safety that concerned him. The locals had already reported that about two thousand men had fled west. Those were the men they'd come for. With them gone, who was left but those whose consciences were clear?

After mounting his horse, Liam kicked his heels into Shadow's sides and followed a stream of cavalry headed for Mingo Creek.

Time's boundaries erased as he rode. Heart pounding to the beat of Shadow's hooves, he watched memories drift across his mind like the snow snaking over the road ahead of him. He remembered this feeling, this surge of energy coursing through his veins. Once it was accompanied by a rush of patriotism, a devotion to America so strong he was willing to die for it. Was he still willing to die for a government that raided civilian homes in the middle of the night? His head ached with cold and bewilderment.

Houses came into view, their silhouettes darker shades of the moonlit night. There were no lights in the windows at one in the morning. Frail wisps of smoke spiraled from a few chimneys. About a dozen cavalry neared the humble log cabins and drew rein. So did Liam.

As he dismounted, frantically preparing in his mind an argument against this madness, the whooshing slide of steel pricked his ears. He turned. They were clicking their bayonets into place.

"Stop!" he cried, all hope of eloquence vanished. "Stop! Do you even know who lives here?"

"Shut up, Irisher!" came a hoarse whisper. The soldiers broke into pairs, bayonets thrust forward, gleaming silver between stars and snow, and made tracks toward separate homes.

They didn't knock. Boots kicked in doors. Women screamed and children wailed, jolting Liam from inaction. Musket in hand, he ran through the snow to the nearest home in time to see two soldiers pointing their bayonets at an old man in his bed.

"Stand down!" Liam shouted with no more authority than that of his conscience.

"We're following orders!" It was Cooper, clearly recovered from his dysentery and eager to redeem his indignity. With the tip of his weapon, he snagged the bedsheets and swung them off the trembling man, clothed only in a pair of trousers. "Out with ye, now! You're under arrest!"

"On what charge?" Rage licked through Liam. His breath plumed white in front of his face, then disappeared.

"On the charge of you shut up!"

A scrubby-faced soldier who had misbuttoned his coat poked his bayonet at the man's bare chest. With a pitiful cry, the old man crept from his bed, hands up, and went barefoot into the snow while his wife wept.

A hand wrapped around Liam's wrist. "Where are they taking him? Why?" the wife shrieked, and her plaintive cry was echoed from house to house.

"I aim to find out."

"Please!" She pulled at him. "He's done no wrong!"

Liam didn't doubt it. He peeled her fingers from his wrist and ducked out of the house.

Four soldiers were guarding chained prisoners in the center of the road. Another two civilians had joined the old man, and more were being marched at point of bayonet in their direction. None of them were dressed in more than nightclothes.

"No! You can't take my brother, you just can't! What'll I do without my brother?" A little girl, about six years old, chased after the soldier corralling her brother toward the guards. Two braids streamed behind her as she ran.

"It'll be all right, Libby, but you have to stay in the house with George!" a young man with a clubfoot called to her. Then he snarled something to the soldier, which earned the butt of a musket in his gut. He doubled over.

The soldier shoved him forward with a laugh. "We ain't keeping you forever. Unless you give us a reason. You an anarchist? Like them Frenchies?"

"I can't take care of him all by myself, Adam! Please! Please don't take him!" The girl sobbed until she tripped and fell in the street.

Liam ran to help her up, and she screamed at the sight of him. He threw down his musket and held up his hands, palms facing her. "See? I won't hurt you, darlin'." He scooped her up, brushing slush and snow from her nightdress and bare feet. "I'll see what I can do for your brother, but you best get back inside before you freeze. Which one's your home?"

The girl pointed, and Liam carried her there, dismayed by the wailing that came from within. "Let me guess," he said. "George?"

"He screams awful loud, don't he? He's just a young 'un, I know, but I can't hardly stand his hollerin'!" She put her hands over her ears to demonstrate.

"Don't you have someone to help watch him?"

"Ma died." She wiped her face with the cuff of her sleeve. "And Pa ran off as soon as he heard you were coming. It's just Adam taking care of me and the baby now."

"I see." Liam clenched his jaw. "Well, you stay right here out of the cold, at least. We don't want Adam coming home to find your toes frozen off."

"All right, mister." She hiccuped with the last of her sobs. "But can you get him back?"

"I can try." Awkwardly, he patted the top of her head and turned back toward the motley group of prisoners growing larger by the moment. Feeling only the heat of his anger now, he marched up to the guards circling Adam and the rest of the civilians.

"You got an issue, Delaney?" Simpson asked.

"I do. I take issue with how you're carrying out whatever order you think you heard. This can't be right. Let these civilians go back to bed where they belong."

"Well, it's you against the generals. And I'm siding with the generals on this one. They said to round these fellows up and stick 'em in town jails, stables, cattle pens—anything will do while they await interrogation by Hamilton. And you ain't got no authority to tell us different."

Another scream split the night, and Liam wheeled to find a woman pulling on the arm of her husband's captor. The soldier cursed at her, but she hung on tight. She spit in his eye, and he slapped her across the face.

"Stand down, soldier!" Liam met them in the street. "You call yourself a friend of order? You are tearing apart this town!"

The soldier turned his bayonet on Liam. "I've had about enough of your bellyachin'. If you're so fond of these whiskey rebels, how about you spend a little more time with them? Chains are on the house." He jabbed his weapon at Liam's middle.

Liam dodged it and stepped sideways, gaze trained on his foe.

"Pick up your musket, you fool, and we'll have ourselves a fair fight."

"Believe me," Liam breathed, "you do not want a musket in my hands right now."

"Is that so?" The soldier lunged again, and once more Liam sidestepped. Cheers from the other soldiers filled the crackling cold air. He knew they weren't for him.

His opponent smiled and half turned toward the attention, and in that moment of unguardedness, Liam grabbed the bayonet and twisted it from the soldier's grip. Blood dripped from his hands as he clutched the blade, but he felt no pain thanks to the numbing cold. Throwing the weapon on the street, he reeled his fist back and pummeled the surprise right off the soldier's face.

In the next moment, he heard the singing of a bullet as it raced past him. Fire seared his cheek and combusted in his ear. Rounding on the shooter, he covered the flaming pain on the side of his face, and his hand came away soaking wet. A metallic smell filled his nose. He'd been shot by his own comrade. Mere inches from certain death.

Then a blow to his skull from behind, and the stars faded from the night.

When Liam awoke, it was to a headache that swelled beneath skin and bone, and to the firm conviction that his left ear was caught in a vise. His hand went to the pain and found a bandage. A swath of his left cheek burned, and the ginger touch of his fingertip found the skin torn away and a scab beginning to form. He opened his eyes to find himself back in his tent by the Monongahela River. The flap opened to sunlight made blinding by the snow.

"You were lucky."

"Alex." Liam's voice sounded too loud in his head. "How long did I sleep?"

"Two days, with a little help from laudanum. I'd offer you more, but we're rationing it. The rebels got a piece of you, didn't they? Better you lend them your ear than they take your head." Alex smiled wryly at his own wit, and Liam knew he was holding back from another comparison to the French guillotines.

"It wasn't a whiskey rebel or Jacobin, and I suspect you know that." Grimacing in pain, Liam turned onto his side, uninjured ear to the ground. "One of your soldiers shot me. I won't ask whether he was relieved or disappointed not to have killed me."

Alex said something, but Liam couldn't hear him. Nor did he really care. Slowly, the events of that night drifted back to him. "Tell me it isn't true, Alex. Tell me you didn't say they could arrest anyone, even if they weren't on those blasted lists."

The words were muffled, but Liam could hear in the cadence of his reply that Alex was justifying his decision. Ever haunted by the hobgoblins of disorder, Alex was in his element now. On a witch hunt for both rebels and martial glory.

"I'm sickened to be a part of it." Liam pushed himself up and felt the blood pounding in his skull. He went to the washstand set up in the tent and picked up the handheld looking glass, his breath fogging the cloudy surface. In front of his bandaged ear, the wound on his cheek reminded him of Indian war paint. After pouring fresh water into the basin, he soaked a towel and did his best to clean himself up.

Light flashed into the tent, signaling that Alex had lifted the flap to leave. Camp smells of coffee, bacon grease, and horse manure took his place.

Liam turned his head toward the opening and listened. Hoofbeats. Were they breaking camp and heading east? He ducked outside to see for himself.

Chilblains again aching in his fingers, he folded his arms and watched the parade before him. The Philadelphia Horse Guard formed two rows as its members escorted prisoners between them. Neat and trim in blue broadcloth uniforms, the guards sat astride huge bay horses, so perfectly matched and powerful they could pull coaches belonging to the urban elite. The bare winter sun gleamed on silver bridles and stirrups, and on the swords the guards held pointing straight up.

211

Between these long lines of soldiers came pairs of prisoners bound for Fort Fayette in Pittsburgh. Liam watched them with the sinking feeling that the army had arrested the wrong men. They looked as cold and hungry as he felt and rode horses of every size, color, and condition. The lucky ones had saddles.

Liam's gaze settled on a man of middling years riding bare-back, his body swaying with the horse's movements. With purpled cheek and his arm in a makeshift sling, he'd clearly not been taken without a fight. Beneath the brim of his weathered hat, a scowl slashed across his face. He looked at Liam with one eye, the other swollen shut.

No. That eye wasn't shut. It was gone.

Comprehension slammed through Liam as he beheld Finn O'Brien, beaten and captured, his eyepatch gone. Liam's mouth went dry, too dry to speak. The world was upside down, the revolution turned inside out.

The columns rattled past him and out of camp, leaving churned slush and mud in their wake.

Chapter Twenty

Weeks had passed since Vivienne told Sebastien about Henri's confession, and he still would not believe it. "*A clever tale,*" he had said, "*but it is not enough to keep him safe. He must not leave the pension at all.*" New pensioners moved in and aroused Sebastien's suspicion. "*They could be Jacobins,*" he said. Or informants, which were just as dangerous.

Even if Henri was not king, the fact that people believed otherwise was all that mattered. A misunderstanding threatened his life. And so Henri was trapped.

This was no way for her boy to live.

After completing her morning work in the Four Winds Tavern kitchen, she walked up to the second-floor dining room for a private meeting. Noise from the Saturday lunch crowd strained up from the floor below her.

"Vivienne!"

Sebastien waved at her from a booth, and she quickly slipped in opposite him.

"Are you hungry?" he asked. "The baker here is the best in the city." He grinned and shoved toward her a basket of her own ginger-raisin scones. "How's Henri?"

Lifting the white linen covering the basket, she pulled out a scone and lathered it with butter. "Lonely, bored, and cramped." The longer Henri stayed in the pension, the less he exercised his rickety legs, for pacing the corridors had long since lost its charm. His stomachaches, too, had increased. Vienne suspected that fear and uncertainty had him in knots. "I'm anxious to get back to him now that my shift is over, so I'll come straight to the point. Has Armand arrived safely in the settlement?"

Asylum, Armand had reminded her, was built with Marie Antoinette and the royal children in mind. But though plans to smuggle out the queen and hide her there had failed, the place was still a refuge for any French people who needed it. Vienne took a bite of her scone, then dabbed the corners of her mouth with a napkin.

Sebastien picked a loose thread from his sleeve and flicked it to the floor. "He has, and I'm sure he is quite at home now. Such a pretty little town, you can't imagine. It's tucked into the wilderness, well away from the crudeness of city life."

Paved walkways lined with roses came to mind, a country retreat for the nobility. Which she wasn't. She smoothed the napkin in her lap and pressed on. "Last Armand and I spoke, he offered to buy a plot of land for me there. With a house on it for myself and Henri. He must have spoken to you about this." She barely kept the disapproval from her tone, for it still galled her that Sebastien and Armand spoke so freely about her.

"Yes, he told me," he confirmed. "He also told me you refused. I assumed nothing less of you. Your penchant for rejecting generosity is astounding." His cutlery scraped his plate as he cut a beef medallion, releasing the fragrance of mushroom and wine sauce. After taking a bite, he shoved the plate to the end of the table. "I must say I was pleased you rejected his offer. Allow me to make one of my own. I bungled it last time."

Vivienne stiffened.

"Marry me." He fished a ring from his pocket and reached for her hand.

Unmoved, she curled her fingers into a fist. "Why?"

A frown wrinkled his young face. "Pardon me?"

"Why should I marry you? And why should you want to marry me?" He was playing a game. He was gambling, and she knew it.

"Armand has given me his blessing. All that matters in life, to me, is your happiness and security. I can give that to you and Louis."

She glanced around the room and spied only one other man at a separate booth, hidden by the newspaper he held. Still, her pulse climbed at his slip. "You mean Henri."

Sebastien shrugged. "Call him what you like. But if you don't give him a father, and soon, there is precious little to stop the Royalist Society from taking his charge. You like to think you are reliant only upon yourself, but you do need me. As I've proven already."

She bristled. As she replayed the memory of Sebastien coming to Henri's rescue in the alley, she saw something she hadn't at the time. Sebastien was the one who'd insisted on the outing to get ice cream and then detained her at the door, making it possible for Henri to be snatched. The attacker, when confronted by Sebastien, barely put up a fight at all, and then somehow managed to vanish. Had it all been a ruse? Had Sebastien arranged it somehow, to make a point about the danger and to prove himself the hero? His story about keeping Henri warm in the tavern with cider didn't sit well with her, either. Armand had checked all the taverns on Front Street soon after they had noticed him missing. Why had Sebastien not come forward with Henri then? Distrust ballooned inside her.

"You have no legal claim to the boy," he was saying. He turned the engagement ring to catch the sunlight slanting through the window, but Vivienne guessed he was thinking of the signet ring of Louis XVI. "All you have is a frightened boy who says he'd like to be yours. But what kind of life are you giving him now?"

"My point exactly."

"So marry me. We'll adopt him together, I'll provide for your needs, and we'll be untouchable. The Royalist Society could make no objection."

Unbelievable, how thin a varnish he bothered to put on the

offer. She leaned forward and whispered, "You propose to adopt the king of France. Is that it, monsieur?"

He did not deny it.

"Then you'd best keep looking, for I have no idea where that poor boy might be, if he has in fact escaped his Paris prison." She nodded to the ring still pinched in his fingers. "Save that for a match who would put you to better advantage."

His complexion fired, then paled, as he pocketed the ring. "You called this meeting." His mouth pulled down at the corners.

"As you said, this life in Philadelphia is no good for Henri. I must know if we could have a home in Asylum." Vienne could almost taste the salt of the Channel as her own adamant words rushed back at her from her conversation with Armand on the schooner. *"I will make my own way . . . If I depend on you for my security, is that not following in Sybille's footstep, too?"*

She poured herself some water and took a sip. "Is it too late to accept Armand's offer, or isn't it?" Her pulse slowed as she waited. On the table between them, the small candle flame bobbed and swayed inside its glass hurricane.

Sebastien stared at her lips overlong before lifting his gaze to her eyes. "I'll look into it Monday as soon as I get into the office."

"Monday evening, then." Vivienne stood and made ready to leave. "Meet me here Monday at eight o'clock with the answer."

Looking none too pleased, he agreed.

It was over, at last. Having handed Shadow's reins to Alex once they were back in Philadelphia, Liam stepped stiffly over the ice-glazed puddles pocking the backyard of the Four Winds Tavern. The chilblains that had plagued him for the last several weeks sent darts of pain up through his shins as he crossed to the well. Drawing a bucket of water, he ladled a frigid stream into his hand, then laved it over his face with a shiver, rubbing the long journey from his skin, if not his soul. Relief to be at the end of that wretched campaign vied with a weariness that was both bone- and spirit-deep.

The bulk of the army was still behind him, by days if not weeks. After they had crossed back over the mountains and made it to Pittsburgh, Alex had insisted on a steady gallop for as long as the horses could handle it at a time. Since his army had made an agreeable number of arrests, now his driving force had been to see Eliza, who was ill. So this evening, Alex, Liam, and the two other guards had arrived in the capital city as the sun was setting.

"Not exactly conquering heroes this time," Liam had muttered, still reeling over the arrests at the Forks of the Ohio, Finn O'Brien figuring large in his mind among them.

"Then you'll be pleased to know that I quit," Alex had replied, rendering Liam speechless. "Tomorrow I'm handing Washington my resignation as Secretary of the Treasury. We have grown apart in our political views, Liam, but I wish you well." And that was that.

Still shocked at Alex's announcement, Liam finished washing his hands at the pump and entered the tavern through the rear door. After the winter's biting chill, the golden atmosphere inside bubbled over with warmth. Ale and rum punch were a subtle counterpoint to the savory smells mingling thickly in the air. He placed his dinner order at the bar, took a mug of Irish tea, and after leaving a message for his sister with the barkeep, climbed to his room on the third floor. He had no appetite to eat in the public dining room right now. Tara would surely bring him his food as soon as she was able.

And in the morning, I'll find Vienne.

Upstairs, Liam unlocked the door to his chamber. Leaving it slightly ajar behind him, he lit the kerosene lamp and set about making a fire in the hearth. As the small flames kindled, thoughts of the campaign melted more easily from his hardened psyche, and his mind turned to the mademoiselle and Henri. Rotten timing, it was, to leave them when he did.

Pushing up from the floor, he hung his hat and cloak, catching his reflection in the mirror above the washstand. A sigh puffed from his nose as he regarded his appearance and wondered if Vienne would be pleased or repulsed to see him again. With his hair pulled back in a queue, there was no hiding that the bullet that had tracked across his cheek had also taken a chunk out of his ear. The scars, at odds with his former schoolmaster self, were befitting a whiskey rebel, he supposed. Every glimpse in the looking glass would be a reminder of the frontier epilogue to the American Revolution. And his role in it.

Hang it all.

Liam sipped his tea and burned his tongue before sitting and removing his boots. From below, he heard a fiddler set his violin strings to dancing. Someone stomped his foot to the rhythm, and a man with a distinctive Southern drawl began a rousing song. Though the words were muffled, Liam knew the lyrics well enough.

> Some chaps whom freedom's spirit warms
> Are threat'ning hard to take up arms,
> And headstrong in rebellion rise
> 'Fore they'll submit to that excise:
> Their liberty they will maintain,
> They fought for't, and they'll fight again.

Liam cringed. He was the only one in the tavern aware of the chasm between the song and reality. Most of the whiskey rebels—but not that mule-headed Finn—had fled beyond the western edge of the country. The U.S. government had arrested more than a hundred scapegoats, and the man who started the entire mess with his infamous excise tax—the illustrious Alexander Hamilton—was quitting his post on the morrow.

The door nudged open with the tap of Tara's shoe. "Liam?"

He turned, and Tara gasped at his half-mangled face. Hurriedly, she set her tray of food on the small desk. "William Michael Delaney!"

He opened his arms to his little sister. With her hair coiled around her head in a thick braid, she was the very picture of their mother in earlier times.

She embraced him, then leaned back, hands on his shoulders,

and inspected the ragged wounds to his cheek and ear. "It might have killed you! And then where would I be?" She threw her arms about his neck and fiercely kissed his right cheek. "What happened?"

Liam blew out a breath. "You won't like it."

She straightened, chin up. "Out with it, then. Quick as a whip."

"In a moment." Stomach cramping, he sat at the desk, silently blessed the parsley-and-bacon-topped goose and turnips she'd brought, and began to eat. He closed his eyes as he chewed, savoring both the heat and the flavor in every bite. "How is Vivienne?"

"I'll let you ask her yourself on the morrow. Missed her, did you?" Tara smiled. "You should tell her that. She'd want to know."

He swallowed, eager to change the subject now, for if any harm had come to Vienne or Henri while he'd been gone, surely Tara would have simply told him. "I assume another postman from Asylum has been here to recover Cherie? I'll have a fine time finding a proper mount to carry me back to the farm now." He took another bite.

A short laugh burst from Tara. Standing before the fire, she crossed her arms over her aproned waist. "Oh, he came here all right, but not until four weeks after you left. Sickness and weather delayed him, he said. But he made it at last and delivered a message for you. Actually, he delivered more than that."

Liam set his fork down on his plate and rested his hands on his knees. "I'm much too tired for riddles, sister. What did he say? Or leave?"

She shrugged, a corner of her mouth turned up. "He came riding in here on Beau, to be sure. But instead of taking Cherie back with him, he quit Asylum completely and left both Narragansett Pacers in my stable. I've been feeding two extra horses all this time."

Liam turned his head to hear better from his good ear. "He quit Asylum? Why?"

Tara turned and poked at the fire to urge it along. "He wasn't being paid his due wages, he said. The French cheated him out of what he was owed, just because he was an American. So he rode that French-owned horse here to get back to Philadelphia and look for different employment. I'd say you owe me for their feed and stabling, Liam, but I know it's not totally your fault the burden of their care fell here. In any case, Cherie and Beau await you, whenever you're ready to go back to the farm."

Shaking his head, Liam sent a silent prayer of thanks for God's provision. But he could only imagine how furious Monsieur Talon must be for both of his highly prized Narragansett Pacers to have disappeared. The sooner Liam could return the horses, the better.

"So tell me what happened to you, now that you've tamed the beast in your belly somewhat." Tara sat on the edge of the bed. "Start with the fellow what's done this to your face and ear. You're as handsome as ever, mind you, just a bit—angrier looking. And I'm angry, too, for you mightn't have come home at all."

Liam rubbed a knot at the base of his skull, and then he told her about the Dreadful Night, as people in western Pennsylvania now referred to November 13. He spoke of the midnight arrests, the prisoners in their bedclothes, about little Libby and her brothers Adam and George. He told her about the civilian woman the soldier struck, and that Liam had been injured while intervening.

Tara balled a handful of her apron into her fist. "What do you mean?"

Liam drank from his mug of tea. "I mean one of our soldiers took a shot at my head, and another one knocked me out from behind with the butt of his musket. When I woke up two days later, Alex's orders had been carried out. Innocent people had been arrested. And at least one who I know was guilty."

She clutched at her locket. "Not Finn. You didn't see him get arrested. I thought you said the whiskey rebels ran off."

"Did you ever know Finn to run from a fight?"

"What'll they do to him? You know the mortality rate in the prison. You didn't stop them from arresting our *cousin*? I thought you believed the tax was tyrannical!" Her speech tumbled out in a torrent.

"There was nothing I could do, Tara."

"Nothing you could do?" She laughed, fury darkening her face. "I've heard that one before, you know."

The words, a mere whisper, were a blow to his gut. Thirteen years peeled away in his mind, and he saw himself telling her that her new husband James had been killed in battle. "*There was nothing I could do,*" he'd told her then, too, and the bride learned she was a widow.

"Tara." But no other words would come.

She rose and slipped from the room. If Liam knew his sister at all, she'd come around, she just needed time.

He speared a turnip and chewed it slowly. Had there been anything he could have done for Finn? Would arguing for his release have done any good? Surely not, since he knew Finn was one of the few arrested who had actually broken the law. Still, Liam felt Tara's disappointment in him—and Finn's—as heavily as if it were a sodden cloak about his shoulders.

December 1, 1794

Dusting the flour from her hands, Vivienne left the baguette starter in the Four Winds kitchen and carried her cloak to the second-floor dining room to look for Sebastien. Firelight and sconces lit the pleasant room, which was nearly as empty as it had been Saturday. Sebastien was already at a table, with paperwork and two steaming mugs before him. Hope sparked.

He stood as she approached, his face as smooth as if he had just shaved it before coming, though the day was almost done. She settled into the booth opposite him, and he sat again. "It's all arranged." He nudged a mug of tea toward her. "Armand made a contingent plan in the event you should change your mind and accept his offer."

Her cheeks burned. Had her initial refusal been so unconvincing? Warming her hands around the mug, she sipped peppermint tea and swallowed her pride. She glanced to the window, but the darkness outside showed only her reflection. She looked as tired as she felt. Straightening her posture, she turned back to Sebastien. "Go on."

His face was wax-pale in the candlelight. "He purchased two lots in Asylum and left a note indicating one would be for your use if you decided to claim it. A different clerk in Senator Morris's office handled the paperwork, so I wasn't aware of it until today." He pointed at one of the documents. "If you didn't claim it, he'd wait until the settlement grew a bit more and then sell it at a profit. Once the value had increased on it, you understand. But since you do want it, you can see about transferring ownership . . ."

He continued, but Vienne ceased to register what he was saying as she studied the document on the table. The letters blurred and danced. "We have a home," she whispered, overcome.

Sebastien slid a paper from the stack and smoothed the curling corners. It was a map, labeled French Asylum. The strong black lines of its streets nestled within a horseshoe bend of a river. He pointed to the grid. "Each house is on a half-acre lot. You'll find most of your new neighbors to be aristocrats and former military officers. There is also a weaver and tailor, a tinsmith, blacksmith, café owner, and a few other artisans. Several priests, of course, including Father Gilbert. This large building, the Grand Maison, was designed to be Marie Antoinette's home of refuge. But, God rest her, now it houses ladies' drawing rooms, card parties, concerts, chess games, and amateur dramatic performances. Monsieur Talon, the colony manager, resides there, too. A dancing pavilion is in a charming wooded islet opposite."

Vivienne studied every line on the paper, tracing the river with her fingertip.

"The land is remote from the fevers and politics of the city," Sebastien continued, "yet in no danger of Indian attack, and the river provides water communication with the coast and with the interior. We expect the settlement to grow to five thousand residents once the river is dredged in a few years' time."

She looked for artifice in his face but detected none. "You paint a picture almost too positive to believe. Are there no complaints?"

He crossed an ankle over his knee, then licked his thumb and rubbed at a scuff on his shoe. "Only that Asylum is not Paris, and the wilderness that cradles it is not the mother country of France. But if you go with an eye to create something new, rather than pine for something old, you'll do well, indeed."

Vivienne read the text of the documents once more. Each one detailed the location and size of the lot and specified that any resources already under cultivation on that land belonged to the new owner, Armand de Champlain. His signature scrawled across the bottom of each page.

Doubt pulled at her hope. "You're sure he meant one of these for me?"

Sebastien fished another leaf of paper from his satchel. "See here. A copy of the note he left."

Should Mademoiselle Vivienne Rivard inquire about a lot, please inform her I've taken the liberty of procuring one for her and her young charge. Please arrange transportation if it becomes necessary.

"He says nothing about transfer of ownership to me." Across the room, domino tiles clattered onto a table.

Sebastien spun the paper around and read it for himself. "No matter. It can be done, I'm sure. The fact that he forgot to mention it is no cause for alarm. The important thing is that he purchased two lots and two houses. He can't very well occupy both."

Vivienne's misgivings bowed to her desperation to leave the city. "When can we go?"

"Now that winter is upon us, the next convoy of refugees will have to wait until spring to go north. In the meantime, I'm afraid you're stuck here. Plenty of time to reconsider my proposal, as you have reconsidered Armand's. Unless you've given your heart to someone else?" He narrowed his gaze.

She shook her head, though her face warmed at the suggestion. What she needed was a home, and now she had one. If she and Henri could only survive the wait.

While most people were finishing their third meal of the day, Liam was ready to start his first. Other than his complaining stomach, he felt better than he had in weeks, thanks to twenty consecutive hours of sleep. His only regret was that he'd missed seeing Vivienne in the kitchen this morning.

Finding the first-floor dining room full, he placed his order with the barkeep and headed to the quieter second floor with a fresh mug of tea. He eased into a booth, grateful for the privacy, and tented his hands about the pewter mug, letting the heat radiate from the metal toward his palms. A waitress delivered a basket of bread.

"Thank you," he told her, ignoring the young woman's doe-eyed stare at his scars. "If you see my sister, Tara, would you please tell her I'm here? I'd like to see her, if she can spare a moment."

She agreed and sashayed away with a flip of blond hair over her shoulder.

Liam drew a warm sweet-potato pecan biscuit from the basket and popped it into his mouth, then helped himself to a thick slice of buttered corn bread. He wondered if Vienne had made it, or if she specialized in baguettes and pastries.

From someplace unseen, a man spoke to his dinner partner. And then she spoke back.

He knew that voice.

Suddenly alert, Liam leaned enough to see the back of Vienne's head. Rising, he began to move toward her, but her name stalled on his lips when he recognized the man she was talking to. Sebastien Lemoine.

The scar on Liam's cheek itched as he silently returned to his seat. Frustration smoldered in his veins that seeing her with another man should affect him so, but he could not convince himself that he didn't care. He had waited this long to see Vienne. He could wait a little longer to talk to her alone.

Liam's gaze drifted until it settled upon a man playing solitaire in a booth along the adjacent wall. His bald head shone in the firelight, and his lips were wide, full, and flat. Prominent golden brown eyes completed his unfortunate resemblance to a frog. He shuffled the card deck, then flipped them thoughtfully into piles. But there was a joker mixed in, and the player didn't seem to mind. He only had eyes for Vivienne.

Something was amiss. Sliding from his booth, Liam ambled toward the frog-faced gentleman. How satisfying it would be to invite himself to a sham card game and interrupt his surveillance.

Before he could reach the stranger, however, Tara swept into the room with a tray bearing a turkey pot pie and crisp potato cakes. "Next time you sleep that long, don't lock the door," she muttered. "I'd have liked to check and make sure you weren't dead." Her tone was void of levity. Pushing past him, she unloaded his dinner onto the table.

He followed and laid a hand on her shoulder. "Sorry, Tara."

"For what?" She hugged the empty tray as she waited for him to respond.

"For Finn. For James. For you."

Her chin quivered as she sniffed. Liam watched the struggle between sorrow and resilience play across her features, and his heart pinched. She'd always hated to cry.

"You could find love again, you know," he told his sister. "You'd be a prize for any man."

She shook her head fiercely. "No, I can't."

"You're still young, and beautiful, and smart and strong—"

"Liam," she whispered, "I'm still in love with James. I don't blame you for his death, but a love like that won't come twice." A sad smile broke through her tears. "I pray someday you'll understand what I mean. Now eat, before it gets cold." She whisked out of the room.

Still standing, he glanced to where Vienne had been seated.

Disappointment dropped into his gut to find that she had left while his back had been turned to her. Sebastien remained, buckling the straps on his satchel. Liam turned toward the card player he'd been about to investigate when Tara had come in. The booth was empty, but the solitaire game was still splayed over the table.

His dinner untouched behind him, Liam crossed to the mess the watcher had left in haste. For the privy, perhaps? He trailed a finger over the cards and stopped, frowning, at the joker's laughing face.

Chapter Twenty-One

Unease tugged at Vivienne as she left the Four Winds Tavern. If Sebastien had not just renewed his ungallant marriage proposal, she might have asked him to escort her back to the pension. But she was humbled enough by accepting a home in Asylum from Armand, the one man whose generosity she had vowed never to need, much less use. Though relieved to have a way out of Philadelphia come spring, she clung to the shred of independence, however slender, that walking home alone afforded.

The wind blew stronger now that the sun had set, but the hour wasn't yet late. Gathering her hood tighter beneath her chin, she dipped in and out of lamplight pooling on the sidewalk, halting for those cutting across her path. A passing chaise clattered by, splattering slush over her cloak.

She moved away from the curb, toward the middle of the sidewalk, to avoid being splashed again. A man wedged himself next to her, forcing her back toward the curb, until she walked mere inches from the street traffic. Through her hood, she heard the muffled hoofbeats of an approaching coach. As the matched pair passed, someone grabbed Vienne and shoved her right for the gap between horses and carriage.

A scream ripped from her, and the horses veered away as she fell headlong onto the cobbles, the iron-rimmed carriage wheels narrowly missing her. Stunned and humiliated, she turned her palms and found them scraped and bleeding. Her knees felt bruised beneath her wet cloak and skirts.

An age-withered hand appeared at her side, outstretched. "You must be more careful, young miss. That could have gone the wrong way in a heartbeat." The old gentleman helped her to her feet, clucking his tongue.

"I wasn't careless, I—I—was pushed!" she stammered. Stepping back onto the sidewalk, she brushed bits of ice from her cloak. Her pulse racing, she scanned the sidewalk but saw nothing unusual among the passersby.

"Is that so?" Frowning, the man looked around. "Well, then. Beware of others who are careless and steer clear of them."

Vienne nodded. "Good advice."

He tipped his hat to her and melted back into the crowd.

Good advice, indeed. Whoever pushed her had done so deliberately. But why? Suspicions slithered over her. Any number of tavern kitchen servants might have said something about Henri's outburst weeks ago. Had word finally reached Jacobin ears? Or was Sebastien orchestrating yet another danger, simply to convince her of her need of him? He was so convinced Henri was Louis-Charles. Perhaps he had boasted of his connection to the boy too loudly, or to the wrong person. Perhaps he had been followed. Shuddering, she looked around once more. A Jacobin would want her gone to clear the way to Henri.

Henri. Was he safe still, with Paulette? Urgency propelled her toward the pension, and caution directed her footsteps away from the well-trafficked street. She knew better than to duck into an unlit alley, but a side street, surely, would be fine. Quickening her pace, she turned a corner, eager to be away from the press of the crowd.

Footsteps followed. Long strides. Heavy gait. She looked over her shoulder but saw no one. Hurriedly, she kept on, though inwardly she railed against her shortsightedness in choosing this path. She hadn't seen who had pushed her into harm's way, but could he not also be the one trailing her now?

Oh no. If Henri was his aim, she could not lead him to the pension. She could not go home, not yet. Her hood fell to her back, and every sound was an alarm in her ears. The squeak of a wooden shingle swaying on its iron hinge. The angry snarling of cats fighting over a piece of fish. The clang of a ladder against a lamppost as the lamplighter began his rounds at the far end of the block.

Vienne's face flushed with heat, but her fingers were freezing cold. She glanced behind her and saw only shadows beneath a deep purple sky. But there, across the street, a man walked alone, bald head shining. He looked at her, then straight ahead again. Surely he wouldn't try anything with the lamplighter still here, lighting his wicks. One by one, the flames beat back the night.

She reached the corner and turned again. The bald man's footsteps were louder this time, faster. She only had to turn halfway to see he was mere yards behind her and not slowing down, his blue woolen cloak flapping against his trousers.

Sweat beaded her brow. "Stay away from me!" She hoisted her skirts and cloak and took off at a dash down the unpaved road. Hard-packed wagon ruts and ridges of ice punched the bottoms of her shoes as she ran, throwing off her balance. She twisted her ankle in one of them and bit down at the searing pain when she tried bearing weight on that foot.

"You break my heart! You're irresistible!" The words were in French and spoken with a pronounced slur. But the man walked with purpose, and he certainly wasn't after love.

"I said leave me!" she screamed. An uproar from the direction of Market Street spun her attention behind her.

"No need to worry, that's just Père Noël making his first appearance of the season. All that cheering you hear—that's the sound of happy families. I guarantee they aren't interested in one lone French girl taking the wrong road home." He was close enough for her to smell the cognac on his breath. His eyes were too large, his face too hard. Wide, flat lips too assured. He was dangerous, and she could not run. Her screams would not be heard.

"How do you know this is the wrong road?" she asked.

"I know." He leered, turning his lapel to show her his tricolor cockade.

His hand shot out and grasped her throat, shoving her up against the nearest wall. He squeezed, trapping her screams.

She couldn't breathe. She clawed at his hand, his face. Kicked his shins, jammed her knee upward against his body, but he dodged the blow. She thought she heard shouting, but sounds became muffled. Black spots crowded her vision.

And then suddenly she was gasping, coughing, breathing, though raggedly, and rubbing at her neck. She heard the sound of knuckles on bone, and of air being knocked from one's lungs. Then the man who'd assaulted her collapsed, unconscious, at her feet, bleeding from his nose.

Only when strong arms came under hers did she realize she'd dropped to her knees, her twisted ankle throbbing. Her rescuer's jaw brushed her cheek as he lifted her to stand. She kept her injured ankle off the ground.

"Vivienne," he said, "let me help you."

"Liam," she gasped, and he captured her to his chest. Overcome, she sank into him, grasping the arms that held her close. The air she labored to draw in felt like shards of ice. "When did you—" But she had neither the time nor voice to spare. "They know where we live. They know . . . I must get to Henri." Her speech concluded in a fit of coughing, and she leaned away from him.

"They. Who is they?" He brushed a curl from her face before placing a steadying hand on her shoulder.

She pointed at the man's cockade. "Jacobins." Her voice was reedy and unreliable. "They think Henri is Louis-Charles, but he isn't."

Only then did she notice the slash across his left cheek pointing to a notch taken from the rim of his ear. "Oh, Liam." She touched his face below the scar, mind racing with questions about who had done this, and what had become of Finn. "You've been gone too long," she whispered and steered her thoughts back to Henri.

Vienne's fingertips on his skin drew Liam's feelings for her dangerously close to the surface. He cast a quick glance at the scoundrel on the ground. Jacobin or not, he'd wake up soon. "Can you walk?" he asked Vivienne.

"I twisted my ankle."

Without another thought, one arm went beneath her shoulders, his other came under her knees, and he scooped her up. She looped her arm about his neck, and he caught her looking again at the nasty scar on his cheek.

"Cut myself shaving," he joked rather than explain the truth just yet, but it failed to lighten the mood. Her neck had already begun to purple where that fiend had dared to squeeze the life out of her.

"Please take me to the Pension Sainte-Marie. I need to—" From the rasping sound of her voice, her windpipe was injured.

He carried her in the opposite direction. "To what? To put yourself where they may be lying in wait for you already?" He shook his head, marching a shortcut through buildings he'd grown up darting between in play. "We can do better than that."

"I need to get Henri," Vienne whispered against his neck. "He's in danger."

"I'll get him."

When they reached the Four Winds, Liam took her in through the kitchen entrance in the rear of the building and set her down. She clutched his arm for balance.

Steam billowed from a cauldron of pepper pot soup, scenting the air with beef, taro root, habanero, allspice, and greens. Lamb roasted on a spit, and potato peels littered a newssheet-covered corner of the floor.

"What on earth?" Ladle in her fist, Rachel came toward them.

"Evenin', Rachel, you're looking well." He made to touch the brim of his cap before remembering he'd left the tavern without one. Nor had he taken the time to fetch a cloak. "Vivienne needs a room, a safe room, for herself and Henri." Arranging lodging was not part of her typical responsibilities as head cook, but Rachel could manage a great deal for a soul in need.

"You in trouble?" Rachel frowned, peering behind them. "Where's Henri?"

Liam answered before Vienne could strain her voice to be heard. "I've yet to get him, but first Vienne needs to disappear. Can you help?"

"Mercy, child!" She stared at Vivienne's bruised neck. "Why, if somebody didn't get a hold of you." Lips pressed together, her nostrils flared in sympathy.

"Twisted her ankle, too, so if you could help her up to a room, I'll explain to Tara when I can. One more thing. Tell the staff that if a bald man comes in here, with a scratch on his face and perhaps a broken nose"—he shrugged—"turn him away at the door."

Rachel's eyes widened. "And if he asks why?"

"He didn't pay his bill before walking out earlier this evening." It was only a hunch, though a strong one. "If he says he'll pay his debt, take his money and have the barkeep throw him out on his ear."

"My lands, Mr. Liam, who's running Four Winds now?"

He turned to Vienne. "I'm off to fetch your boy."

"I'll write a note for you, or they'll never let him leave." She grimaced as she spoke, and anger coursed through him afresh at the man who had caused her pain.

Rachel scurried off, returning moments later with paper and pencil on a platter, which Liam held while Vivienne wrote a note on its surface. A ringlet coiled against her cheek as she handed it to him.

"Please hurry," she whispered.

He did.

If Vivienne could have walked, she would've been pacing the small room on the third floor of the tavern. But as she couldn't, she sat on one of two beds in the room, staring at the door. On the small table beside her, Rachel had left a mug of chamomile tea, but one sip had been all she could tolerate. Wonder, fear, hope, and dread flipped her stomach first one way and then the other.

A knock on the door sent a jolt right through her. "It's me. Tara."

Metal scraped the lock, and Vienne immediately envisioned a man on the other side of that door, forcing Tara to turn the key. A bald man with a broken nose.

But when the door eased open, only Tara slipped through before latching and locking it once more. Relief flooded Vienne.

"Ach, Viv. Rachel told me what happened, or at least what she knew of the story." Her gaze dipped to Vienne's throat. "So the devil did get his paws around you, then. 'Twas one of my own patrons, too, I hear! He'll not be coming back if I can help it." Tara towered above Vienne, unconcerned with the tendrils of burnished hair straying from her pins.

"I don't mean to bring trouble to the Four Winds. I'll stay only until I have other arrangements. Take the fee for the room from my pay." Vivienne hoped that would be enough to cover it.

"Not to worry about that." Tara chafed her arms, then rounded on the small hearth, knelt, and added more wood to the glowing embers. As she blew on them, flames leaped up again. "There now, that's better."

Voices floated down the hall. Liam, Vienne thought. And a woman's? Forgetting to favor her ankle, she swung her feet to the floor, winced, and hopped to the door.

Hand on the latch, Vienne peered through the peephole and saw Liam and a red-faced Paulette, her mobcap crooked on her head. Both of them carried boxes from Vienne's room at the pension. Stepping back, she swung wide the door.

Henri bounded into the room. "Mademoiselle!"

She knelt on the floor and embraced him. He threw his arms around her tender neck.

"Easy," Liam murmured.

Henri relaxed his grip. "That bad man hurt you?"

"Not so very much." She hoped he didn't notice the waver in her voice. She pulled him in again, breathing in his scent. He smelled of the herbs he'd been grinding for Paulette: basil, sage, rosemary. Her heart cramped. She had prayed to love him with a mother's love, a love she'd never felt herself and had never before bestowed. Maybe this ache, big enough to swallow her whole, was close.

When she caught a glimpse of Paulette's worried face, she stood and hugged the maid.

"Vivienne!" Paulette cried. "I couldn't believe it, even though I read it in your own hand. I could not let this man take Henri away without coming myself to see that it's true."

"Thank you for that. And it's true." She sighed. "Every word."

Tara laid her hand on Vienne's shoulder. "I'll come check on you later. Do you need anything now?"

"No, thank you."

After a few words with her brother, Tara left the room.

Liam locked the door behind her while remaining inside the room. Under any other circumstances, it would have been highly improper to have a man alone in a bedroom with two women and a child. But as Vienne was more comfortable with the door closed and locked than left open, she didn't protest.

He nodded at the boxes he'd stacked along the wall. "Miss Dubois was good enough to pack your things."

Vienne grasped what she'd been distracted from acknowledging until now: she would never stay at the Pension Sainte-Marie again. She'd known her days there were numbered, since she hoped to relocate to Asylum soon, but to leave like this—it felt too much like running away. Like escaping. And she'd had her fill of that in France. Vienne sat on the bed to relieve her throbbing ankle, and Henri nested beneath her arm.

"I'll wait in the corridor to escort Miss Dubois home again." Liam let himself outside.

Paulette blew out an exaggerated sigh, then sat on the bed opposite Vienne and whispered, "I don't understand. Why did that man attack you? Why do you think he'd try it again?"

Vienne reached for the tea and drank it. Now that Henri was

with her again, the warm brew felt far more soothing. "He was a Jacobin."

The maid's mouth screwed tight to one side as questions crimped her brow. "But why did he target you? Jacobins don't go around choking women at random. There is a purpose to their actions. What kind of trouble are you mixed up in?"

Vienne shook her head and drank again. This, she could not reveal.

Frowning, Paulette moved to the fire frolicking in the hearth now, and held her open hands to the heat. When she faced Vivienne again, her countenance was drawn. "It's one thing to work here, but something else altogether to take up residence. I'm uneasy leaving the two of you in a tavern, outside the French Quarter, at that."

"We'll be all right here." But for how long, Vienne could not say. "Rest easy."

"Well." Paulette rubbed her hands together. "I'll have a fine time explaining to Madame where you've disappeared to. I've half a mind to let her think you've gone to bed, and then you can tell her the state of things yourself tomorrow."

"Thank you, Paulette. Please, if anyone comes calling, don't say where Henri and I are staying now. Tell no one. Not even Monsieur Lemoine."

The maid's hazel eyes narrowed. "I thought he was sweet on you. I thought the two of you . . ." She bit her tongue. "You have my word. Your secret is safe with me."

Vienne could only pray it was.

Chapter Twenty-Two

Liam's dinner was stone cold by the time he found it waiting for him in his room, but that didn't stop him from downing the potato cakes and turkey pie when he saw it. Paulette was back at the pension, Beau and Cherie were sleek and healthy in the stable, and Vivienne and Henri were safe in their room on the other side of Liam's wall.

For now.

Swallowing the last bite of turkey, he went to the basin and washed his hands and face. He had to go back to Asylum. But how could he leave Vienne now? If someone had followed her away from the Four Winds Tavern, it was only a matter of time before that same someone came back here looking for her. Tara would be in jeopardy, too.

No. He couldn't allow it. Leaning on the windowsill, he looked out into the night, alert for any movement between lampposts. He'd been powerless to prevent James's death and absent when his mother died last summer. He'd done nothing at all to help Finn. With such a record, he did not seem qualified to protect anyone. And yet, if he didn't look out for Vivienne and Henri and Tara, who would? Certainly not that young dandy, Sebastien Lemoine, who hadn't even the decency to see Vivienne home. *Lord, show me the way.*

His conscience pricked him. Vienne was smart and strong, perhaps stronger than she knew. She would have something to say about the path she should take from here, if only he would ask.

The night watchman had yet to start his rounds, so the hour couldn't be too late. Half past nine, perhaps. Liam stared at the wall separating him from Vienne. Then he rapped his knuckles on it. "Vivienne?" he called. "It's Liam. I'd like to talk to you without this wall between us."

Her soft voice called through. "Just a moment, please."

"Certainly."

After leaving enough time for her to make herself presentable, Liam smoothed a hand down his shirtfront, slipped into the hall, and tapped on her door.

She opened it, fully dressed, hair bound loosely at the nape of her neck. Fatigue smeared shadows beneath her eyes.

"Would it scandalize you if I were to come in?" He kept his voice low. "We need to talk without being overheard."

One hand on her bruised throat, she stepped back to admit him before closing and locking the door again. "Henri's sleeping," she said, and Liam assured her he'd try not to wake him.

Already the room held the faint scent of Vienne's rose water. She sat on the bed while he stoked the fire. Then he grabbed the back of the only chair in the room, turned it around to face her, and lowered himself into it. He kneaded his hands together, rubbing absently at the calluses he found.

Vienne grasped his hand, stilling it. "Thank you. Liam, you saved my life."

His gaze went to the mottled skin of her neck. The desire to protect her unfolded within him, crowding everything else away. "I was almost too late."

"But you weren't."

He covered her hand with his for a moment, then released it. It would be too easy to draw her closer. "We were fortunate this time. Do you know what you'll do now? I'm sure you realize you won't be safe here for long."

She crossed her arms and grimaced as she swallowed. He should not keep her talking long, if he could help it. "I need asylum."

"That you do," he agreed.

"French Asylum. It's an actual place," she corrected. "You've heard of it?"

His eyebrows rose. "Lovely piece of earth. Are you considering moving there? It would be far safer than Philadelphia for you and Henri."

Light sparked in her green eyes. "I've secured a home there for us."

"You have?" Surprise jolted through him at this answer to his prayer.

Vienne adjusted her fichu, but the marks of her attacker remained visible beneath the lace. "I want to go soon, but Sebastien says I can't until spring."

So that was why she had met with him this evening. Liam held her gaze, weighing what he was about to suggest. "What if I said you can leave tomorrow? With me?"

Her lips parted. "What?"

In the hallway, a floorboard creaked as someone passed by. Pulling his chair closer to Vienne, Liam leaned forward, elbows on his knees. His fingertips brushed the soft folds of her skirt before he clasped his hands together. "My farm is on the edge of Asylum. I've been gone far too long, and I have two horses in Tara's stable that need to go back with me. If that's not Providence I don't know what is. You and Henri can have Cherie, and I'll ride Beau."

Vienne cast a glance at Henri's sleeping form before facing him again. "If it's safe to travel, why did Sebastien say otherwise?"

Wind howled outside the tavern, and the window quaked in its casing. Liam crossed the room to make sure it was closed tight, then quietly returned to his seat. "He's talking about convoys of refugees. Groups of people travel by wagon to Harrisburg, then paddle upstream on the Susquehanna the rest of the way. It can take between ten days and two weeks that way, sometimes even longer.

With the river and weather being so cold now, it's too dangerous. He's right that they'll need to wait."

She pinched at the ruffles on her sleeves. "Your route is better, then."

"It's more direct, and faster, but the way is rugged, especially the last sixty miles or so of the journey. It takes four days in ideal conditions to make the trip. Maybe six with the days being shorter, though. You'd be unchaperoned, but there's no way around it. You have my word I'll do nothing to dishonor you."

"I trust you." She leaned forward, a faint pink staining her cheeks. "I trust you completely."

Vienne's words were a seal upon his intent, stamped with the responsibility of conveying two souls to their refuge. It was a press and a burden he gladly bore. Liam vowed not to betray that trust.

Vivienne's breath steamed and then froze on the inside of her muffler as she and Henri rode beside Liam. Icicles striped the rock face looming on one side, while dried grasses poked through the snow like blond stubble. The wind whipped about them, but by now, after five days of the same, the little boy had ceased to complain.

Clumps of snow rested on evergreen branches like clotted cream. With Henri's body slouched against Vivienne's back in sleep, she grasped his arms about her waist with one hand while keeping Cherie's reins loosely in the other.

Henri stirred. The warmth of his body separated from hers as he straightened. "Mr. Delaney, won't you tell us a story? One about Indians, with war ponies and tomahawks and all the rest."

"Another time." Liam's voice was subdued behind his scarf.

So was his manner. He was working through something.

Vienne let another quarter mile go by before venturing, "Do you want to talk about what happened? Out west, I mean." Henri leaned against her again, his arms about her middle.

Liam glanced at the boy before looking straight ahead. "No."

But he pushed his wool layers below his chin to speak, revealing the scars that brought a twinge to Vivienne's gut, for he'd already explained how they came to be.

"Your mind is still there, I can tell. We have time, and I'm certain you won't be overheard by gossips." Hoofbeats plodded softly on a trail so lonesome, even the creak of leather saddles and the clinking of bits in the horses' mouths could be heard. Snow-powdered hills gently rose and fell, like the folds of a discarded garment. Their crests were fringed with bare trees, their black branches a delicate embroidery on a gray wool sky.

Liam's breath puffed in white clouds as he shifted Beau's reins in his hands. "Finn was arrested. Did I tell you that? Did Tara?" He glanced at her, and she shook her head, heart sinking for this man, who took so seriously his role in his cousin's life. "I saw him, beaten and bound, and he saw me, too, among the soldiers that ordered and carried out his arrest. I've always been on Finn's side ere this."

When he didn't continue, Vivienne said, "You can't think he blames you."

"Who he blames is the least of my concerns right now. The journey he's making over the mountains and across the state into Philadelphia is at least as rugged as this one we're making. Except he's walking it, and he doesn't have the food or clothing we do." He brought his muffler back up over his nose, holding it there for a moment, before letting it drop once more. "I don't know if Finn will make it. But you will, Vivienne. You and Henri. The way is rough, but the weather may hold. God help me, I'll not see harm come to you."

Liam's face, bared to the cold, showed faint furrows at the brow and starbursts at his eyes, the marks of a contemplative man who had both frowned and laughed much, and opened himself to the same sun which shone upon his fields. Vienne drew strength from his fierceness, and comfort from his tenderness, for he was both, and more, to her.

"Would that we did not require anyone's protection. But since we do," Vivienne conceded, "I would have no one but you, Liam, for the job."

The nod he gave her was solemn. Pulling their scarves back over their faces, they slipped into a comfortable quiet as they put more miles behind them, step by horseshoed step.

Vivienne lost count of the distance they covered. Bare trees amassed on far-off slopes in a haze of bronze and silver filigree. At last, gaps through the trees yielded glimpses of the Susquehanna River, a silver-armored snake carving its own path through the wilderness. There was a desolation about this place that could frighten her, if she let it. For a refuge, it seemed inhospitable, even to the horses. At Liam's word, they dismounted and led Beau and Cherie by their bridles, all of them picking their way over the narrow, ice-glazed trail. Roots crisscrossed the path, as thick as ropes and rigging, so that Vienne held back her skirts to see where she placed her feet.

When Henri faltered, Liam crouched down, bidding the boy climb up on his back.

"Oof!" Liam said as he rose, Henri's thin limbs twining around him. "You're big as a mule, you are!" Their laughter bounced and echoed against the wilderness. "Take heart, Vienne," Liam added. "We won't always need to so closely watch our steps."

Catching his eye, she smiled at the unspoken meaning before crossing a stream of melting snow. "I trust you are right." For however difficult it was to reach, Asylum was that much more hidden from those who would bring them harm.

Vivienne marveled at the distance they'd traveled from Philadelphia and at how far she'd come in her relationship with Liam from the first night he'd danced with her at the Binghams'. True to his word, he had not touched her on this journey. At night, they had slept in separate rooms in ordinaries and inns he was familiar with along the way. With each day that passed, her respect and affection deepened, until she could no longer think of him as a mere friend. She felt herself being drawn to him, as the sun turned a flower's face, and as the moon pulled the tide.

Ahead of her on the trail, Henri laughed at something. Liam looked over his shoulder at her. "Just making sure you're still there," he said.

She smiled. "I'm here."

With a grin and wink, he turned and continued up the trail with Henri clinging happily to his back.

Vienne would follow wherever he led.

Part Four

Gaul's exiled royalists, a pensive train,
Here raise the hut and till the rough domain.
The way-worn pilgrim to their fires receive,
Supply his wants; but at his tidings grieve;
Afflicting news! For ever on the wing,
A ruined country and a murdered King!
Peace to their lone retreats while sheltered here,
May these deep shades to them be doubly dear;
And Power's proud worshippers, wherever placed,
Who saw such grandeur ruined and defaced,
By deeds of virtue to themselves secure
Those inborn joys, that, spite of Kings, endure,
Though thrones and states from their foundations part;
The precious balsam of a blameless heart.

—Alexander Wilson, *The Foresters*, 1804

Chapter Twenty-Three

Secrets, Paulette Dubois knew how to keep.

So when she opened the pension's front door to find Sebastien Lemoine, she remained unruffled. He was always so shiny and spotless, like a portrait on the canvas of milky sky behind him. She had half a mind to take her feather duster to his waistcoat and see if she couldn't transfer a bit of dust. It wasn't fitting for a man to be so clean all the time. A little dirt was good for the soul.

"Paulette," he was saying, and she wondered if he'd had to say it more than once.

"Monsieur Lemoine, forgive me." The bite in the chill air refocused her attention.

"I've come to call on Vivienne. May I?" He stepped forward, unwrapping the wool from his neck until it draped neatly over both shoulders.

She crossed her arms, rubbing the goose bumps forming beneath her thin dress. "She's not here." She glanced at the fire in the parlor hearth, where the flames leaned away from the door.

He lifted his timepiece from his pocket, consulted it with a frown, then put it back. "What do you mean, she isn't here? She's always here in the afternoons. She doesn't leave. She and Henri both stay home." His nose was pink from the cold.

"Well, a little variation to the routine, then. Vivienne and Henri are gone."

Sebastien clenched both ends of his scarf in his fists. "You don't mean it."

"I assure you I do." At five feet tall, and slender as a weasel, Paulette did not cut an imposing figure, this she knew. But what she lacked in stature, she made up for with spirit and confidence.

Something flared in his face, a passion she hadn't known such a clean man could possess. Without another word, he pushed past her into the pension and bounded up the stairs to Vivienne's room.

Paulette threw the door closed against the swirl of winter wind. By the time she reached him, he was already in the empty room, which she'd just cleaned to ready it for the next pensioner.

"Gone? Gone where?" He rounded on her, and she took a step back in spite of herself. "Why did they leave? Without telling me? Tell me what you know. Tell me!" His face was close enough to hers that she could see the fine pores on his fine nose and smell the coffee on his breath.

"I don't scare easy, you'll find." Paulette pressed her lips into a resolute line, backed against the wall though she was. Her hand reached around the corner, gripping the banister to steady herself.

"Forgive me." He stepped back. "I am shocked, and perhaps scared myself. Wherever she is, she shouldn't be alone with Henri. She can't take care of him like I can." He rubbed a narrow hand over his face and muttered, "I was going to marry her."

So the monsieur was used to having what he wanted and had no idea what to do when things didn't go his way. Oh, the lessons she could give him on that.

"Is there nothing you can tell me?" His words were measured, but the tone was hard and impatient.

"What do I know? I'm just the maid."

His shoulders slumped. He leaned back against the wall in the corridor and stared at a spidery crack in the plaster ceiling.

"I'll see you to the door, then." Let him mull and sulk in his own home. She still had work to do. At a flick of her feather duster toward the stairs, he trudged down to the parlor, and she followed.

But at the door, Sebastien turned to her. "Do forgive me, Paulette. I meant no disrespect to you. I don't tell many people this, but my own mother was a maid back in France. My father a valet. So you see, you and I have more in common than you think."

She squinted at him, from the top of his pomaded hair to the tips of his polished shoes. "Is that right?" Either he was lying or this explained why he worked so hard at his personal grooming and wardrobe.

A lump bobbed behind his cravat. "Yes, I tell the truth. We're not so different, you and I. Both making our way in a new world. And we both care about Henri. Vivienne and Henri. This city is a dangerous place, so you can understand why I have been shocked out of my manners to find they aren't here. If there's something you aren't telling me . . ." He fished a bill from his pocketbook. "Information is money, mademoiselle."

The suspicion that had begun as a cold knot in her belly now snaked throughout her middle. She shoved the cash away. "Put that to better use and drink your troubles away like a normal man."

"But that's just it!" He shoved the money back into his pocket. "I've been to the tavern where she works, or used to work. She wasn't there either, hasn't been there for days."

"What?" She dropped her duster into her apron pocket and set her hands on her hips.

"The bread has been awful, and when I asked the owner how to account for it, all she said was that they were looking for a new baker. Every other question I asked was soundly ignored."

Paulette tucked a stray strand of brown hair up under her cap, absorbing this news without comment. Vivienne and Henri lived at the tavern now. Would Vivienne also have quit her job to remain even further out of sight? Even though she needed the money and enjoyed the work? Whatever secret Vivienne held, perhaps it was bigger than Paulette had thought.

"I worry for the child," Sebastien said. "And for Vienne, of course. We had plans."

Paulette looked at him sideways. That was the second time he'd mentioned Henri first. Odd priority for a jilted lover.

"Where is he?" Monsieur Lemoine asked again, this time grabbing Paulette's arms.

She stomped on his foot with the heel of her boot and brought her other knee up hard to his groin. "Unhand me!" she cried out, though no one else was in the pension to hear her.

He did. Bending at the waist, he clutched his knees and trapped a whimper behind his puffed cheeks. How quickly he had resorted to a bribe and to physical force. Perhaps he really was a former street urchin, prone to violence and dishonesty, who tried to hide his past behind fancy clothes.

Sebastien slowly straightened and glared at her. "I'll come again. If you hear anything about the boy—anything at all—I'll make it worth your while to tell me." Grimacing, he left the pension.

Paulette shuddered as she returned to dusting the parlor, feathers skimming Madame's gilt-framed mirrors. She looked through her own reflection, inspecting the glass for smudges to be removed. What she saw instead was clearly blazoned on her mind. Sebastien Lemoine was not in love. Vivienne was an afterthought, Henri his main concern. The boy was in danger—she felt it in her bones. And Paulette aimed to find out why.

ASYLUM, PENNSYLVANIA
DECEMBER 1794

Vivienne's head ached with cold and confusion as they stepped off the flatboat river ferry that had brought them across the Susquehanna's horseshoe bend. Henri grasped her hand and asked where the settlement was.

Liam led the horses by their bridles off the ferry and onto the bank. "This is it."

She flexed her fingers, coaxing them to be nimble again, and drew from her cloak pocket the map Sebastien had supplied. On the paper, neat black lines indicated a developed wharf right where now there was merely a narrow plank walk jutting from river to land. On the map, a grid of streets organized dozens of lots. She looked up and watched smoke lift from several chimneys in the distance, only to drop down to the earth, snaking among the cabins like sooty wraiths.

She tugged her muffler below her chin. "Liam, how do you explain this?"

He looked over her shoulder. His scar stood out more starkly against his cold-whitened cheek. "That's the *plan* you're holding. And that"—he gestured to a collection of log cabins—"is the current reality. Welcome to Asylum." Remarkably, his tone held no sarcasm. "Well done, both of you. I know the journey was arduous."

"How many houses are there?" Henri asked.

"Twenty-three, at present." Liam patted Beau on the neck. "Did Monsieur Lemoine paint a different picture for you? Le Petit Trianon, perhaps?"

Vienne bristled at the mention of Marie Antoinette's extravagant nature retreat, where the animals were shampooed for the queen's royal eye, their droppings disposed of as promptly as they appeared. "Let's just say Sebastien didn't give this place its proper due in his description," she replied, determined to adapt. She had not come here for ease of living, but to be safe from those who had designs on Henri's life. If Asylum's sole appeal lay in its remoteness and inaccessibility, that was enough.

"You'll grow accustomed to it, I have no doubt." Liam smiled, but the bands beneath his eyes revealed that the trip had taxed him, too.

The sun slipped behind the hills backing the settlement, darkening the sky from bleached linen to gray velvet. There were no lampposts here, but the stars piercing the cloudless canopy gave an ethereal light of their own.

Moments later, a lantern bobbed toward them through the darkness, and a shout split the night. "Two adults and a child! A boy! A boy!"

Vienne held Henri close as more lanterns joined the first, the lights resembling fireflies on a summer's eve. In no time, eager white faces surrounded her. Silk gowns and embroidered suits hung loosely on their frames. A flash of panic shot through Vienne, for want of food was a terror to her and had been ever since the bread famine during the year of the Great Cold in Paris, when lacework stopped because fingers were too numb to move, and beggars died in doorways.

"Let me see him!" Thin hands reached out to Henri. Beneath formal white curls, their eyes were hungry. "Is it him at last?"

"Louis-Charles!" breathed another, reverently. "We've been waiting. Your room is prepared."

Vivienne shook her head, chest constricting. She was about to dash their hope. "He is not the king," she said, "I vow. His name is Henri Chastain." Her words suspended in glittering clouds before scattering on the wind.

"Not Louis-Charles?" a woman asked. "We heard he was coming . . ." Her voice cracked and faded away.

"No, madame," Vienne told her. "This boy is not the king."

"I'm sorry." Henri's small voice spiraled up. "I would be your hero if I could."

"Ach." Liam scooped him up, holding him easily in one arm, and said in English, "Who says you must be king to be a hero?"

Henri's smile shone to match the stars.

"Mademoiselle Rivard? Is that you? Saints be praised!" Father Gilbert pushed through the small crowd to stand, beaming, before them. He, too, had lost weight since last spring, but his countenance was as kind as ever. "And Mr. Delaney, too. Welcome home!"

Liam shook his hand in greeting.

"I don't know if you ever met Henri Chastain," Vienne added. "This is Martine's son."

Father Gilbert squeezed Henri's shoulder. "This is just the place for you, I'm sure. How is your mother?"

"With the angels now," Henri replied.

Father Gilbert sighed. "I'm so sorry to hear that. I'm sure you miss her very much." A moment passed in reverence before he turned to Vienne. "Madame Suzanne Arquette is here, too," he told her, though she doubted the poor woman's troubled mind would remember her. "You have a house, I take it?"

She told him she did, though her confidence flagged. Craning her neck, she searched for Armand among those who had gathered to welcome them. If he was there, she didn't see him. "Do you know a Monsieur Armand de Champlain?" she asked.

Murmurs rippled through a few of the women present. "Who doesn't?" one said in a tone that implied much.

Embarrassment scorched Vivienne's face. She should have known Armand would create such a reputation for himself. And she should have used more discretion instead of inquiring about him so openly.

"It's late," Father Gilbert said. "Your house is likely bare and cold. Stay this first night in the Grand Maison, at least. Tomorrow, after you're rested and fed, you can get your first look at your new home in daylight." He leaned in and added in a whisper, "If you've business with Monsieur de Champlain, you'll find him at breakfast, I'm sure."

Liam set Henri down and began unstrapping the bundles of her belongings from Cherie. After handing his lantern to Henri, Father Gilbert took one bag from him, and Vienne took the other.

"Thank you," she said to Liam. So inadequate, those two little words. "Thank you for bringing us home."

The corners of his lips curved up. "I would do nothing less for you."

She believed him. The journey now complete, Vienne suddenly wished they were not surrounded by others, and that his hands were not full of reins.

"You're in good hands now, I see. I hope you find your house to your liking. I may have built it myself." He touched his cap and led the horses away. As she watched him go, the ache between her temples sank to her heart.

"This way." Father Gilbert's voice recaptured her attention. Those who had lingered with their lanterns formed a guiding light as they walked in a wobbly line from the small wharf to the Grand Maison, the great house that loomed up ahead. "This was to be the queen's house," Father Gilbert whispered. "A shelter for her and her children."

"So I've been told."

In the moonlight, four brick chimneys rose from the roof, and the wood-shingled walls were pierced with many glass windows. She tried to imagine the queen and her children living here and failed. By the time they reached the enormous double doors, most of the others in their procession had dropped away to cabins of their own.

Inside, a wide hall ran the entire length of the building, with rooms opening to either side. She could tell as she passed that they were nearly bare, but the few furnishings she saw were reminiscent of Versailles. Oil paintings, carved sofas, plush chairs. In one room, a pianoforte. In another, a long, polished table topped with silver candlesticks.

"You will breakfast there in the morning." Father Gilbert pointed to the long table, then led Vienne and Henri to a staircase of polished rosewood. The walls were covered in fleur-de-lys paper, which could have come only from France. But the symbols of the monarchy rippled, belying the hewn and squared logs beneath.

At the top of the stairs, Vienne found the layout of the second floor identical to the first. Father Gilbert led them to the second room on the right. "You may sleep here tonight. Keep the lantern." He set her bundle on the floor. "The room across the hall was meant for the dauphin. Monsieur Talon, the colony manager here, handpicked the toys and furnishings he thought would please Louis-Charles. Perhaps Henri might enjoy playing in there sometimes." He gave the boy a tender smile.

"Thank you," Vienne said, quickly feeling the exhaustion of her journey. "Will we see you tomorrow?"

"My dear, you will see all of us, every day. Rest well tonight. God bless you."

Vienne and Henri stood in the hall with the lantern until the former priest reached the stairs and called out that he could make his way from there.

"Come, Henri," she whispered. "You can explore the toys tomorrow if you like. For now, it's time to rest."

The large room was cold, despite the four hearths to heat the house. Too exhausted to bother with the warming pan leaning at one end of the fireplace, they laid down on canopied beds fully dressed, their cloaks still on, and extinguished the lantern. Vienne barely had a chance to recognize that the curtains the starlight shone through were lace before she tumbled into sleep.

The aroma of coffee roused Vivienne from her slumber. Her eyelids fluttered. Sunlight, harsh and cold, streamed through the curtains. She stared at the scalloped edges and the sunflowers woven through a hexagonal ground. For a moment, she was back in her Palais-Royal apartment above the lace shop she shared with Tante Rose. She closed her eyes and slid back in time to a showroom that frothed with Alençon and Chantilly. There was Tante Rose having tea with a patron, while Vienne arranged samples of lace on deep blue velvet pillows. Then Rose's hand went to her neck, and her fingers bled red.

No, it wasn't her fingers that were bleeding.

Vienne's eyes popped open, and she sat up, heart racing, chest heaving.

Henri awoke and looked at her. "It's all right," he said. "We're safe now."

She nodded. "Yes. Yes, of course."

Rising, Vienne went to the window to see what darkness had veiled last night. Fields silvered beneath winter's breath, and the river curving through them was a satin blue-sky ribbon. Gray wisps curled out of chimneys like fragile flags. Scanning for a chimney not yet smoking, she wondered which log home would be hers.

They had slept late, she realized. Too late to make a good impression. But perhaps late enough to find Armand at breakfast. Availing herself of the washstand, she scrubbed Henri's face and hands and performed her toilette as well as she could. Folding screens divided the room, and she used one for privacy as she changed into the freshest gown she had, which was still hopelessly rumpled and held the odor of the horse that had carried it. Henri changed his clothing, too, but his hair would not be tamed by brush or comb. Even without mirrors, she knew they'd done nothing to erase the evidence of their travels.

Downstairs, they followed the smell of coffee into the room Father Gilbert had pointed out the night before. Two women and a man were seated at the table, drinking coffee from their bowls and piling ham and yellow-hued biscuits onto their plates. Their hair was powdered white, and the women wore formal gowns of pastel silk.

"Ah," said one. "Newcomers." Her eyebrows were painted high on her forehead. "Children don't eat at this table."

Vivienne looked around and saw no other. "This one does." She placed her hand on Henri's back, and they sat.

Introductions were stiffly made. Born to nobility, the man was David du Page but likely preferred to be called "Count." His wife, Aurore, had been the first to speak, and their daughter, Zoe, sat between them.

"I didn't catch your title." Aurore blinked with false lashes, drawing attention to the beauty patch near her eye.

Vienne smiled. "No title. Just Vivienne Rivard. I was a lacemaker. For the queen," she added, though it was prideful to say so. "And more recently a baker."

"A tradeswoman. At table. With a child." Aurore wrinkled her nose with disdain.

Henri swung his legs beneath the table, moving his chair back and forth on the hardwood floor. Ignoring the glare coming from Aurore, Vienne gently placed her hand on his leg. "Be still," she whispered, but she understood his nervous habit. The Du Page family did not exactly set one at ease. Quietly, she sipped her coffee.

And nearly spit it out when Armand blustered in. Vienne brought her napkin to her lips and forced a swallow.

He paled. "Vienne," he breathed. Three powdered heads turned at the use of such a familiar name.

She smoothed her napkin over her lap. "Monsieur de Champlain."

"You two are . . . well acquainted?" Aurore asked.

Ignoring her, Armand seated himself across from Vivienne and poured his coffee. "Forgive me, I was not expecting to see you so soon. Certainly not until the spring, at least. However did you manage to find transport from Philadelphia?"

"Mr. Delaney brought us on horseback!" Henri offered. "Mademoiselle and I shared Cherie, and the Irishman had Beau all to himself."

Zoe's eyes rounded. "Mr. Delaney? I've seen him around the settlement, building houses and clearing trees. He seems quite . . . strong."

"And rough," her mother added. "How inappropriate. I do wonder why you couldn't have waited until spring to come in a larger convoy. It isn't as if you were in danger of fever at this time of year. But then, some women's virtue isn't worth guarding as much as others'." She dabbed the corners of her mouth with her napkin.

Anger surged through Vienne. "How efficient of you." She sipped her coffee, then peered over the rim of the bowl. "My drink is not yet cold, and yet you've already determined my character." And placed her in the same category as Sybille.

Count du Page buffed his fingernails against his waistcoat, then ran his thumb along their edge as he stood. "I believe we're done here. Come, *mes chères*."

They left the room.

Armand speared a slice of ham from a platter and dragged it

onto his plate. "You must ignore Aurore's cutting words. Everyone else has learned to do so, especially her husband. I can empathize. My own wife—" He stopped himself, shaking his head. "Forgive me. Now, let us begin again. You wouldn't be here if you hadn't changed your mind about my offer. Am I right?" He sliced his ham into small squares and ate.

"Yes." She sighed. "Sebastien told me you purchased two lots, and I must say, I am grateful for your foresight. I do have need of a home." The words sat bitterly on her tongue. Had Sybille said this to him as well, so many years ago? But this was different. "Philadelphia proved unsafe. Political passions still run high."

"I am rejoiced to hear you finally accept my help." He smiled and sipped his coffee. "My own house is right in the middle of the settlement. Yours is on the far side of it, which I hope will not inconvenience you too much. I thought, as I chose the lots, you'd prefer as much distance from me as you could get, although in a colony of this size, distance is a relative term. I took the liberty of inspecting the property, and I believe you'll be pleased with your accommodations. That is, if you bear in mind that this is the wilderness and not the rue Poissonnière."

Vivienne tried not to chafe at the mention of the street where Sybille had lived. "The ownership is in your name."

Henri tucked a bite of bread into his cheek, eyebrows knitting together. "I thought it was ours now. Isn't the house ours?"

"It was my money that bought it," Armand told him. To Vivienne, he lowered his voice. "I was under the impression you lacked sufficient funds. Or else you'd have bought a lot yourself."

Her lips pressed into a line. As much as she hated to be indebted to him, could she really ask for the deed to be transferred to her name? "While I live there, I expect you to respect our privacy. You will not enter the house without knocking, even though it belongs to you." Indeed, she hoped he would rarely visit at all.

"But of course, Vivienne. I'm not without manners and common courtesy. I'll take you to see it at once. Consider it a loan, if that suits you better."

After a moment's hesitation, she agreed. Even this arrangement was more than generous, and despite her efforts to push him away, Armand had been nothing but kind to her.

And she had no other options. Swallowing back her bitterness, she returned his tentative smile and thanked him.

Chapter Twenty-Four

Inside the barn, Liam stood a length of log on a chopping block, then brought his ax down through the middle. After he repeated the process on each half, he tossed the firewood into the wheelbarrow. Red looked on with large, limpid eyes, a welcome companion after months away. Liam was eager to visit Jethro, and he needed to explain to Talon how Beau and Cherie had reappeared in the stable last night, but first he wanted to get some firewood into the house, where it could do some good.

Wind whistled through the trees outside. It wrapped around the barn, slicing in through the door he'd left open to allow sunlight to guide his work. Even so, sweat filmed his skin as he chopped. His thoughts wandered to Vivienne and Henri. He hoped they would adapt to yet another new home in Asylum. He hoped they'd fall in love with the land, as he had, with appreciation for what it gave and respect for what it couldn't.

But surrounded by French aristocrats as they now were, he wondered if Vivienne would still insist on speaking English. She had been eager to embrace America. Would she remain so here, where the rest of the residents lived for the day they could return to France?

"Ach." He split another log, admitting to himself his real question: would she still choose the company of a recently disfigured Irishman when she was surrounded by genteel French?

He thought she might.

He hoped she would.

Red nickered. Resting his ax on the ground, Liam rubbed the horse along its jawline and reined in the hope that threatened to carry him where he wasn't ready to go. The last time he'd given his heart away, it had come back to him in shards.

Vivienne had needed him until this point, to bring her and Henri here. He would wait and see how things went, for Maggie had needed him, too. But she hadn't wanted him. There was a difference.

When Maggie had pressed Liam through letters to come home from war and marry her sooner than planned, he had longed for the day he could but asked Maggie to wait until his service was over. "I need you," she'd written. "I need you now, please, please come home to me." What she needed was a hasty wedding to hide the fact that she was with child. Whose child, Liam never knew, but it most certainly wasn't his. He couldn't decide which shocked him more upon learning the truth from Tara, that Maggie had married the British officer billeted in her home, or that the baby arrived five months later. They lived in England, last he'd heard, on a fine estate.

Maggie was a taker. She used people for what she could get from them. "Vienne is nothing like that," he muttered, rubbing Red between the eyes. Her dedication to Henri and her insistence on working proved it.

After a final pat to his horse, Liam took up his ax again and swung it through the next log with more strength than was required. The blade lodged deep into the block, and he left it there. Gathering up the rest of the wood from the hay-strewn floor, he tossed the pieces into the wheelbarrow and rolled it toward his house.

Inside the parlor, he built a fire in the hearth, then piled wood in the iron rack beside the fireplace. Next, he took the remaining pieces upstairs to his bedroom, where he washed his hands and face before heading back down the stairs.

Voices stayed him on the bottom tread. They were coming from the parlor.

With long strides, he marched into the room to find Vivienne, Henri, and Armand, all of whom appeared as surprised to see him as he was to see them. He scratched the stubble on his chin. "'Tis customary, in America, to knock when going calling. But I do welcome the visit. Right neighborly of you." He shook Armand's hand, thankful he'd swept the cobwebs and dust from his house that morning.

"I understand I have you to thank for bringing my—for bringing Vivienne and Henri from Philadelphia," Armand said. "I can't imagine the journey. I'm indebted."

Liam told him he was welcome. "If you'll stay for coffee, I'll make it."

Vienne pushed her hood back and unwound her muffler, folding it over one arm. The winsome flush in her cheeks might have been from the cold, Liam told himself. Or the fire. A curl brushed her neck as she regarded him. "Have you been here all morning, chopping wood and stocking it? For us?"

Armand frowned.

So did Liam. "Well, it was for me, really. Your coming this morning is a surprise."

"But how did you know?" she pressed.

"I didn't know." Liam crossed his arms, then stuffed his hands in his pockets instead, confusion furrowing his brow. Was she not listening? "I just told you, I didn't know you were coming."

Henri looked all around the room, then scampered into the hall and back. "This is our house now? Our very own?"

Oh. Oh no. "What's that? You don't think—"

"You said you may have built my house, but I didn't think you'd also chop the firewood for me," Vivienne said. "Thank you, Liam, but are you not anxious to tend your own home now that—"

Liam held up his hand. "There's been a mistake."

"I should say so." Armand cleared his throat and stared at Liam.

"Vivienne, this is not your home. It's mine." He watched the color leach from her face.

She spun toward Armand, then back to Liam. "How can this be?" She spread a map upon the table, and Armand pointed to a lot circled in gray ink. Liam's lot. "There. You see?"

"If it's my word against a circle of ink, I think I win." Liam fought to gentle his tone. But this was his house, his land. His dream.

"Armand, this is Liam's property." Vienne's voice was stronger than it had been in days. "I will not take it from him. We'll find another lot instead. Henri, come."

Wide-eyed, the boy took her hand.

"I will handle this, Vivienne." Armand puffed out his chest. "Young man, I purchased this lot from the Asylum Company via Senator Robert Morris in Philadelphia. I don't believe you mean any harm. Clearly, we have a misunderstanding, but one I hope we can resolve straightaway. The fact is, you're trespassing."

"Trespassing!" Liam's mind whirred. "They've sold you the wrong property. As you see, this one's taken. I really was building my own fire here." The flames popped and snapped. He no longer needed coffee to keep him awake.

"If anyone's mistaken, my dear fellow, it's you." Armand drew a deed from his cloak pocket and showed it to him.

Quickly, Liam parsed it, a groove forming on his brow. That was his lot identified on the paper. "A clerical error. The sooner we set it to rights, the better."

White-faced, Vienne agreed. "Liam," she whispered through colorless lips. "I had no idea. This wasn't my plan at all."

Armand glanced at her and Henri. "Monsieur Talon is already expecting an interview with the new colonists."

And more than likely, he was already furious with Liam.

While Henri played in the dauphin's room upstairs, Vivienne stood in Monsieur Talon's office below, nerves buzzing. The adjoining music room was silent at this time of day, and the quiet between Liam and Armand was thick with tension.

Talon sat behind his desk, face drawn, the two deeds laid before him. She had never met Talon before, but she knew he'd been head of the king's secret police—when there was a king. He'd managed an impressive network of operatives and guards when the stakes were entire kingdoms. As she stood before him with a claim that paled in significance, she wondered if he was bored to delirium. Or if he realized that she belonged neither to France nor to America, and that a home of her own was *her* kingdom.

Just as it was Liam's. He tapped his hat against his leg, obviously as impatient as she was to hear the verdict.

"Mr. Delaney. I wondered if I'd see you today, since I was surprised to see my horses returned to my stable at last. Do explain to me, please, why you saw fit to keep my property from me all this time."

With an economy of words, Liam explained the circumstances. His tone was even and calm.

Talon's face was stone. "The other mail carrier quit because of a wages and property disagreement. And now here *you* are with another one. These land disputes are so tedious." Talon drummed his fingers over the deeds. His hair was powdered, his fine coat pressed and brushed, and his office windowless, so that even during the day, candlesticks defended against the dark.

"Monsieur Talon," Armand began, "Senator Morris assured me everything was in order when I purchased my two lots, including the one Mr. Delaney says is his. I have no quarrel with Mr. Delaney personally and believe him to be an upright man. But obviously we cannot both own the land."

With the leisure of one accustomed to others hanging on his words, Talon did not respond right away. At length he said, "One of these claims is invalid."

Vienne's mouth went dry as starched cloth. She shifted her weight, fingering the lace at her sleeves.

"Mr. Delaney, you purchased the land from whom?"

Liam supplied a name, unfamiliar to her.

"A Connecticut man," Talon verified.

"Yes. But I don't see what difference that makes."

"A great deal," the manager declared. "It makes a great deal of difference when that Connecticut man had no right to sell you this land to begin with. The Asylum Company owns that land."

Liam's smile was thin and tight. "No, monsieur. I do."

"Under false pretenses. See here, look at these dates." Talon pointed to the two leaves of paper, and Liam bent over them. "Our claim to that land precedes yours. The land belongs to Armand de Champlain."

Armand exhaled. Vivienne sucked in a sharp breath.

"I protest. I dispute," Liam sputtered, his face darkening to a furious shade of red. "I've cleared my land, planted crops. I built my home—and half the houses in Asylum, by the way. And now you're saying it isn't mine?"

"Correct. It isn't your land, and none of the improvements you've made to it can be claimed by you, either. According to de Champlain's deed, he owns it all. The house, the outbuildings, the crops, the livestock. You have nothing, Mr. Delaney, unless you purchase it directly from him."

Vienne could scarcely breathe. "There must be a different lot we could take in exchange," she said. "Leave Mr. Delaney's to him, for I refuse to evict him so Henri and I can move in."

Talon made a short, scuffing noise against his teeth. "Utter nonsense. Mr. Delaney has no lot. He is a squatter. Monsieur de Champlain, if you wish to void the purchase, the property reverts back to the Asylum Company, and we'll sell it to someone else. If you wish to sell the property yourself, you may do so, but you cannot just let him have it."

"Ma chère," Armand inserted, the endearment raking her nerves, "if the Irishman has done all that work to the lot, it sounds like you could not do better for yourself than to simply move in."

"To be sure." Liam's tone was ice cold. "'Tis so convenient. For you. I was just hopin' and prayin' that all my labors could benefit someone else so I could be landless again."

263

"This isn't what I wanted," Vienne whispered.

"But you'll still take it, won't you?" A muscle bunched in Liam's jaw.

"It's not up to her," Armand interjected.

"I've made my decision." Talon waved his hand dismissively. It was over.

Vienne swept out of the office and into the sunlit music room. Mercifully, it was empty, save for the pianoforte and some chairs lining the walls. From within a gilt frame, a shepherdess in a flowing white dress looked down upon them. "We need to talk." She pressed the ache behind her temple, then dropped her hand to her side. "All of us."

"What is there to discuss?" Armand folded his deed and tucked it into his coat pocket. "It's done."

Liam cast a sidelong look at her, nostrils flaring. A vein throbbed on his forehead, visible anger that complemented his scars too well. But behind his fierceness, Vienne knew he hid fresh wounds. *"I needed to sink my roots deep into a place of my own,"* he had told her once. *"Sounds strange to you, maybe, but my land and I take care of each other."*

Her fingernails bit into her palms. "I tell you, I refuse to take Liam's home from him. I won't do it." Not after everything Liam had done for her and Henri. Not after all he'd become to her.

Armand wiped a hand over his face. "I regret it has come to this. But did you not understand what Monsieur Talon said? If you truly refuse, Mr. Delaney still won't keep his land. I would have to sell it so I can buy you another lot, and he would lose it to someone else."

Vivienne's stomach rebelled at the truth. She put her hand to her middle as her mind whirred, searching for some kind of solution. At least if she lived there, she could work to make sure it was returned to him.

"Please listen." She drew a steadying breath and smoothed her skirt before clasping her trembling hands. "If it must be this way, then I need Liam."

Both men raised their eyebrows. Good. At least they were paying attention.

"I'm a single woman with a child, and suddenly I'm tasked with not only managing a home but managing fields, as well. I know lace and bread, not farming. And I know nothing of life in the wilderness."

Armand frowned. "You have a house now. I thought you'd be happy."

"I'm grateful for the roof over our heads, though I hate how this has turned out. But I see no reason to let Liam's cultivation go to waste because of my ignorance. I've no intention of any such negligence. Armand, when you sell the grounds again—for you've already confessed yourself a sojourner—you want them to be increased in value, don't you? Then don't let the wilderness reclaim what Liam has worked so hard to wrest from its grip."

Liam's gaze pierced hers, but his face was a mask she could not read.

"Everything that pleases you about the lot you purchased for my use," she continued, "that's all the fruit of his labor. He knows that land better than anyone. Hire him to maintain it and improve it further. That land can yield a profit, Armand, but neither you nor I can bring it forth."

Armand crossed his arms and rocked back on his heels. He was at least fifty years old and too soft to drive a plow himself. "I suppose I could rent the land back to you."

"I paid for that land already," Liam growled. "I'll not pay you again to be toiling at it."

"Not for cash," Vienne jumped in. "No yearly rental, Armand. Let him work the land and give you a portion of the crops. Crops that otherwise we wouldn't see at all."

Liam stalked away, tugging at the tie in his neckcloth, but did not leave the room.

"What does the land yield?" Armand asked.

Muttering beneath his breath, Liam paced back toward them.

"Flax and rye. Corn. Maple sugar. Molasses and vinegar, tar and potash for them that know how to make it."

It did not take long for Armand to see reason. "I've no time for such things. Let us draw up the terms."

"To give you more of what's mine, you mean." Liam fumed.

But Vivienne saw past his bluster. He would not let go of the land he loved. And if she had any influence at all over the situation, she would not let Liam lose his dream.

Chapter Twenty-Five

"I've already told you all I know: they aren't here, they've sent no word, and as far as I can tell, they're not coming back!" Done repeating herself by now, Paulette slammed the front door of the Pension Sainte-Marie on a very upset Sebastien Lemoine.

"Who was that, dear?" Madame Barouche bustled into the room, eyes like an owl. "I hope you haven't turned away good business? We still have one room to let."

Sunlight poured into the cold parlor. Paulette moved to the fireplace and knelt to stoke it. "Monsieur Lemoine, madame. Looking for Vivienne and Henri." A log collapsed, and she added another with iron tongs before replacing the grate. Standing, she brushed off her apron.

Madame's eyebrows rose. "Ah. Yes." Her silver curls quivered as she shook her head, and her blue-veined hands flitted over her beribboned bodice. "Well, their sudden departure was a shock to all of us. I wonder . . ." Then she clipped her thin lips shut. "Listen."

Paulette inclined her ear toward the door. On the other side, two male voices thrust and parried. Moments later, a pair of footsteps receded, and a hard rap shook the parlor door.

Madame folded her hands before her waist, waiting while Paulette straightened her cap and answered the knock.

"Yes?" Paulette eyed the visitor through a five-inch gap between the door and its frame. Snow swirled outside in big feathery flakes, making the street look like a chicken coop right after a fox came through it.

"Let him in!" Madame urged.

Grudgingly, Paulette swung wide the door, and the tall man filled its frame as he entered.

He swiped a red wool cap from his bald head and crushed it in his hand. The other arm, bent at the elbow, he held against his middle. Half-moon bruises rested in the canals beneath his eyes, framing his crooked nose. "Was that man bothering you?" he asked.

"Not much." Paulette grunted. "I should ask who's been bothering you. Broken nose? Dislocated shoulder?" She squinted at a faint scratch on his cheek.

Madame clucked her tongue, a chastisement for saying too much. At least, from the older woman's point of view. But Paulette was tired of always being the one answering the questions. Couldn't she ask a few herself? After all, this man was in her territory now. She crossed her arms over her apron.

His grin was broad and thin. "Good eye. I wonder what else you've seen."

"Pardon me." Madame Barouche glided forward, hand outstretched. "I am Madame Ernestine Barouche, the proprietress. Are you in need of a room, monsieur?"

Taking her delicate hand, he gave a slight bow. "I am Corbin Fraser. And I *am* looking for a room, in fact. My friend, Vivienne Rivard, said this was the best place in the French Quarter."

Madame brightened. "Did she now? Well, we certainly enjoyed having her here."

Snowflakes melted on his shoulders. "No longer here, then." Small puddles the color of dishwater spread from his boots. "Did she leave a forwarding address? I have a letter to send."

At this, Paulette threw up her hands. "Then you'll be just as disappointed as her other caller."

"We all miss her," Madame admitted. "Her and Henri both." Corbin's wide lips spread in what might have been a smile. "I'll bet she misses you, too. She'll come back to visit, I wager. Or at least send word by mail."

Madame sniffed. "Yes. Well. Paulette, why don't you show him the room and explain the terms? If all is satisfactory, we'll draw up the contract."

"Yes, madame." Paulette bobbed in a curtsy, then bade Corbin to follow her up the stairs. "You're in luck." She ushered him inside Vivienne's old room and hoped the garret's slanted ceiling would not bother him. He was a good bit taller than its previous tenants. "It opened up last week."

"Whose room was it? Was it theirs?" He inspected it, opening drawers, looking out the window, running his hand over the green toile counterpane. Like he was looking for something.

Her eyes narrowed as she regarded him. "Would it matter if it was?" The small space still smelled faintly of Vivienne's rose water.

Corbin shrugged. "Call me sentimental."

An admirer, then, though he didn't seem Vivienne's type. Strange, though, that Paulette had never seen him before. Perhaps he was a patron of the tavern who had fallen in love with her bread. In any case, she explained the terms of lodging, and he agreed.

"You'll tell me as soon as you hear from her, won't you? I'd really like to send my letter." His lips stretched in that frog-like smile again, and Paulette's eye fell on his lapel. Beneath a dusting of snow, a tricolor cockade showed through. She glanced at his hat again. The *bonnet rouge*.

She screwed her mouth to one side, considering. "I'll tell you right now, Madame Barouche is a royalist. If you hadn't already guessed." They'd never had pro-revolutionaries stay here before. "She's old and set in her ways, and if you don't mind my saying so, her views aren't doing anyone harm. I don't want trouble. Is this going to be a problem for you?" She eyed his injuries afresh.

"I don't have a problem with your madame, as long as you don't have a problem with me. You and I are going to get along fine, aren't we, citizeness? Unless it's you who causes trouble for me."

Heat washed over her face. "I'm just a maid." She gritted her teeth.

"Clever girl." He laughed. "Be more."

ASYLUM, PENNSYLVANIA

It was dusk before Liam could bring himself to knock on Jethro's door, hat in one hand. Dread and guilt cinched his middle.

Light flickered around the edges of the door. It opened, and Jethro filled the frame with a build more muscular than Liam remembered. "Well!" His dark brown eyes went immediately to the notch taken out of Liam's ear. The ragged scar on his cheek. "How does the other guy look?"

A smile curled Liam's lips. "You know, I didn't have a chance to find out."

One eyebrow raised, Jethro beckoned Liam inside. "Coffee's hot."

Liam slipped inside the kitchen house and shut the door against the cold. Hanging his hat and cloak on a peg on the wall, he rubbed his hand over his face and sat at the table, listening to the fire. So much had happened since he'd last been here, none of it pleasant.

Jethro reached for a cup and the kettle of coffee.

Holding up his hand, Liam shook his head. "Not thirsty."

After topping off his own mug, Jethro sat across from him. "You want to start by explaining your face?"

Liam chuckled, then gave him the scaffolding of events. He wasn't proud of any of it, and it stung to confess his ineptitude. "They got Finn," he added at the end. "I saw him, and I couldn't do a thing about it." It sounded more and more like an excuse, rather than an explanation.

"Tara knows?"

"I told her." He blew out a sigh. "You can imagine how that went."

Jethro whistled low. "Where is he now, do you expect?"

"On his way to Philadelphia, under guard." Suddenly, Liam was very, very tired of this story. Weary of the shame it brought for his own inaction, for Alex, and for the government he and Jethro had both fought to establish. Besides, his other news pressed on his chest.

He stalled, extracting from Jethro every update, which didn't take nearly long enough. Jethro had traded some labor for chickens, and one of them had pecked another to death. But the hens were laying, and Jethro had gotten pretty good at cooking eggs. Food stores for winter seemed to be on the thin side, so they'd have to ration carefully and plan to take meals at the inn.

Reluctantly, Liam took the plunge. "Well. I had a bad day."

Lines carved Jethro's brow. "You did?"

He winced. "And so did you." Piece by excruciating piece, he regaled to Jethro the events and people that had dispossessed him of his property, and the new arrangement that allowed them both to stay.

Jethro's face set in hard lines. A log crumbled behind the grate, releasing a spray of sparks. "Mr. Liam. I left a decent job because I trusted you. You said I'd be investing in my future, and I believed you. I been clearing land and building with the understanding that this is for a family of my own someday, God willing. I don't mind working hard with little return for a while. But now you're telling me that the land you promised would be mine isn't yours to give. Is that right?"

"I wish it weren't."

"But is it?"

Liam swiped his hand over his hair. "Hang it all. That's what Talon says." This felt like confession. Tara, Finn, Jethro—he'd disappointed all of them in the ways that hurt the most. All he did was fail people. "Listen. You can stay in this house, or you can return to Philadelphia with me on my next mail run. I'm sure Tara would have a job for you."

"Empty-handed? After all this time away?" His voice filled every corner of the room.

Guilt raked through Liam. "I'll give you what I can to put rent money in your pocket. But I'm going to work this land. I'll give Armand de Champlain a share of the crops, but the rest I keep. The Frenchman is going to leave eventually. I'm staying here for the long haul."

Jethro left the table and knelt at the fire, stoking its embers. He stayed there, staring at the flames, for an uncomfortably long time. "When you say you're staying here, you mean *right* here, don't you? Here in *this* house." He stood, towering over Liam.

Kneading a sore muscle in his shoulder, Liam stood as well. "I can't stay in mine while Vivienne and Henri are there, now, can I?"

Jethro cast his gaze heavenward and shook his head. "A house of my own, he said, Lord. A house of my very own."

With a sheepish smile, Liam extended his hand. "What do you say? Roommates?"

Vivienne and Henri stayed at the Grand Maison, giving Liam time to move his personal belongings out of the house. Armand had also paid him to construct two new bedframes and a bureau for their clothes. Using what little funds Vienne had left, she purchased bed linens and towels from the weaver and tailor's shop. The joy of preparing for a new home was dampened by the knowledge that it wasn't truly hers. For ousting Liam, she felt like a usurper. For living in a house Armand owned, she felt like a bird in a cage—and a hypocrite, for accepting an arrangement that resembled Sybille's.

During Vienne's residence at the Grand Maison, a feast day for one of the saints gave the colonists reason to gather together. She dressed in a gown that had belonged to Martine and entered the dining hall with Henri.

The long table was filled on both sides with men and women in formal attire suitable for the court at Versailles. The overpowering smell was not of food, but of powder, pomade, and perfume. With her own black curls pinned up but unpowdered, Vienne felt like the black sheep among a flock of white.

The men's embroidered silk suits rivaled the women's gowns in their finery and sported no less lace. Ostrich-feather fans rested on the table beside blue-and-white French china.

Struck by the contrast with the wilderness outside, Vienne took her seat beside Henri. Armand was at the far end of the table, and she was glad of it, though she knew he hadn't known the land he purchased for her was Liam's. Setting those thoughts aside, she caught Father Gilbert's eye and smiled. Next to him, Suzanne Arquette stared at Vienne with vacant gray eyes, void of recognition.

The woman across from her introduced herself and her husband as Evelyne and Philippe Sando. "We were silk merchants in Lyons." Before the revolutionaries burned all the silk factories down, Vienne understood. But such unpleasantness was not spoken at this table. The Sandos looked to be of middling years, but ages were so hard to guess among those who had known terror.

Vienne introduced herself and Henri.

"Another artisan." Evelyne's tone was warm. "You are very welcome to Asylum, the both of you. It was beginning to get rather stuffy in here, if you catch my meaning." She flicked a glance down the line of aristocrats, then smiled conspiratorially at Vienne, who liked her immediately.

"Henri." Philippe leaned forward to speak across the table to him. "There aren't many children here now to play with, but that will change soon enough."

The boy's legs stopped swinging. "What do you mean?"

"Haven't you heard? This was meant to be the queen's house, but it will yet shelter her son. You must have known Louis-Charles, yes?"

Henri paled slightly. "He was my best friend."

Along the table, several powdered heads turned in their direction. Forks suspended over plates and cups stalled in the air as their owners stared at Henri. Did he embody for them the hope

273

of seeing the child king? Or did some secretly believe they were looking at him already?

"What news do you have?" Vienne asked in a hushed tone out of habit, for surely there was no danger to them here.

"There are plans," Evelyne offered cagily. "And won't Louis-Charles be so pleased to find he already has a friend here, waiting for him! He will be missing his parents and sister. But you will be a most welcome companion to him, I'm sure."

Henri looked at Vienne with such confusion in his eyes. His bottom lip pulled in. "He is coming? From the prison?" What she heard was, *Dare I hope?*

Compassion made her swallow the reasonable answer that sprang to her lips. Was there any harm in hope? "We must pray for him," she said at length, and the Sandos agreed. "We will pray for Louis-Charles and for those who plan his escape." She touched Henri's knee, and he tucked his hand inside hers.

The rest of the meal passed with gentler talk of Mozart and fashion, Rousseau and Crusoe, while they sipped squirrel soup and nibbled dry bread made from corn. Afterward, they all gathered in the music room.

Madame Aurore du Page seated herself at the pianoforte, and her daughter, Zoe, stood beside her to sing an aria from Grétry's *Richard the Lionheart.*

> O my king!
> The Universe abandons you!
> On earth, it is only me
> Who is interested in you!
> Alone in the universe
> I would break the chains
> when everyone else deserted you!

The royalist anthem brought several in the room to tears. For all their finery, Vienne mused, they were lost in the wilderness, mourning a world that no longer existed. A world that might never be again.

Henri tugged on her hand, and she sat on a plush sofa, patting the blue velvet beside her.

He sat, as well. "I'm going to be very good from now on." His small face was solemn and grave. "I will always obey you, and I won't lie or complain, or run away."

Vienne studied him for a moment before responding. "I'm happy to hear that. What made you decide on this?"

"I promised God that I would be the very best I could if He will only bring Louis-Charles back." With his little finger, he traced a line in the sofa's carved frame. "I might be his only friend left. If he feels bad, the way I feel bad in my stomach, I will stay with him so he doesn't have to be scared anymore. Like you've been staying with me. He will come back, won't he?" He dropped his hand back to his lap and looked at her, so earnestly. In a whisper, he added, "Do you think God heard my prayer?"

Throat aching, she wrapped her arm around his slender shoulders and squeezed. Hot tears slipped from her eyes. The rest of Asylum longed for a king, but Henri just wanted his friend to be safe from harm. "Yes, mon cher, God heard your prayer. I think He is pleased that you want to care for your friend. But if—if you don't get the chance, that doesn't mean God is punishing you for not being good enough. I don't think He works like that."

Henri pulled back to look at her and brushed his own tears from his face. "Then how does He work, Mademoiselle?"

She offered a tremulous smile. "In ways I don't understand myself. But He hears you. If nothing else, trust that He hears when you pray."

He frowned for a moment before responding. "I'd prefer it if He also agrees with me."

A chuckle escaped Vienne as she hugged him one more time.

"Mr. Delaney!" Henri cried and bounded from the sofa.

She rose to face Liam, and uncertainty pulsed beneath her skin. If he despised her, she'd understand why. But how bereft she felt at the thought.

Liam rested his hand on Henri's shoulder, his brow creasing

as she swept a rogue tear from her cheek. "I'm interrupting." He removed his hat.

"No, it's fine." Beyond that, small talk failed her. "I'm sorry." Two small words, when what she longed for was an hour of conversation with which to reconcile.

"You and I both." He scanned the room. His face was freshly shaven, his queue tidy. The faint scent of balsam surrounded him.

Conversations broke off. Behind fluttering fans, women peered at them, eyebrows arching. She could only imagine the gossip that would come of this.

Henri turned to Liam. "Is it ready for us? Is our new house ready?"

A sigh blew over Liam's lips. "'Tis indeed. Can we talk?" He gestured toward the hall, and she followed him out of the room, Henri in tow.

Away from the candlelight, shadows threw them into an unintended intimacy. The fire raging behind his eyes the last time she'd seen him had dimmed to a smolder, but the intensity in his gaze still held her captive. "Are you ready to move in? Or do you want to stay one more night with your friends here?"

"I'd hardly call them friends." Aside from the Sandos and Father Gilbert, as a whole, they seemed to disdain her as a tradesperson far below their rank. "But yes, I'm ready."

"Boxes packed?"

"It won't take long. We don't have much, as you recall."

"I'll do it!" Henri took off running for the stairs.

"I should help him," she said.

"I'll wait." The resignation in his tone unsettled her. Turning from her, he lowered himself to a chair in the hall and stretched one leg out as he crossed his arms. She'd never seen him so subdued. Defeated. She hated that she'd had a role in that.

Moments later, she and Henri carried their meager belongings down the stairs, where Liam took Vienne's from her. Henri insisted his burden was light.

The walk to Liam's house wasn't long, but it was cold, as usual, and dark. Though the feast had begun at four o'clock, the sun had set before they'd been at table even three quarters of an hour. Silver moonlight reflected on patches of ice as they traveled away from the river and past the few rows of log houses. On the far side of them, unsettled lots provided a buffer between Liam's house and the rest of Asylum, a distance she was sure the Irishman appreciated. Pearl gray smoke lifted from its chimney, and the glazed windows glowed amber from the firelight inside.

As they approached, Liam pointed to the outbuildings. The springhouse, the cookhouse, the dining house, the barn, the woodshed, the privy. "I stocked the woodshed, so you should have enough to keep you for a while." Arms full of her bundles, he went to the main house door, and she opened it.

Henri grunted as he dropped his burdens on the table. "That wasn't heavy at all."

She raised an eyebrow.

"I mean, I thought it would be heavier than that."

The tour Liam gave them was brief and terse. The house was sparsely furnished, simply because he hadn't had the use for or the time to make more. While the Grand Maison held only imported goods, everything here was handmade. The table and chairs, the beds and bureau upstairs.

"Thank you." She stood in the parlor before the fire he'd built for her warmth. "I never meant—I never thought the house—" Fumbling for words, she removed her cloak and folded it over her arm. She could not bring herself to hang it on the peg where his coat and hat should be. "I hate this situation as much as you do."

He rubbed his chin. "Really? As much as I do?"

"I'd love nothing more than for you to buy this place back from Armand as soon as you can."

Light and shadow chased over his features, betraying the struggle within. "I'm leaving Asylum. For Philadelphia."

Vienne's mouth went dry. "Will you come back?" She pushed a lock of hair from the side of her face.

Liam glanced to the fire and held his hand toward the flames. "You know I can't stay away." He looked at her again, the fight gone from his eyes. "The mail rider due to go next is too ill to travel. I'm going in his place."

A familiar clatter in the hallway told her that Henri had set up his ninepins already. She pressed her fingertips to her temples.

"I don't know how long I'll be gone," Liam continued. "It depends on the weather. Your nearest neighbor is Jethro Fortune, a free black man who used to be Tara's barkeep at the Four Winds. His house is half a mile that way." He pointed. "I asked him to check in on you. If you need anything from him, be sure Armand will pay him a fair wage for the work first. I'll not have him treated like a slave, you understand."

"Of course."

"Is there anything you require of me before I go?"

She shook her head, dismayed at the transactional nature of the question, for now he would be paid by Armand for any service rendered. "Liam," she whispered, "have a cup of tea first? The hour is not yet late."

"'Tis too late for that. I go early in the morn."

"You're leaving?" Henri burst in from the hall, piercing the tension in the room.

Liam bent on one knee. "I am. You'll be the man of the house now. Will you take good care of it? And be good for Mademoiselle?"

Henri responded with vigorous nodding. "I promise. I was already planning on it."

Tousling the boy's hair, Liam stood. With one last glance at Vienne, he said, "Welcome home," and then walked out of his house.

Chapter Twenty-Six

After he'd completed the mail exchange and they'd attended the service at Christ Church, Liam and Tara shared the holiday feast that had been served to Four Winds diners an hour ago: roast goose and baked ham, boiled potatoes, roasted parsnips, brussels sprouts, cabbage, and a Christmas plum pudding half drowned in whiskey. Of course.

"Vivienne and Henri are settled in a house, then?" Tara asked between spoonfuls of pudding.

"That they are." But he wasn't up to telling her which one. Not yet.

"You do realize you've now stolen both my barkeep and my baker, don't you? I should stay mad a little longer for that, but I can't. You did the right thing, whisking her and Henri out of here the way you did. It's a shame it had to happen, though. She's a hard worker and a giving soul. We miss her around here. I like her, Liam. I'll bet she wasn't even scandalized by your unchaperoned journey. Sensible to the needs of the moment, she is. A woman like that won't come twice." Tara paused to take a bite. "Wait a minute. I forgot about me. I guess a woman like that *does* come twice! Maybe just not three times, eh?" Laughing, she slapped the table.

Begrudgingly, he chuckled with her. Swirling a brussels sprout through melted butter on his plate, he recalled Vivienne with Henri in the Grand Maison's music room, surrounded by upturned noses. She didn't fit in with that lot. He should have had that cup of tea with her before leaving. There were things he needed to say, that she likely needed to hear. Setting down his fork, he took a drink of coffee and looked out the window, wondering if she'd had need of Jethro yet.

The glass panes rattled in their casings. Cannons boomed, and plates and cutlery jangled on the board. A rumbling crescendoed into the full-blown shouts and cheers of an approaching mob. On Christmas Day.

Was the city mad?

"Stay here," he told his sister, who pretended not to hear him. Without grabbing a cloak, he rushed into the damp chill outside and ran to the corner of Market Street. Up and down the block, people spilled from doorways and teemed on the sidewalks. The crowd pressed toward him.

"What's this all about?" he shouted over the roar of the masses. Wind pulled strands of hair from his queue.

"Didn't you hear? It's a Christmas gift for President Washington!" a woman said.

"Of what sort?" Liam asked.

"It's the whiskey rebels! Brought to justice at last!"

"Where?" Wild-eyed, Tara spun around, her wool dress a blur of blue and green.

Liam caught her hand before she bolted in any direction she took a fancy to. Up the road, people were turning, pointing, shouting in a fever pitch. Then he saw the glint of sun on silver. The drawn swords of mounted soldiers. Church bells pealed madly, not for the coming of the Messiah and peace on earth, but for the returning of the army from the West.

Looping his arm through Tara's, he held her tight and pushed their way to the edge of the sidewalk. Cheering drowned out the hoofbeats of the approaching guards. Between redbrick buildings, their snow-dusted blue uniforms were a surreal tribute to America's patriotic colors.

Liam craned his neck. Twenty prisoners walked between two lines of horses. Most were barefoot. All were gaunt and in rags after their journey over the mountains, and they wore white paper badges pinned to their hats. Around their necks hung wooden boards the size of schoolroom slates, with the words *whiskey rebel* scrawled on them in white paint. Their heads were bowed as they put one foot before the other. All heads but one.

"Finn!" Waving frantically, Tara lunged into the street, but Liam pulled her back as a soldier swung his sword in her direction.

"Stay back!" the guard shouted.

Liam held her fast, but his gaze followed his one-eyed cousin. Despite whatever kind soul had given him a replacement eyepatch along the way, twenty pounds had melted from his frame since Mingo Creek. He was a walking wisp of a man.

Finn locked eyes with him as he shuffled on bandaged feet. "Liam!" he bellowed. "I paid the tax!"

The words stunned him. Perhaps he'd misheard. He angled his good ear toward the prisoners. "You paid it?"

"Aye! And they're throwing me in jail just the same."

"Soldier!" Liam shouted. "Is that right?" He elbowed his way through the edge of the crowd, keeping pace with the motley parade. "You're taking them to jail, then?"

"What else?" the guard sneered.

"On what charges? What are the charges?" But Liam's question went unanswered.

"They won't say, Liam! I lost everything," Finn yelled hoarsely. "It's all gone."

"Enough from you!" The guard brought the tip of his sword to Finn's concave chest.

Liam felt that metal point over his heart as surely as if it had touched him instead. Tara's voice sounded far away as she hurled insults at the guards. Fury consumed him, a combustion of anger and frustration and sorrow.

"Liam!" Tara shouted in his ear, the one torn apart by a bullet. "*Do* something!"

He didn't need to be told. Hang Alexander Hamilton and the Watermelon Army. Hang the excise tax and this farcical show of strong government. If they weren't playing by their own rules anymore, neither would Liam.

After squeezing his sister's hand, he disappeared into the throng. He dashed back to the tavern, slipping on slush and mud, and shouted to the stableboy to ready Cherie. Energy thrumming through his veins, he ducked inside, took the stairs two at a time, and snatched his cloak and satchel. Clapping his hat on his head, he left just as quickly.

In the yard, he pressed extra coins into the stableboy's hand and mounted Cherie. The jail was only a few blocks away. He could get there before the prisoners arrived. Having no plan to guide him, he acted only on instinct—and rage. He had no weapon, save his hands. No authority beyond his gut. But this time, he would not stand idly by.

Heart hammering, he dismounted in an alley near the jail and looped the reins over the horse's neck. Even from here, the prison stench of illness and rot stung his nose. Quietly, he sidled closer to the stone building, halting when he heard an officer say to another, "Remember, they are to get no food and no light once they're inside. We're to break them before they even go to trial."

"If they ask about charges?"

"We don't know the charges, exactly, either. Not that it would matter—the judges will be under strict orders to convict."

Liam's senses stood at attention as the mounted soldiers escorted their prisoners near. With one quick glance at Cherie to make sure she was waiting in place, he peered around the corner again. The arrested men weren't even chained together. Did they really assume they were all resigned to their fate? He saw Finn and gave a whistle that mimicked birdsong.

Finn caught it and found him waiting in the shadows. Liam gestured with his thumb over his shoulder, and Finn's eye lit with steely resolve. Beyond that, he made no sign he understood.

In the jail yard, the soldiers sheathed their swords, trading them for muskets instead as they readied for the ceremonial transfer of prisoners to the local jail. After dismounting, they all stared straight ahead while the officer on the steps before the door read to them from an official-looking paper.

Liam remained in the shadows, every nerve and muscle pulled taut, trusting Finn to make his move. When the call came to "ground arms," every musket butt hit the ground at once—and with perfect timing, Finn took that split second to break formation. Darting between the surprised soldiers, he wielded the board from his neck, cracking it over the soldier quickest to attempt shouldering his weapon. The wood splintered over the soldier's head, and he dropped to the ground among the shards.

Finn sprinted toward Liam, who shot out his hand and grabbed his elbow, jerking him around the corner. He shoved his cousin toward Cherie. "Get on!"

Pulse roaring in his ears, Liam mounted as well, Finn behind him, then dug his heels into the animal's flanks. He looked over his shoulder in time to see two guards round the corner, then kneel to fire. Two oblivious little boys ran out in front of them, waving wooden swords, and the soldiers lowered their weapons.

Liam faced front and urged Cherie to continue her gallop. Navigating through alleys and back streets, they eventually turned the horse back into the thousands that had gathered on the streets. Finn ripped the white slip of paper from his hat, releasing it to the wind.

"Clear the way!" Liam shouted. Cherie thundered over the cobbles, carving a path through people and around corners, until the streets narrowed into lanes of frozen mud. He didn't look back.

"Where are we going?" Finn was winded already, a shell of the man he'd once been.

Setting his jaw, Liam trained a wary eye on a full-bellied sky that threatened snow. But his course was set. "Where do you think?"

ASYLUM, PENNSYLVANIA
DECEMBER 27, 1794

Fog hung low over Asylum, curling around Red's knees and twining through the wheel spokes of the wagon. Pulling her cloak and skirts clear of the axle, Vivienne climbed up and sat on the bench beside Henri and Jethro, who had waited for her outside the inn.

"Success?" Jethro clucked to Red, and the wheels rolled forward through the mist.

Vivienne put her arm around Henri. "I can bake at home and deliver the food to the inn in batches. With only sixteen families in the settlement, they won't have as much need as the Four Winds Tavern, of course, but it's employment nonetheless and allows me to be with Henri more. There isn't much cash in circulation here, but he'll add credit to my account at the general store—or the tailor's or the blacksmith's, wherever I need to shop. I'd call that a success." She pressed Henri against her side before releasing him.

"That's good news, mighty good news indeed." Jethro glanced at her. "All God's children need something to do. Especially to help get us through the winter."

"And that's what we're doing now, right, Mr. Fortune?" Henri asked. "Helping folks get through the winter?"

Jethro steered Red onto one of the streets that ran parallel to the river. Neat houses of squared logs flanked either side. "Only a few deliveries today, and they'll be quick," he explained, voice as muffled behind his scarf as Red's hoofbeats. "I just load the firewood into their woodsheds. No need to chat at each stop."

"Have they paid you yet?" Vivienne could only guess how many hours of labor were represented by the bundles of chopped wood, bound with twine, nestled in the wagon behind her.

"Oh yes." Jethro smiled dryly. "Learned fast that if I don't get payment up front, I may not see it at all. Seems some of these French from Saint-Domingue are used to having colored folks do their work for free. Some of them even brought their own slaves with them. Have you seen the shanties down by the river? Their owners call them servants, but they're slaves all right, and that's where they live, God help them." He shook his head. "Those days are over for me. Yessir."

"'Yessir'?" Henri repeated. "What does that mean?"

Laughing, Jethro pulled his wool cap down over his ears. "Yes sir," he enunciated. "Say it fast, 'yessir.' In this case, it means, 'Yes, indeed. Sure enough. That's certain.' Or, 'Those days—of my slavery—are over for me. Yes, indeed. I'm never going back to that.'"

"'Yessir' means all of that?" Henri rubbed his mittened hands together to warm them.

"Mm-hmm. Yessir." Flashing a smile, Jethro halted Red beside someone's property and handed the reins to Henri. "Don't run off on me now." Winking, he climbed down from the bench and hefted two bundles of firewood from the wagon.

"Mr. Fortune is a good neighbor to have, isn't he, Mademoiselle?" Henri held tight to the reins.

"A very good neighbor, indeed." Whatever grudge he might have felt about the land dispute, he did not take it out on Vivienne or Henri. Instead, he had come by the day after Liam left, pointing out to her the stores of food in the cellar and cookhouse. She kept careful notation of these, determined that any food she and Henri consumed should be paid for. Jethro's offer to take her into the settlement today was an unsolicited kindness, and she was grateful.

But it was Liam who occupied her innermost thoughts. As the damp cold seeped through her cloak and into her very bones, she could not help but wonder how he had fared on that arduous journey through woods and mountains. And when he might come home. But she did not go so far as to hope he'd be pleased to see her, occupying his home as she was.

Jethro whistled as he returned to the wagon and loaded his arms with more wood for the shed. The front door of the main house opened, and a woman in a formal silk dress stepped out. She watched him, hands on her hips, while he completed his task and climbed back into the wagon.

At this, she stalked down her steps toward them, her neck

mottling with the cold. "Where do you think you're going?" Her shrill voice cut through the fog. Her finger was pointed at Jethro.

Vivienne recognized Suzanne Arquette, the poor woman who had lost her mind. Jethro looked to Vienne for translation.

"She's confused," she told him. To Suzanne, she called, "Mr. Fortune is delivering your order of firewood, that's all."

"You're running away from me! Brazen slave! And me, all alone in this place, with no one to do my bidding."

At a sharp intake of breath from Henri, Vivienne bade him be quiet, and she climbed down from the bench herself. "Suzanne?" she said, approaching her. "I don't know if you remember me, but my name is Vivienne. We lived in the same pension in Philadelphia."

With eyes the same white-washed gray as the sky, Suzanne searched Vienne's face as one who grasps for a light in the dark. "Vivienne? Philadelphia. I don't—" She shook her head.

Vienne's heart squeezed, remembering Sybille's own struggles. "It's cold outside, Suzanne." She took her by the hand. "Let's go in where you can be warm."

But Suzanne looked past her, at Jethro. "That's my slave. He keeps running away. I'm tired and I miss my family, and I don't know what's become of them. I don't know what's become of any of my people, except for that man." She pointed again and stamped her slippered foot on the hard earth. "I paid for him, he is my property, and I will not have him disappear on me again! I won't have it!"

Vivienne angled so Jethro could see her mouth. "Go." His nod told her he understood. He would take Henri with him for the rest of his deliveries and then go home. If Vivienne had to walk back after visiting Suzanne, so be it.

Slipping an arm around Suzanne's shoulders, she steered the woman back up the path to her house. "It looks like you had flowers there last summer." Bare beds lined the walkway, partially patched over with snow. "Tell me, what do you grow here?"

Regaining her bearings in the simple topic, Suzanne spoke of roses and lilacs, and of more exotic species that Vienne guessed had grown in her gardens on Saint-Domingue. Before Suzanne knew it, she was back inside her parlor, sitting on the damask sofa with Vienne. She had lost weight since Philadelphia. Her skin was translucent, blue veins visibly throbbing at her temples. With her frizzled blond hair a nimbus about her head, she had the look of a dandelion. If Vienne had not heard the venom in her voice when addressing Jethro, she would have thought Suzanne insubstantial.

"I'm sorry," Suzanne said suddenly. "Do I know you?" She twisted the ring on her finger.

Vienne caught her breath.

The ring.

"I—I'm Vivienne Rivard," she stuttered, but all she could think of was the signet ring of Louis XVI. She hadn't seen it when they unpacked their things. Where was it? "We met in Philadelphia. I'm one of your neighbors here in Asylum." She heard herself say the words as one listening from a distance. "And I'm very sorry, but I need to go now."

Rising, she flew back outside into the fog, ignoring Suzanne's protests behind her.

It wasn't a long way home. Trusting Henri to Jethro's care, Vivienne hurried through the blocks of matching houses and up the gentle slope until she reached Liam's property. Without bothering to remove her cloak, she bounded up the stairs and searched the bedrooms, taking everything out of the drawers.

Nothing.

On her hands and knees, she looked under the bureaus and beds, searched with her fingers along the grooves of each floorboard, looking for a chink into which the ring might have slipped. But the planks were smooth and tightly joined.

Heart sinking, she descended the steps and searched the first floor, though she knew it would be futile. Their belongings had been unpacked upstairs. If the ring were anywhere, it would be there. Wouldn't it?

When she heard the jangle of Red's bridle, she waved to Jethro from the door and ushered Henri inside.

"Henri, do you have the ring?" she asked.

He gaped at her. "No! But we brought it with us, didn't we?"

She racked her brain. "I thought surely we did!"

But it was not she who had packed their things.

Henri sagged against her, still buttoned into his cloak. "Louis-Charles will need that ring when he's king." His tone was mournful. He spoke of Louis-Charles every day now. Which of Talon's toys might please him, how they would play together, what he could teach him about living in the woods.

Head aching, Vivienne took off Henri's hat and smoothed his hair. They hadn't seen the signet ring since she'd packed it away the day Sebastien brought him home full of hard cider. She had wrapped it in something—a stocking? a glove?—and tucked it deep into a bureau drawer until she knew what to do with it.

Vivienne had never known what to do with it. But she hadn't intended to leave it behind, and it wasn't here. So either it had somehow gotten lost on the way to Asylum, or it was still at the Pension Sainte-Marie.

She prayed it was the former. Nothing good could come from possessing it. But something worse might come from losing it.

Henri shrugged off his coat and unwound the scarf from his neck, then laid firewood in the cold hearth. Vivienne remained at the window, looking through lace at a world still wrapped in fog.

ASYLUM, PENNSYLVANIA
DECEMBER 31, 1794

Smoke spiraled from Liam's old kitchen house, and the leaded windows shone bright against the lowering sky. Dismounting Cherie, Liam plowed through the snow and pounded on the door before bursting inside.

"Vivienne, I need you. Will you come?" Steam rose from his ice-glazed scarf.

"Liam!" The oven door slammed closed as she whirled to face

him, skin aglow. A fine sheen of sweat formed a beaded diadem on her brow. Apple pies cooled on the table beside loaves of bread. After the miserable journey behind him, the warmth and fragrance, the sight of her there, went to his head like strong ale.

Henri bounded from the table, knocking a book to the floor. "What's wrong, Mr. Delaney?"

Liam clapped the boy on the back in greeting. "It's Finn. He's in bad shape, but . . ." There were no doctors in Asylum. "Please—I don't know who else could help." She had sewn up Armand without liking him. Perhaps she'd take pity on a whiskey rebel, too.

Vivienne's expression snapped from surprise to steely determination. "Henri." She pointed to the loaves on the table. He gathered two of them into a basket while Vivienne snatched up jars and herbs. "You have needle and thread?"

"I don't know," Liam said. "Maybe Jethro does."

Wiping her hands on her apron, she dashed from the kitchen house without her cloak. Moments later she returned, dusted with snow, and patted the bulge in her apron pocket. "Henri, stay and bank the fire."

"I'll send Jethro for you, all right?" Liam assured the boy. "It won't be but a few moments."

He took Vivienne's cloak from a peg and draped it about her shoulders lest she forget it again. After fastening only the top hook, she pulled up her hood and plunged into the cold, basket over her arm.

Liam helped her onto Cherie, then climbed up to ride in front of her, urging the poor, tired beast to carry them the final distance home.

Vivienne's arms wrapped his middle, and her basket bounced against his hip. "Is Finn very bad off?" she asked.

"Likely. But he could have been worse." *He could have died on that march.* Liam clenched his jaw.

"And how are you? Liam?"

Grunting, he focused on the column of smoke ahead. "Glad to be home." The word stung his tongue, but not so much as it had before he left.

They rode the rest of the way in silence, as if storing up their energies for what lay ahead.

Liam drew rein before Jethro's kitchen house, where he'd deposited Finn minutes ago. It was no hospital, but neither was it a jail. Liam dismounted first, then took Vivienne's waist in his hands to help her down. "Thank you," he said, and led her inside.

With a word of greeting, Jethro took Vienne's basket and unpacked it on the table. Finn looked up from where he sat in a chair and mustered a smile for Vivienne. "As I recall, you're pretty good at this sort of thing."

"That remains to be seen, but I'll try." She unhooked her cloak, and Liam took it from her, hanging it on a peg.

"That's all I need." Finn's breath rattled before erupting into a cough that folded him in half.

While Jethro went to stay with Henri, Vivienne told Liam how to help her, and he gladly did her bidding. Peppermint leaves were crushed and spread on Finn's bare chest, then covered with a rag soaked in warm water. Another treatment was applied to his back, which Liam held in place. When the coughing subsided enough, Finn grabbed a loaf of bread and began to eat.

"Easy, now," Liam told him. "You eat too fast, it'll all come right back up."

With a nod, Finn reluctantly chewed slower.

Vivienne knelt at his feet, black curls tumbling over her shoulder from where her hair was tied at the nape of her neck. With a sponge, she soaked the encrusted bandages covering his feet until they loosened. "Tell me how this happened."

Carefully, she unwound the ruined linens, and Liam unspooled the story at the same methodical pace. Layer by layer, he tugged free the ugly truth that had been coiled inside him, so that by the time she reached the battered feet beneath their bindings, he'd laid bare all that had brought them here. The odor of Finn's wounds pinched his nose.

"Faith, lads," she whispered, and Liam smiled at the French accent on the Irish term. If there was any scold rising in her for their heedless flight from Philadelphia, she held it back. Law and liberty. Order and freedom. It was all a tangled mess.

"What have you got down there?" Liam asked. Finn's feet had already suffered during his forced march over the mountains and hadn't fared any better during the hard ride from Philadelphia. They'd been fools to attempt the journey in this weather, but they'd have been bigger fools to stay in the city.

She took one wretched foot and then the other into her aproned lap to examine them from every angle. After pouring water from a kettle into a basin, she mixed in some snow to cool it. At her bidding, Finn immersed his feet. "Possible frostbite on the toes. Untreated cuts."

Liam swallowed a groan. He'd seen this in the war. Dirty wounds didn't heal. They grew worse and worse, until the surgeon lopped off the offending area altogether. But he would not speak of that.

Exhaustion battled to take Liam under, and he felt every one of his thirty-eight years as he forced himself to stay awake. Time blurred. He was eating Vienne's bread but did not remember taking the compress off Finn's back or when his cousin had donned a fresh shirt. Mugs of steaming tea appeared on the table, and she made both Finn and Liam drink. The smell of comfrey sharpened in the warm kitchen as she pounded out a salve. She stitched, she soaked, she spread the ointment. Vienne was a marvel of remedies.

"Where did you learn all of this?" Liam asked her. "Or are lace-makers routinely trained in the healing arts?"

She smiled up at him. "During the winter of the Great Cold in Paris, pneumonia and frostbite were all too common. It was too cold for the nimble work of lacemaking, so Tante Rose and I volunteered at the convent, caring for the sick who flocked there. All of this, I learned from the nuns."

Finn cried out in pain.

"That's good." Vivienne winced in sympathy as she gingerly dried his feet and wrapped them. "If you can feel anything, that's a good sign."

The door scraped open, and Jethro returned, Henri in tow.

Snowflakes swirled in with them, melting as soon as they hit the wooden floor. The boy darted to sit at the table across from Liam.

Jethro whistled. "You're right lucky I got used to the idea of having company while you were gone, Liam. Looks like Finn here ain't going anywhere for some time." Arms crossed, he leaned against the side of the fireplace, one ankle crossed over the other. "Anything I missed?"

Finn cleared his lungs with a cough far too large for his frame. "The long and the short of it, then. I paid the infernal tax." His sigh was punctured by another round of coughing. "And then my neighbors burned down my still. When the army came over the mountains, them that never paid fled farther west, into Indian country. I didn't go because I had nothing to fear. But as Liam knows, them as made the arrests didn't bother with petty concepts such as guilt and innocence. They just rounded us up. For sport. No charges were ever made." His speech was slow, made more so by his frequent breaks to cough. "Marched twenty of us all the way to Philly, where we were greeted by our adoring fans."

"Twenty thousand of them," Liam added, still impressed with the figure he'd seen in a newspaper. Twenty thousand people more interested in a ragtag bunch of broken down men than in celebrating Christmas with their families inside.

"Then Liam saw me, came to the jail, and we lit outta there just in time."

Jethro's brow wrinkled. "Will you stay here until the spring and then go home?"

"Ain't no home anymore, lads. How do you like that? All three of us, landless."

"Five." Vivienne poured more hot water into Liam's mug before refilling Finn's. She replaced the kettle on the crane above the fire and sat on the bench beside Henri. "You've not forgotten, surely, that Henri and I are landless, too."

Swallowing a gulp of tea, Liam met her gaze over the boy's head. Reluctantly, he conceded, for she was right. And right to point it out. Her position was as temporary as any of theirs. A common bond for an uncommon group. The mademoiselle and her courtly orphan, a free black man, and two Irish cousins all bunched into a kitchen house on a piece of earth that belonged to none of them.

Jethro broke his reverie. "They burned your still, but you still have your land, don't you?"

Finn spoke into the fire. "I may not have told you the full truth about my . . . situation."

"Out with it, then." Liam wrapped his hands around his mug.

"I thought I was buying that land when I traded in those worthless paper bonds after the war. But as it turns out, I was only renting it."

Had he feared Liam would think less of him for not owning the land outright? After all these years, Finn still wanted to impress the cousin he'd grown up shadowing.

"With the stipulation," Finn continued, "that I could stay only so long as I improved the land. When the still burned down and I could no longer make whiskey, the landlord gave me thirty days to yield *something* or he'd evict me. But your army came and evicted me instead." He wheezed, catching his breath. "I've got nothing left to go back to. The land was never mine to begin with."

Jethro caught Liam's gaze and shook his head as if to say, *You two and your imaginary land.*

"We'll get you sorted out." But expenses for three men piled up in Liam's head. "We'll all be fine. Come spring, there's plenty of work to be done at the settlement for those who can't—or won't—help themselves."

"And before spring?" Jethro asked. Hail pelted the windows. "'Cause I see a whole lot of winter still ahead."

"I aim to pull my weight, Liam, as soon as I'm back on my feet," Finn insisted.

Who knew how long that would be? "I can fix this. I can . . . I can . . ." The heat of the fire in the enclosed space made Liam light-headed.

"Teach again." Vienne's soft voice was bright with confidence and persuasion. "With private tutoring, even in winter. Teach Henri."

"Oh, would you, Mr. Delaney?" The boy's blue eyes shone. "Mademoiselle can pay you. She bakes for the inn now."

"Apple pies and bread?" Liam asked, recalling the industry he'd walked in on.

She nudged a chunk of bread toward him, which he took. "I was fortunate to find a store of dried apples in your cellar. I bake at home, and Henri helps me walk it over, with warmed stones in the baskets. If you would teach Henri—for fair wages, of course—he and I would both be grateful. Surely some arrangement can be made."

"You have a talent for making such arrangements, I've noticed." He smiled at her, and at Henri, growing red from holding his breath, and knew he would not tell them no.

Chapter Twenty-Seven

Henri's chalk hovered over the figures on his slate. Lips rolled between his teeth, he glanced at the snowshoes propped up against the wall, wishing he was already wearing them. Mr. Delaney had promised to take him to the woods to try them out after his lesson.

Indulging a small sigh, he turned back to his slate and tried to concentrate. Which was difficult when Mr. Delaney was talking to Mademoiselle while she baked. Lessons were always held in the kitchen house. It saved on firewood, they said, to heat one room instead of the kitchen and the parlor both. But Mr. Delaney didn't seem to mind being close enough to sample whatever Vivienne was baking for the inn.

"Have a taste, Henri." She leaned over the worktable to hand him a spoonful of filling for some kind of tart. "Too sour, yet?"

The blend of dried cherries, softened and sugared in the saucepan, melted in his mouth. "Oui."

Mr. Delaney's laugh rumbled below Vivienne's. "Well, I think it's just right."

"You always say that." Henri licked his lips and handed the spoon back to her.

Truth be told, he didn't really mind having school here. Probably he thought better around good smells. His stomach didn't hurt anymore, and he saw so much more of Vivienne than he did in Philadelphia, too. Mr. Delaney was a fine teacher indoors, but he also said that not all learning came from books, that nature had its own lessons to teach. Henri couldn't wait to go snowshoeing and call it school. When the time was right, Mr. Delaney would show him how to tap trees for maple syrup, too.

Restless, Henri rested his chin in his hand, frowning at his numbers. "Is this right?" He tapped his slate.

But Mr. Delaney didn't hear him. He was talking to Mademoiselle, their voices a comforting undercurrent to rolling pins and tapping knives and whisking, scraping spoons. But how much was there to say about cherries and sugar, anyway?

"Mr. Delaney?" Henri said again, and his teacher looked almost surprised. As if he'd forgotten that he was here to teach and not keep Mademoiselle company. "Can you look at this?"

"Absolutely." Mr. Delaney slid onto the bench beside Henri. "Ah. There. What's six times eight?"

"Fifty-eight."

Mr. Delaney narrowed one eye.

"Forty-eight! Forty-eight."

"Once you fix that, the rest of the problem should be straightforward. Your method is correct, just make sure the basics are right at every step." Mr. Delaney squeezed his shoulder, then went to the hearth and fed wood to the fire. Henri let him do things like that when he was here, but it was Henri's job when Mr. Delaney was on a mail trip.

Sparks danced above the flames like fireflies. With the pop and hiss of the fire in his ears, Henri worked on the rest of his problems. The rest of them were easy, and his thoughts drifted while his chalk seemed to work on its own. Henri liked living here in the wilderness. It made him feel brave and important to be the man of the house in such a place. When Louis-Charles arrived, he would likely be afraid, but Henri would teach him how to get along. Henri would take care of his friend.

He glanced out the window, gauging the daylight, before turning over his slate and copying his spelling words. Night seemed to fall in the middle of the afternoon here, quick as a window dropping its sash. But even the long winter evenings were interesting when spent in the company of their neighbors.

"Are you going to help me with my horse after dinner tonight?" Henri pulled a misshapen piece of wood from his pocket.

Mr. Delaney took it in his hands, turning it over, pretending to admire it, which made Henri laugh. Someday it would be a horse for Louis-Charles, to replace Bucephalus. But Henri had only just started learning how to whittle.

"I can see where the tail will be." Vivienne gestured with sticky, floured fingers. "Well done!"

"Mademoiselle," Henri said, "that is his nose."

Vivienne flushed. "Oh dear. My mistake, I'm sure." She flashed a sheepish grin and returned to filling her crusts.

"I can see it," Mr. Delaney said. "If you come visit me and the lads, I'm happy to give you a hand. Bring Mademoiselle, too." He smiled.

So did Henri. He loved whittling with Mr. Delaney before the parlor fire, with Mr. Fortune and Mr. O'Brien there, too. Mademoiselle usually made lace on her pillow. Sometimes one of them would pick up a book and read aloud. But mostly, Henri looked forward to having help carving the horse. He still felt awful about losing Bucephalus and wanted his gift to be ready in time. Wouldn't Louis-Charles be impressed when he learned Henri made it himself?

"When will you all come to *our* house in the evening?" Henri asked. Last time they paid a visit to Mr. Fortune's house, Mr. O'Brien's lungs still sounded gravelly.

"Everyone is welcome, of course." Vivienne poured her cherry mixture slowly into her pastry-lined pans. To Henri, she added, "But it's still not good for Mr. O'Brien to be out in the cold, even to come to this house. Hopefully his cough will clear before too long."

"Are his feet better yet?" Henri rolled his ankles under the table, trying to imagine they were frozen blocks of flesh.

Mr. Delaney opened the oven door while Vivienne slid in her

tarts. "He lost a few toes this week. But he had ten to begin with, so he'll get around just fine real soon. After all, he's made do with just one eye." He shut the oven.

Henri paused to consider this, sorry that Mr. O'Brien kept losing his body parts. Handing his slate to his teacher, Henri hopped down from the bench and walked about with one eye closed, toes curled inside his shoes, to see for himself what it was like. It felt funny. He stumbled a bit, balance thrown off, but he still made it over to the pegs on the wall, where he tugged on his cloak and hat.

Mr. Delaney chuckled at Henri's experiment, but as he looked over the slate, he could find no fault with his work.

Good. It was hard being so well behaved all the time, but this was the bargain Henri had made with God, and he wasn't going to forget it. He hoped God wouldn't, either. *Please bring Louis-Charles back to me,* he prayed again and pulled his boots over his feet. "Coming?"

"Of course." Mr. Delaney tapped a smudge of flour from Mademoiselle's nose before pulling his own cloak off its peg. "We'll be back before dark," he told her, picking up the snowshoes.

When they left Vivienne, her cheeks were red. She shouldn't stand so close to the fire.

Like water wearing down a canyon, Vivienne and Henri were eroding Liam's boundaries, their presence coursing through his life in ways he didn't expect.

Or mind.

Sconces illuminated Jethro's parlor beyond the firelight's reach, casting halos upon the whitewashed walls. Liam sat in a wooden chair of his own making, Henri standing at his side, watching him whittle. Across the braided rug from them, Vivienne bent her head over the lacemaking pillow in her lap. With a ready smile, she looked up from the bobbins dancing between her hands whenever Henri had more progress to show her.

The boy took his wood to where Jethro and Finn were hunched over a game of chess. "What do you think that is?" he asked.

Jethro leaned back, taking the object in his broad hand. "Well now! Could be wrong, of course, but I do believe . . ." He glanced at Liam, who scratched the side of his nose. "The muzzle," Jethro proclaimed triumphantly.

"Correct!" Henri cried. "Do you see it, too, Mr. O'Brien?"

"Aye, lad." He paused to clear his throat. "You'll out-whittle ol' Liam there in no time."

Looking pleased as a peacock, Henri resumed his spot on the rug before the fire. Vivienne caught Liam's eye with a gleam in her own. Shaking her head, she concealed a laugh, then looked down at her work again.

"Make your move, man!" Finn boomed as Jethro brooded over the board. After weeks of brooding himself, Finn's outburst was a good sign, more in keeping with his natural temperament. Between the illness in his lungs, the frostbite in his toes, and all that the Whiskey Rebellion had entailed, he'd had much to recover from. And as much as Liam sympathized with the loss of Finn's home, he was grateful that his cousin was recuperating here, away from influences that might have steered him toward revenge. Granted, there were fools enough among the laborers who worked at Asylum, Derek and Ernest Schultze topping the list. But under Liam's watchful eye, surely Finn would mature beyond their sway.

"Check," Jethro said, and it was Finn's turn to contemplate his next move. Not something that had ever come easy to him, even when they were kids.

Liam pulled his chair closer to Vivienne's. A mess of silk threads splayed from the pins stuck in her pillow. How she managed to weave those strands into such intricate patterns defied his understanding. "Making lace is a lot like whittling, isn't it?" He kept his face blank as he teased her.

Her eyebrow popped up. "In what way?"

"Well, with whittling, we carve away the excess wood to free the art locked inside. That's what Michelangelo said once about carving marble, anyway, and I agree with him."

"Aye, you and Michelangelo, the best of friends, always seeing eye to eye on art!" Finn ribbed. "And how is that like making lace?"

"It's similar, because with lace, you . . . you . . ."

Game forgotten between them, Jethro and Finn stared at Liam expectantly. They looked about ready to burst.

"Ain't a blessed thing like about it!" Jethro hooted. "You couldn't do what she does in a million years."

Finn slapped the table, bouncing some chess pieces out of their squares.

Liam and Vienne joined their laughter. "They're right," he confessed. "It's not at all the same, except for the fact that we both make something with our hands. How did you ever learn it?"

"My Tante Rose taught me when I was a child." A smile slowly curved her lips.

"She raised you, didn't she? You mentioned her before. What was she like?"

Vivienne's hands slowed a notch but kept moving. "Wonderful." She slipped into French, perhaps without realizing it, as she spoke her memories. Sipping chocolate together at outdoor cafés. Filling vases in their shop with white roses. Making lace while strolling violinists played Mozart in the public gardens of the Palais-Royal. "When the Jacobins killed her, I lost the only person in the world who really knew me and loved me."

Liam was not sure if her voice was serrated from love or anger or grief, or all three. "How did you get out?"

"The grace of God." The bobbins flew between her fingers.

"Tell him about Félix!" Henri came between them, the unformed horse in his hand. Of course Vienne and Henri would have shared their escape stories, and many other memories of which Liam could form only the barest concept.

"Yes, tell me about Félix." Liam coached Henri on his whittling before resuming work on his own project. The child crossed his legs on the floor by Vienne's skirt.

Her eyes remained on her work. "Félix is the man who let me get away. I rode in a market wagon to leave the city and was stopped like everyone else at the barricade. They were searching for enemies to the revolution, which, as a lacemaker, included me."

"But would they have known that by looking at you?" Liam asked.

"Not unless they already knew me and knew my trade. The inspector assigned to my wagon was such a man. Félix and I grew up together. We were friends once, and he let me pass."

"More than friends," Liam guessed. For what man would not have wanted more with Vivienne?

"He courted me but proved faithless, just as Armand—" She stopped, laying down her bobbins and folding her hands. "Félix was not courting me during the revolution. We had broken it off before then, and glad I was of that, for he proved as untrue to his country as he had been to me."

"Untrue? In what way?" Finn abandoned the chessboard, swiveling in his chair to face her.

"Like so many other revolutionaries, he disguised his love of self with a claim for love of liberty."

Liam caught Finn's eye and stayed him with a look, for her comment was a spark that could ignite him. In truth, Liam's own blood began to warm.

"Félix said he loved me, but he loved his own ideals more than anything else. The liberty he worshipped included the freedom to take a secret lover while courting me. It was for liberty's sake that he turned his back on the teachings of the Church, calling them too confining. And it was for the liberty of 'the people' that he became a citizen soldier working for the Committee of Public Safety, which sent to the guillotine people who did not agree with them. Félix cast off moral authority as easily as he threw off the monarchy's rule. And so you see, it was only the grace of God that kept him from detaining me that day at the barricade. For certainly he was 'at liberty' to arrest me."

Liam tried not to chafe at the equation of liberty and moral failure. He strained to focus on her personal experiences, but despite his best efforts, he felt a thin veil of judgment drape the room.

"What of us, then?" Firelight flickered in Finn's eye. "All three men here fought for liberty, too, though it's true we cut off no heads to do it. Do you say we fought for selfish gain? Out of moral corruption?"

Vivienne met his gaze. "I say nothing of the kind for your American Revolution. You fought a conventional war, and you won."

When she did not tack on a commentary about the Whiskey Rebellion, Liam relaxed a bit and put blade to wood once more. He glanced at Jethro and wondered how he felt about white people talking about liberty for white people, when countless souls had none at all, just for the color of their skin.

Finn gave a huzzah and burst into a racking cough. An elbow over his mouth, he hobbled out of the room. Jethro bade them a good night and followed him.

Sympathy etched Henri's brow as he inclined his ear to Finn's coughing. "Mr. O'Brien would be so much worse if he was in jail right now, wouldn't he?"

"He would."

The boy nodded. "Then it's good you rescued him. When I grow up, I want to be like you and Robin Hood. I want to do what's right, no matter what the law says."

Eyebrows plunging, Vivienne pressed her lips together. "Henri, it is important to obey the law. Isn't that right, Mr. Delaney?"

"Then why did he take Mr. O'Brien away before they could put him in jail?"

Liam rubbed the back of his neck. "It's complicated, lad."

"For a boy, it is not. Rulers are to be respected, for their office alone, if nothing else. The law is to be obeyed." Vienne leaned toward Liam, a curl swaying near her cheek. The aroma of the cherry tarts she'd been baking wafted from her dress. "Remember, his father was killed by those who defied both order and authority."

"Those were bad men who did that," Henri protested. "Mr. Delaney is a good man."

"Sometimes even good men make bad decisions." Her voice was soft but cutting.

Bristling, Liam felt the rebuttal gathering on his tongue. "You refer to French revolutionaries now? Or to me? Or maybe to Armand, for surely you don't agree with every choice he's made?"

Henri frowned. "I guess Mr. Delaney knows which laws should be followed and which ones shouldn't. And there are some laws which should not have been passed. Right?"

Liam scraped at the wood in his hand. "I would say so."

The wrong thing to say.

In a flash, Vivienne gathered up her work and tucked it into her basket. She rose, and Liam stood, too, leaving his whittling project and knife on the chair. "In the future, Mr. Delaney, I would thank you to restrict your lessons for Henri to his official schooling and leave his moral education to me."

"His *moral* education?"

Her nostrils flared. He'd hit a nerve. Well, so had she.

"If anyone's got the right to be offended just now—"

"Ah, yes. More talk of rights. Forgive me, Liam, but I've had enough of that to last a lifetime. Henri, we're going."

"Vivienne. Not like this." He held her by the shoulders until she looked at him.

"And why not?" she said at length.

"Because tomorrow I'm going, too." And another two weeks would pass, at least, before he'd return. Blast these winter trips to the capital. Since he had switched trips with the rider who had been ill, Liam had been able to stay in Asylum since bringing Finn back. But his turn had come again.

"Then Godspeed. Give Tara and Rachel my best." Vienne twisted from his hold, assuring him she needed no escort back.

Moments later, Liam stood in an empty parlor before a fire that sputtered behind its grate. He scooped up the wood he'd been whittling, the rough edges sharp against his thumb. Maybe Michelangelo had been wrong. Not every mess held something beautiful inside. He stepped toward the fire and tossed his half-shaped wood into the flames.

Chapter Twenty-Eight

Asylum, Pennsylvania
March 1795

Winter in Asylum proved severe, but it was a savagery not without beauty. February passed in pearlescent splendor. Snowdrifts dazzled like crushed diamonds in the sun, and ice encrusted trees with crystal. The stillness of winter in the wilderness was like nothing Vivienne had ever known. Still haunted by the lost signet ring, she took comfort in the settlement's isolation. *The remoteness means safety*, she told herself. *This is asylum, indeed.* Most of the time, she and Henri were cocooned in warmth and light with books and baking, whittling and lacemaking, and with their landless American neighbors.

A wry smile curved her lips when she recalled how strongly Sebastien had argued that Henri needed a man in his life. Well, now the boy had plenty, even without a hasty marriage to the eager Monsieur Lemoine. Fleetingly, she wondered if she'd ever see Sebastien again. She could not imagine him in this setting, for all his sparkling words about the place. And now that she was here in this isolated hamlet, she could not imagine leaving.

Liam did enough of that for both of them, and Vivienne did more than her share of looking for his return. She should not have said so much when last they were together. Or perhaps she should have said more. And now he was gone. Could he be arrested, she wondered, for snatching Finn the last time he was in Philadelphia? Worry made a cold companion.

She closed the curtains in the dining house as night blotted out the blank expanse of snow. At six o'clock, the first week of March, the sun had already set.

Henri sat at the table and surveyed their meager spread. Bread made with rice, since there was no more wheat flour, baked beans, and smoked pork chops, the latter a gift from Mr. Fortune.

She bowed her head and prayed over the meal.

"And please bring Mr. Delaney and Louis-Charles home to us soon," Henri added, as he did every night.

A knock at the door, and Henri's fork clattered to his plate. "Mr. Delaney!" he cried and bounded from the table to greet him.

Vivienne rose, pulse quickening, as Henri opened the door. But it was Armand instead of Liam on the threshold, holding a hatbox, and she felt her relief snuff out.

"May I come in, monsieur?" Armand bowed to Henri but looked past him to Vivienne. The age that showed in the sag of his earlobes had not yet taken the aristocratic grace with which he moved. His back was straight. His shoulders, though thin, did not slouch.

"But of course." Henri stepped back, and Armand entered, bringing a raw wet wind in with him. He set the box on the floor near the door, its lid slightly askew, then hung his cloak and hat on a peg.

Staying, then. Vienne sighed.

"You don't take meals at the Grand Maison." Armand smoothed his graying hair back into his queue, then straightened his lavender silk waistcoat. "But I can see you're not suffering for that."

She knew she should invite him to dine, so she placed another setting on the table before resuming her seat. "You know as well as I do that children are not welcome there. And we get along fine on our own."

"I expected nothing less of you." Smiling, Armand sat and helped himself to a serving of pork. His cutlery scraped his plate as he cut through the pink meat. "You are comfortable here?"

"I am well provided for. I'd be more comfortable if my gain was not Mr. Delaney's loss." But Vivienne had no appetite to talk in circles about this property tonight. She told Henri to serve himself before she spooned beans onto her own plate.

"How are you this evening, Monsieur de Champlain?" Henri asked, displaying manners she seemed to lack at the moment.

"I can't complain. But I am a little lonely." The embroidery that ran like a vine among his buttons swayed as he reached to pour himself a drink.

"You are?" the boy asked. "Have you no friends here? Father Gilbert seems very nice. And Monsieur Sando, the silk merchant. Or would you rather a count? Count du Page?"

Armand sipped his wine. "All fine men, indeed. But I really wanted to see you. I brought you something." His gaze slid to Vivienne.

She swallowed and let her napkin drop beside her plate. "Armand, you really, truly shouldn't have." Their relationship was muddied enough as it was. A personal gift would do nothing at all to clear it.

But when Armand lifted the lid of the hatbox, it was to Henri he showed the contents.

A cry of wonder burst from the child. "For me?" he gasped, and then turned sideways in his chair to lift a tiny, mewling ball of gray fluff from the box. "A kitten for me?"

"If your—If Vivienne says it's all right, of course."

As if she could say no now. Not that she was tempted to in the least.

Vivienne left her dinner to see the kitten for herself. With the tip of her finger, she stroked the silken fur between its ears, laughing with Henri over its tiny nose and paws. "You'll have to take good care of her, mon cher. You don't happen to know anything about cats now, do you?"

"Oh, *mais oui*! There were cats everywhere, just *everywhere* in Versailles! Dogs, too, but they were so noisy. I'm very good with animals, you know." Cupping one hand beneath the kitten's hind legs, he held her close, and she promptly fell asleep. "Thank you, monsieur. Thank you. I will name her . . . Madame Fishypaws."

Vivienne rolled her lips between her teeth to catch her laughter.

"It suits her, for she will grow to love fish, I'm sure of it." Armand's smile creased his face. "We found this little one all alone in the visitors' stable. No telling what happened to the mother, but she hasn't come back for it in too long."

A look of solemn understanding came over Henri. "Ah. So her parents are dead. She's an orphan."

"Not if you take her." Armand slipped his finger under the kitten's paw. "I thought you might enjoy having a little friend of your own. Something to care for, yes?"

"Yes." Henri dropped a kiss between the kitten's ears. "My friend is coming. Madame Fishypaws will keep me company until then." Thoughtfully, he looked to Armand. "Would you mind very much, Monsieur de Champlain, if I give her to Louis-Charles when he comes?"

Armand placed his hand on Henri's shoulder. "Young man, what a fine notion. If that would make you happy, then that is what you should do."

"He loves cats as much as me. And in prison, I don't suppose he got to see a single one."

Vivienne's hand went to the pang in her chest. "No, Henri. I don't suppose he did."

Smiling, Henri slipped down from the table. "She's very small, you see, and so she would like to be near the heat." He paused. "Oh—may I?" With Vivienne's permission, he abandoned his food and sat cross-legged on the rug before the fire.

Vivienne watched him cradle the tiny creature and turned back to Armand. "Thank you. You surprised me tonight."

"Then I consider this a good night, indeed." Seating himself at the table once more, he refilled his cup of wine and raised it. "To surprising you. In a good way."

In spite of everything, she laughed.

"You're doing so well with the child, Vivienne. He is thoughtful and courteous, a marvel considering what he's been through. He is fortunate to have you."

Vienne smiled. "We are fortunate to have each other."

Quietly, they ate together, until she gathered her courage and asked, "Are you lonely for your family, Armand?"

His scraggly eyebrows shot up before lowering back into place. "And now it is you who surprises me, Vivienne." A sadness flowed into his voice. "Yes. If I am truthful, I miss them more than I can say."

She took a sip of wine, swallowed, and prayed for grace. "You loved your children very much, didn't you? You miss Angelique and Gustave."

He rubbed the stem of his goblet with his thumb. "Hyacinthe, too. And their mother. And yours."

Her glance swept over Henri and his kitten before returning to the careworn face before her. She forced herself to see the pain in his eyes, to acknowledge that he had experienced loss and grieved the loved ones no longer in his life. He was imperfect—selfish, stubborn, and given to carnal temptation. But a villain? Perhaps not.

"You must know, Vivienne, that your mother missed you, too."

She wiped a napkin over her mouth before she could call him false. Instead, she asked, "When was that?"

"More than she admitted, I'm sure. There were two times, in particular, that I recall." He inclined his head. "Shall I go on?"

The armor over her heart screwed tighter. "Do."

"Once when you were eight. She had just met you for the first time since placing you as a baby in Rose's arms. You were so bright and so—wholesome, Sybille said. Yes, that was the word. Wholesome. Just shining with innocence, like an angel. You lavished attention on her, though she felt she didn't deserve it. Over ice cream, was it?"

Le Caveau. Chocolate ice cream. White lace.

"Well. She knew then that placing you in her sister's care was the best thing she could have done for you. Sybille was too far down her own road to ever hope to make amends—these were her own words, understand—and she knew she ought to stay away from you from then on. She felt she would be a polluting influence on you." He rubbed a hand over his face and looked into the distance.

An ache swelled within Vienne. "Did she?"

"Yes. I didn't like hearing that she suddenly felt soiled, of course. I loved her with a passion and didn't want to think that acting on it was a sin. Forgive me, Vivienne, but I didn't want to think of a little girl without parents. I told her I didn't want to hear about you again."

The air went out of Vivienne's lungs. Her hands functioned separately from her mind, twisting her napkin in her lap, refolding it. She might have taken another sip of wine to hide the tremble of her lips, but if so, it was like one in a deep fog, for Armand's words clouded everything around her.

"I was wrong." His voice pierced through. "God help me, I was wrong in so many ways. And she did talk about you again. I was tired, and Hyacinthe had just died, but I didn't tell Sybille that. All she could talk about was that she had seen you through the window of Rose's shop. She hadn't dared to go in. It was enough for her to see the poised young lady you had grown into. You were consulting with a patron, perhaps. Bah." He waved his hand. "I don't recall how it went."

But Vivienne did. She had seen Sybille on the other side of the glass and recognized her at once, for her own reflection matched so nearly the image of her mother. "*You don't serve courtesans like her, do you?*" a patron inside had asked. It was the first time Vienne understood what Sybille did and why Vienne had come into this world. By mistake.

Armand kept talking. "I was grieving the loss of my own girl. I didn't want to hear about any other. Even though you were as much mine as Hyacinthe and Angelique ever were. The fact that I didn't claim you—until too late—does not change that fact. And you deserve to know that Sybille loved you in the only way she knew how. By staying away."

Until she didn't. For Sybille had come back to visit Tante Rose a couple of times, and then returned during the revolution to help Vivienne and Rose both.

Armand pushed back his plate and leaned forward, the lace at his throat quivering as he spoke. "You should know that the note you intercepted—the one inviting Sybille to Le Havre? It was not the first one I'd sent. I had asked her to leave Paris, if not the country, right before the monarchy fell. She refused, Vivienne, because you and Rose were there. She wanted to be near you more than she wanted to escape with me. Do you hear me, ma chère? She wanted you."

The lines of his face blurred as she stared at him. Words and memories formed a lance to her blistered heart, and tears were the relief that spilled free. She had not dared to believe Sybille when, during her illness, she had told Vienne she loved her. Vienne had convinced herself it was only madness that made her say it. But perhaps it was the one thing that made any sense. Her mother had loved her, after all, in the only ways she knew how.

"Judging by how much you cry when I am near, I am beginning to think I would do well to follow Sybille's suit. You've been telling me as much for months now, but I finally understand. If the best way for me to show you love is by staying away from now on, I will."

Henri appeared at Vivienne's elbow, Madame Fishypaws nestled in the crook of his arm. "You will what, monsieur? What did you say?"

By degrees, Vienne realized how weary she was of guarding herself from Armand. She cautiously lowered the shield that had become more burden than protection. And prayed she would not regret it.

"Monsieur will come again, sometime," she said, "to see how Madame Fishypaws grows into a lovely fat cat."

Armand smiled as he rubbed the kitten's downy belly. Eyes welling with tears, he looked at Vienne. "I would be delighted."

PHILADELPHIA
MARCH 1795

Paulette glowered as she headed down to the wharves, empty pail bumping against her threadbare dress. With all the rooms full again at the Pension Sainte-Marie, Paulette worked from sunup to sundown, picking up after more French refugees who couldn't look after themselves. Even though only breakfast was served to the boarders, she still cooked three times a day for Madame, and the cleaning and laundry for the entire pension kept Paulette's hands chapped and raw. She peered at her knuckles as she gripped her bucket. Almost as red and rough as a fishwife's. And now Madame wanted oysters for dinner.

Oysters. Paulette's least favorite food. Their odor whisked her back to the French coastal town of Marseille, where she'd wished, more than anything, that she could sail away. The memories attached to these mollusks were ones she'd much rather forget. And yet, those hard years had made her who she was. Tough, resilient, strong. Which came in handy for a pension maid, especially when a man like Corbin Fraser was among the residents.

He could bully, and he could charm. But Paulette was moved by neither, for she didn't have the information he wanted.

Lips clamped tight, she marched to the vendor calling out his prices and made quick work of the transaction that filled her pail with oysters.

"Paulette?"

She turned at the sound of her name, skirt billowing, hair lashing about her neck. Gulls circled against a tarnished sky that promised rain. "Monsieur Lemoine."

He strolled over to her, using an umbrella like a walking cane. As ever, he was spit-polished to a shine, even down here at the docks. What a fop.

"Fancy meeting you here," she said when he was near enough to hear, with an emphasis on the *fancy*. She snickered at her wit. If she wasn't intimidated by Corbin, she certainly wouldn't be daunted by the dandy before her, even if Vienne had reason to distrust him.

"It shouldn't surprise you. Didn't Vivienne tell you I recruit at the docks for Senator Morris's settlement?"

"As it happens, Vivienne did not tell me every detail about you." And if that surprised him, he was even more arrogant than she took him for.

Blinking, he held up his palm and looked at the clouds, then wiped a bit of drizzle on his breeches. "It's for Asylum. Sometimes French refugees arrive with no idea where to go, you see, and if they are looking for land, they're more than happy to consider what Asylum has to offer."

Sebastien spoke as if she knew all about this place. She let him.

He leaned on the handle of his umbrella, one ankle crossed at the other. "I might have guessed that's where Vivienne and Henri disappeared to. Arranged the details myself, all except for her transportation. How was I to know she'd go in the middle of winter like that?" He shook his head. "You might have told me that's where she'd gone and saved us both a headache or two. But I expect she told you to keep that a secret, for Henri's protection, in which case—well done, good and faithful servant."

A Bible verse? How quaint. She might have known he was religious. "So I suppose you know they're all right now," she tried.

"Oh yes. Armand de Champlain and I are on quite friendly terms, and he assures me they get on splendidly."

Fat drops of rain spotted the brick sidewalk like copper coins. "You seemed in such a hurry to find them before. I'm surprised you're not with them now, if you know their location."

Sebastien leaned in closer. A sharp wind sliced and swirled between them, mixing the smells of his pomade with that of her oysters. Paulette muscled back a gag. "Between you and me," he confided, "the boy could not be in a better place. I confess I want to be with them again, but now?" He gestured toward the swollen river and toward the unpaved roads, so thick with mud that planks of wood from the shipyard were required to cross them.

"No one is getting to Asylum until the river slows and the roads dry out, that much is sure. And in the meantime, Louis—I mean, Henri—is not going anywhere."

Paulette made her face a mask as pieces flew together in her mind. Sebastien opened his umbrella, raindrops pattered on the oysters in her pail, but she did not feel the water on her skin. With searing clarity, fragments of information and shards of memory snapped into place, creating a picture so bright she marveled that she'd been blind to it before.

Sebastien drew his satchel closer to his body, beneath the protection of his umbrella. "A convoy of refugees will make the trip later, when the season allows for travel. I daresay I'll join them. Really, I don't know why she felt the need to keep her whereabouts a secret from me, of all people. I only want what's best. For everyone."

Thunder rattled, sending stevedores and porters running for shelter. With a simple, "Good day," Sebastien left, too.

Paulette stood with her pail in his wake. It grew heavier in her hands until she realized it was filling with rainwater. Carefully, she tipped out the rain and began walking home, turning a single truth over in her mind.

Henri was Louis-Charles Capet. Vivienne and Sebastien knew it. And so did Corbin Fraser. But Corbin didn't know where he was.

Rain plastered her hair to her neck and smeared the dirt on her hem into mud. Wet skirts slapping her ankles, Paulette rolled her discovery this way and that, looking at it from every angle, deciding what to do. If a stinking oyster could turn sand into something precious, she could do something wondrous, too. Her knowledge was one small grain, hidden inside her shell. And there she would keep it, until the right moment came to harvest that pearl.

Asylum, Pennsylvania
May 1795

Liam smoothed the soil around the bushes he'd just planted, relishing the feel of damp earth between his fingers and the smell of it in the air. Spring had come to Asylum almost as an afterthought this year, the ground reluctant to thaw, trees hesitant to bud. Liam could relate.

Standing, he brushed dirt from the knees of his trousers and returned his shovel to the barn, casting a glance toward the kitchen house on his way. He had come and gone on two more trips to Philadelphia. On each return, he found the atmosphere surrounding Vivienne considerably cool. And it was she who made the weather, at least for him. Her smile could shine like the dawn, but a clipped word pelted hail. The only thing predictable about her was that she was as stubborn as Tara had ever been, but far more difficult to ignore. Which meant he'd have to be the one to crack the ice between them. He would not leave her again with their differences unresolved.

So when Jethro had volunteered to take Henri fishing that evening, while Finn went wherever he went these days, Liam had stayed back with Vienne. After placing the shovel with his other tools, he crossed to the kitchen house and knocked.

Vienne opened the door with a tub of dirty dishes on her aproned hip. Curls strayed from the braided hair that crowned her head.

"Let me help with that. Free of charge," he added, lest she think he expected Armand to credit this service to his account.

With a sideways glance, she agreed.

Liam took the tub from her, and she walked beside him toward the creek. Wind billowed like cool sheets against his skin. Above hills lush with forest green, shades of lavender banded the sky. Words amassed on his tongue, arguments and apologies tangling together. "I'm not Félix," he blurted.

"What?" She tucked a strand of hair behind her ear and looked at him.

Clover crushed beneath their footsteps, releasing its sweet scent into the air. "I've had plenty of time to think about what you told me about your escape from Paris. And I'm not like Félix. I'm not a man who loves a principle more than he loves a person."

Vivienne slowed her pace but said nothing. Her cotton skirt

ballooned before her as they walked, and he saw for the first time that she was barefoot in the grass.

"It would be easier," he continued, "if I did not care how you regard me. But I do. And I care about Henri a great deal. The fact that you don't trust me as a moral influence for him—" He had no words for how that made him feel. He'd always been a shepherd for his family, especially for Finn. His mother and Tara relied on him, and he'd never betrayed their faith.

"Liam." Vivienne touched his elbow. "I trust you, but you must tread lightly where law and revolution are concerned. I understand your point of view, and I understand your point. But do you see mine? Or are you so concerned with being right that you have no time to consider other perspectives?"

He lowered the tub to the bank of the creek and knelt. Cold water covered his hand as he plunged a jug into the creek to fill it. "My trouble is not that I don't see other viewpoints. It's that I see them all, all at once." He poured water over the dishes and dipped the pitcher back into the creek for more. The shade from the overhanging trees was restful to his eyes.

Kneeling beside him, she took a sponge to the pans. How different she was from what he'd first assumed her to be. How mistaken he'd been.

"I've been wrong before," Liam admitted. "You are right to teach Henri that laws are for obeying. They are." Except in the case of tyranny, but he knew better than to pull that thread right now. "I'll talk to him about it, if you like. And if I have hurt you, I have erred there, too." For it was not just Henri's father the revolutionaries had killed, but her beloved Tante Rose, as well. "Forgive me."

Vivienne handed him a pan to dry, then watched a family of ducks paddle downstream. Dragonflies winged silently above the water, and a cricket perched on a moss-furred stone and began his nightly song. "I do. And I share my portion of the blame. I don't remember what I said, but I do remember regretting how it all shook out."

"'*Even good men make bad decisions.*' Sound familiar?" The line had lingered like an illness in his mind. After swiping a flour sack towel over the pan, he set it aside.

Her lashes dropped to her cheeks. "You are a good man, Liam. But—"

He braced himself as she peered up at him. "But what?" he asked. "I followed the rules. I went on that campaign against the whiskey rebels, as I was ordered."

"Yes, but then you broke the law when you took Finn home with you on Christmas Day. I've been sick with worry each time you return to Philadelphia! Are you not fugitives, you and your cousin both? Could they not arrest you, too, for helping Finn evade his sentence? Every time you leave, I tell myself I might not see you again. And when you come home—I'm angry that I spent all that time worrying, and angry that you don't seem worried at all! As if you're above the law entirely. But you aren't."

"You can't be siding with the authorities on this one. They arrested anyone they pleased, even the innocent. They refused to bring charges or set a date for trial."

Vienne's dishes sat forgotten in their tub. "I'm not after a quarrel. I'm telling you that I was afraid. To lose you." She looked down, rubbing the stitching on her apron hem between her fingers. When she spoke again, her voice was as quiet as the riffling stream. "You mean more to us than you know. And I could only conclude by your lack of caution that we mean less to you than I had hoped."

Liam let her words wash over him while a blue jay chattered in the tree above them. This was not what he'd expected. "If anything happened to me, Jethro could take care of your needs on the land."

"That's not what I meant."

Hope flickered inside him. Vienne reached for a dish, but Liam caught her hand and held it. "Then what did you mean?"

She made a tight seam of her mouth, when what he longed for was an honest answer. He was too old for anything else.

316

He released her. "I'm sorry you were frightened. There is truly nothing to fear now. While I was in Philadelphia this last time, Washington finally pardoned them, five months after they were imprisoned. Every man arrested for the Whiskey Rebellion is free to go. If they have any place left to return to."

"So Finn, and you . . ."

"It's over."

Vienne handed him a pie plate. "Just like that?"

He shrugged, wiping it dry. "Be at ease."

Heaving a great sigh, Vienne bowed her head, clenching the sponge in her lap, heedless of the water soaking through her skirts. "I don't know whether to feel foolish, or relieved, or both."

"Feel whatever you want." He swallowed. "When we're done here, I have something to show you."

At last she looked at him with eyes the color of spring itself. They finished their task and went home.

After depositing the tub of dishes inside the kitchen house, Liam led her to the front of the main house and pointed to the bushes he'd just planted on either side of the front door.

"Roses," he told her, in case she couldn't tell by the thorny stems alone. "I picked them up in Wilkes-Barre on my way home. The man who sold them to me told me they'll bloom white, not red." She never wore red, and he could guess why she didn't favor the color. "You like white, don't you? They were in your lace shop, you said."

"White roses!" she gasped. "Yes, white roses, white lace, and my Tante Rose." She covered her mouth with one hand, her brow crimping. A tear rolled down her cheek.

"Oh no." He stepped toward her. "I didn't mean to upset you. I should have asked you first, before planting such a visible reminder—"

"I love them," she whispered, gazing at the bushes in wonder, as if they were already blossoming with snow-white petals. Then she grasped his hands and repeated, "I love them, Liam. I can't believe you remembered."

A smile warmed slowly on his face. If he could only bottle what he felt right now. Her happiness poured his youth back into him, and he realized he would bend himself to the purpose again and again, God willing.

Félix, she'd said, was the man who let her get away. But Liam Delaney would be the man who kept her.

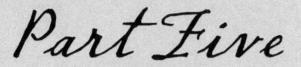

Part Five

To me remains nor place, nor time;
My country is in every clime;
I can be calm and free from care
On any shore, since God is there.

While place we seek, or place we shun,
The soul finds happiness in none;
But with a God to guide our way,
'Tis equal joy to go or stay.

—Madame Guyon

Chapter Twenty-Nine

Still damp with morning's dew, the cool earth soiled Vivienne's apron as she knelt in her garden, tugging weeds from between iris and yarrow. Geese soared overhead, soft brown chevrons against a sky of robin's-egg blue.

Before she lived here, Liam had planted garlic, chives, mint, rosemary, and thyme in the beds around the house. But these flowers, and the rose bushes Liam had planted for her, were her own. The plantings were small and vulnerable, and she cultivated them with tender care, like most of the women in Asylum. It was no surprise that French women preferred the beautiful, perhaps even over the practical. But Vienne suspected that they, whose memories were haunted with the blood and death of the French Revolution, were even more inspired to nourish life and beauty where they could.

The door slammed behind Henri as he ran out of the house. "I'm going to help Mr. Delaney!" His little cat, Madame Fishypaws, romped after him.

She sat on her heels and watched them dash to let Liam through the gate in the paling fence. Beyond it, fields of flax, rye, and grass for hay shimmered in the morning sun. The breeze that whispered through their stalks and toyed with the ends of her hair carried the taste of sunbaked grain.

Clapping the dirt from her hands, she gathered the herbs she'd cut onto her lap, then bunched the hem of her apron into one fist to make it a sack for her harvest. Rising, she went to greet the man who meant more to her than he likely knew.

"Like this? Right here?" Brow furrowed in concentration, Henri held a section of lattice in place on the summer house Liam was building.

"That's the way." Liam hammered the wood into place in three spots before turning to reach for more nails. When he saw Vienne, he touched the brim of his cap. "It's almost finished. Before I leave this morning, it will be done, as long as my assistant doesn't tire on me."

"I don't get tired." Henri's chest lifted. "I'm very strong," he added through gritted teeth, curling his fist.

Vivienne smiled, gratitude filling her, for truly Henri was stronger than he'd ever been. The more time he spent outside, the less his legs ached, and it had been more than four months since he'd complained of the stomach pains that once plagued him. God was healing Henri in Asylum, body and soul.

With a low whistle, Liam patted Henri's bicep. "Why, you're near as strong as me!"

He held out his arm, and Henri grabbed it with both hands, then lifted his feet off the ground while Liam spun in a circle, much to the delight of the shrieking boy. Henri let go in a fit of laughter, collapsing to the ground. Fishypaws pounced on his chest.

Liam lifted his face to the sunshine, then turned back to Vivienne. "Monsieur Talon has returned from his travels."

"Oh?" Talon was often abroad, and no one blamed him. Many resented that he had somewhere to go, however. Most of those who came to Asylum in fear for their lives now found they could not leave. The Reign of Terror was over, but the revolution was not, though it had been six years since the fall of the Bastille. Vienne felt the chives warming in her apron and the dirt beneath her fingernails. Grass stained the hem of her muslin gown. Had it been only six years since she'd made lace for a queen? It felt like twenty.

"There will be a dance this evening at the pavilion," Liam added. "You'll want to go. I can keep Henri, if you like."

Her eyebrows lifted. "Are you certain?"

"Yes!" Henri leapt to his feet, holding his cat and scratching her under the chin. "We've got work to do together, I'm sure, Mademoiselle. Let me stay with Mr. Delaney and his friends. I'll be no trouble at all to them."

Liam spun his hammer end over end into the air and caught it again. "Actually, I was hoping you could help me try out a canoe on the river. I could use another strong oarsman. If you're up to it."

Vienne smiled at the look on Henri's face. Of course he was. She left them to finish the latticed summer house, enjoying the promise of its cool shade.

The afternoon heated to a golden simmer, with sunshine thick as honey, and the evening was nearly as warm. Reluctantly, Vivienne traded cool muslin for sage green silk. Lace ruffled at her elbows and squared neckline. After Liam came to take Henri, she went alone to the pavilion.

Cicadas ticking in her ears, she held the hem of her skirt higher than the dust clouding about her steps. Though the Americans had cleared trees to allow for the settlement, the French had quickly planted Lombardy poplars in pleasing rows between homes, and young weeping willows swayed here and there. After winter's palette of whites and grays, summer gardens and flower boxes burst with color and hummed with industrious bees.

Violin music drew her to the pavilion on a wooded islet behind the Grand Maison. The waters of the Susquehanna rolled like cloudy cider beneath the footbridge that carried her across.

Arriving late by intention, she lingered on the edge, smiling as she watched former silk merchants Evelyne and Philippe Sando dancing. They were the lucky ones—those who loved the ones they held. Count David and Aurore du Page danced, too, but only the music, it seemed, held them together. Near a table that held cups of lemonade and wine, several widows traded gossip while poor Suzanne Arquette craned her neck for a husband who would never again ask her to dance. Zoe du Page was paired with a man Armand's age, a former officer in the French military and one of several constitutionalists who'd been driven from the country along with moderation.

"Ah, Vienne. How lovely you are." Armand approached her with a smile. "Tell me, how is Henri? And Madame Fishypaws?"

"Very well, both of them. He loves that cat more than you can imagine." It really was a thoughtful gift. Since then, Armand had shown respectful restraint with only the occasional visit. When he came, Vienne showed him the gardens, the grains growing in the sun, or the fields Liam and Jethro had cleared for more crops. And Henri proudly showed him his cat. "How are you?" she asked him.

"In good health, I suppose. But lonely." The Madeira on Armand's breath pinched her nose.

Sunlight gilded the dust suspended in its slanting rays. Warm sap from surrounding hemlock trees spiced the air. "I hear you have company often." Vienne fanned herself. "Usually women."

"Bah." He waved at a fly. "They are nothing to me. And I'm quite sure I'm nothing to them. But if you and Henri ever cared to stop by . . ."

"And risk walking in on your activities?"

"My activities?" Laughing, he bent over the walking cane in his fist before straightening again. "Cards, dominoes, idle chatter." He wrinkled his Roman nose and whispered, "I mostly invite them just to be rid of the silence."

Vienne eyed the man before her. He had missed a button on his waistcoat. No woman would have let him leave the house like that. Gently, she pointed it out so he could fasten it. Maybe, one day, she and Henri would go see him. But she wasn't quite ready to promise it. "We'll see."

He raised an eyebrow and bowed to her. "Why, thank you." Drawing himself to his full height once more, he added, "You'll tell Henri I said hello, won't you? And give Madame Fishypaws a scratch behind her ears for me."

She smiled. "I will indeed."

"I do apologize that *your* gift has been so long in coming, my dear. But I believe that's about to change."

Her fan stilled against her fichu. "Gift? There's no need, Armand."

Crickets chirped, and dragonflies flitted between powdered wigs. Armand's chest rose and fell with a sigh. "You work so hard. Allow me to take care of you. It really is a gift of the most practical nature. There's nothing personal or scandalous about it."

The violinists played the final note in their song, and the messieurs bowed to their curtsying partners. Vienne frowned. "I can't imagine—"

"Lovely night for a dance, no?" The familiar voice of Sebastien Lemoine startled Vivienne. He and Armand exchanged a hearty greeting.

"Armand," she said behind her fan, "tell me this is not your gift to me."

Armand laughed. "No, he isn't. Although he seems to think he is, does he not?"

Bronzed by what must have been a recent trip up the river, Sebastien grinned. "Truly, Vienne, I'd be hurt by the way you ran off last winter if I didn't know the reason for your secrecy. And how is our little boy?" He scanned the area behind her.

"Well. You two have some catching up to do." Armand bowed to them both and glided away. "You can thank me later for your gift."

The nerve of him. The nerve of *both* of them. She swatted at the flies peppering the air. "Henri is not yours," she reminded Sebastien. "But he is well. When did you arrive?"

"This afternoon, with a few more refugees who've decided to settle here. We would have been here weeks ago, but we were waiting for all the paperwork to be in order, and one of the refugees was too ill to travel for a while. You'll see a familiar face among them. Paulette Dubois."

The name drew a smile to Vivienne's face. "She's here?" She looked around.

"Not here at the dance, of course, unless she has a fairy godmother to turn her into nobility. She's come as domestic help."

"But why? She was so faithful to Madame Barouche."

"That she was. But the madame is no longer in the pension business, as I understand it. Paulette can tell you the details."

An owl hooted from his unseen perch as Vivienne tried to digest this news. "Where is Paulette?"

Sebastien glanced in the direction of the Grand Maison. "Resting. You'll see her soon enough, and she will rejoice to see you. Faith, but she was true to keep your secrets, even from me. For now, she recovers. Travel by boat did not agree with her, I'm afraid."

Paulette would do well to rest, for she would have more work to contend with here than she ever had in the city, even if she gained employment for the most lenient of residents.

Sebastien took Vivienne's hand. "Dance with me."

As the violin played an introduction, she allowed him to lead her out on the floor. Mechanically, her feet performed the steps as Sebastien swept her about. Fireflies twinkled, and lanterns rimmed the pavilion with their soft yellow glow. Inside the lit perimeter, the music and dancing continued. Outside, night dropped over the wilderness. Surely Monsieur Talon would come soon.

"I missed you." Sebastien's whisper tickled her ear. "Did you not miss me, too? Surely, you can confess as much. A woman, all alone in the wilderness. That isn't right."

She hadn't missed him at all. She certainly had not missed his posturing to influence Henri. "I wasn't alone. I had plenty of help when I needed it."

"For half the time," Sebastien countered. "You refer to that Irish squatter who brings the mail to Philadelphia, do you not? The man Armand pays to take care of you. Small comfort, that. You didn't think his attentions were sincere, did you? Or for purposes other than mercenary?"

"Enough of that," she whispered, when what she really wanted was to stomp on his foot. "Liam was here with me a fine sight more than you were."

"A problem I'm only too willing to remedy." He shrugged, a gleam in his eye. "You brought it up."

Vivienne shook her head. "Then I'll drop it. And you'll do the same." She glanced at the couples swirling about. "People talk."

He pressed her closer. "Let them." His lips brushed her cheek as he said it, and she jerked away from him.

"You overreach, monsieur." Liam Delaney tapped Sebastien on the shoulder. "I'm cutting in."

Sebastien stopped to glare at him. "And what if I won't let you?"

"Come now." Liam's smile was terse. "Don't be greedy."

Making her own decision, Vivienne moved toward Liam, and Sebastien gave a stiff, awkward bow before retreating.

Liam's hand settled gently in the hollow of her waist. Gratefully, she took her new partner. The muscled shoulder beneath her hand spoke of unending labor on the land they both called home. The warm hand enveloping hers was calloused, yet more welcome than Sebastien's smooth touch had been.

"The hour grows late," she admitted. "I'm sorry to keep you waiting."

Effortlessly, it seemed, he guided her through the waltz. "Henri is right there." He nodded to the log bench where the boy sat, then turned so she could see him. Henri waved to her, smiling, then sipped a cup of lemonade. "He's fine. Are you?"

She looked into his eyes, their peerless blue deepened by evening's shade. "If he is fine, then so am I."

"Have you been caring for the boy so long, you tend his wants and needs with no thought of your own? You're allowed to be your own person. With your own feelings." His hand slid to the small of her back, and with the slightest pressure, the distance between their bodies grew smaller. Head bowing toward hers, he trailed his gaze from her neckline to the pulse at her throat, then to her lips and finally back up to her eyes. "How do *you* feel?"

Summer's musky heat pressed against her. She scarcely knew

what she felt, let alone how to describe it, or if she should. An ache to be known swelled within her, but fear and doubt surged. She was assigning too much to his question. She was a fool to savor his attention this way, to long for more from their friendship. Because of her, he'd lost his land and house. And yet, of all the men she'd ever known, he remained the only one who could stir her heart.

The music ended. Their feet stilled, but Liam held her a moment after the last note died away before releasing her. He bowed, and she curtsied.

"Thank you for the dance," she breathed, then threaded through the couples to find Henri.

The boy stood when she reached him, and he had barely begun to regale her with tales of his adventures with Liam when a stronger voice rang out, hushing those gathered.

"The news I share comes hard." The lanterns at Monsieur Talon's back lit the outline of his frame as he raised his hands, then dropped them limply to his sides.

Henri pressed into Vivienne's side. With wariness etched into his brow, Liam glanced at them both before facing Talon.

"According to reports, the king, Louis-Charles, is dead."

Henri stared at Monsieur Talon, shocked into silence. Talon was lying. Henri had prayed and prayed, and had been so very good, and Louis-Charles was sure to come home now!

"Oh, Henri," Mademoiselle whispered. Murmuring rippled through the crowd.

"No," Henri said quietly. Then louder, "Louis-Charles is not dead!" Suddenly his legs could not hold him. He dropped to the bench, shaking.

Vivienne sat beside him, wrapping her arms around his shoulders. Mr. Delaney sat on his other side, his broad hand spanning Henri's back.

"It isn't true," Henri whimpered. "It's a lie." *Please, God, let it be a lie.* His belly felt wrong, like it was full of hard cider again. He thought he was going to be sick.

From the shadows, a voice called out, "How can he be dead? He was only ten years old."

"My friends, this was but one report," Talon stated. "I have other information that would refute it. There is reason, yet, to hope."

Henri lifted his head with a sharp intake of breath. "What do you mean?"

"Some poor child died in prison, in the cell meant for Louis-Charles, of neglect—or, if we be honest, abuse by villainous guards. But *which* child was it? Too many unanswered questions remain for us to believe in a simple death and burial."

Oh, God! Did You spare my friend?

Henri held his breath as Talon laid mysteries before them all. Louis-Charles's sister, Marie Therese, lived doors away from her brother and was not allowed to see the body. Not only that, but no one who had known the dauphin before imprisonment was brought in to confirm the dead boy's identity.

"Guards changed frequently," Talon continued. "We believe a switch was made sometime in the last fourteen to sixteen months. A child posing as the dauphin took his place in the cell, and now in his coffin, too."

Relief flowed through Henri, tempered only by the thought that some other boy had not been saved. He broke free of Vivienne. The colonists stepped back, allowing him a path to approach Monsieur Talon. He felt a hand on his shoulder, smelled the rose water that marked Vivienne's presence. "A boy died in Louis-Charles's place?"

Whispers shuddered through the royalists. Henri did not have to understand each word to grasp their hope and wonder. Of course they were happy. Louis-Charles was still alive!

Monsieur Lemoine looked from the colonists to Henri. Talon tented his fingers before his waist. "It seems a more likely explanation than the little king's death. Consider this. Visitors allowed to see him in early 1794 reported him in good health for the circumstances. Intelligent and articulate. Two months later, those who saw the child prisoner said he was bedridden, full of vermin, unable to speak a single word. The first child had rickets, the second, scrofula."

"My rickets bother me much less now," Henri offered, hoping to encourage the rest of the group. If Henri's legs could gain strength here in Asylum, his friend could heal here, too! "Louis-Charles is alive." He knew it. God had heard his prayers and answered him.

Mr. Delaney and Vivienne exchanged a glance before Monsieur Lemoine caught her eye. He knew what all of them must be thinking. *Perhaps Henri is right. Louis-Charles is still alive.* Of course, he was right. Henri beamed. Around him, voices crescendoed to exclamations and questions thrown out to the wind.

As though from a dream, Paulette Dubois emerged from the shadows in a travel-rumpled gown. Ignoring Mr. Delaney completely, she reached for Vivienne, who embraced her in greeting, almost as a long-lost friend. "I heard there was an announcement here tonight," the maid whispered. "I never dreamed . . ."

"There is more." Talon lifted his hands to quiet them. "Three doctors called in to treat the child with scrofula suggested it was not the same boy they'd seen earlier. All three are now dead, by circumstances too strange to be natural. After the boy's coffin was buried in secret, the four men involved in the burial also died suddenly, again in ways that cannot be explained except to allow for foul intent."

"They saw inside the coffin," said Philippe Sando. "They must have remarked that the corpse was taller, or shorter, or otherwise markedly different than Louis-Charles had been."

"And the observations cost them their lives," suggested Evelyne. "But where is he? Where is our boy king now?"

"Alive!" Henri insisted again, this time shouting, for he could not contain his joy.

In the hush that followed, a goblet dropped to the pavilion floor, and blood-red wine trickled out. "Behold, the king!" Suzanne Arquette curtsied low to Henri and held it as if frozen in place.

Ah. Poor mad Suzanne. Henri touched her gently on the shoulder. "Arise, madame. You needn't bow to me."

Someone gasped. But as Henri scanned the lantern-lit faces, all eyes were not on the unhinged woman from Saint-Domingue, but upon him.

"It's only Suzanne," Vivienne whispered to Paulette.

But the maid stood transfixed, her face pale in the moon's silver light, staring at Henri.

Chapter Thirty

It was early in the morning the following day when Sebastien appeared on Vivienne's doorstep, though she'd already been awake and dressed for hours. Stepping outside, she met him on her front step.

"We need to talk," he began. "Won't you let me in?"

Hastily, she wound her braid into a bun and pinned it at the nape of her neck. "We can talk here." Dawn barely skimmed over the hills. She led him away from the house and leaned a hip against the white painted fence. "What is it?"

"The time is now. Marry me."

"How romantic." She laughed, a short puff through her nose.

Sebastien removed his hat and ran a hand over his black hair. "I'm serious, Vienne. For your sake. For Henri's."

She smiled, genuinely amused at his redundant strategy. "And most importantly, for yours, no? You still think he is Louis-Charles, don't you? He isn't."

"How can you say that?"

"Sebastien, I know him. He is Henri Chastain, as I've told you time and again."

"What if there was no Henri? What if this was just about you and me?" He slid his hands over her shoulders and down her arms.

Somewhere deep inside her, an alarm sounded.

"After everything we've been through, do you feel nothing for me at all?" he was saying. "Do you still not understand what I feel for you?"

Then his lips were on hers, warm and insistent. His hand held her head, and the other went behind her waist, pinning her body to his. With his fingers roving through her hair, her braid dislodged from its pins, unraveling down her back. He deepened the kiss, and the alarm inside her became a scream.

Vivienne wrenched herself free and slapped him with all the force she could muster. "How dare you!" She started to back away.

Sebastien's hand shot out and gripped her wrist, squeezing until her fingers lost feeling.

"Let go of me," she gasped.

"I don't like being hit by a woman."

A shadow fell over Sebastien just before a fist smashed into his jaw from the side.

"Did you like being hit by a man?" Liam's voice was fierce, his hand still clenched. "Or should we try that again? So you can really think about your answer."

Sebastien touched his mouth, and his fingers came away bloody. "What do you think you're doing?" he growled through swollen lips.

Liam nodded to where he'd dropped his poles on the ground. "Going fishing. You weren't exactly what I thought I'd catch this morning. I do believe I'll throw you back where you came from." He moved his body in front of Vivienne's, a wall between her and Sebastien. "I might ask what *you* were doing, but I already know the answer."

"You don't know anything."

Lips still burning from the stolen kiss, Vivienne rubbed the red welts on her wrist. She stepped aside to see the man so lustful for position that he would hurt her. "Go."

Liam walked over to Sebastien. He was taller and broader and every bit more a man than Sebastien had ever been. "I'll escort you."

"Don't be a fool, Vienne." Sebastien licked his lip. "They will come for him. Henri is not safe. Nor are you."

Liam grasped his elbow and marched him toward the road.

"I warned you!" Sebastien called over his shoulder. But she would not look at him again.

The men disappeared. Smoldering against Sebastien, Vivienne circled her rose bushes, pulling spent blooms from their stems and dropping them to the earth. When she had picked both bushes clean, she cupped the last withered rose in her palm, peeled back the tan, crusted outer petals and plucked a still-soft white one from the center. As she rubbed the velvety texture with her thumb, Sebastien's last words echoed in her mind. Was there any truth in them? Would anyone come for Henri?

When Liam returned, she let the last petals fall from her hand. "What did you do?" she asked him.

Liam put one boot on the front step, knee bent. "Ushered him to Armand and told him what happened. Armand will keep an eye on him until he leaves town this morning. You should have seen how upset Armand was. He does care for you a great deal." He paused. "We both do."

Vivienne willed her heart to calm.

Liam lifted her wrist to inspect it, his thumb circling over her racing pulse. "Sebastien hurt you, didn't he?" He searched her face for a moment, then looked back down at where his thumb still brushed her skin. Bringing her wrist to his lips, he pressed a lingering kiss to the welt.

Her breath caught at the touch of his lips. In his eyes she saw both a question and an answer, restraint and longing.

The front door banged open behind him. "Mr. Delaney!" With his hair sticking up like straw from the back of his head, Henri stuffed his shirt into his trousers. "Are you ready?"

"I am." Liam smiled at Vienne, slowly released her hand, and turned to Henri.

In the road in front of the general store, Paulette handed her letter to Sebastien Lemoine for him to mail upon his return to Philadelphia. He'd never recognize the address, since Corbin Fraser had taken new rooms.

She frowned at his swollen lip. "What happened to you?"

Sebastien moved his jaw sideways with his hand. "I tried. It's up to you to protect Henri now. The Jacobins have been rumbling in Philadelphia lately. I think they have a plan."

"Count on me." Adjusting the strap of her bag on her shoulder, she thanked him, then strolled away as if her heartbeat were not a tocsin within her chest.

Slapping at a mosquito on her neck, she smashed it beneath her fingertips, then bent and wiped the mess on a patch of weeds sprouting along the road. She did not relish the wilderness, but her purpose for being here outweighed personal discomfort. Those who suggested she wasn't tough enough for Asylum were sorely mistaken. And she'd prove it.

With the sun at her back, her brow filmed with sweat as she made her way through the settlement toward Vivienne's house. Paulette paused at the paling fence to straighten her cap and rehearse in her mind what she would say. She tightened her grip on the strap of her bag, the contents of which were the sum of her belongings.

In the yard, sheets snapped from clotheslines, releasing their clean scent on the wind. A laundry basket on her hip, Vivienne stepped out from behind one of them, an apron over her sprigged muslin dress and a ribbon gathering her hair at her neck. A smile broke over her face when she spied Paulette. "Come in!"

Paulette unlatched the gate and entered, then took the basket from Vivienne. "That's enough of that, now that I'm here."

"Pardon me?" Wind tossed Vivienne's curls over her shoulder and blew a strand across her cheek. She pushed it away.

"You don't have any other help about, do you?"

"Help? Liam—Mr. Delaney helps a great deal around the property."

Paulette bit back a sharp reply. She still didn't trust that man. "Don't be stubborn, now. I'm to be your maid."

A ripple moved across Vivienne's forehead before her lips curved at one corner. "I'd love to have your companionship again, but I've learned to help myself."

"I'm sure you have, but just the same, I'm here to serve." Without waiting for permission, Paulette carried the load of wet laundry to an empty clothesline, let her bag drop to the ground along with the basket, and began hanging Henri's breeches.

Vivienne followed her. "Paulette, I rejoice to see you again. I want to hear how you've fared since we parted in December. But though it pains me to admit it, my financial situation has not improved enough for me to afford your services. And I won't have you laboring for me without compensation when you might easily be hired by any number of residents wealthier than me by far."

As if Paulette could stomach working for one of those white-wigged snobs. Undeterred, she draped a petticoat over the line. "Then how do you afford the Irishman's work?"

"I don't."

She already knew that, but she used the opportunity to probe. "You mean his assistance is motivated by something else? Are you two . . ."

Vivienne's cheeks bloomed pink as she pinned a petticoat and breeches into place. "His assistance is *paid for* by someone else."

Paulette smiled. "Of course. Monsieur de Champlain has paid for me, too." It was perfect. "A gift for you. If you please." She held out her hand and nodded at the clothespins sagging in Vivienne's apron pocket.

After a moment's pause, Vivienne transferred them to Paulette's waiting palm. "*You* are my gift from Armand? You two arranged this without consulting me?"

"We've been writing letters. Sebastien told me of the arrangement you two had here, and when I suggested my services, he was only too happy to write a letter of introduction for me to Armand."

Vivienne clasped her hands. "I'm so relieved. He told me last night he had a gift for me, and I couldn't begin to think what it was."

So she was pleased. How nice. Paulette smiled. "I was told you have room enough and work enough for me."

Relaxed now, Vivienne looped her arm through Paulette's. "Come, you'll want to see the house."

The interior of the house was plain but clean. Without wallpaper to disguise the log walls, it was far more rustic than the Grand

Maison but had small bursts of charm here and there. Lace curtains fluttered at open windows. Bouquets of roses and yarrow set in pewter pitchers brightened tables and mantels hewn of wood.

Upstairs, Vivienne pointed to the room where she and Henri slept.

Paulette cocked her head. "He still sleeps in the same room as you? Isn't he ten years old now?"

Vivienne shrugged. "He doesn't like sleeping alone. In the winter, at least, it saves on firewood."

"And where is he now?" Paulette schooled her voice to nonchalance.

"With Mr. Delaney, fishing. I think after that, they are harvesting hay with Mr. Fortune. Henri's taken to the outdoors much better than he ever took to kitchen work." She chuckled. "Or maybe it's the company he favors. They've been so good to him. And for him."

A breath of sultry summer wind puffed through the window. "The country suits him, then. I'm glad. He seemed so frail in the city. But then, I'm sure the news of Louis-Charles last night has bolstered his spirit." Her voice lifted at the end, an invitation for Vivienne to agree with her.

"Absolutely. He's been so concerned about the young king."

Paulette tried not to stiffen. Louis-Charles was not the king. There was no king of France. Even if the boy was intelligent, kind, and mannerly, and if blue blood flowed in his veins. What else was the revolution for, if not to destroy the monarchy and let the people rule themselves?

"And if Louis-Charles were to come to Asylum . . ." Paulette prompted.

"We would rejoice, of course! No child deserves what he has been through."

She should have expected such a sentiment from Vivienne Rivard. Paulette bit her tongue before she could point out what the poor children of France had been through. And didn't those lives matter as much, if not more, than the life of one spoiled boy?

"May he be well, wherever he is." Vivienne led her down the hall and stood in another doorway. "Here you are."

Allowing the conversation to shift, Paulette entered the room and looked about. There was nothing but space to recommend it, but it would do.

"Mr. Delaney will need to make you a bed frame. I have enough leftover ticking that we could sew up a mattress for you straightaway and fill it with fresh hay. We'll also see that you have your own washstand and bureau. Will you want to stay in the Grand Maison until the furniture is made?"

"Not at all," Paulette said lightly, as though she did not still simmer beneath her skin. "I can sleep on the floor in the meantime and get to working for you right away. I see tomatoes in your garden ripe for canning. But show me the state of your cellar first. Let's see what we have to work with."

"Thank you, Paulette. Truly, you are a gift to me."

Paulette's lips curled in a smile. She couldn't have planned this better.

Vivienne seemed to hesitate for a moment. "While I'm thinking of it—I think we may have left something behind in the pension. A gold ring. It would have been shoved back into a corner of a drawer. Did you happen to come across it, perhaps when cleaning after we left?"

"A gold ring, you say?" Paulette's face pinched. "Can't say that I did. I wiped out every drawer in the bureau myself, too." Who else would have done it? Madame Barouche made her do everything.

Vivienne pressed her lips together. "Oh. Well, you would have remembered if you'd seen it, I'm sure."

"Quite." Paulette slipped her hand into her apron pocket and fingered the false lining she'd sewn inside, pressing between her thumb and forefinger a metal circle large enough to fit a man's finger. A king's finger, in fact. Who else was a signet ring for?

Water slid over Liam's chest as he dipped into the gurgling creek. Even after hours spent cutting and stacking hay to dry in the sun, Vivienne remained firmly on his mind. Spreading his arms, he lay on his back, indulging in the cool water on his skin. He stared at the branches swaying overhead and replayed the events of the morning.

What had he been thinking, to kiss Vienne, even on the arm, right after Sebastien had stolen a kiss from her lips? She might have preferred being left alone, considering.

Then again, she might not have minded.

Liam groaned. He was terrible at reading women, and worse at interpreting any moment that wasn't completely straightforward. The only thing he was sure of now was that he yearned for her with a depth and strength that kept him awake into the night and opened his eyes again each morning. He had never felt this way about a woman, ever. And Henri was much more than a pupil to him.

Frowning, Liam recalled Sebastien's outbursts this morning. What had he said on the way to Armand's? Something about Jacobins. But here, in Asylum? It was hard to credit. Holding his breath, Liam submerged his head completely, rinsing bits of straw and grass from his hair and skin.

Sluicing water from his limbs and torso, he emerged from the creek, then stepped back into his trousers. He swung his shirt at the flies, then draped it over his shoulder as he strode toward home, whistling. The tune on his lips had been playing in his head since he'd danced to it with Vivienne last night. A wave of heat washed over him as he recalled how she looked in the moonlight. How she felt in his arms.

Hoofbeats sounded behind him. Liam turned to find a stranger, apparently lost. "Can I help you?" Water dripped from his hairline to the tip of his nose, and he swiped at it with the back of his hand.

The man rode close enough for Liam to see the perspiration darkening his shirt. He mopped his fleshy, sunburned face with a handkerchief, then tugged the brim of his hat into place. "Joseph Cowley. Excise officer. I'm here to collect tax on any whiskey stills in these parts, according to the law passed in 1791."

Liam hooked his thumb into the pocket at his hip. "I'm aware of the law, officer. You'll not find any stills around here. You'd best move along."

Cowley squinted at him. "You certain of that? Never met an Irisher who didn't have a penchant for whiskey and the wherewithal to make his own—or acquaint himself with those who do."

Liam gave a little bow. "Now you have. And don't call me a liar. It makes me cross. As you might have heard, we Irish are prone to a temper." He poured a full brogue into his words and angled his head, displaying his scarred cheek and notched ear to their best advantage.

Eyes rounding, Cowley's gaze scurried from the marks on Liam's face and over his muscles, still wet from the creek. Finding it vastly amusing, Liam slammed a fist into his hand. The officer jumped.

"You best be on your way," Liam repeated.

"Don't you threaten me. I have the full weight of the law on my side."

"Threaten you? No such thing. I'm but giving you a bit of advice. There's a tavern eight miles from here." He pointed. "If you head straight that way and don't look back, you might reach it before the catamounts come out to find you."

"Catamounts?"

"Wildcats. Also, be mindful of wolves. Good day, officer. May the road rise up to meet you, et cetera." Feet planted wide on the path, Liam crossed his arms and waited until the officer's horse trotted away, bouncing him in the saddle. A born horseman, the officer was not.

Liam shrugged off the encounter, grateful that it was he and not Finn who had met the tax collector. Who could guess what Finn would do if he'd chanced upon the likes of Joseph Cowley?

Grasses tugging at his trousers, Liam placed a hand on a knee-high stone fence and vaulted over it, the sunbaked stone warming his palm. The summer air was perfumed with freshly cut alfalfa hay and Jethro's roasted rabbit. Inhaling deeply, he entered the kitchen house he shared with two other bachelors and wondered what it would be like to share a home with a woman instead.

"Hungry?" Jethro ladled a steaming helping of rabbit stew into a wooden bowl and slid it across the table toward Liam.

"Famished, thank you." He tossed his shirt into a corner, lowered himself onto the bench, and bowed his head, blessing both food and friends.

"Thirsty, too, I hope." Finn slammed a tumbler on the table in front of Liam, then sat across from him, staring like a puppy.

Oh no. Liam knew that look. He brought the tumbler to his nose and sniffed. Whiskey.

"Go on, taste it. Not as dark as Monongahela rye, but still better than anything in that Frenchie's inn. I call it Susquehanna rye. Or maybe Pennsylvania rye. Which is better, d'ye think?"

"Short memory, friend. Whiskey isn't my drink."

Jethro laughed, a deep rich rumble, and tucked into his own stew. "It's not bad, though."

"Are you in on this?" Liam asked Jethro. "Did you both use your shares of the rye harvest to make whiskey?"

"Plan to." Jethro swallowed. "Why not? It's still the most profitable use of the grain and the easiest way to get it to market."

"You should see the still, Liam," Finn added. "I've been working on it for months. Didn't want to tell you about it before I knew it would work. Well, it works."

"I don't want to see it." He pushed the tumbler away. "An excise officer came through today, looking for stills to tax. Which means he was looking for you two."

"Don't forget Ernest and Derek Schultze. They use it for their own rye, and all I ask in return is a small share of the whiskey they produce."

"Quite the operation you have." Liam kneaded the muscles in his shoulder, still stiff from cutting hay. "And I told the officer there was no such thing around." Was it a lie, if he believed it true at the time?

Finn grinned, pushing his ruddy cheeks back from brown-stained teeth. "Well done, lad. A toast." He lifted his tumbler. "To second chances. To crops that pay. To a future rising from *your land*, whatever Armand may call it."

Liam poured a glass of water and lifted it. "To a future. To the land," he said, and drank. But it did not sit well with him.

341

Chapter Thirty-One

A week had passed since Paulette's arrival, and every day the young woman offered assistance Vivienne hadn't even realized she needed. From boiling old potatoes into a starch to planting onion ends in the garden to grow new plants, she had a use for everything. Vivienne shadowed her movements in order to learn and try to help, but today she sensed she was merely underfoot. So she turned to what she did best.

Sunshine checkered the lace pillow on her lap as it streamed through the lattice on the summer house. Her baking for the inn delivered for the day, she was glad to be out of doors. Deftly, her fingers crossed bobbins tied to the strands over, under, and across the delicate threads. A pattern emerged, fit for a king. If Louis-Charles were to arrive in the settlement, he would be in dire need of, well, everything. Evelyne Sando had volunteered to embroider fleur-de-lys onto a new silk coverlet, while Vienne worked on lace cuffs, using Henri as a model for size.

"Care for some company?" Without waiting for a response, Paulette carried her two pails into the summer house and sat across from Vienne on the bench. She scooped a mess of beans into her aproned lap and began shelling, dropping the peas into the empty bucket at her feet and letting the hulls patter to the floor.

"Thank you for doing that," Vienne said. Beyond her, across the fields of alfalfa hay, butterflies flurried like snow.

Paulette grunted. "You have the harder work, by far. It scarcely takes a single thought to run a thumb along the seam and pop these peas out. Oh—will my being here bother you? Break your concentration?"

Vienne smiled without looking up. "You can talk. As long as I watch what I'm doing, I'll be fine."

"Good. Henri isn't back yet, I see. Don't you worry?"

Vienne shook her head. "He's only fishing in the creek. Mr. Delaney is with him."

"And you trust him with the boy?"

Wind rustled through the space between them, ruffling the hems of their skirts. "Yes. He has more than proven himself on that score." Though her personal feelings for Liam had tangled and grown wild, she knew beyond a doubt that he was good for Henri. And the child adored him. "But I'm not quite decided on his cousin, Finn, and the company he keeps."

"Oh?"

"He has a good heart, but he tends to act without thinking. And the two American laborers who have befriended him—the Schultze brothers—are known for sloppy workmanship and drunkenness." But the Schultzes were not foremost in her mind today. "Paulette, I must ask you to forgive me. I've never inquired about your family or how you came to be in Philadelphia. You know plenty about me and Henri. Won't you tell me about yourself?"

For a moment, Paulette's hands stilled. Then, with characteristic spirit, she resumed her shelling. "My goodness. Can't say as I've ever been asked that by my employer before."

"But don't think of me that way." After all, she was not the one paying her wages. "You've done so much for me. You changed my life by teaching me how to bake. So, please, I'd really like to hear your story. Unless the telling of it brings you pain." Why had she not considered that until now? Perhaps this was the reason the girl hadn't already mentioned a parent, a sibling, a friend. Vienne should tread lightly. "How long did you work at the Pension Sainte-Marie?"

Odd, that she didn't respond right away. The question was innocuous enough. But then, "Six years. Madame Barouche hired me when I was fourteen. I was young, but I knew how to work. And I suppose Madame couldn't afford the wages of an older, more experienced maid."

Vienne's hands suspended, bobbins held between her fingers so she could glance at Paulette. "That must have been hard. I was working by that age, too."

"With your aunt, you said. But not your parents."

"No. My aunt raised me as her own child, or as close to it as she could." Not for the first time, Vivienne wondered if Tante Rose had felt as out of her element as she had felt with Henri. "And your parents?"

"I watched them die."

"Oh!" Vienne clutched the bobbins in her hands and looked up. "I'm so sorry."

Calmly, Paulette went on shelling peas, never breaking her rhythm to sniff or wipe a tear. No emotion of any kind changed her features. "It was a long time ago."

"But it's not something one ever forgets."

"I was very young. I barely remember them. I only recall the moments they died. I wish the opposite were true, you know? That I remembered their lives and not their deaths. I don't know for sure, but I think they might have been good people." She poured a pile of hulls onto the floor and scooped another handful of beans into her lap. "After that, I lived on the charity of others for years, until I could work in domestic service in Marseille. But my employers were . . . not kind. I hid on a ship, finally landing in Philadelphia. That was in 1789. Right before the Bastille fell, actually. I found Madame Barouche and have worked for her ever since. That is, until she decided the pension was too much for her advancing years and took a room above a *parfumerie* on South Second Street."

"Such a hard life, Paulette. I had no idea. Thank you for sharing that with me." Vivienne could not think what else to say. Her own life could have paralleled that tale, had it not been for Tante Rose.

They grew quiet, with only the sound of dropping peas and the patter of bobbins dropping on the pillow as Vienne traded one silk strand for another. A black-capped chickadee fluttered into the summer house and alighted on the lattice, apparently content to watch the women work.

"Well." Paulette rose, brushing off her apron. "I know my story didn't make for good telling. The living of it was even worse. But we're here now, aren't we? No looking back."

"Indeed," Vivienne mused. For she had nowhere else to go. "Paulette? Sebastien said something about a possible danger to Henri. Have you heard any whisperings about that? I hate to see hobgoblins where there are none, but I don't want to play the fool, either."

Paulette reached over and patted her knee. "Never you mind about that. If anything's amiss, I'll know it before anyone else, you can count on that. I'll keep a good watch on you both."

Smiling, Vienne returned to her work. "It's so good to have you here."

Night lay thick as molasses on Liam's skin, though the window was open to invite a breeze. Hay crunched in the mattress as he turned onto his side, a fly buzzing in his ear. If Jethro and Finn could sleep in this heat, no doubt it was only with the help of whiskey.

Whiskey. The word had come to mean so much more than a drink and could scarcely be uttered without thought of the excise that went with it. Liam didn't agree with the tax any more now than he ever had, but the fire that had once burned in his belly against it was gone. He had spoken and fought against it. And he'd lost.

A Bible verse, long buried, surfaced in his mind. *Render therefore unto Caesar the things which are Caesar's; and unto God the things that are God's.*

Liam turned onto his back and stared at the ceiling. He had always tried to do the right thing, as he saw it. But it had been far too long since he'd asked God to show him the right, as He saw it. That the two could be different unnerved him. He pushed himself out of bed and went to the window, leaning on the sill for a breath of air, if not a fresh wind.

Then he heard a man screaming for help, clearly terrified. *What on earth?*

Liam hastily pulled on his trousers and grabbed a knife from his bureau before bounding down the stairs and outside. The man in distress couldn't be far. The cries intensified, leading Liam in the direction of Vienne's house, until he came upon a large pale form at the edge of the woods.

"Help me! You have to help me!"

Moonlight filtered through the clouds. "Joseph Cowley?" The excise officer was stripped naked and tied to a tree.

"You," Cowley snarled. "You said there were no whiskey stills in these parts. Then I sampled some at that tavern you sent me to, and they told me it came from here."

"Who did this to you?"

"Two men. German accents. Took my clothes and ran."

The Schultze brothers. Holding back an unholy oath, Liam unfolded his knife as the smell of burning tar met his nose.

Shadowed by night, Derek and Ernest arrived, carrying a pot of tar between them. Two long sticks topped with sponges jutted from Derek's right hand, while Ernest clutched the neck of a burlap sack, undoubtedly full of feathers. Watching Liam, they set down the pot.

"Evening, boys," Liam said. "Lovely night for a walk, isn't it? Only it seems to me it's past your bedtime."

Derek glared at the knife in Liam's hand. "What do you think you're doing here, old man?" A thatch of red hair fell over his brow.

"Preventing the two of you from doing something very stupid and very cruel." He hoped.

Ernest dipped his sponge in the tar and held it up, the dripping black liquid a perfect match to his hair. "I heard tell you fought the whiskey rebels out in Washington County, but I also heard you helped Finn O'Brien escape before he was thrown in jail. So which is it, Delaney? Are you a friend or foe to liberty?"

Liam clenched his teeth. He certainly didn't have it all figured out, but he knew that severely burning a man with hot tar was not the answer. "The tax is the law. I'll not stand by and let you destroy a man for doing his job."

"So you're for tyranny, now," Derek sneered. "Strange, for a veteran of our revolution."

Liam stood his ground, silently calculating how many seconds it would take to cut through Cowley's bindings. Too many. If the brothers had a mind to, they could simply pick up the cauldron and heave its contents over the naked man in a shorter time. He ducked behind the tree and placed the hilt of his knife in the tax man's hands. Let him cut through his bindings himself.

"Oh no, you don't." Derek lunged, but Liam caught him by the shoulders and shoved him backward, hard. The young man fell on his rear, dangerously close to the pot of hot tar. While he scrambled to his feet, Ernest plunged his stick into the pot once more and thrust it toward Liam.

He dodged it, then yanked the stick from the reckless young man's grip and threw it as hard as he could into the woods.

"Look out!" Cowley shrieked, then took off running through the trees. Derek lit after him, dripping stick in his grip.

Ernest charged into Liam, knocking the air from his lungs as he plowed him into the ground. Liam rolled until he had the upper hand. Unwilling to break Ernest's nose, Liam slammed his fist into his jaw just hard enough to slow him down and take the fight out of him.

He should have punched harder. Infuriated, the younger man lashed about, all rage and no strategy. Still, he managed to connect his fist with Liam's nose.

Derek ran out of the woods alone, poised to dunk his sponge back in the cauldron of tar. The taste of blood in his mouth, Liam wrenched free of Ernest's flailing limbs, dashed to the pot, and overturned it, spilling the tar on the ground.

"We're done here," he growled. "Go home."

Clouds passed over the moon, and in the sudden darkness, Liam lost track of Ernest. He felt a blow to the back of his knees at the same time hands grabbed his shoulders and yanked. Hands outstretched, he fell to the ground—right on a puddle of congealing tar. It coated his hand and splashed onto his chest.

A lantern came bobbing toward them. "Who's there?"

Pain warbled her voice in his ears. He understood by the sound of their footsteps that Derek and Ernest grabbed the pot and made a hasty retreat.

As the light came closer, Liam stood and backed away from the spreading tar, holding his burning hand away from his body. He glanced at Vivienne and saw her feet were bare beneath the hem of her dress. "Stay back!" he said through gritted teeth. "There's tar on the ground."

She stopped, glancing to the earth, then up to his blackened hand and the flecks of tar on his torso. Her eyes widened. "Cold water?" she said.

He grimaced. "The creek." He had to stop the burning.

Quickly, she led the way with her lantern to a grassy bank downstream from the springhouse. Jaw clenched, he strode into the water and knelt on the muddy bed so the creek came up over the burning spots on his side and chest. He squeezed his eyes shut and moaned, more from frustration than the pain.

Vivienne stayed quiet as minutes ticked by, but he knew by the presence of light that she remained. When he opened his eyes, he found her sitting on the bank beside the lantern, her dress tucked modestly around her. Her hair fell in a thick braid over one shoulder.

"What happened?" she asked.

He told her.

Moths fluttered against the lantern casing. "You were defending the tax collector?"

"I was defending a victim of pointless violence. He happened to be a tax collector." Who also happened to be after his cousin to pay the excise.

Vivienne twisted the end of her braid around one finger. "I'm so sorry you were hurt. You were doing the right thing."

"Aye." Just like he was doing the right thing at Mingo Creek, right before a bullet tore a path through the side of his face. "It's such a pain." His lips twitched up, as did hers. But it could have been much worse. The tar had already cooled somewhat before he'd come in contact with it. Still, if he felt like this now, he could only imagine the agony Joseph Cowley would have suffered if the Schultze boys had managed to coat his naked body. "I've made more enemies tonight." He climbed out of the water and sat on the bank beside her.

"Maybe so. But I'm on your side." She took his hand in hers and bent her head to inspect the tar. A breeze stirred the lace at her elbows.

He tried flexing his palm beneath the shell of hardened tar.

"No, don't," she said. "Don't pick at it or peel it off. It might take good skin with it. Wait until it loosens on its own. Does it hurt very terribly?"

Liam withdrew his hand and rested it, palm up, on his own lap. "Less terribly. It feels like a crust on a hand I'm rather fond of using." He spread his good hand over the tar scabbing his side. "It's a good thing I've never been vain, or I'd be disappointed at my diminishing good looks."

A smile curving gently on her lips, she wiped the creek water beading on his scarred left cheek before tucking her hand back into the folds of her skirt. "Some of us are marked on the outside."

"And some on the inside?"

"Yes." She peered out over the creek, though he knew she couldn't see a thing beyond the pool of lantern light they shared. He couldn't see anything past Vivienne. He didn't want to.

He skimmed her profile, from the dark eyelashes to the graceful arc of her neck. She'd taken the time to trade her nightgown for a dress before coming outside, but he hadn't even bothered to grab a shirt. Their legs stretched out in front of them both, guiltless of stockings or shoes. With her ankles crossed, bare toes peeked out from beneath her hem.

Perhaps he should look away from her. He didn't. "Are you scandalized, sitting in the dark, alone with me?"

"Only a little." Her tone held no guile or artifice. "I'm not a maiden of tender years, all innocence and naïveté."

He did not want a maiden of tender years, untested by life's trials.

"I'm an old maid, at nine and twenty. And feel far older still."

"As old as me?" he teased, for he had ten years on her. Sobering, he added, "I'm too old for games. There's something bothering you, and I have a feeling it's not an excise tax. Please, Vienne. Let us be honest with each other."

She drew her knees under her chin. "You're right. You need to know something about me, Liam, though I'm ashamed to make it plain." She paused so long, he wondered if she had changed her mind about telling him.

"Is it something you've done?" he prodded gently. "I've made mistakes, myself. We all have."

"No. It's who I am." A sigh lifted her chest and released. "I'm the illegitimate daughter of a courtesan, thanks to Armand." A small laugh broke from her. "And there you have it. No wonder I have no shame in talking to a half-bare man, unchaperoned, by the light of moon and lantern." She hugged her knees tighter. "I expect you think less of me now."

Disoriented, Liam swallowed. "No. I don't think less of you. You're not stained by the sins of your parents."

"I never wanted to take advantage of Armand's guilt over—" She swirled her hand in the air, and he understood. "But then with the danger in Philadelphia . . . and my funds were running out as it was, even with baking at the tavern. I suppose we always have choices, but I felt it was the only decision I could make. So I let Armand provide for me, though it galled me then and galls me now. This is *your* land, Liam. Whatever any piece of paper says." Her voice trembled with conviction. "And there's the rub. I wish we hadn't taken it from you. I'm sorry."

"If there was anything to forgive, I would. You've done no wrong."

"Thank you. But Liam, now that we're here, I don't want to live anywhere else," she whispered.

"Then don't." Nothing mattered to him more than her, more than keeping her by his side. He angled to face her. Moved closer. Vienne's glance skittered over his chest before meeting his eyes. The pain from the tar receding, Liam swallowed, trying to master the longing unfurling inside him. "I won't steal from you what you aren't willing to give, and I won't take liberties that aren't mine to take. So I'm asking for your permission. I'd like—I'd *really* like—to kiss you. Properly. If I may."

Her breath shuddered as she gave the barest of nods.

Gently, he lifted her chin and bent his head to hers, his hand cupping the slender column of her neck before sliding behind her back. Vienne flattened a hand against his chest and kissed him tenderly, then with an urgency that felt like hunger. He felt her plunge her fingers through his hair at the back of his head. If she leaned in any closer, he doubted he'd have the strength to stay upright.

He trailed his lips to her cheek, then her earlobe, her jaw, her neck. Then broke away.

"Maybe we do need a chaperone," he said, taking her hand for the simple pleasure of holding it.

Vivienne's smile told him she agreed. "That was"—she paused to catch her breath—"proper." She laughed and squeezed his hand.

A clover-scented breeze fluttered the leaves in the branches overhead, and a frog croaked from somewhere along the moonlit creek. At length, Liam mustered the courage to break the spell. "Will you stay, Vienne?" As the question left him, he realized how little he had to offer her. He had no land anymore, only hope and determination. She deserved more than that. "Will you remain, at least, in America?"

"This is where I belong." But a shadow passed over her features.

"And Henri believes he belongs in France. When the time is right. Is that it?"

She nodded. "Yes."

He studied her for a moment before replying. "So will you do what's right for you? Or will you do what a ten-year-old child believes is right for him?"

Her jaw set. "I will pray, mon cher, that God leads us on a path that is right for both of us. For *all* of us." She placed a tender kiss on the scar on his cheek and stood. "I should go."

And like a firefly whose glow vanishes into the night, she was gone.

Chapter Thirty-Two

Paulette should have burned the reply she received from Philadelphia as soon as she'd read it. Perhaps she was weak, to need to read it so many times. Perhaps she was weak to be clutching it in the dark even now, when what she really needed was to sleep. Or to think. And right now, she could scarcely do either.

Starlight fell in fleur-de-lys patterns across the floor in her room through lace curtains. If Vivienne's aunt had not been guillotined, and if Vivienne had not been charged with caring for a child raised at Versailles, perhaps she would be more sympathetic to the revolution. As it was, all that seemed to matter to her was a little boy who was not even her own son. Her narrow focus was foolhardy. The entire world was at stake. Even the American Thomas Jefferson had said so. Whatever blood must be shed would be worth it for the cause of liberty, for the rights of the common man.

And, of course, the common woman.

Flipping her thin braid over one shoulder, Paulette slipped from bed and lit a taper, resolved to do what she'd said she would. Dipping the tip of her letter into the flame, she waited until it caught, then dropped it into the fireplace, where she watched the words curl and shrivel into ashes.

Kill him.

Bullfrogs twanged, and crickets sang. But those two words roared in her ears. She knew why it must be done.

Since Monsieur Talon had announced that the boy who'd died in prison was not, in fact, Louis-Charles, hope flourished in Asylum. Building supplies had been moved out of the dauphin's room in the Grand Maison, and new furnishings were collected with an eye to pleasing the true Louis-Charles. All the while, the people here would ask Henri, "Would Louis-Charles like this? Would that suit his fancy?" And Henri replied with confidence. He knew every preference, every dislike, without hesitation.

It wasn't long before more people than Suzanne Arquette were conjecturing that he might be king. And all they had to go on was circumstantial—his age, his coloring, his comportment. His rickets. They had no idea he'd also been custodian of Louis XVI's signet ring and the boy king's stuffed horse. Paulette had found the toy while cleaning Corbin Fraser's room one day and recognized it as Henri's at once. Only when she turned it over and saw the embroidery on the hoof did she realize its significance. Henri had lost it during an attempted abduction, she remembered, and it had found its way into Corbin's hands.

While possession of the ring and the toy was not enough to prove without doubt that Henri was Louis-Charles, it was too much to ignore. *The revolution is not yet over,* Corbin had written from Philadelphia. *If there is the slightest chance the boy could be Louis-Charles Capet, there must be an end to the matter, and soon. Kill him.*

Paulette rose and walked to the washstand, where she laved clean water over her sweat-glossed face. In the mirror above the basin, she studied her shadowy reflection. Was this the face of a murderer? She looked at her hands, rough from scrubbing, washing, cooking, gardening. But could these same hands also kill a child?

Groaning, she sank onto the edge of the bed and held her head in her hands. All this agony over the fate of someone else's child. Had anyone agonized when Paulette's child had been killed? She clutched her middle, rocking back and forth as the pain of memory ripped through her. She had been a fourteen-year-old scullery maid when the master of the house decided to take her to his bed. An abortion ended the life he'd planted in her womb and obliterated the hope of ever having children of her own. She was not supposed to want her baby, and yet she had. With her parents dead, that little life had been her very own, her flesh and blood, and even that was stolen from her.

That was what she fought against. A system that created classes, that made the rich richer while taking from the poor. Just because she had fled her country prior to the Bastille's fall did not mean she cheered for it any less. The poor bore the brunt of France's financial burdens, while nobles and priests were never taxed—in coin or in any other way. That was why there had to be a revolution, and why the revolution must succeed. Somehow, she had known ever since her baby had been murdered inside her that she would atone for his life.

She just hadn't imagined the atonement meant taking the life of another child. But of course it did. And what better child than one who might be king?

The taste of bile filled her mouth. Inexplicably, she felt an urge to pray—but she did not believe in God. "Reason," she whispered to herself. "I believe in reason." And what could be more reasonable than this? Still, she hoped for some sign.

Shouts from outside pricked her ears. Remaining still on her bed, she strained to listen. There it was again. From the next room, where Vivienne and Henri both slept, shuffling sounds betrayed that Vivienne was dressing. Footsteps faded down the hall. The front door opened and closed, and the cabin shuddered.

So did Paulette. She was alone in the house with Henri. *A sign.*

As if propelled by some unseen force, she quietly stole into the hallway and slipped into Henri's room. Even in his sleep, he clutched that small whittled horse, a replacement for Bucephalus. His blond hair curled about his head like a halo. But he was neither angel nor saint. He was either the son of Martine Chastain, whose chief concerns before the revolution related to fashions and parties—or he was the son of Marie Antoinette. A likeable child, perhaps, but one who must be sacrificed for the greater good. The revolution must not fail. The royalists must not be given their king, or even one who may pretend to be king. They must not even be allowed to hope. Not at any cost.

With her pulse rushing in her ears and sweat dripping down her sides beneath her nightdress, Paulette could barely draw breath in the suffocating room. Her weakness appalled her. She loathed Charlotte Corday, who had assassinated Jacobin leader Jean-Paul Marat two years ago, but the action had taken strength and singleness of mind that even Paulette could admire. The twenty-four-year-old Charlotte had traveled from Caen to Paris, purchased a kitchen knife with a six-inch blade, and entered Marat's home when he happened to be bathing. If her palms had been slick on the hilt of her knife, she plunged it into his chest anyway and made a martyr of the revolutionary leader, though she knew her action would send her to the guillotine. "*To save your country means not noticing what it costs,*" she had said in her trial, right before her execution.

On this, Paulette and Charlotte Corday agreed. But Paulette would save her country for the Jacobins. She would save the revolution from the royalists. And dismiss the cost. In the same way royalists esteemed Charlotte Corday, revolutionaries would remember the name Paulette Dubois. Forever.

The "Ça Ira" played in her mind. *It'll be fine, it'll be fine.* Vivienne's pillow became a weapon in her hands. But would Henri awake, without air, and fight? She moved his arms to his sides as he lay on his back. A cloud passed over the moon, extinguishing the silver glow in the room. In that moment of utter darkness, she gathered her shift to her knees and eased herself onto his bed, straddling him, pinning him. She suspended the pillow above his head.

What? He died in his sleep? she would say in the morning to a weeping Vivienne. *How tragic! No, don't blame yourself. You couldn't have known . . .*

Paulette pressed the pillow over Henri's face. Gently at first, then harder, until she thought she could feel the small protrusion of his nose beneath it. He struggled beneath her, legs kicking against the sheets, torso twisting. Ignoring his muffled cries, she held fast. She would kill this boy in his sleep, just as Charlotte Corday had killed Marat in his bath.

Charlotte had been ready to die for her crime. If anyone suspected

Paulette, was she ready to suffer the same consequence? *No one will ever know I did it.* But another voice screamed louder: *Maybe.* Henri was tiring, or losing consciousness, or both. Was she willing to die for this act? She did not fear the righteous judgment of a God who did not exist, nor did she believe in an afterlife. But she did believe in pain. What would Talon, former chief of secret police, do to her if he thought she had killed the sole heir to the French throne? Perspiration filmed her entire body. Her arms shook.

Downstairs, the door closed, its latch resounding in her ears with the force of a cannon blast. She rolled off Henri, placed Vivienne's pillow back on her bed, and darted from the room. The tread on the stair grew louder as Paulette scrambled back to her chamber.

Henri roused and cried out.

Footsteps ran to him. "What is it?" Vivienne's voice through the wall.

Crying and gasping. Words Paulette could not decipher. What did he know? What did he tell her? Paulette cursed herself for her sloppy half attempt. If he accused her—

"A nightmare," Vivienne soothed, and the air whooshed back into Paulette's lungs. "Another bad dream, but all is well. It'll be fine, it'll be fine. . . ."

A chill spiraled down Paulette's spine as she heard in Vivienne's consolation the chorus of "Ça Ira." Another sign. She had failed tonight, but she would try again. Outside, the sky cleared, and shadows once more formed across her bed in the shape of the symbol of the monarchy. She traced the outline of the lily with her finger, an anthem on her lips.

> Ah! It'll be fine, It'll be fine, It'll be fine
> the aristocrats, we'll hang them!
> If we don't hang them
> We'll break them
> If we don't break them
> We'll burn them.

Vivienne sat next to Henri on the bed and swept the hair off his sticky brow. "It was just a nightmare," she murmured to him. "Yes, but it felt so real! It was one of those where I couldn't see anything, couldn't scream. I tried calling for you, but I couldn't." Madame Fishypaws leapt onto the bed and walked up Henri's body, standing on the boy's chest while he stroked behind her ears. "I couldn't even breathe."

"That sounds awful. I'm right here." She hadn't been, minutes ago, but it wasn't as if Henri had been left home alone. If he had truly called out much longer, if he really had some need, Paulette would have heard him. Paulette would have come to his aid.

"Do you suppose Fishypaws had any role in this dream?" Vienne suggested. The kitten had a habit of insisting on attention at night, rubbing its body across Vienne's face until she awoke and petted it. Perhaps Madame Fishypaws had draped herself over Henri's face while he slept.

"Oh." He yawned and rolled to his side, and the kitten tumbled beside him. After kneading her small paws into the mattress, she curled up beside Henri. "I don't know. Maybe. I think I can go back to sleep if you stay here for a while."

"I'll be in my own bed across the room. That's close enough, mon cher. You'll be fine." Rising, she stooped to brush a kiss to his temple, and his arm came around her neck and squeezed. "I love you," she whispered.

"I love you, too," he said.

Vienne smiled at the dimples fading in and out of his cheeks as he nestled into his pillow.

The floor was warm and smooth beneath her feet as she walked through a gossamer moonbeam. She slipped behind the folding screen and changed into her nightdress before climbing into her bed. Drowsiness was slow to join her. As Henri's breathing steadied and slowed in sleep, her thoughts swung back to Liam, as they often did while she lay in a bed he'd made, in a house he'd built, on land that once belonged to him.

But tonight was different. Tonight there was more to think

about than wood and earth. Hay crunched in its ticking as Vienne rolled over and scooped a paper fan from the floor. Closing her eyes, she stirred a breeze toward her face and waited for guilt or shame to pounce.

It didn't. The only thing she felt was a thrilling wonder. And if she were honest with herself, a longing to belong to Liam. He knew her and wanted her still. When he asked permission to kiss her properly, a yearning, long subdued, had awakened for the man she loved. She had hoped but not dared to believe, until now, that his feelings for her reached beyond friendship. Now she knew. Faith, but he had certainly banished all doubt.

Perhaps they should take care not to be alone together like that again.

With a smile, she worked the fan faster.

Footsteps.

Squinting against the sunlight filling his room, Liam swung his legs over the bed and followed the sound into the hallway. As much as he'd like to linger in memories of last night with Vienne, the events that had preceded their unplanned moment by the creek surged in his mind. He needed answers. Now.

"Finn." Liam's voice boomed at the top of the stairs, catching his cousin on his way down. "Did you know?"

At the bottom of the steps, Finn turned. "And a good morning to you, too."

"I've had better." Descending to join him, Liam raised the hand that was encrusted with hardened tar. Pain pulsed beneath its surface. "I asked you a question. Sit down." He jerked his chin toward the parlor.

Eye widening as he took in Liam's hand and the black splatters on his chest, Finn slinked into the room and folded his wiry frame into a chair.

Jethro appeared in the doorway. "What's this?" His gaze caught on Liam's black scabs.

"A little gift from the Schultze brothers last night. And I need to know if Finn, or you, had something to do with it."

Mouth pulling down at the corners, Jethro leaned against the parlor doorframe and crossed his arms over his work shirt. "I have no idea what you're talking about. Do you, Finn?"

A fly buzzed in languid lines near the fireplace. Finn dropped his head into his hands.

Liam's jaw clenched. "Then I'll tell you what I know. The excise collector, Joseph Cowley, was tied up to a tree, naked, when I found him last night. Surprised you didn't hear his screams, too, by the way. Or maybe I shouldn't be. Because Derek and Ernest Schultze came moments later with a pot of hot tar and bag of feathers. I got in the way of the plan. Mr. Cowley is fine, in case you were worried. Now, I'll ask you again. What do you know?"

Jethro shook his head. "You think I'd be fool enough to have any part in such a plot against a white man? I'd lose my freedom, maybe more than that. No sir, I'd never try it, even if I wanted to, which I don't. I've seen the likes of tar and feathers before. Ain't no way I'd do that to someone. And if I'd heard tell of such a plan, you can bet I'd have spoken against it."

Liam believed him and told him so, and Jethro left to make him a salve of comfrey and feverfew. Liam sat across the game table from Finn and waited. Outside, a woodpecker drilled into the silence stretching between the two cousins.

"You weren't supposed to get hurt."

"Hang it all, Finn!" Liam slammed a hand onto the chessboard and launched from his chair. He paced across the braided rug, the thick fibers cushioning his feet. "You knew about this? Did you help plan it? I know you've got an ax to grind on this tax issue, but this is beneath human decency."

"Slow down. I'm not as fully to blame as you think."

"Oh no?" Liam swiveled to find Finn on his feet, hands up to halt his tirade. "How fully to blame are you, then?"

Air puffed sharply through Finn's nose. "After you told us Cowley had come through here, I mentioned it to Derek and Ernest. We joked about what we'd do if he ever came back. I said I wouldn't pay, because I have no cash. They said they wouldn't pay, even if they did."

"And then?"

"Ernest asked me what had happened to the excise officers in Washington County when they came around to collect. I told them the truth." He scratched the patchy whiskers on his cheek. "Some were scared off with just words, one or two that I know of were tarred and feathered. But I have never been part of that myself, Liam, not out west, and not here." His voice tapered off at the end.

Liam angled his good ear toward his cousin. "What are you not telling me?"

Finn pinched the front of his shirt and flapped it back and forth to fan himself, for already the day was too warm. Then he crossed his arms and studied the mantel behind Liam. "Derek asked me how tarring and feathering was done. I told him to use his common sense and figure it out himself. It couldn't be complicated. I didn't mean that he should actually carry it out on someone. You've got to believe me, cousin. I never thought this would happen, and I certainly never thought you'd come to harm in the process."

That Finn never thought, Liam believed. Struggling to keep Finn's past indiscretions out of the argument, Liam held his tongue before he said something he would regret later, for he could feel his temper rising. *Think it through, Finn. Just think.* How many times had Liam told him that? He'd always been far too easily influenced by careless comrades.

And yet somehow not influenced enough by Liam. If Liam was at fault for that, he prayed God would forgive him. Staring at his blackened palm, he exhaled as much frustration as he could. If what Finn had told him was true, he'd been thoughtless, but not the merciless scoundrels the Schultze brothers were. He hoped.

"Tell me this, Finn. If you had come across Cowley about to be cast into the most intense suffering he'd ever known, what would you have done? I want the truth."

Finn walked to the window and opened it wider. Humidity

infused the room without a breath of wind to carry it. He swatted at a mosquito on his arm before facing Liam. "The truth is, I don't know. Maybe I'd have intervened like you did. Maybe I'd have looked the other way. I truly don't know. And that's the most honest answer I can give. I'm certain that disappoints you, but we can't all be Liam Delaneys."

Liam rubbed his hand over his face. "I don't want you to be anyone but yourself. But I want you to be the best version of Finn O'Brien you can be."

"And what would that be? The kind with two eyes, ten toes, and a thriving carpentry trade?" The edge in Finn's tone belied the pain beneath the words. "Do you think I like living on charity? Do you think I don't know I'm a burden, just like I was when I first moved into your household?" His shoulders hunched slightly upward, as they had when he was a boy, caught in some kind of trouble.

"Finn." Liam crossed to him and gripped his shoulder until it settled back down into place. "You're not a burden, you're family. And I'm living on the same arrangement as you, remember? This land and house don't belong to any of us. But as long as you do live here, we must come to an agreement. If Joseph Cowley comes back around, or any man he sends in his place, there will be no violence. We'll settle your debt. We will live inside the law, cousin. This is the country we fought to establish. It's time to play by this country's rules. If you need to cut ties with Derek and Ernest to make this easier—and I strongly suggest you do—the sooner, the better."

Finn nodded, his expression serious. "I am sorry about your tar, you know."

"I forgive you." Liam released him and wondered if Jethro was about ready with that salve. "And I trust this won't happen again."

Henri kicked a plank in the paling fence, only mildly caring if it came loose. No one had time for him anymore.

Sweat made his scalp itch under his straw hat. He picked up a stick and dragged it along the fence as he walked. *Ta-ta-ta-ta-ta-ta-ta.* All along the perimeter he went, sometimes slower, sometimes faster, listening to the stick sing against the wood. *Ta-ta-ta-ta-ta-ta-ta!*

Boring.

With a sigh no one heard, he squatted at the edge of Vivienne's garden and plunged the stick into the earth between her flowers. He stirred the soft soil until he found a big fat worm and tried to pick it up without using his hands, but it writhed away.

Boring.

He couldn't wait for Louis-Charles to get here. One day, they'd be together again—here for a while, and then back in France.

Henri plunged his hands into his pockets. "Mademoiselle!" he called, marching toward the kitchen house. He stood in the open doorway but would not go in. The building was cozy in the winter, but midsummer made it like an oven. "Mademoiselle, how long will it be, do you suppose, until we can all go back to France?"

She leaned on the table's floured surface and dropped her head for a moment. When she looked up again, she didn't look happy. Not mad, though, either, though he asked this same question fairly often. "We can't go back yet," she told him quietly. "You know that, mon cher. No one knows how long it will be until it's safe to return."

Henri gripped his whittled horse inside his pocket. Waiting was such hard work. "Let's go for a canoe ride," he suggested. "It will cool you off. Won't that feel nice, to be out on the river?"

She punched down a bowl of dough. "Not now, Henri. Perhaps later."

Perhaps later. He'd heard that before.

"What's Mr. Delaney doing today?"

"I don't know." She didn't even look up this time.

Henri crouched and called to his cat. "Here, Fishy Fishy Fishy Fishy!" When she came, he scooped her up and held her beneath his chin. He liked to smell her silky fur. "What about Mr. Fortune? Or Mr. O'Brien? Sometimes they need help. Do you think I could help them?"

"They would have come to get you if that were the case."

That meant no. Probably the men thought he wasn't strong enough for the work even though he'd told them his legs felt so much better. Madame Fishypaws squirmed, and he tossed her to the ground.

Henri pressed his back straight against the doorframe and walked his feet up the other side of it. He was getting pretty good at this. "Look! Look at this, I'm doing it!" Hands gripping the frame behind his back, knees bent, he pushed his feet against the doorway as hard as he could to keep himself locked in place, suspended above the floor. Slipping, he jumped down. "Did you even see that?"

Vivienne looked up and smiled. "I've seen you do that many times."

"That time was the best, though. What are you making? Are you saving some for me? Is it ready?"

"Faith, Henri! Go read a book in the summer house."

"What's this?" Paulette crossed the yard toward him, an empty laundry basket in her hand. Behind her, sheets flapped on the clothesline beneath the cloudless sky. Like sails against the ocean. "Nothing to do, I see."

Henri knew better than to agree with her. Once when he'd done that, she'd set him to shelling black walnuts, and his hands were stained brown for days. Another time, she made him grind coffee beans. He'd much rather stay outside.

"I have it." Paulette tapped her temple, hazel eyes as sharp as the point of her chin. "Vivienne, could you use any raspberries?"

Mademoiselle looked up. "Oh, yes! That would be wonderful. Would you? Would you take him?"

"My pleasure." Paulette picked two small baskets off a shelf and handed one to Henri. "I don't suppose you could show me the way, could you?"

"I most certainly can." A little surge of energy shot through him as he led her through the small settlement toward the winding river.

It didn't take long to reach the place Henri had in mind. Nestled between sighing trees and laughing river, a clearing spread before them where grass bowed low in the wind, a sea of changing greens and ochers. Grasshoppers leapt through undulating blades. Bees hummed from one wildflower to another.

At the edge of the clearing, thorny bushes as tall as his nose were loaded with red, ripe fruit. "Watch out for the stickers," he told Paulette. He'd been poked by them plenty before.

The broad brim of her hat shadowed half her face as she dropped berries into her basket. "We should have worn gardening gloves to protect our hands."

A warbler flickered on a nearby tree, a small yellow flame against the green. "I'm very tough," Henri informed her, "and my arms are smaller than yours. If you want, pick the easy ones, and I'll go in after the rest." He popped a raspberry into his mouth, crushing the flavors with his tongue until he felt the seeds against his teeth. So good. But it would be even better with sugar.

He glanced toward the river. Even from here, he could see the sun sparkling off its churning surface. "Do you know, Paulette, of all the rivers I have known—the Seine, the Delaware, and this one—I love this one best." He smiled at the Susquehanna.

"Is that so? Why?"

Henri ate another berry before adding more to his basket. "I'll show you. But we'll have to leave our baskets here." He looked at her skirt. "Can you climb in that?"

Paulette's hand hovered over her basket. "What do you have in mind?"

He grinned. "Trust me. It will be worth it."

After tucking their baskets where they could find them again later, Henri took Paulette to a path that wound around tree trunks and through underbrush.

"Where are you taking me?" Paulette puffed as she followed him up stony curves.

"Prospect Rock." It was a hard climb, and he'd only done it once before. In the spring, Vivienne had said she felt suffocated by how close the hills were, and Mr. Delaney responded with a hike. He had needed to help Henri in the toughest parts that time, but Henri was stronger now. He could do this. And wouldn't Vivienne and Mr. Delaney be surprised to hear he'd done it without any help? "You'll like it at the top, I know you will."

The trail dipped and climbed, and soon he was panting, too. He'd forgotten how steep it got. In some places, they had to grasp a small tree or branch to keep from falling backward. It was harder for Paulette, because she also had to keep her skirt out of the way. But she did it.

Finally, they reached the top. "See." Henri was short of breath. "That's why I love this one best."

Paulette stood beside him, hand on his shoulder. She put her other hand to her heart, and he smiled. He knew she'd like it.

To the west and south, mountains rose in layers, ridge after ridge. Across the river, hills hundreds of feet high were covered with green trees. Out from the north flowed the Susquehanna River in giant sweeping curves. In the great horseshoe bend lay log houses, all the same except for the Grand Maison, and straight streets crossing each other in a perfect grid. From this distance, it looked like a toy town made of pieces Mr. Delaney had whittled.

Henri sat on the rock, then lowered himself to his back. Soft clouds blotted the blinding blue sky with restful, dove-breast gray. They seemed low enough to touch. He reached up to bury his hand in the feathers.

"I'm going to bring Louis-Charles here one day, too," he said. "But he'll have to be extra careful." He pointed to the loose rocks at the edge. "It's a long way down from here."

Paulette stood over Henri, mind racing. The boy could have an accident up here, if he wasn't careful.

A squirrel skittered out onto the rock, and Henri jolted up. "Do you think I could catch it?"

Sweat beaded on her neck. "Yes," she whispered. "Try."

Henri pushed himself up to a crouch on the rock. It was broad enough that he could scramble about without going near the edge. She inched closer to the drop-off and looked down. Her heart slammed against her chest.

"Next time," Henri said, and she turned to find him clapping dirt from his hands. "He can climb trees. No fair."

Below, some little creature scattered a spray of pebbles.

"What's that?" he asked. "Another squirrel?"

"I think—" She could do this. The boy had set it up for her perfectly. One lie. One push. And it would be over. "I think it's Madame Fishypaws down there."

Henri blanched. "Are you sure?"

"Come see." She pointed to a narrow outcropping below.

"Oh no." He came close, and she wrapped her hands around his shoulders.

Gently, she moved his body in front of hers. "I've got you," she told him. "Do you see her?"

He leaned forward, trusting her to hold his weight. "Here, Fishy Fishy Fishy!" he called. His toes edged closer to danger.

Paulette's hands grew damp on his shirt. *Courage!* This was the moment. This was her chance to act for the good of her country.

Still she paused, envisioning what might come after she pushed him over the edge. What a mess.

And the alternative: he might not die. What then? Would she try to convince him he had slipped from her grasp? Would she have to kill him with a rock?

Paulette shuddered. She tightened her grip on the boy, her pulse throbbing.

"I don't think she followed us up here." Henri backed away from the precipice.

So did Paulette. She sat on the rock to catch her breath. How very weak she was.

Chapter Thirty-Three

AUGUST 1795

After leaving a basket of food on the blanket, Vivienne and Paulette approached the edge of the woods where it seemed all of Asylum had gathered. In the spirit of improving the settlement for the arrival of Louis-Charles, Monsieur Talon had called for a tree-felling contest, to be followed by a picnic afterward.

Soft lemon sun shone on the rainbow of silks the French wore and glowed on the plain linen shirts of the Americans. Vivienne remarked that the latter looked far more at ease with their axes and saws than their high-heeled, waistcoated counterparts, and Paulette, at her side, agreed. Not surprisingly, Henri had already dashed off and found Liam, who was walking him back to Vivienne.

"But why can't I help?" Henri's voice lifted, all sincerity.

"It would help if I didn't have to wonder if you were about to be hacked by a wayward ax or smashed by a falling tree," offered Vienne.

Liam grinned at her predictable speech, then turned to Henri. "Tell you what. I'm tasking you with an important job. Keep a careful watch on all the contestants." Ever the schoolmaster, he pulled a piece of foolscap from his pocket, along with a stub of pencil. "Make a chart to track how long it takes each team to fell their trees. On axis Y, write the team names. On axis X, write minutes. Then shade in how long it takes each team to fell their tree."

Henri accepted the paper and pencil with a wary frown. "Is this schoolwork?"

Liam laughed and handed him his timepiece to borrow. "We'll clear some trees, and then we can eat."

"Will you at least eat with us?" Henri asked.

"Of course." Liam's gaze lifted to meet Vivienne's, smile lines fanning from his eyes.

"Liam, how is your hand?" she asked, ignoring Paulette's bored expression. "Have you been using the ointment Jethro made?"

"Every day." He spread open his right hand. The skin looked pinker than usual and lacked the callused ridge of his left palm, but the healing was remarkable.

"But will this hurt?" She waved a hand toward the trees about to be slain.

He flashed a smile. "Not until it's over."

Henri bounced on his toes. "I don't see your cousin, Mr. Delaney. Is he coming?"

"Afraid not, lad. He has other matters to attend to. Besides, swinging axes is better left to those with both eyes. Here, I'll show you why. Cover one eye, like this. Now—"

Monsieur Talon interrupted the impromptu lesson. Standing on a stump, he raised his arms. "Contestants, take your places!"

"Good luck!" Vivienne called as Liam walked away.

He turned and winked at her. "Don't need it. But thanks." He touched the brim of his hat and went to meet Jethro.

"Impertinent backwoodsman," Paulette mumbled.

Vivienne didn't bother to conceal a laugh. "The contest will be no contest."

"Look!" Paulette whispered. "Do you see those two Americans over there? One of them just spit at Mr. Delaney as he walked by. Look how they glare at him. What's behind all of that, do you suppose? Who are they?"

Vienne watched the two young men distort their faces while

taunting Liam, who soundly ignored them. "Henri, is your chart ready?" While the boy knelt and drew his lines, she leaned toward Paulette and whispered behind her fan. "Those are the Schultze brothers, roughly your age. Derek is the one with red hair, and Ernest has black hair." Derek was shorter and more robust, but Ernest's wiry frame was likely equally strong.

"They look as though they've put a hex on the Irishman. Why?"

In hushed tones, Vienne told her about the confrontation surrounding Joseph Cowley. "Liam foiled their plans to tar and feather the tax man, and I suppose they've been riled up about it since."

Paulette watched them with obvious interest. "Frustrated young men know how to hold a grudge."

"Ready!" Talon's voice boomed. Eight pairs of men gripped their tools, focused on the trunks before them. "Begin!"

Cheering erupted from women usually more prone to whispers as they clapped for their favorite contenders. Henri's boyish shrieking drowned them out. The Frenchmen hopped all around their trunks, hacking in a ring around the tree.

"Which way is it going to fall?" Armand cried to David du Page.

"I don't know! Just keep cutting all around and see what happens!"

"Ach! Look at your father, Zoe." Aurore's voice transcended the rest. "I haven't seen him move that much in years. Like a little bird hopping about!" She and her daughter bent in peals of laughter.

Flying chunks of wood nicked the Frenchmen's silk breeches and snagged their clocked stockings. Their faces grew red beneath crooked white wigs. But they were trying in all sincerity, and even Vivienne found herself lauding their efforts.

"Look at the Americans!" Henri pointed to an entirely different method. Rather than chipping away in circles, Liam and Jethro worked in an admirable rhythm, swinging their axes at the same spot on the trunk, first one and then the other, over and over. Liam's shirt strained across his shoulders when he hefted the ax and swung it. Sweat darkened the linen over his chest and glistened at his temples, but his labor was precise and orderly. He knew what he wanted and how to get it.

"You're smiling." Paulette's tone hinted at contempt, as if she'd added, *Like a lovesick fool*.

Maybe she was. Vivienne shrugged. "Why shouldn't I smile?" Though she and Liam had had few moments alone together since that night at the creek, she still reveled in his company no matter who else was around.

Eventually, Liam and Jethro sliced a large wedge away. Then, on the opposite side of the tree, they notched the trunk with a smaller gash. Chests heaving, they stood back. "Timber!" Liam pointed to where the tree would fall, then they both pushed the trunk. With a great crack and a whooshing of air through the canopy of leaves, the tree crashed to the earth, exactly where he'd said it would.

"They won! Mr. Delaney and Mr. Fortune won first place!" Henri skipped around the blanket before remembering to check the timepiece and record the minutes on his chart.

Liam and Jethro shook hands, congratulating each other. Liam looked over at Vienne, and she smiled her approval. A grin on his face, he offered her a quick bow.

"As if he chopped down that tree just for you," Paulette remarked. "How sweet."

With a critical eye, Paulette watched Mr. Delaney and his friend Mr. Fortune hustle over to offer Armand de Champlain some advice. *Liam*, Vivienne called him. Well. Those two would be very happy together, she was sure. How nice for them.

"Look at those sore losers now." Vivienne nodded at Ernest and Derek Schultze. Their faces looked like thunder as they gestured to the felled tree.

"Madame Arquette!" Zoe du Page screamed.

Paulette's gaze jumped to where she pointed. Mad Suzanne Arquette levered an ax out of the tree stump and ran toward Mr. Fortune with it, blade out. "It was you!" she cried. "You killed my family, every one of them! Didn't you?" Face purple with rage, she charged forward, tripping on her gown.

Needing no translation to understand her intent, Mr. Fortune shouted at her to stop, holding his ax at both ends of the handle, ready to block her blows.

Henri gasped.

"Suzanne, no!" Vivienne leapt up and ran toward Suzanne. "He didn't do it. You're confused. He's innocent."

"Then who did kill my family?" Suzanne raged. "Someone did. Many of them did. Slaughtered and burned them all! Where are the rest of the slaves?"

While Mr. Delaney, Monsieur de Champlain, and Monsieur du Page circled Suzanne, Paulette glanced around. Jethro Fortune was the only black man present. The rest of the slaves—or servants, as their owners called them—were likely laboring near their shanties. Scrubbing, cooking, laundering. Mr. Fortune was the scapegoat for them as much as he was for the slaves who really took the lives of Suzanne's family.

"Calm yourself, madame." This from the count.

"Calm?" Suzanne shoved her ax toward him in a jerky, thrusting motion. "Would you be calm if your family was murdered? No, no, I won't be calm. I can see it now. I can see everything." The ax wobbled in her grip. She was weakening.

"Be careful, Mademoiselle!" Henri cried out, but he remained rooted to his spot.

Vivienne entered the circle of men and spoke to Suzanne in tones too low for Paulette to hear. Suzanne shook her head again and again. But the ax blade lowered to the ground, and the men wrested it from her grip. Suzanne shook with sobs, and Vivienne comforted her.

But it was people like Suzanne Arquette who'd made the revolution necessary. Oppressive rulers lording over their subjects. The classes must be equalized.

The revolution must succeed.

Resolve hardening her spine, Paulette returned her attention to the Schultze brothers. They, too, lost interest in the drama, gripped their ax handles near the blades, and stormed off.

"Where are you going?" Henri asked.

Paulette snatched a fresh baguette and a wheel of cheese from the basket. "I want to see if I can cheer those American boys up," she tossed over her shoulder. But she didn't look back.

Neither did the brothers. She had to run to catch up to them. Ernest, the dark, lanky fellow, moved like a catamount through the woods. But Derek heard her coming.

He wheeled around. "Who are you?" Freckles spotted his ruddy round cheeks.

"Your new best friend. Hungry?" She held out her offering. "I understand there's something else gnawing at your middles, something bread alone can't take care of. Or should I say, *someone*."

Derek frowned at her. "Speak plainly, woman." But he reached for the cheese, and she let him have it.

"Liam Delaney." Satisfaction filled her as she watched scowls slash across their faces at the mere mention of his name. "I thought so."

"That old man—"

She lifted a hand to stop his speech. "I have no interest in your complaints. Only in what you're willing to do about it."

The brothers exchanged a confused glance. Ernest swallowed and said, "He'll get what's coming to him sooner or later. You wait and see."

But Paulette had tired of waiting. "Sooner is always better than later. Have you a plan? No?" She smiled. "I do."

Chapter Thirty-Four

Vivienne tipped her face heavenward, her straw hat falling to her back. Sunset spread across the sky in spills of burgundy and merlot, setting the river ablaze with its reflection. Liam's oars dipped into the water, pulling their canoe in a slow, rhythmic glide.

"Don't look now, mon cher, but they're gaining on us." A tease lilted in her voice.

He swiveled. Armand and Henri paddled a canoe behind them, both faces flushed with concentration and the lingering heat of the summer day. Armand's silk suit shimmered as he shouted encouragement to Henri. "That's it, faster now! Oh dear, we're turning sideways—the other side, Henri, row on the other side! No, the *other* other side! We'll catch them yet!"

Henri's tongue poked from the corner of his mouth as he switched the child-sized paddle Liam had made for him from the right side of the canoe to the left. "We're going to pass you!"

"Oh dear," Armand huffed, resting his oar across his knees for a moment as the canoe spun toward a bank again. "Good effort. Let's keep trying!" He plunged back into the race.

Something like joy swelled in Vienne until it broke free in laughter.

Liam turned to face her again, amusement dancing in his eyes. He moved his oars through the water, but he had turned them so the blades sliced the river without really moving them forward. "They're catching up!"

A turtle crept along the cracked mud where the river had receded from the bank. Dragonflies flitted through a thatch of reeds. Almost at a standstill in the water, Liam and Vienne allowed Armand and Henri to near.

"Go faster!" she told Liam. "They're almost here!"

Henri's gleeful laugh bounced off the water. "Too late, Mademoiselle!" A smile wreathed his face as they passed.

Armand mopped his brow with a kerchief, chuckling. "How far did you say the wharf is from here?"

"Around the bend and straight ahead a little ways." Liam gave him a reassuring smile. "You're nearly there."

"Ah. Good. Onward, my boy! We shall win this race home yet!" Tucking his kerchief into his pocket, Armand thrust his paddle back into the water and pulled.

Touched by Armand's enthusiasm, Vienne waited until they had made some progress before leaning toward Liam and whispering, "Do you think they'll get there all right?"

"To be sure. A little on the slow side, but they'll get there. If there's any trouble, we'll come across it soon enough. But let's give them some time to get ahead, shall we?" He rowed the canoe toward a weeping willow overhanging the river. As the water grew shallow, he pulled the vessel until it came to a slow stop, wedged into the soft riverbed. "That's better."

Wind stirred through the tree, and the branches dangled their fingertips in the water beside the canoe. Twilight fell in pieces through the leaves.

"You're leaving for Philadelphia in the morning, aren't you?" she asked.

He nodded. "If there's no rain to turn the roads to mud, I'll be back in ten days."

Vienne checked a sigh. She did not begrudge him the chance to see Tara, and she knew the fee he earned would go toward buying back his land. "I'll miss you."

Fireflies throbbed among the branches that swayed behind him. "And I you. You make it difficult to leave."

"Really?" She smiled. "How difficult?" The call of a loon floated across the river.

His lips curved as he reached for her. He gently drew her off the seat until they both knelt on the bottom of the canoe, his knees against the green-striped cotton dress puddling about her. "Very."

Water lapped quietly against the vessel. Liam enfolded Vienne in his arms, and she molded into his embrace. Her hands moved along his arms and shoulders, then swept up to loop behind his neck as she answered his kisses with her own.

The canoe rocked beneath them. Crickets began to chirp. With effort, she pulled away, hand against Liam's chest, where she felt a pounding beneath her palm.

"Vienne." His voice was husky as he touched his forehead to hers. "When I get back from this trip . . . we should talk."

"We're talking now."

After pressing a kiss to her brow, he sat back and shook his head, his expression soft and serious all at once. "That's not what I mean."

She tilted her head, imagination soaring. "Then what do you—"

"When I get back." He took her hands in his. "Promise me you'll take care of yourself while I'm gone, and then we'll have our conversation."

She laced her fingers through his. "Of course. But it's you who should take care. Your journey poses far more challenges than we face in Asylum. Hurry home," she added with a smile. The next ten days would surely prove longer than she wanted to wait.

Cicadas whirred outside the windows while Vivienne sat stiffly in the music room of the Grand Maison. Sleeves sticking to her arms, she fanned herself, wishing her ocean-blue silk was as cool as the water it resembled.

"So nice of you to join us." Aurore du Page's tone was thick with sarcasm as she crossed to the pianoforte. It was expected that all would gather here in the evenings, and Vienne had skipped it too often to be polite, much preferring evenings spent with Henri, Liam, Jethro, and Finn. Instead, she was here, listening to Zoe sing, while Henri played with toys he'd helped curate for Louis-Charles upstairs, accompanied by Paulette.

Evelyne Sando lowered herself onto the velvet sofa beside Vivienne, face glowing with humidity almost to the shade of her rose brocade gown. "Never mind her." She smiled. "How are you, Vienne? I haven't seen you since the tree-felling and picnic, what, almost two weeks ago now? Poor Suzanne. You were so good with her. That aside, you seemed quite content with your company."

Vienne raised an eyebrow. "Do you mean with Henri? And Paulette?"

Evelyne pursed her lips. "No. I mean the fellow who won first place and then gave lessons to every Frenchman who cared to learn. Delaney, is it? Handsome. A woman could do far worse." She took out her fan and stirred the air with it. "Will he come tonight?"

"Here?" Vivienne laughed. "You know Americans aren't welcome at our events unless by special invitation. Like the contest, for instance."

"I do know. I'm asking if you've given him a special invitation. It's plain you're smitten with each other, and rightly so. Why not be with the one you love?"

Vienne felt a flush creep into her cheeks. "If Liam were in Asylum, I would be with him right now, but not here," she admitted. She favored the chorus of crickets and wind through the trees over the Du Page women at the pianoforte. The gurgling creek as it ran over her feet. The splash of stones as Henri tossed them into the water. Liam's rich laughter. That was the music she craved on a late summer's eve. Swatting away a fly, Vienne labored to pull a breath from the soggy air. "He's gone on a mail run." She hoped the evening in the Grand Maison would help the time pass faster. Liam was due back tomorrow.

"Ah yes. Perhaps we may hear something of Louis-Charles this time." Across the room, Zoe hit a false note, and Evelyne cringed behind her fan. "And how is Henri, our Little Prince?" Her eyes sparkled. She was not the only resident of Asylum who had taken to referring to Henri in this way.

Vivienne took her cup of lemonade from the table beside her. Condensation beaded on the outside of the glass, soaking her palm as she drank. "Henri is overjoyed at the prospect of Louis-Charles arriving. But the nightmares he's had lately—they seem as vivid as those he had in Philadelphia. I don't know why, all of a sudden, these fears have roared back to life. Especially here in Asylum, of all places. Asylum is safe."

"What kind of dreams?"

Vienne took one more sip, then licked the sweet-sour taste from her lips. "He said—he said someone is trying to kill him."

Evelyne crossed herself. "In his dream, you mean."

"Yes. It's one recurring nightmare. He seems to be fine in the daylight, but he has the most difficult time at night. He won't retire until I do, so I go to bed early and read while he falls asleep." She smiled. "I've been getting a lot of reading done. But I confess, I grow weary of this unfounded fear. His mother was fearful, too." But it wasn't right to speak ill of the dead. Still, she wondered if Martine's terror hadn't somehow burrowed itself into Henri only to be revived again with this fresh dream.

"We have all known horrors, have we not?" Evelyne fluttered her fan. "If he remembers why he left France, he has fears enough of his own, without any inheritance from his mother."

"Of course. You are right." Perhaps Vienne was the unreasonable one for so resolutely shutting a door on the memories of slamming guillotines, of plazas sticky with blood, and of the masses who cheered for more. For daring to hope that life in Asylum was beyond the clutch of terror.

Zoe finished another song, and this time Vivienne clapped politely as the young woman curtsied. It was not difficult, here in this enclave in the wilderness, to pretend all danger had gone. Still, Sebastien's final warning echoed in her mind.

Henri glided into the room, Paulette faithfully behind him. Vivienne did not miss the smiles that greeted him as he placed his small hand on her knee. "If you please, Mademoiselle, the hour grows late, does it not? I'd like to go home."

Gladly. She bussed Evelyne's cheeks and made her farewells, walking home in the moonlight with Henri and Paulette.

"He's so tired, but he doesn't seem to be sleeping well," Paulette observed once they reached the house. "Let me make you both some tea to relax you. You deserve a good night's rest."

Vivienne tousled Henri's hair. "Thank you, Paulette. I'm sure we'd both love to sleep well tonight."

If the night went according to Paulette's plan, they'd sleep so well they'd never wake up. Of course, it was only Henri who truly needed to die. But as Paulette had failed at that twice, this plan was her final hope of success. It was unfortunate Vivienne was in the way. A cost Paulette tried not to notice.

She shooed them into the parlor to wait, then went to the kitchen house and put on a kettle of water. When it was boiling, she made a chamomile tea, then pulled a flask from the back of the cupboard and added enough of the Schultze brothers' whiskey to send them both into a deep slumber.

She nipped two generous chunks from the sugar cone and stirred them into the tea. Tasting one of them, she wrinkled her nose. The sweetener didn't quite compensate for the whiskey's bitterness. After adding a little more sugar, she brought the cups to Vivienne and Henri back in the main house. Medicine didn't always taste good, after all. "Drink up, now."

They did, and retired for the night.

Once she was sure they were sleeping, Paulette slipped from the house before she could lose her nerve. She had waited too long to carry out her plan. Corbin Fraser and the other Jacobins in Philadelphia called that weakness. He'd threatened to come do the job himself if she would only grant him directions. No need for that now. She would prove him wrong tonight.

Heart pounding to the drumbeats of "La Marseillaise," she

hiked her skirt above her ankles and raced behind the settlement. *To arms, citizens, Form your battalions! March, march! . . . Drive on, sacred patriotism.* When she came to the cabin she sought, she banged on the door until it opened.

"Tonight," she said breathlessly. "You remember the plan?"

Ernest bared his teeth as he smiled. "I've been waiting."

"You have enough whiskey? You and Derek both? You must be thorough."

"We have plenty."

"Then it's time." She forced the words through her closing throat as the "Ça Ira" clanged in her head.

If we don't break them, we'll burn them.

She felt like she was going to be sick.

Chapter Thirty-Five

Gradually, the sound of Henri's moaning pierced Vivienne's slumber. He was in the throes of another nightmare. But she was tired, so tired she could not lift her eyelids, let alone reach out to soothe him. Sleep was a giant pinning her down. She was powerless against its weight.

How much time passed, she could not measure, before something stirred her into consciousness. Smoke, and the heat of a fire here in the bedroom. In August.

Lurching awake, she sat straight up. The window glowed orange and red. She dashed to it and stared in horror at Liam's fields of grain. Hours ago, they were nearly ripe for harvest, and now they were up in flames. She could almost feel the heat.

No, she *did* feel the heat. In the floor. In the walls. Smoke snaked across the ceiling, gathering between the beams like skeins of wool.

"Henri!" She shook him. "Wake up!" Fighting panic, she yelled until he shuddered awake, suddenly alive with fear. "Let's go."

With his whittled horse for Louis-Charles clutched tight in his hand, Vivienne grabbed the other and burst from the room, then cursed herself and darted back inside it, Henri still in tow. Yanking open the bureau drawer, she grabbed two towels, dropped them in the washstand basin, and poured water on top to soak them. "Over your nose and mouth, like this." She handed one to Henri and demonstrated by folding and holding the wet towel over her face.

Back out into the hall they dashed. "Paulette!"

The maid's door was jammed. Vivienne banged on it, shouting for the young woman to wake up. Sweat poured from her hairline, stinging her eyes. Running back into her room, she grabbed her pitcher, then went to Paulette's door and smashed it against the handle until it gave way. She kicked the door in and felt her way to the bed. Empty.

A piece of the ceiling crumbled in a shower of sparks to the mattress, and the hay in the ticking caught fire. Vivienne started to beat at it with her wet towel but then realized the cloth had already baked dry beneath her hand. *Lord, help us!* How much time had they lost?

"Is this a nightmare?" Henri cried. Flames licked from the bed and chewed through the curtains, which dropped in pieces to send fire rippling across the floor.

Vienne shook her head. It was nightmare and reality, both.

"Madame Fishypaws!" the boy shrieked. "Where is she?"

Frantic now, she pulled Henri down to the floor. She could barely think straight. The cat. He was asking about his cat. "In the barn," she remembered. "Let's go!"

They crawled beneath gray haze, knees scraping over the warping floorboards. Smoke stole her breath and pressed in around her, shrouding her senses. Even her brain felt clogged, and she could not find the door to the hall. Pinpoints of pain told her where sparks burrowed into her nightdress, and she struck at each prick as it came.

"Henri." Her voice rasped against his coughing. She wanted to tell him to mind the sparks, but he wouldn't hear her. She could barely hear herself. A spot on his shoulder glowed orange, and she slapped it before it spread.

The washstand collapsed as its legs became charred stumps, sending the basin and pitcher rolling across the floor. The crash restored her bearings. Blindly, Vienne led Henri away from the noise, finally finding the hall.

Blisters bubbled on her palms. The timbers in the roof above them cracked as loudly as a falling tree. A beam fell onto the steps, engulfed in crackling fire, blocking the way downstairs and out of the house. Stair spindles burst into pillars of flame.

She tightened her grip on Henri, her heart pounding as though to break through its cage. The taste of things burning filled her mouth. Vienne clutched at her middle to cough and inhaled flakes of ash.

Henri cried out, dashing out a spark on his sleeve. "Your hair!" Panic pitched his voice high.

Lungs burning, Vienne batted at hair that felt too hot to the touch, and she felt Henri's small hands beat at the wild locks falling down her back.

An explosion, and then another. The windows shattering. She could barely swallow around her thickened tongue, let alone cry out for help. If she and Henri were to survive this, it would have to be with God's help alone.

Dread corkscrewed through Liam as he galloped toward the smell of smoke and a sky that glowed orange in the night. He stood in his stirrups, thighs burning as he leaned low over Cherie. The horse thundered over the land and splashed through the shallow bend in the river before carrying him to the chaos that was now Asylum.

The slave shanties. All of them, up in flames.

Dismounting, he ran to join the line of settlers passing buckets of water between the creek and the burning shanties. "What happened?"

Armand de Champlain passed him a bucket. "Suzanne Arquette. She finally got her revenge for what the slaves did to her family in Saint-Domingue."

Liam passed buckets from Armand to Derek Schultze as quickly as they came. "Suzanne did this? All by herself?" It didn't add up. The woman was angry and had lost her wits—so many wits, in fact, that she couldn't have organized such complete destruction on her own. "That odor," he said. "Do you smell it?"

Armand sniffed.

"Beneath the smoke," Liam clarified.

"Alcohol, is it?"

"Whiskey." Derek laughed beside him, more whiskey on his

breath. Mischief sparked in his eyes. "You're back early, but you're still too late."

"What do you—" *Oh no.* Liam jerked his head toward home. Without another word, he abandoned his post in the line and mounted Cherie again.

His crops were lost, he could smell that straightaway. But his house—Vivienne's house. Flames leapt to the sky from the sagging roof, or what was left of it. Energy exploded through him as he took it in. In a split second, he grasped the sum of it. Whether or not Suzanne had her revenge tonight, Ernest and Derek Schultze most certainly had. They'd used their whiskey to ignite the fires that destroyed his crops and house. But where were Vivienne and Henri, and Paulette?

"Vivienne!" he shouted, dismounting Cherie and racing toward the flaming house. "Henri! Vienne!" The windows were gone, leaving gaping black holes rimmed with fire.

Armand appeared, panting, beside him. "You don't think—" Then he ran around the perimeter in the other direction, calling for them, as well.

Liam heard something. They were in there, alive. "I'm coming!" He charged to the front door but found it locked.

"You can't go in there," Armand shouted over the roaring flames. "Look!" He pointed through one of the windows at a wall of fire. The heat washed over them in waves, even standing outside. "They must be on the second floor."

"They have to jump. We'll break their falls." Liam sprinted around the side of the house again, Armand right beside him. "Vienne!" he shouted.

"The north side! My bedroom!" she cried.

"Jump out the window! We'll catch you!"

A pause before she responded. "Count to three!"

Liam and Armand exchanged a glance. Then, arms outstretched, they shouted, "One, two, three!"

Henri came flying through the window, straight for Armand. The older man caught the boy admirably, and both rolled on the hard earth.

"Vienne!" Liam yelled. His eyes watered from the heat. "Now!" A flash of white appeared in the window, then plunged into Liam's arms. He collapsed to his knees, still holding her, and buried his face in her smoky mass of unbound hair. "Are you all right?" She covered her coughing with her elbow, but nodded and clung to him.

It took him several seconds to realize they were missing someone. He lifted his head. "Is Paulette coming?"

"She's gone," Vienne gasped.

"Oh no. I'm sorry."

She shook her head. "Gone before the fire woke us. I don't know where she is."

Strange, but at least no one had died. He tightened his arms around her for one last moment, then said, "Come away from the fire."

He and Armand led Vivienne and Henri a safe distance away. Their faces were both smudged with sweat and soot. They looked at the house they had all three called home. Walls and roof broke and crumbled, every crack and shudder resounding in Liam's chest. The house, and his long-held dreams, surrendered.

"Oh, Liam!" Vienne brought her hands to her cheeks. "It's lost!"

"But you aren't, and neither is Henri, thank the Lord." He could rebuild the house, he wanted to say, but his words stalled. He could only stand there and stare at the raging fire.

Footsteps pounded the ground behind him, and he straightened.

"Liam! We had no idea," Finn cried. "Jethro and I were trying to stop the fire in the fields this whole time, and he's still there—we didn't know—" His voice cracked. "Are you all right, Vienne?"

"I will be," she rasped. Liam wrapped his arms around her waist, and she leaned against him. He would never let her go again.

Finn turned his worried eye to Henri. "And you, lad? How do you fare?"

"Were they trying to kill me?" the boy wheezed and dropped to his knees, coughing. Madame Fishypaws bounded from the shadows and rubbed against his leg.

Vivienne broke from Liam's hold and sat on the ground, gathering

Henri in her arms. He curled into her and she kissed his head, swaying gently with him. Silently, her shoulders shook.

A muscle worked in Liam's jaw. "This was the work of Ernest and Derek Schultze and the whiskey they made with your still," he growled to Finn. "They knew this was my house. Whether they knew it was occupied in my absence, I can't say yet. Find them and hold them for me, would you?" Anger boiled in his veins.

Finn's face darkened with understanding. "I was never a part of this, cousin, I swear it. I'll serve them up on a silver platter, I will."

"Wait." Liam stayed him with one hand. "If I see those two again, I can't guarantee I won't hurt them. It would be better—for them and for me—if they find themselves in the care of the sheriff without my so-called help. I'd consider it a personal favor if you see to it. I'm certain they lit the shanties on fire, as well, so Talon will surely lock them up until the Wyalusing sheriff can collect them."

"I'll take care of it, Liam. I vow."

Armand brushed grass and soot from his silk lapel. "I'll help."

As they left, Liam sat on the ground by Vienne. If there were any hope of saving anything inside, he would have done so. But the house had been expertly torched, the fire's blaze an impasse impossible to breach.

With the smell of charred crops and burning timber cinching around him, he watched the roof of the house collapse onto the second floor, which broke with the weight of its flaming burden. He had placed every shingle, hewn every log, pounded every nail in place himself. Even the furniture had come into being from his hands.

"I'm so sorry," Vivienne choked out on a ragged breath. She gestured from the smoldering house to the smoking fields. "Everything you labored to bring forth, everything you love, gone."

"Nay. Not everything." But he could say no more around the blade in his throat.

She looked at him, eyes glassy and rimmed with red, and her composure left her at last. Tears spilled down her cheeks. As he pressed her head to his shoulder, Henri reached out his hand, and Liam ensconced it with his own.

Thunder rolled above them, and almost as quickly, heavy drops splashed his face and hands. He shrugged out of his jacket and draped it over Vivienne. Rain drummed to the earth in sheets, sizzling onto the burning house and fields, pouring over his head. A deluge. Now. When most of the damage had already been done.

The ground turning to mud beneath them, Liam rose and helped Vivienne to her feet.

Paulette stumbled over a tree root as she ran through the woods toward Vivienne's house. Finn O'Brien and Armand de Champlain had come charging toward the bucket line, accusing Derek and Ernest of exactly what they'd done. But neither had mentioned whether Henri had survived. She had to know. She had to see for herself whether she'd succeeded or failed.

She didn't know what she hoped to find.

Rain speared through the branches overhead, splattering her hair. Wiping her face, she fisted her skirts and threaded her way through the edge of the forest. In her mind, she rehearsed what she would say when the Schultze boys blamed her. *Why would I want the house to burn down? I live there!* Besides, she hadn't told them to do it, hadn't given them any tools or weapons. All she had done was fan the flames of their hate and told them when Mr. Delaney was gone. No one could convict her on such flimsy facts as those.

Branches snapped behind her. Was she being followed? Thunder continued to roll, and lightning bleached the gray curtain of rain. In that instant, she looked over her shoulder and saw him, his bald head gleaming in the storm's flash. Suddenly she was as rooted to the earth as the trees around her.

Corbin Fraser, however, suffered no such paralysis. Mere moments later, his hand clapped onto her shoulder, fingers digging below her collarbone. Though shadowed by night and forest, she could see his lips spread in a grimace. "I told you to get the job done or I'd come do it myself."

"But how?" She hadn't told him how to get here, and unless a guide like Sebastien Lemoine showed the way, Asylum was all but impossible to find, as had been intended.

"Delaney came to the Four Winds Tavern. The staff hadn't forgotten to bar my entrance, but there was no stopping me from listening outside the window while they ate. Or from waiting and watching the door. When he left the next day for Asylum, I followed. And here we are. Where is the boy?"

"I was just going to see myself." She led him the rest of the way until they could see the ruins of Mr. Delaney's property. The flames were dying down beneath the rain.

"Were they locked inside?"

"Of course."

"Did they *stay* locked inside?" Rain streamed down his face like water over a rock, and he did not blink it away.

Paulette chewed her lip. She hadn't been able to stomach watching it burn down around them. If she had heard them cry for help, who knew but that in a moment of weakness she would have gone to their aid and set them free? "I wasn't here," she confessed. "Didn't you hear? This was the work of two young whiskey rebels bent on revenge."

"Clever ruse. But if the boy is still alive, all in vain. Ah. Look." With a hard shove, he released her to point to three figures in the summer house. Two adults and a child. "All in vain, I see." He pulled a pistol from his waistband. "And I thought you were more than a maid. You've proven yourself a miserable failure. It all ends now."

Her mouth went dry.

Corbin cocked his pistol. "Step into the clearing. Call to him. He will come to you, yes? Then step aside."

She looked at the gun, imagined the bullet that would tear through Henri's throat. Her hand went to her own.

"You have one chance to help make this right. Or I'll end your life right after I end his."

Something pulled at her gut as she forced her feet to move. *It is the right thing to do,* she told herself. *The boy must be killed for the sake of the revolution. I will save my country and not notice the cost.*

She stepped from the thicket and into the clearing, where rain poured over her in waves. She felt at sea in a world gone mad. A tide of conviction welled within her, and she waited for it to recede. Charlotte Corday had killed a man in his bath. Women were not just scullery maids and cooks; they were arbiters of justice. *Corday killed Marat because he called for thousands of heads to roll. What harm has Henri brought to anyone?*

The ebb and flow of her conscience was a thorn to her enlightened mind. She beat it back with reason.

"Henri!" she called in a wobbling voice. She tried again. "Henri! Are you well?" That was better.

The silhouettes of three people stood. When lightning illuminated the sky, all three left the summer house. Did they suspect? Did they wonder where she'd been?

"I was helping at the shanties!" she cried out. "I came as soon as I heard the fire had been here, too! I was so worried!" The lies were getting harder to grind out. She licked the water from her lips. "Henri, come here, let me touch you for myself." *Let me draw you into my trap. Let me separate you from those you love so this man behind me can put a bullet between your eyes.*

Henri came toward her, his thin limbs swinging, his white nightshirt ghostlike as it drew near, begrimed though it was.

Paulette bent down, arms outstretched. She heard Corbin move into place behind her.

"We tried to get you," Henri said. "We tried to save you from the fire, but you weren't there. We were worried."

He stopped right in front of her, and she caught him to herself. Made herself remember that she would never hold her own child this way. Told herself this boy belonged to no one. He was an orphan. As she had been.

Blast Henri. Blast her aching, unreasonable heart. Years of pent-up tears gathered and burned until they all seemed to spill over at once, mingling with the rain on her cheeks.

Thunder cracked violently overhead, and the boy cringed. She released him. He'd always been afraid of loud noises. He'd always been afraid of so much. He was right to be. He should have been afraid of her.

Don't do this.

"Paulette," Henri whispered in her ear, his body stiff with fear, "there is a man behind you with a gun."

"Step away," Corbin growled. Liam and Vivienne were getting closer.

Paulette kissed the top of Henri's head, though his hair held a paste of ash and rain. She whispered in his ear, "Run."

Then she shoved him toward Liam and wheeled on Corbin Fraser, knocking the pistol from his hand.

Cursing, he pummeled her jaw with his fist. Ignoring the pain, she dropped to her hands and knees in the mud, searching frantically for the gun. She found it, but before she could discharge it into the woods, Corbin tore it from her grasp. She tackled him in the dark, bowling him over onto his back. Vivienne screamed.

"Run!" Paulette cried, and felt knuckles fill her mouth. She bit down as hard as she could while scratching and clawing like a catamount at whatever she could reach. Her hand came around his, and she felt the gun beneath it. She tried to wrest it from him, prying at his fingers while kicking him in the groin.

Paulette's head jerked back as Corbin yanked her hair. A kick to her kidney sent her sprawling in the mud. A shot fired. The taste of sulfur filled her nose and mouth. *Henri?* She meant to call but had no voice.

More footsteps pounded the earth. Men were shouting, grunting, fighting. Had Finn O'Brien returned with Armand? She heard voices but could not recognize the words. They were patterns of sound, that was all. Rain streamed over her body, and the water seemed to rise around her. Still, she could not move. Lightning stabbed the sky, and she saw that the puddle she lay in was red. She closed her eyes and thought of Jean-Paul Marat, who died in a bath stained with his own blood.

Chapter Thirty-Six

Thunder rattled the barn walls as Vivienne held Henri close, praying with all her might—for the second time that night—that God would be their refuge. They had stayed rooted in the mud outside when Liam came to blows with the attacker. As he had knocked the pistol from the man's hand, Jethro had come from behind, kicking the weapon away and striking the Jacobin at the knees so he stumbled. While the men fought in the dark, she had finally moved, scooping the weapon from sodden ground and pulling Henri with her to the barn.

Minutes later, the door burst open, and rain sprayed in around Liam, who was bare chested and bleeding from his lip as he carried a young woman in his arms. Behind him, Armand held a lantern, banishing darkness into the corners.

"Paulette!" Vivienne covered her mouth with her hand as she approached. Vaguely, she was aware of Armand gathering Henri and steering him away from the gruesome sight.

"Shot in the stomach." Liam laid her gently on bales of hay stacked waist-high. His shirt was tied about her middle, already dark with blood. "By the same Jacobin who strangled you in Philadelphia. Name of Corbin Fraser. Finn and Jethro took him to Talon, where he'll stay in custody along with Ernest and Derek."

"What?" Vienne's thoughts turned laboriously, unable to gain any traction. She grasped her friend's cold, wet hand, rubbing away the mud and grass between her fingers, then plucked a piece of hay from her hair. Paulette wouldn't like to be so dirty.

Liam cut his voice low. "Fraser confessed they were working together. He and Paulette."

Vivienne dropped the maid's hand as if it burned her.

"Vienne." Liam came to her side, cupping her shoulders in his broad hands. "Their aim was the boy's life, in the chance that he might be king. The revolution—"

"Stop," she hissed. "Do not speak to me of revolution, here. This is a *refuge*." Her voice shook. "We are *safe*. It is why we came." She choked on the words, trapping a sob in her throat. "Not Paulette. Not her." She covered her face with her hands, felt Liam pull her against his chest.

Something fluttered against her nightdress. Paulette's fingers. She was trying to speak. "Here." She fished into her pocket and struggled to pull something free, pinched between her thumb and forefinger. The gold signet ring of Louis XVI.

Vivienne gasped as she took the ring. Comprehension sliced through her. "Oh, Paulette. What has become of you?"

A crying wind blasted through the slats in the walls, and Red's bridle creaked as it swayed on its hook. The smells of leather and straw and wood clashed with the iron scent of blood.

"I couldn't do it," she whispered, tears tracing her cheeks. "But I brought the danger to your doorstep. I'm sorry."

Sorry? For deception, betrayal, attempted murder? Vienne knew Paulette was a troubled soul from what little she'd shared of her life, but she had no idea how far the young woman had allowed her pain to carry her.

"I tried not to believe in God. I tried to think I had no need of Him, but I—" Paulette licked her lips and labored to breathe. "I still don't want a king, but I do think there is a God. A God who is not pleased with murder or the planning of it. Do you think— could He forgive even me? Even now?"

Vienne looped the signet ring over her thumb and gripped Paulette's hand. She seemed so frail, so vulnerable. "Yes. He can." In time, He would help Vienne forgive her, too.

Paulette closed her eyes, and the lines on her brow relaxed. She squeezed Vienne's hand, and then dropped it.

Noise scraped Vienne's ears. The storm gnashed against the barn, nearly rocking it, and Red snorted and stamped in his stall. Thunder crashed, and yet somehow, she could still hear the bewildered beating of her heart.

The door groaned, more rain rode in on a thrashing wind, and Father Gilbert's voice turned Vienne's head. "I came as soon as I heard." Quickly observing that only Paulette was injured, he rushed to her, removing his sodden hat. Water streamed from his clothing and soaked into the hay at his feet. "Not too late, am I?"

Vivienne backed away, teeth rattling. Her hands and limbs would not stop shaking. Liam held her close while Father Gilbert knelt beside Paulette to speak, listen, and pray until the maid breathed her last.

The next day, after Vivienne had bathed and dressed in a borrowed gown from Evelyne, she sat in Louis-Charles's room on the second floor of the Grand Maison. Henri, uninterested in play, curled next to her on the sofa. No one had told him that the fire and bullet had been meant for him, but she sensed he knew.

"The bad men are locked away now, yes?" he asked for the eleventh time.

"Yes. The king's chief of secret police has them in his keeping. Monsieur Talon knows what to do."

A soft knock on the doorframe turned her head. "Talon would like to see you now," Evelyne said. "I'll stay with Henri."

"Merci."

Downstairs in Talon's windowless office, tapers flickered, perfuming the already warm air. Vivienne stood before him between Armand and Liam, as she had the first week of her arrival.

Monsieur Talon tented his fingers. "I have questioned all three men in my custody. The sum of the matter is this. The Jacobins, who believed Henri could be Louis-Charles, infiltrated Asylum in order to kill him. Your maid, Paulette Dubois, exploited a feud between Mr. Delaney and the Schultze brothers over some whiskey tax. According to their side of the story, she planned for them to use whiskey to start the fires we suffered through last night. First in the slave shanties, to occupy the colonists. Then Mr. Delaney's fields and house." He turned his appraising eye on Armand. "Monsieur de Champlain. You were the one paying for Mademoiselle Dubois's service, were you not?"

He paled. "I was. I did. But I had no idea, none whatever, of her designs on—"

"And you and Mr. Delaney have quarreled over that particular plot of land. Your arrangement was that he could live on the land and draw income from the crops. Which are now destroyed, along with the house. This has all but ruined the property he hoped to regain, while your fortune remains quite intact. Correct again?"

"Why, I—I—I reject your insinuation, sir," Armand sputtered.

"I stated the facts, monsieur. Only the facts. You cannot deny that you stand to benefit from Mr. Delaney's recent misfortune, for he might now give up on the land and start over somewhere else. And now I invite you to make your case. Were you or were you not in any way involved in these dreadful events?"

Vienne watched the sweat bead on Armand's brow as he ran a finger between his cravat and neck. He swallowed. "I was not in any way involved in the cause of these events, but I did aid in the capture of the offenders. Would I have done that, if I'd been an accomplice in these crimes? Would I not have set them free for fear of them divulging my role—a role which does not exist, mind you."

Talon stood and looked down his nose at Armand. "Perhaps. Or perhaps you have used your considerable means to buy their silence. After all, two American laborers and two self-professed Jacobins—one of whom is already dead—I can't imagine that their fates would trouble you even a little. They could be your tools."

"They are not." Armand dabbed a handkerchief to his face. "I promise you. Are you forgetting that Vivienne Rivard lives—lived—in that house with Henri? I would never harm her, nor would I harm the boy in her keeping."

"Or maybe you set all of this up in order for her to trust you. Because you wanted to get rid of the boy without the messiness of getting your own hands dirty. The perfect arrangement for another secret Jacobin, if I do say so myself."

"I tell you the truth, I would never harm either of them or see any harm come to them! On my honor." Armand's voice grew in volume and pitch.

Vienne could no longer stay silent. "If I may, Monsieur Talon," she interjected, "Monsieur de Champlain is innocent of these crimes. He would not hurt me, I vow."

"Oh? How can you be so sure?"

She drew a deep breath and looked at Armand. "*Forgive me, Vienne.*" How many times had he said it since she met him? Too many to count. Finally, she realized, she did. "Because he is my father."

A small cry escaped Armand. "Ah! Vivienne!" His face crumpled, and he hid his trembling mouth behind his handkerchief while tears flowed freely from his eyes.

Something inside her broke at the sight. She squeezed his shoulder, and he covered her hand with his own. Liam caught her eye and sent her a tender smile.

Sniffing back her own tears, she released Armand and brought the signet ring from her pocket. She held it out to Talon. "This should be in your care."

He took it from her and examined it, furrows etching deep across his brow. Lines carved from the corners of his lips to his jawline. "Where did you get this?"

"Henri's mother had it in her possession. She was lady-in-waiting to Marie Antoinette."

"I heard she had smuggled it out to some trusted person before she, too, went to the guillotine. But a lady-in-waiting? I would not have guessed it."

"But then, who would have guessed an imposter child would be in the prison in the dauphin's place?"

The wrinkles in Talon's face grew fainter. "Indeed. Thank you for this. I will keep it for Louis-Charles. What do you require in return for its safe delivery into my hands?"

She glanced at Armand, then at Liam, before returning Talon's stare. "The land, monsieur, of course. I require the land returned to Mr. Delaney's ownership, and Armand compensated however he chooses, either with a different plot and property, or with the money he would get from the sale."

Armand turned to Liam. "Do you still want that land, such as it is?"

"That I do." His eyes misted. "'Tis still good land beneath its scars."

"Then take it." Armand pushed back his shoulders and lifted his chin. "I'll work with Talon here to make sure the paperwork is drawn up. And Mr. Delaney—I'm not much hand at felling trees, but if I can be of any other use to you as you rebuild that house, by all means, I'm at your service." He offered a gallant bow.

"Anything else?" Talon asked.

"There is one thing more," Vivienne replied. "I want to adopt Henri. Officially. Legally. I don't know where to begin, since his parents are both deceased, but I don't want him to ever wonder whose he is." She knew how that felt and didn't want that for Henri. Beside her, Armand colored.

"I'll see to it. It may take some weeks, but you can trust I'll see the matter through."

"Thank you." Vivienne curtsied. The men bowed their thanks, and all of them left the office.

In the music room, Armand shook Liam's hand, and Vienne allowed her father to kiss her cheek. The way the older man smiled at her, she knew he saw her and not just Sybille. He was smiling through fresh tears when he left the room, leaving her alone with Liam.

Her heart rate quickened as he gazed at her, full of wonder.

"You could have asked for anything, unto half the kingdom. And you asked for my land. For me. Thank you."

"It's your land, Liam, no one else's. No one could love it as well as you."

He nodded slowly. "'Tis rare I find a thing to love with my whole heart. But when I do, I never stop." He took her hands. "I promised you a conversation when I returned. You once said you never wanted to leave. Picture in your mind for a moment that the house isn't a smoldering ruin. It's been rebuilt, with the help of Finn, Jethro, and Armand, if I can find something for him to do. Imagine it the way it was when you loved it, but with an extra room on the second floor. For a nursery, perhaps. And flower boxes on all the windows, and Lombardy poplars lining the drive. An orchard full of apple trees, for pies and sauces and jellies. What would you say if I asked you to stay?"

She cocked an eyebrow, though her pulse throbbed at the picture he painted. "As the maid and cook?"

"Nay. The land is just dirt without you there living on it with me. A house can't be a home without you in it. Vienne, I love you. I've loved you longer than I'm sure was proper. And now I'm asking you—let me serve you the rest of my life. Not out of duty, but for love. Let me be a husband to you and a father to Henri. And to any other babies you want to give me."

Heat flashed over her at the thought, and longing filled her. "I'd love nothing more than to be your wife."

His lips curving, he cupped her cheek with one hand, the other coming around her waist. Reflecting his smile, she rose up on her toes and linked her hands behind his neck. He swayed, his lips against hers, stealing her breath away. Melting into his embrace, she savored his touch, his smell, his love. He was an Irish-American who'd fought for his revolution, and she a French-woman who'd fled another. And yet this, at last, was where she belonged. Her refuge was in the Lord, and her heart firmly in Liam's hands.

"Mademoiselle?" Henri's voice floated to her.

Liam released her, and she beckoned to Henri, while Evelyne smiled from the doorway.

"Henri," Vienne began. "I will never replace your mother. But what would you say about becoming part of a new family? With me and Mr. Delaney, from now on?"

His eyes became wide blue pools. "With both of you? Forever?"

"We're getting married, lad." To hear him say it sent a thrill spiraling through Vienne's middle. "And we want to adopt you, officially. If that's all right with you."

"Could I call you Maman and Papa? Is that what it means? I'll have parents again?"

"Yes, of course!" Vienne cried. "If you like."

"I do. I will. I will like it very much!" He hugged her about the waist tighter than he ever had, and Liam enfolded them both.

Enveloped by the two she loved most, Vivienne realized Asylum wasn't just a place on a map. It was wherever they were together.

Epilogue

Vivienne Delaney laid her lacework aside as a breeze whispered through the summer house, heavy with the fragrance of roses and clover. Closing her eyes, she let the air feather over her face and through her hair. The dress trim she was making for her daughters could wait. A deep and abiding contentment filled her, and she savored it.

"Sweet dreams, beloved?" Liam stepped into the summer house and bent to kiss her lips before holding out a teacup full of fresh, ripe blueberries.

"Getting sweeter all the time." Smiling her thanks, she popped a warm berry into her mouth, relishing its perfect flavor. "These must be the last of the season, or nearly. Have some."

Liam obliged, sitting beside her in a sunbeam that glinted on his russet hair. He'd been cutting and spreading hay to dry with Henri, and the scent of alfalfa clung to his linen shirt. "And how is our babe today?" His hand spread over her middle as the baby kicked. Liam's laugh tumbled over her, as deep as it was contagious. "Active enough for the both of you, eh?"

"By October, it will be your turn to carry him. Or her," Vienne reminded her husband.

Footsteps announced a visitor. Armand removed his bicorne hat from the gray hair crowning his head. The lines pleating his face carved deeper with each passing year. "I'm not interrupting?"

"Not at all. Come in." She held her cup of berries aloft in offering, but he declined.

Liam shook Armand's hand and bade him sit. While the men spoke of the harvest and market prices, Vivienne peered beyond them. At the edge of grass grown tired of summer's heat, goldenrod and purple asters swayed in the wind. A fluffy little bluebird flitted from between the stalks, hunting insects.

"And how are Finn and Jethro lately?" Her father often asked after the two men who'd helped bring Corbin Fraser to justice. "Their own farms getting along as well as this one?"

Pride lit Liam's eyes, and rightly so. Their land was the most fruitful of all the lots in this horseshoe bend of the Susquehanna. "Aye, the lads both had a good year. Jethro's wife is doing a brisk trade in milk and cheese from their goats and cattle, too."

"I've had some." Armand licked his lips. "Delicious. And what of the one-eyed whiskey rebel? I'll bet he's rejoicing that President Jefferson just repealed that excise tax, is he not?"

Liam chuckled. "That he is."

"Thankfully, he's as committed to farming—and to being a good neighbor and uncle—as he ever was to distilling," Vivienne added. She was glad Liam had Finn nearby, for visits to Tara were rare, though she was never far from their thoughts.

A joyful shriek split the air, followed by another. Vienne's heart swelled as Henri strode from the direction of the creek, swinging four-year-old Kate and Rosalie, aged six, in the air. Vivienne set her teacup beside the lace pillow, saving the remaining berries for the children.

"Ah." Armand regarded Henri. Light fell through the lattice upon his emerald green suit and white stockings. "My news will concern him, too. Perhaps it will affect him most of all."

Uneasy, Vivienne waved a mosquito away before resting her hands on her belly. Liam called to Henri and the girls, drawing them all to the summer house. Rosalie flipped her dark braids over her shoulder and crossed her ankles as she sat by Armand. Kate pushed a copper curl from her freckled cheek and drew circles in the air with her dangling feet.

Henri's brows knit together. His blond hair was pulled back in a queue, and his features were chiseled, like Martine's had been. But his boyhood frame was transforming into a man's. "Something's wrong." He glanced to where Vivienne had laced her fingers over her middle.

"No." Smiling, she shook her head and grasped Liam's proffered hand. "Please sit. Armand brings news."

On the bench opposite her, Henri pulled Kate onto his lap and tugged her skirts down over her grass-stained knees. Rosalie sidled closer to him, nudging his elbow. Obeying her signal, he wrapped his arm about her shoulders, and she sank against his side.

Spine straight, Armand met Vivienne's gaze. "It comes as a shock, even though it has been so long looked for, but we can go back. We can return home."

"But we're already home!" Kate declared. She slid from Henri's lap to sit on the floor, and Madame Fishypaws climbed gingerly into her lap. With dimpled hands, Kate stroked the cat's fur, and her purring mingled with the whirring and ticking of insects.

"You mean France." Henri leaned forward, hands clasped, elbows on his knees, a habit he'd picked up from Liam.

"Napoleon Bonaparte has granted a general amnesty for us émigrés. We can go home. At last."

Liam's hand tightened gently over Vienne's, and a rush of emotion and memory washed over her. The France she had escaped was not the same France now inviting its lost sons and daughters back home.

But neither was Vienne the same. The Lord had mended her spirit and reshaped her to fit a new place, with new hopes. New loves. This was where she was meant to be, with her husband and children surrounding her. "Kate is right. I'm already home."

Armand's lips pressed flat for a moment. "I agree." A lump shifted between the cords of his neck. "I've heard from my wife and children, Angelique and Gustave. They are ready to make amends."

Staring at him, Vivienne struggled to register his words.

"After all this time?" Liam asked.

"We have been corresponding." Armand rubbed the light brown spots on his hands. "I am not young, I know. But—" He spread his hands, palms up.

"It is never too late to reconcile." Vienne reminded him of the words he'd once told her.

"Indeed." Armand's voice quavered. "Indeed. And now I must ask forgiveness from you once again, Vivienne, for I have purposed to return to them. With the years I have left, I will be the husband and father I should have been all along."

Vienne couldn't speak right away for the sharpness in her throat. She rose, and he stood and took her outstretched hands. This man, whom she had been so determined to despise, had truly become her father. The blood that throbbed in her veins was his as much as it was Sybille's. "There's nothing to forgive, for it's the right thing to do." She managed a smile. "I wish you the very best."

Rosalie climbed over to Liam, who pulled her close and kissed her cheek. A bullfrog twanged from the rippling creek.

Armand released Vienne. "I will take Henri. If he wishes to go." He addressed her son. "If you wish to return to the land of your birth. Your heritage. We may be able to secure for you some inheritance, or at least a portion of it, that your father would have wanted you to have."

Henri's eyebrows arched. Slowly, he stood and paced the small summer house, each step a drumbeat on Vienne's heart.

"You're a man now, Henri," Liam said. "Old enough to choose your own future."

"What?" Kate looked up from petting the cat. "Henri, what is it?" No one answered her.

"Maman?" Henri's voice cracked as he faced Vivienne, questions swimming in his eyes. He would stay if she begged him to.

Instead, she took his smooth face in her hands and looked up at him, for he had long since surpassed her height. "Henri, you are our son. As much as Rosalie and Kate are our daughters. I know you. I love you. I want you." She blinked back the tears that threatened, shoved away the knowledge that if Henri left with Armand, she would likely never see him again. "But you must choose what *you* want now."

High above Asylum, wind flapped Henri's linen shirt as he squinted at the sun-spangled Susquehanna hugging the settlement. There stood the Grand Maison, there was the market square and boulevard, there was the chapel, and there were the fifty houses lining straight streets between riverbank and fields. Easily he spotted his family's farm at the farthest edge from the river, and Finn's and Jethro's, their fields a patchwork of rippling golds and greens. And there was the land Henri meant to claim as his own as soon as he turned eighteen.

Unless, of course, he was in France by then.

Mist snagged on tree-filled ridges that hinted at autumn's coming fire. Henri's thoughts winged over them, eastward, toward the ocean he'd crossed once before. Contemplating a return to France with Armand led directly to pondering the fate of Louis-Charles, the rightful king.

Muscles knotted in Henri's shoulders. He scuffed his boot at a scattering of pine needles and sent a spray of gravel clattering over the ledge. He had come here to Prospect Rock so often to think, to pray, to watch for new arrivals—one in particular.

As he plunged his hand into his pocket, Henri's fingers closed around the small wooden horse he had whittled during his first winter in Asylum. He knew every edge and curve, from the sharp points of its ears to the flanks worn smooth by his worrying thumb. How much smaller it seemed now that he was seventeen. How unlikely that he would ever give it to his friend.

A downy woodpecker drummed its beak against a tree. Below,

the river roiled and purled around boulders and fallen trees. As the water curved around its bend, the past several years swept over him. While Henri had thrived in the love of his family, on land that healed body and soul, news had filtered in of a dozen young men who, one by one, had laid claim to France's throne. All false. Hope, once bright, took on a mellow patina.

A squirrel scampered over the rock, bushy tail twitching, before scrabbling up a pine tree that grew straight to the sun from a small patch of earth between the rocks. Countless times, Henri had prayed that wherever Louis-Charles was, he grew straight and tall toward the sun as well.

Henri's eyes burned. Bending, he scooped up a pinecone, turning it in his hand and pressing the scales with his thumb. Sap stuck to his skin and spiced the air, mingling with the smell of a rotting log.

He was done bargaining with God. And he was done being scared for his friend. Louis-Charles would never come to Asylum, nor would he ever assume his throne. *But he found a refuge of his own, didn't he, Lord?* Henri felt it in his bones as surely as he felt the carved horse in his pocket and the pinecone sharp against his palm. No more secrets. No more plots or danger or hiding. Only heaven. And what better place for Louis-Charles could there be? He was with his parents, and with the King of Kings, in a place where no tears were shed, wrapped in love and joy and light.

And where was Henri's place? Crickets trilling in his ears, he thought and prayed over the crossroads until fireflies pulsed in the gathering twilight and in the settlement below. Pinpoints of light to lead him home.

Henri reeled back his arm and hurled the pinecone over the precipice before beginning the rugged hike downhill. With practiced steps, he crossed roots and slid down slopes, jumped over cracks in the rocks and vaulted over fallen logs. The river's rushing was music in his ears. He emerged at last into the clearing and, with wild grass tugging his trousers, threaded toward his house.

As he neared, his sisters' laughter pealed. Maman stood when she saw him, her hand to her heart. Papa draped his arm around her shoulders. Rosalie and Kate raced from the summer house, knees pumping beneath their skirts, Madame Fishypaws bounding at their heels. Squealing, his sisters plowed toward him.

"First one to slap my hand wins!" Henri dropped to his knees, arms spread wide to either side. The little girls crashed into his arms, and peace billowed over him, an answer to his prayers.

Louis-Charles was safely home.

And so was Henri.

Author's Note and Acknowledgments

While the main characters in *A Refuge Assured* are entirely fictional, the events and attitudes with which they interacted are straight from history, from prologue to epilogue. When I learned that lacemaking was deemed a crime worthy of the guillotine in 1794 France, I knew I wanted to tell the story of a woman who escaped her country's revolution to find asylum (and Asylum) in a nation still finding its footing after its own.

Several historical figures appear or are referenced in *A Refuge Assured*, including the royal family of Louis XVI, the Marquis de Lafayette, radical French revolutionary leaders Robespierre and Jean-Paul Marat, the young assassin Charlotte Corday, Alexander Hamilton and his wife, Eliza, George Washington, Thomas Jefferson, Anne Bingham, Senator Robert Morris, Dr. Benjamin Rush, Dr. Edward Stevens, French Ambassador Genêt, Albert Gallatin, David Bradford, and Monsieur Omer Talon, manager of Asylum.

Louis-Charles was one of the most tragic figures I encountered in my research for this book. I'm sure I was especially sympathetic to his plight because my eight-year-old son, Ethan, is the age Louis-Charles was when he was taken from his mother's prison cell and isolated in his own until he died two years later. The mysteries surrounding his fate, laid out by Monsieur Talon in this novel, went unsolved for centuries, and the legend of the "Lost King" was especially popular after the restoration of France's monarchy in 1814. By this time, close to one hundred claimants had come forward pretending to be Louis-Charles. But a DNA test performed in 2000 proved that the boy who died while imprisoned was, indeed, the son of Marie Antoinette.

The French Revolution affected America in integral ways, one of which was Hamilton's sincere belief that the Whiskey Rebellion was a Jacobin attempt to overthrow the recently birthed American government. (Francophile Thomas Jefferson repealed the whiskey tax soon after becoming president.) For more on the link between France and America in the 1790s, read *When the United States Spoke French* by François Furstenberg and *These Fiery Frenchified Dames: Women and Political Culture in Early National Philadelphia* by Susan Branson.

The signet ring of Louis XVI was delivered to Marie Antoinette after her husband's execution, and when she was sentenced to death, as well, she managed to smuggle the ring to her former secretary. The ring finding its way to a lady-in-waiting was my own fictional invention.

Asylum, Pennsylvania, was a real place, truly built as a refuge for Marie Antoinette and her children. The French who lived there did hire American laborers, though there was some disdain between the nationalities. There really was a tree-felling contest between them, and an express mail carrier for the settlement. Land disputes were also not uncommon. History buffs already familiar with Asylum, I hope you will excuse my decision not to incorporate more of the real people who lived there for the sake of simplifying the cast and story. After Napoleon declared general amnesty, most of the émigrés in Asylum returned to France, but some chose to stay in America. The site of French Azilum, or Asylum, can still be visited today. Many thanks to Lee Kleinsmith and Deborah L. Courville for accommodating my family's visit even before the grounds were officially open for the summer season.

Readers who wish to dig deeper into the history behind *A Refuge Assured* may want to read *Marie Antoinette: The Journey* by Antonia Fraser or *The Whiskey Rebellion* by William Hogeland. Recipes for food mentioned in scenes at the Four Winds Tavern come from *The City Tavern Cookbook* by Chef Walter Staib. Visit the historic City Tavern in Philadelphia and taste them for yourself! I was fortunate that Chef Staib took time to talk with me when I went. Thanks also to Chef George for extending my tour of the building and for answering all my questions about eighteenth-century tavern life.

I also owe thanks to dear friends Lisa and Micah Reyes, and Bettina and Rob Dowell, for hosting my family on my research trip/spring break "vacation." (Psst, Elsa and Ethan, I know you didn't love the historical stuff as much as I did. Don't forget, we did take you to Chocolate World in Hershey, Pennsylvania, and the Spy Museum in D.C. Remember how fun that was?) To my husband, Rob, thank you for joining in on my adventures and for supporting my efforts to get this book right!

I'm so grateful to my friend and fellow author Laura Frantz for partnering with me to subtly link our heroines. When we discovered we were both writing about lacemakers for our novels, we had fun creating a shared French ancestry for Vivienne and for Laura's heroine Liberty in her novel *The Lacemaker*. Eagle-eyed readers will catch the connection tucked into each novel.

Thanks also to my agent, Tim Beals of Credo Communications, for unflagging support, and to my editors, Dave Long and Jessica Barnes, for their brilliant suggestions for improving this story.

Everlasting thanks to kindred spirit Susie Finkbeiner for walking with me through every stage of novel writing. Your encouragement is balm to the ragged writer's soul.

For help with horse research, thanks to Pegg Thomas, Debbie Lynne Costello, Susan Page Davis, and Chris Jager, who also had the honor of naming Beau, Cherie, and Red.

I'm blessed by and grateful for my critique partner Joanne Bischof for her candid feedback; the Cedar Falls Public Library interlibrary loan staff, for securing every obscure volume I request; my parents, Peter and Pixie Falck, for watching the kids and giving me pie; my brother and sister-in-law, Jason and Audrey Falck, for prayers and French crepes; and Trinity Bible Church's Pathfinders class for praying me through my deadlines. Special thanks to Trent and Jennifer Simpson and family for playdates and meals during crunch time!

Most importantly, thank you, Lord, for being a refuge for all of us, and a trustworthy heavenly Father.

If you remember nothing else from this story, I pray you remember this: No matter who you are, or where you've come from, God knows you. He loves you and wants you. If you are a follower of Christ, you are a child of the King.

Discussion Questions

1. For a long time, Vivienne feels that the more people know about her, especially her parentage, the more likely she is to lose their esteem. Can you think of a time when you shared something you weren't proud of, and the response surprised you? What happened?

2. Vivienne has a difficult time forgiving Sybille and Armand for their life choices. Have you also struggled to forgive a family member? What happened when you finally did?

3. Fleeing the French Revolution uproots Vivienne, requiring her to reinvent herself in a new country. When have you been uprooted, either by a physical relocation or by an emotional/social/economic upheaval? How did you find your footing again after that?

4. Liam struggles to reconcile his love of liberty with the need for order in the new nation of America. What parallels do you see in America today, in the balancing act between personal rights and freedoms and the need to govern and be governed?

5. After Martine dies, Vivienne is charged with raising a child, which is something she feels the least qualified to do. When was the last time a task was thrust upon you that you weren't sure you could manage? What happened?

6. Liam feels responsible for the well-being of the people closest to him, even though Tara and Finn are adults and Liam lives far from them. Do you ever feel responsible for people who are outside your sphere of influence? Why or why not?

7. Throughout the book, Vivienne seeks refuge in settings that promise safety. Today, we may not be hiding from physical danger, but what do we try to escape? Where do we seek refuge in our modern culture? What are typical results of those coping mechanisms?

8. Liam's injuries during the book were a direct result of his defending people from harm. When have you experienced a negative personal outcome for standing up for what you believe in?

9. Armand gives Henri a kitten because he knows Henri would enjoy having something to care for. Has there been a time in your life when caring for someone else has also helped you in some way? Explain.

10. Themes of home and belonging are important to Vivienne, Liam, and Henri. Where, or with whom, do you feel the most profound sense of belonging? Why?

About the Author

Jocelyn Green is an award-winning author of multiple fiction and nonfiction works, including *Faith Deployed: Daily Encouragement for Military Wives* and *The 5 Love Languages Military Edition*, which she co-wrote with Dr. Gary Chapman. Her first novel in the HEROINES BEHIND THE LINES series, *Wedded to War*, was a Christy Award finalist and the gold medal winner in historical fiction from the Military Writers Society of America. She and her husband live in Cedar Falls, Iowa, with their two children and two cats. Her goal with every book is to inspire faith and courage in her readers. Visit her at www.jocelyngreen.com.

Sign Up for Jocelyn's Newsletter!

Keep up to date with Jocelyn's news on book releases and events by signing up for her email list at jocelyngreen.com.

More from Jocelyn Green

After being unjustly imprisoned, midwife Julianne Chevalier trades her life sentence for exile to the French colony of Louisiana in 1720. She is forced to marry a convict in order to sail, but when tragedy strikes, her hopes for a new life are shattered. Now she must find her own way in this dangerous, rugged land while bearing the king's mark—the brand of a criminal.

The Mark of the King

You May Also Like...

At the outset of WWI, high-end thief Willa Forsythe is hired to steal a cypher from famous violinist Lukas De Wilde. Given the value of his father's work as a cryptologist, Lukas fears for his family and doesn't know who to trust. He likes Willa—and the feeling is mutual. But if Willa doesn't betray him as ordered, her own family will pay the price.

A Song Unheard by Roseanna M. White
SHADOWS OVER ENGLAND #2
roseannawhite.com

In 1772, Lady Keturah Banning Tomlinson and her sisters inherit their father's estates and travel to the West Indies to see what is left of their legacy. On the island of Nevis, every man seems to be trying to win Keturah's hand and, with it, the ownership of her plantation. Set on saving their heritage, can she trust God with her future—and her heart?

Keturah by Lisa T. Bergren
THE SUGAR BARON'S DAUGHTERS #1
lisatbergren.com

After being branded during the battle of Jericho, Moriyah has had no prospects for marriage—until now. She hopes to please the man, but things go horribly wrong and she is forced to flee for her life. Seeking safety at one of the Levitical cities of refuge, she is unprepared for the dangers she faces, and the enemies—and allies—she encounters on her way.

A Light on the Hill by Connilyn Cossette
CITIES OF REFUGE #1
connilyncossette.com

CPSIA information can be obtained
at www.ICGtesting.com
Printed in the USA
LVOW03*2312050318
568804LV00002B/19/P